WALKING
INTO OCEAN
THE

DAVID
WHELLAMS

A PETER CAMMON MYSTERY

ECW Press

Published by ECW Press
2120 Queen Street East, Suite 200, Toronto, Ontario, Canada M4E 1E2
416-694-3348 / info@ecwpress.com

LIBRARY AND ARCHIVES CANADA CATALOGUING IN PUBLICATION

Whellams, David, 1948-
Walking into the ocean / David Whellams.

ISBN 978-1-77041-042-8 (BOUND); 978-1-77041-103-6 (PBK)
ALSO ISSUED AS: 978-1-77090-232-9 (PDF); 978-1-77090-233-6 (EPUB)

I. Title.

PS8645.H45W35 2012   C813'.6   C2011-906946-6

Cover images: man with umbrella © Steve Hamblin/Corbis;
blue stain © Panupong Roopyai/iStockphoto
Cover and text design: Tania Craan
Author photo by Jennifer Barnes JB Photography
Printing: Friesens   2   3   4   5

The publication of *Walking into the Ocean* has been generously supported by the Canada Council for the Arts which last year invested $20.1 million in writing and publishing throughout Canada, and by the Ontario Arts Council, an agency of the Government of Ontario. We also acknowledge the financial support of the Government of Canada through the Canada Book Fund for our publishing activities, and the contribution of the Government of Ontario through the Ontario Book Publishing Tax Credit. The marketing of this book was made possible with the support of the Ontario Media Development Corporation.

PRINTED AND BOUND IN CANADA

for Ann and Diana

PART ONE

The Shore

CHAPTER 1

He stood at the end of the garden lane, alone, waiting. He had once beheaded a sunflower in that same garden.

Chief Inspector Peter Cammon might have been from a work by Magritte. He wore a high-buttoned black suit and a small bowler, also flat black. He held a black umbrella, which might have been mistaken from a certain distance for a walking stick, though the effect was not Chaplinesque. His moustache, trimmed short and neat, added to the impression of compact self-control, though the effect was not Hitlerian; it had long ago turned grey and distinguished.

Another growing season had come and would soon be gone, and the ripe sunflowers, as planned out by his wife, Joan, marched all the way along the snake-rail fence that hemmed the lane. If Cammon, stiff and monochromatic, seemed oddly posed against this backdrop of Impressionist extravagance, the juxtaposition didn't interest him. He was simply waiting, he told himself, for this latest investigation to begin, that's all. It was still a fresh morning but warming up fast enough for him to remove his hat and suit coat and fold them over the top of the Gladstone bag at his feet. He regretted bringing the too-formal hat, but leaving it to crown one of the fence posts seemed too capricious a farewell, given how edgy Joan could get when he started a case. The sunflowers did not lead him to think of gardening or marital dissonance or Van Gogh; rather, and he wasn't sure why, they made him jump to a memory from the last case he had been involved in before his semi-retirement.

As part of that investigation, he had paid a visit to an Alzheimer's ward in the thin hope of getting information out of an old woman who might, or might not, have seen a killing from her hospital window. Arriving during a routine cognitive test being administered by the hospital psychologist, he watched as the woman misidentified the most ordinary of objects. She thought knuckles were coins and shoelaces were blankets. She responded with such certainty that the psychologist just let her go on, without correction. Peter had ached at her distress; an interview would have been useless. What interested him more and more as he approached the age of sixty-eight was memory itself. After forty years of examining witnesses, he understood that the machinery of the subconscious could spit out a stored image for its own reasons — what counted for a detective was where the recollections led you — yet with this woman the gears had worn through. She had enjoyed looking out her window at the garden, yet what, if anything, imprinted itself on her mind? The tumblers of memory were but a stumbling block away from senility, where memory became a betrayer rather than a faithful guide through the wilds of a difficult universe.

Peter understood that the woman, whom the psychologist let ramble, found solace, from what Peter did not care to guess, by moving into another world entirely. He had no intention of entering her world. He had worked too hard to create his own.

But these were idle thoughts, a warm-up exercise to burn off the morning's mental fogs while he waited for his colleague to pick him up. They didn't lead him any further into the incident with the old woman; nor was there any danger that he himself would slip into daftness in the imminent future, although sunstroke was possible in the growing heat of this late September morning.

He had been told enough about his new assignment to book six days in Whittlesun, the coastal town that reluctantly laid claim to the murder-suicide. Sir Stephen Bartleben, who had made the call to him from Yard Headquarters in London and who was the point man for liaising with Whittlesun Police, hadn't ordered Peter to block in six days, but only suggested it. It probably would not take that long but, Peter knew from experience, there was no way to tell. One presumed the locals were competent, but then again, they had called the Yard for assistance, not the other way round, and so there might be complications of which Peter was currently unaware. On the other hand, wife-murders, and the flight of the husbands, just as often turned out to be routine. Peter would soon know — the degree of complexity, that is. One of his virtues was patience.

André Lasker, a mechanic, had beaten his wife to death and thrown her body off the local cliffs. Or perhaps she had been alive when he pushed her into the Channel. The husband then took off his clothes and walked into the ocean. Her body had been found; his had not.

Sir Stephen Bartleben, who held the title of Deputy Commissioner, had disclosed these simple facts over the telephone. There was never any question of Cammon refusing the assignment, even though he was semi-retired. While it might be said that they had an "understanding" about his availability, Peter Cammon himself was somewhat unsure about his own definition of his status. He had been determined to retire three years ago, then immediately shaky about the decision. Sir Stephen had resisted his departure, for it implied that he ought to be next; they were of the same generation, if not the same class. Their careers had paralleled, though Peter was the field operative and Sir Stephen's role was to back him up from the remove of London. Peter had worked on contract seven months out of the last twelve, and since leaving his post he had spent about half his time freelancing for the Yard. Yesterday, Bartleben had assumed full cooperation; he would not have called otherwise.

Peter hadn't asked for details over the phone. Tommy Verden, his friend and frequent partner, would have an information packet with him. Peter would read it over in the car during the two-hour drive to Whittlesun.

The more problematic question was why the boss was sending Peter in particular. There were probably more diplomatic, and younger, choices for a routine case like this one. Within the Yard culture, Peter was notorious for working solo. He cooperated when necessary, and he had a fondness for the collaborative work of forensic analysis, and after a second glass of ale would offer speculation as blue sky as anyone's in the halls of Scotland Yard HQ. But he had aggravating habits, such as wandering off on his own to track down peripheral witnesses or tying up crime scenes for long periods, driving local authorities crazy. Bartleben was used to fending off complaints from regional police chiefs.

And Bartleben had explained, if only in selective part, one startling feature of this case that might quickly increase the potential for friction. Over the phone, he had gone out of his way to say, "Oh, yes, one of the reasons they could use a little help is that the police in Southwest Region, along the coast, are a bit preoccupied with finding a serial murderer. See Inspector Maris in Whittlesun as soon as you get there. Sounded frazzled over the phone. Good luck."

Tommy Verden arrived fifteen minutes behind schedule and apologized mildly. He placed Cammon's grip in the back but didn't open the door for him. Years ago such a formality might have been expected, but now, Tommy felt, such a gesture would represent condescension to Peter's ineluctable age. Cammon was the most amiable of superiors, but respect, in the right forms, was still key to their working relationship, and so he didn't hold the door.

As Verden left the cottage, Peter looked back down the lane. The house was out of view and he did not expect to see Joan, but he turned anyway. Their understanding required no ritual parting gestures, yet he looked out of formal respect for her, even though she couldn't see him doing it. He did note the flowers again before they drove away. He had topped the doddering sunflower in a flash of anger one evening during the latter days of the Yorkshire Ripper affair. In 1981, Peter Sutcliffe, a lorry driver and sometime factory worker, was finally arrested after murdering thirteen women in Britain, but not before a massive, unprecedented manhunt had been launched and had drawn in — and exhausted — every police force in the country, including New Scotland Yard. Inspector Cammon had worked on the investigation for fifteen months. One day the insanity had followed the weary detective home. It was a time when no one was safe, he had judged — not Joan, not civilization, not fields of innocent sunflowers. But the farcical act of decapitating the flower (dead-heading was too laden a term) had pulled him out of his anger, and he was fresh at work the next morning.

Peter forgot all about gardens as they accelerated away from the lane. Verden passed the sealed packet over the headrest. Peter ripped it open and began reading. Tommy drove fast, as he always did, but did nothing sudden that would jog his friend out of his concentration, which was total. He wasn't offended by Peter's silence; besides, he had already read the file.

Peter read steadily for an hour. It wasn't significant that he sat in the back; he merely needed the room to lay out the contents of the envelope. Otherwise, he and Tommy would have shared the front seat and theorized the whole way about the bare-bones facts of the Lasker case. For now, he stayed silent. As they shot up the slip road onto the motorway, Verden could hear Peter behind him, grunting while he thumbed the file. Tommy had started out as a constable and was content in an inspector's career. Thick-shouldered and dead-eyed, but alert and quick as well, he was a reliable backup to field officers like Peter Cammon. He downplayed his physical strength; Sarah, Peter's daughter, described him as a "quiet grizzly bear." He usually wore neat flannels and a casual tweed jacket, which somehow seemed just the right uniform for a man who was willing to please but was also aware of his ability to break your neck.

Peter lowered the sheaf of papers and photographs. He and Verden hadn't been in touch for months, but their habits were set. Verden had worked with Peter for thirty years but he often began conversations formally. "What do you think, sir?"

"The beaches," Peter said.

"Thought you would notice that," Verden replied, looking in the rear-view mirror.

Peter thought of telling Tommy to pull over so that he could move to the front seat, but he held back.

"Tommy, do they mean that the husband dumped the wife on one beach but then walked into the sea at a different beach?"

"Factually true. The way I've experienced it, you cannot throw a body into the surf from the heights and then walk into the waves at the same spot. Hence, two beaches."

"Yes, but if your object were suicide, wouldn't one method do as well as another, even if you had a particular modus terminus in mind at the outset? Following her off the same cliff would be quick, at least."

"Yes, but keep in mind that women favour certain methods, like poison and gas. Men are willing to be more dramatic."

It didn't matter that this made little sense; it was warm-up banter, to get the conversation moving. Did Tommy think that walking into the sea was more dramatic than a swan dive off a windswept cliff? It could depend on which Gothic romance he was reading, Peter supposed; as a regular driver for Sir Stephen, Verden had a lot of time to read. He leaned across the seat back so that Tommy wouldn't have to crane his neck.

"Go on."

"In my experience, it's men who pursue the stagy scenarios. I'm talking dramatic in the sense of melodramatic. But once they plan their exit, men think they have to follow the framework to the letter, so to speak. Lasker folded his clothes and left them in a neat pile. That had to be pre-planned, he had the image in his head. Somehow he found himself *on top* of the cliff but he felt compelled to stick to the idea of walking naked into the sea. Jesus, Peter, you're the English Lit specialist."

Peter saw where his colleague was heading with this. Lasker had indeed planned a showy exit and had stuck to the scheme, the kind of drowning Byron or Hardy would have appreciated. Perhaps André was making a statement, although the message was as yet obscure. It was hard to imagine someone piling up his clothes and jumping off a cliff, naked. That scenario flirted with farce. Thus, he must have selected a spot along the shore where he could wade gradually into the sea. Peter appreciated the logic of the plan, but his instincts weren't buying it. It took a cold killer to toss his victim off a precipice and then drive away.

Still, did Lasker confuse himself? Did he lash out at her, improvise her disposal and then go back to the original plan? Peter had no idea of the answers. Of course, if it had *all* been planned, then there was no farce and no happenstance, only deadly calculation.

Or had André Lasker faked his own death?

By the time the sea came into view, Peter had finished reading the file. He instructed Tommy to drop him off at the shore, as near as possible to the strip where the murderer had walked into the Channel. Tommy would leave his bag at the hotel, the Delphine, off the high street. Peter could walk into town when he was finished; he was sure that the centre of Whittlesun wouldn't be far from the beach.

They found the tourist beach by following the posted signs. The poured cement parking area that extended out onto the shore contained only one other car, and Tommy was able to loop around the lot without doing a three-point backup. He offered no parting advice when Peter opened the door and got out with his umbrella and, reluctantly, the bowler. Verden had driven Peter hundreds of times, often as an active partner, just as often as a drop-off service, but he never told anyone, including Joan, with whom he was good friends, that he found these partings a little bizarre. The protocol was clear when Peter worked alone. He got into these distant, impenetrable moods at the beginning; no one should try to interfere, Tommy knew. He wasn't afraid for his colleague, and he expected to hear from him soon, but he would check the valise to see if Peter had brought along that ancient Smith & Wesson. But Peter Cammon ruminating against the backdrop of a cold, lonely sea — that was just about perfect, Tommy thought as he drove off.

His old knees popping, Peter scrooched down on the pebble strand of Lower Whittlesun Beach and looked out to the calm English Channel. A family of four, the owners of the sedan, with their rickety fold-up chairs and primary red and yellow plastic buckets and spades, traipsed towards the parking slab, giving him a look as they passed, as if he were responsible for their bruised feet. He ignored them. Like everyone else, he endured England's shape-shifting weather with stoicism. Right now the sea was the colour of worn-out pewter, with a lowering sky to match. He heard the motor start up behind him. Alone now, he stared out to a flat, unpromising horizon. It did not take long for a heavy melancholy to settle on the shore. This was a place for disappointed tourists, and perhaps for lonely individuals with desperate plans. Even as his joints stiffened, he continued to examine the sea.

Whittlesun claimed two beaches, each providing half a tourist site. The stony one here, murder on a bather's heels, nonetheless offered a calm, wadeable sea. Way off to his left, he knew, beyond an obstructing promontory, lay a narrower beach of sand; however, his package of notes warned that it backed up against crumbling cliffs and ran steeply into choppy, treacherous waters. Anna Lasker had fallen into the tide at this point. He had a clear view of about a half-mile in each direction. To his right, the shore ended at a long, wooden pier; the massif bracketed the left extreme. He could see a ruined church on the clifftop.

If Lasker hadn't been washed out irretrievably, the sea would serve as its own net and cough up the body eventually. With his pointed index finger, Peter drew an arc, a decisive line across the near horizon from land point to point, penning the zone of investigation into an area about a nautical mile wide, from the promontory to the pier. What had happened out beyond this perimeter would likely remain unknown until Lasker crossed back into this zone, one way or another.

How did it feel striding out to the vanishing point, until the salt water closed over your head? Was the urge to swim irresistible? The metaphor became literal: swim or sink. At what point did your decision become unretractable, André?

He had spent enough time here for the moment. He had just wanted to take a look, gain an impression. He creaked to his feet but remained focused on the Channel for an extra minute. What made Peter Cammon a good detective was a kind of free-roaming patience (Bartleben's phrase); he was willing to stare at a scene without knowing what he was looking for, until something lodged in his mind, even if only in his subconscious. Not many detectives were willing to partner with him.

Did you plan your walk into the depths for a day like this one, André? Not likely. Verden was right: you followed a tight schedule shaped by more compelling forces than the weather.

Just one more minute, he decided. The tide was moving in by detectable inches. The wind had come up to create distinct waves. Dickens might have had this place in mind when he described "the waves of an unwholesome sea." Matthew Arnold had imagined "the grating roar of pebbles" in the tidal flow, although he had been talking about religion, the Sea of Faith retreating.

He shook his head in an effort to reset his thinking. He had once regarded homicide in almost literary terms. Whether or not he was naturally inclined this way from four years at Oxford, he came to understand that most criminal acts were sordid and unimaginative. Violent, driven men followed classic patterns — not to mention that they told themselves cheap stories to justify their deeds — and his task was to follow the storyline back to the standard founderous bog of greed, envy, ambition and the breakdown of self-control. In other words, Peter Cammon was a romantic, always searching out the melodrama. His febrile mind had served him well in the early years. Young Inspector Cammon proved instrumental in solving several revenge crimes back then, including three killings by the Kray organization. The murders, and a bank robbery in Durham, had made his reputation. Rapid promotion had followed.

But it was also his duty, he came to realize after a few years, to try to comprehend the hot anger at the core of most crimes. Some dismissed this darkness as imponderable, but he saw that the attacker's rage and the victim's terror clashed on a tilting plane, where pain and hope rose and fell, and that was where the uniqueness of each case would be found. The anger and the terror had to be engaged before he could parse the criminal act.

André, did you begin that night in hot anger? Did you run from the horror into the shallow waves, fearing to meet the undertow? Did the chill sea then turn passion to panic?

At Peter's retirement reception, Lord Paymer, the current head of New Scotland Yard, had urged Peter, given his decades of exposure to violent offences, to assemble an encyclopaedia of crimes. This had been his unsubtle way of edging Peter towards fully leaving; the chief hated the "half measure" of semi-retirement and the cost of keeping consulting detectives on the rolls. But Peter had little interest in reducing his career experience to a list of pigeon-holed sins, and if he had undertaken such a taxonomy, "walking into the sea" would have been a sub-genre of a sub-class, at best. And from the literary perspective, were there any precedents? Didn't someone in *Far from the Madding Crowd* choose that way out? It seemed a cowardly form of suicide, and if a deception, a contrived one. The catalogue entry would note the conventions in exiting via the ocean (whether intending to stay under or planning one's resurfacing to a new life). Clothes are to be stacked in a squared pile above the high-tide line, so that they will be found. A note is superfluous. Civilization's deserter, overwhelmed by a need to leave his old life behind, walks steadily into the water at a precise right angle to the horizon. It should be a neat, formal departure. Almost a British thing.

André Lasker had followed all these rules, but Peter suspected that he had over-planned his exit. That was why Chief Inspector Peter Cammon gave fifty-fifty odds that Lasker was still alive.

He counted to the seventh wave and turned back to the town.

CHAPTER 2

The sea road climbed by a series of hairpin bends to the centre of Whittlesun, but it was faster to walk straight up the pedestrian steps that crossed the road at a right angle, like the straight lines on an American dollar sign. Rain threatened, but it would hold off for an hour or two, he guessed, although he was having trouble judging this coastal weather. At the top of the stone stairway, he took off his suit jacket and paused to look back at his first vista of the harbour off to the west. There was a boldness, a defiant confidence in the way the town engaged the sea. Whittlesun had been a significant Channel port for four centuries. His briefing stated that the port still offered moorings for fishermen and a marina for boaters, but larger ships no longer used the silted harbour. And if Lasker had jumped a ferry, it wasn't out of Whittlesun; the nearest boat left from up the eastern coast.

The upper road became the high street and led him right into the town. He reached the Delphine without a wrong turn, and found his bag and the Lasker dossier waiting in his room. He hadn't bothered with his laptop, since apparently none of the hotels in Whittlesun offered wi-fi service or any other mode of in-room Internet. He wasn't sure about using the computer facilities at the local station. As he unpacked, he noticed a card on the faux refectory desk that, indeed, offered a connection for a token fee. He thought about asking Tommy Verden to retrieve his computer from the cottage. He hung his spare clothes in the closet.

Leaving his umbrella and hat in the room, he took the lift to the lobby and asked directions to the central police station. It turned out that the main, and only, police offices for Whittlesun were located farther up the hillside, but within walking distance.

Against all logic and topography, the upper reaches of Whittlesun had been laid out on a right-angle grid. Major streets that would have flowed better if contoured around the foothills instead ran straight uphill at steep, stubborn angles. The hotel concierge told him to expect a serious climb no matter which route he took; there used to be a funicular tram running to the cliff plateau but it had "rusted out," as he put it.

Daubney Lane, the main commercial street in central Whittlesun, was bustling with traffic at this hour, and the town seemed prosperous enough to Peter. There was nothing startling or unfamiliar in the Whittlesun core; the renovators and the modernizers could only do so much with a traditional high street in a moderate-sized English town. If anything, the town was evolving into a tourist village, where quaintness becomes the touchstone and the imposed Dickensian veneer risks parody. Peter supposed that Whittlesun might have revived its maritime tradition, but instead it had opted for standard Victorian street lights and adding an Old English *e* to just about every shoppe name. It takes money to make the old new again, he thought. He sensed the struggle going on in Whittlesun. Workmen toiled on the decaying, oxidized roof of a 17th-century church, replacing green cladding with brown copper; the repairs looked long overdue. Otherwise, there did not appear to be any publicly funded renovation along the main avenues, aside from the street lamps.

The concierge had overstated the steepness of the climb, and Peter had a pleasant hike. He found the station by the sound of police motorcycles entering and leaving the car park. The building, about four streets uphill from the commercial area, had once housed an insurance company or a bank; grandiose pillars framed the main entrance. He guessed that the police had taken it over when they outgrew their old digs. The Whittlesun Force was autonomous, serving all of Dorset but remaining officially under the control of Southwest Regional Police. Bartleben had informed him that there were eighteen constables, five detectives and twenty or more other ranks. "Not so many," Sir Stephen had opined, "if you have to patrol for a serial killer."

Peter hadn't called ahead. Inspector Maris had been told by Bartleben to expect Chief Inspector Cammon sometime that morning. Peter counted six motorcycles and four police vehicles with decals on the doors, and two that he knew were unmarked police cars. A seventh bike was leaving by the far exit. Was anybody policing Whittlesun? They all seemed to be here, Peter thought. He entered the reception area at the front, which immediately disillusioned anyone expecting the pillars to have a stylish follow-through. The former grand entrance had been partitioned for security reasons, and now a female officer in a Plexiglas booth confronted each visitor. She was cheerful enough and, through the scratched and smeared plastic panels, sized him up, probably as an elderly victim of a break-in or an auto theft. His identity card did the usual trick; she recoiled in impressed disbelief from his Scotland Yard credentials. She stabbed a button on her phone console, then another for good measure.

"Just a minute, Chief Inspector," she said through the round grill in the booth.

It took a full five minutes before an officer in shirtsleeves clicked the door lock and came out to greet him. The man was overweight and whey-faced, but he smiled broadly and openly. His whole manner indicated awe at being in the presence of a Yard senior detective.

This couldn't be the heavily burdened Inspector Maris. This rumpled young man was cheerful and welcoming, and lacked the executive gene. Bartleben had warned Peter not to expect enthusiasm. Maris had made it clear that Peter was coming down to help with the work-up on André Lasker; he would not officially supervise the dossier, nor determine the offences to be charged, should Lasker be nabbed.

"Hello!" the young detective said, and offered his hand. "Sorry. Sorry to keep you waiting. Come in. Down from London, then?"

He stood aside and Peter had to squeeze past him around the Plexiglas box and through the doorway. It would have been easier for the officer to go first.

"Peter Cammon."

"Ronald Hamm. We're just finishing up our staff meeting. I'd invite you in, but we're about done. If you wait out here, I'll be back in a flash."

Detective Hamm rushed into a room and the door closed behind him. Peter remained standing in the main room. It was open concept: few walls, with cloth-panelled partitions that seemed to him to create the worst of both worlds, eliminating real privacy but preventing spontaneous gatherings. The retention of the heavy interior pillars from the previous business gave the place an odd feel, as if some general and his staff had temporarily taken over the premises of a chateau in wartime. Glass-walled offices had been constructed in the four corners of the big space. Peter suspected that the bureaucratic dictates of police administration had compromised the original design of the refit.

In his short talk with Bartleben, Peter hadn't revealed his first reaction to the assignment, but all detectives from the Yard knew the drill when they descended to the Regions. Local police were always ambivalent, conceding that they needed the help but resisting any implication that they lacked the expertise necessary to crack the case. There was an inherent contradiction in this resentment — don't ask if you don't really want the assistance — but Peter ran into it just about every time. He knew that Stephen would have pledged the fullest cooperation and deference to local powers over the phone, but, in practice, the arm-twisting would all have to be done by the Yard man on the spot. Peter's lone-wolf habits weren't going to help, and Bartleben had known that. For his part, Peter wished that Bartleben would get out in the field more.

He could hear a lecturing voice in the closed room but no clear words. Officers began to come out of the meeting, one at a time, the door flapping, and he caught bits of sentences out of context.

". . . want those numbers in shape by noon tomorrow."

A very young man with red hair and the air of a junior staffer or an earnest executive assistant rushed out, and the door swung back again.

". . . coastal communities where people see things."

A minute later the meeting broke up. Peter had to step aside to avoid being trampled. Three uniformed officers rushed out together and made for the front door. Other detectives returned to their desks out in the open area and began making phone calls. There was nothing extraordinary about this police activity, but someone had put a fire under them, he noted.

Hamm emerged, his shirt even more dishevelled now.

"Inspector Maris said we should go to his office. Won't be a sec."

And it wasn't, since Maris, the last one out of the meeting room, was right behind him. The inspector was in his late thirties, and everything about him seemed constricted. His suit lapels were narrower than was the current fashion, and the jacket pinched him at the waist. His hair was gelled and brushed straight back from his temples. His shoes had pointy toes; they needed a polish. Peter judged that he didn't lift weights or otherwise get much exercise. All of this supported a generally harried look.

"Maris. You're Cammon?"

"Yes."

Without further greeting, Maris led him to one of the glass rooms in the corner. He closed the door and heaved a bundle of notes and files onto his desk. Only then did he glare at Peter. Maris's look was laden with deep irritation.

"Sit down. This is a devil of a business."

He could have been referring to the series of killings along the coast or to Lasker's slaughter of his wife. Peter assumed the former, although he was unsure. A gratuitous thought occurred to him: were the two investigations destined to overlap?

15

Maris had trouble sitting still; he twisted in his chair and sighed with impatience even before starting his spiel. Give him time to vent; he was allowed, Peter reasoned. Perhaps it's that the staff meeting didn't go well. The time for asserting the Yard's role would come soon.

Maris rose and smacked the desk. "Have you ever dealt with a mass killer?"

Peter nodded. He decided to demonstrate that he could be collegial. "Peter Sutcliffe."

But the question had been rhetorical. So was Peter's response, in effect, since he wasn't about to debate the Yorkshire Ripper.

"You know the biggest thing with a serial murderer?" Maris said. "It's that we never seem to catch them early enough. The numbers grow until he makes an obvious mistake."

Peter nodded again. He had no stake in the killings but he resolved to be both frank and forthcoming. Maybe it would garner cooperation. "I agree. There's an argument that serial killers and rapists are different than other criminals. Maybe, but they're messy, reveal more information to us than most. Yet we often have trouble figuring out what they're telling us." Why did he feel that he was babbling?

He sized up Maris. Peter tried not to be judgmental but the tension was already in the air. It seemed to Peter that Maris's already sweaty brow and his sawing hand gestures were an overreaction. Maris was probably raised in a south coast county and remained suspicious of outsiders. He was a believer in the humanity of the citizens with whom he grew up; outsiders didn't get that break. The chance that a local was calculatingly killing off young women was an affront to the values that had been poured into his upbringing. Such indignation could distort his perspective on the murders.

There were many ways this conversation could go, Peter felt. His gambit hadn't won any concessions from the inspector, not even eye contact after that first look. He understood that Maris needed to control his small kingdom and not be embarrassed by a parachuted expert out of London. On the other hand, another local caliph might simply have welcomed the help. So be it, Peter decided, but he needed certain protocols in place, if only to speed up the Lasker investigation. The crime scene was already turning stale. He had to make sure Maris understood that the more information and resources he made available at the outset, the less Peter would need to bother him over the next week.

The pleasantries ended. Maris remained in a heightened state, ready for sparring, it seemed.

"Inspector, I don't even begin to understand why Bartleben dispatched you down here. He sent you, what, to fix a problem?"

"No, to help in any way I can."

"This is purely a manpower challenge. I don't really need a chief inspector. Whatever Lasker's sins may turn out to be, I can handle it. But we have a serial rapist on the loose on the south coast and there's no spare help to do the Lasker interviews. I'm not sure they require a Scotland Yard chief inspector."

Peter's neutral look masked his annoyance. Bartleben expected him to be diplomatic, and that was his natural policy. He would help out wherever he could. And Maris had given him a prompt: if the Whittlesun force was overwhelmed, Peter would pick up the slack in an unthreatening way. That would be his principal angle on the assignment. But then . . . He disliked dismissive people, like Maris, who gave speeches and then foreclosed discussion. And there was that cheap shot about chief inspectors. What was that, a form of reverse condescension?

He couldn't help himself, and said, "Want my suggestions for dealing with the other forces?"

Peter was aware from Bartleben's information packet that a Task Force had been set up to reassure the public about the killings. J.J. "Jack" McElroy, an old colleague, was leading it, but he worked out of Devon, not Dorset, where Whittlesun was located. As far as Peter knew, none of the victims came from Dorset. Maris was a member because both counties formed part of Southwest Region.

For a second, Maris was confused about whether Peter was referring to Lasker or the other case. He settled on the serial murders. "No."

"Be proactive." Peter was leaning forward now. This whole thing was about to go off the rails, and it would be his fault. Maris sat down and tilted back a few inches in his chair. Peter shifted tone, adopting the bureaucratic jargon of modern police management. "Yes," he said, "I suggest you show the lead on the exchange of information. Perhaps volunteer to chair any subcommittee on evidence sharing. Set up a database, and here's the thing, set it up so that everyone is using the same software with the same protocols for adding information."

Peter regretted going too far. It wasn't his business and he had nothing against Maris. But it was fun to watch the impact.

For the first time, Inspector Maris scrutinized the older man's face and was immediately taken aback by the coldness in Cammon's eyes, and his steady gaze. Maris surmised that Cammon knew more than expected about the serial predator. Bartleben, that snob who admitted never visiting the south edge of England, must have told his man all about the killings, and that there was a Task Force in place. Worse, the chairperson, Chief Inspector J.J. McElroy, was undoubtedly a full member of the old boys' network controlled by Westminster. As for the Dorset inspector himself, his defensiveness towards the Scotland Yard detective had been instinctive, not even personal. He decided to relent for the moment.

"Let's confine ourselves to the Lasker killing," Maris stated. "Whatever you do for us and whatever comes out of the Lasker case, the accountability remains mine. I don't think you can do any better than my own people, and I definitely plan to fulfil my duties, accountability-wise."

Peter backed off. He looked for something conciliatory to offer. "You're right. I won't interfere. But I'm guessing that your workload will only get heavier, including increasing patrols and meeting with local residents. You may not get to Lasker and his wife for a while. Let me do what I can. I'll hand it all over to you when I've done the interviews."

None of this explanatory effort connoted an apology or real

compromise on his part. He didn't work that way. Ultimately he would track down André Lasker, as Bartleben expected; it wouldn't be Maris's people, he was already sure. But at this juncture, he was playing his cards from a position of weakness. The forensic work-up to date had been done locally, and the Whittlesun police knew where to go and whom to ask about the marriage and Lasker's business activities.

Peter's flattery, if that's what it was, suddenly paid off. Maris sighed under the weight of the whole world. "I'll let you run with it until week's end. You can have Constable Willet to guide you. Also, use him as your liaison with me. I appreciate your help."

Peter wasn't concerned about the thinness of this commitment, or Maris's underlying hostility. He had enough to start, and was already planning on making use of the corpulent Detective Hamm.

The Whittlesun chief evidently considered the meeting over. He unwound himself from his chair and stood. Peter proffered a hand and promised to deliver a progress report in two days. He asked Maris's permission to deal directly with the Regional Lab on forensic matters. He didn't need his go-ahead, since the laboratories weren't beholden to local police agencies; on the other hand, most of the initial forensics on the Lasker home had been initiated by Whittlesun detectives, whose testimony at trial would have to dovetail with Peter's own analysis. It was best to avoid Maris sniping later about going around channels with the pathologists. Maris gave him a file which Peter guessed was the initial autopsy on Mrs. Anna Lasker.

Peter smiled. "Thanks for all this." He left the glass enclosure. He would report back to Maris when he was good and ready.

Rather than immediately searching out Constable Willet, Peter explored the open zone of cubicles until he found Ronald Hamm. The detective ruled over a partitioned space that was smaller than a penitentiary cell. He seemed glad to see the older policeman, and again pumped his hand. Peter glanced back and reckoned that Maris couldn't quite eyeball them though his office wall.

"You're a veteran of the Yard, then, sir?"

Peter leaned forward to bring his head below the top of the partition. "Many years, Detective Hamm."

"No problem. Town treating you right?"

"Thanks. I wonder if you could do me a favour. Is there a standard package of public material, even if only press material already in the can, on the recent assaults on the Devon cliffs?"

"Oh, yes, that's available." Hamm showed no surprise at the request. Had Maris not been clear with his staff about Peter's narrow duties? "By the way, the papers up in Devon have dubbed him 'the Rover.'" Hamm turned sombre and lowered his voice. "Tough case."

"Having a tough time with it?" It wasn't exactly a question. He was feeling mischievous. He hoped Hamm would expound further.

"They call him the Rover because he works up and down the coast. UNESCO has designated the Jurassic Coast a World Heritage Site. Some people figure that the Rover will stop once he reaches the end of it."

Even Hamm seemed to realize the silliness of this speculation, which was born of the need of every investigator to put some kind of frame around a rampaging killer. Peter guessed that the Task Force hadn't made a lot of progress. As far as he knew, there had been three killings that appeared to be linked. Already the media had slapped a misleading label on the perp. J.J. McElroy would hate it and would forbid his officers using it, but Peter guessed that the name would stick. Throughout his career Peter had avoided the press, and he still saw no virtue in courting them. That was one advantage in letting Maris run both shows, he supposed.

"Would that material be available now?" he asked.

"Oh, sure! I'll need to have Services photocopy a package. I have to go up to the Kingsway, that's a suburb north of town, to pin down a sighting reported by an old man. If you're free about five, we could meet for a drink. Which hotel are you at?"

"The Delphine."

"There's a pub, the Crown, up the street from you. Let's meet there at 5:00 p.m."

Peter nodded. He convinced himself that his end run around Maris was, at worst, a venial sin. If he had time later, he would find a Net feed and Google "The Rover."

CHAPTER 3

Peter left Hamm and tracked down Constable Willet in a cubicle by the south wall of the sprawling station. Willet was just finishing his lunch and preparing to head out on his afternoon beat. His massive proportions made it likely that it had been a large lunch. Unfortunately, his surplus fat tended to settle around his belly and across his shoulders, so that when he stood he loomed over Peter like an iceberg. He was just over fifty but in some ways seemed older than Peter. Management indulged him, allowing him to grow his yellow-grey hair to the collar and sport a thick, Teutonic moustache. Willet would die of a heart attack on the upward slope of a cobblestone Whittlesun street somewhere along his beat, and Maris would deliver a eulogy praising another workhorse Peeler who had died in harness.

Peter understood why Maris had partnered Willet with him. He was the local constable, the man known and trusted in the neighbourhoods. Every police force had these characters. Willet could introduce Peter to the residents along the street where the Laskers had lived, and he would know the driving and walking routes to the Whittlesun beach fronts. And he would report every detail back to Maris.

"Good morning, Guv'nor," Willet said, even though it was after twelve. "I'm the one in charge of the Lasker house."

Ah, Peter thought, that's the other reason I'm being hooked up with the constable. The Lasker residence was in his patrol area. He had taken the first call and he considered the crime scene his personal domain.

Overweight though he was, Constable Willet raised no objection when Peter suggested they walk. The house keys jangled in Willet's pocket as they made their way down the cobbled road one street over from the high street. Peter was thankful that he didn't lead them up any of the streets that climbed farther inland; he knew CPR but had no desire to apply it. The Laskers' street curved around the hill away from the main commercial area, but still within the boundaries of the town centre. Willet stopped before a narrow house, much like every other in the row except for the glaring police tape and *Keep Out* notice stuck to the door. That would have to go, Peter decided. While Willet sorted through his ring of keys, Peter took a moment to check the front view. If you craned your neck from the top floor, he estimated, you might find the sea. The former council houses along the row were identical, only the colour of the heavy front doors varying. Ever since various cities in the British Isles began flogging posters of the "doors of pick-your-city," homeowners had been painting their entrances bright crayon colours. On this strip there were doors done in shiny orange, blue, red and pink. The Lasker door was Lincoln green.

"Typical two up, two down," Willet volunteered.

The house appeared to be well maintained, and Peter knew from the file that the Laskers had owned it mortgage-free. Willet jiggled the supplementary lock, which resembled the lock boxes used by estate agents. You had to open the box in order to get the key that let you into the house. The police notice read: *No Entry, by Order of the Police. Leave no mail or flyers.* The phone number of the Whittlesun station completed the notice.

Bartleben would have insisted on the call with Maris that his people preserve the killing ground as found, without any further disturbance except for the taking of blood samples and the impounding of documents found in the rooms. The Yard hated nothing more than arriving, as consulting experts, at a crime scene that had been trampled by eager policemen. Peter had seen Yard detectives pulled out of crime sites before they even started. He was sure that the demand had offended Maris, since Bartleben was, in effect, challenging his competence, and further implying that Maris shouldn't have waited three days before calling in London, by which time some of the forensic evidence would have mouldered.

They stepped inside. A storm might have come up from the sea and blown through the house. The complete disarray and the immediacy of the frozen drama in the home sent a sickening thrill through Peter Cammon, even though he had probed hundreds of crime scenes. A light had been left on in the vestibule and he could see blood on the right side of the corridor. He flipped the nearby switch and another ceiling light went on at the end of the hallway. A third overhead had been smashed. He moved gingerly into the space. Passion, fear and spite were stamped in blood along the hall and the entry to the back kitchen. Red smears, at hip level, ran along the corridor like some demented wainscoting.

A plastic runner had been laid on the bloodied carpet. Peter asked Willet to turn on every light on the ground floor. He took a pair of pigskin gloves from his pocket and put them on; he had meant to leave them behind in his hotel room with his hat and umbrella. They would serve his purposes now.

"Constable, could you search in the kitchen for a lightbulb and install it here?"

"Right you are, Guv," Willet replied. The use of "Guv" was only marginally tolerable within police protocol but Peter didn't care about ceremony. Willet disappeared. Peter stood stock still in the corridor, trying to gain an initial impression of the Laskers. The outside of their house was well kept, up to the standard of the street, and the entranceway was recently painted too. Even before examining the living room, he understood that the Laskers were solid middle class.

Willet returned with the bulb; he was tall enough to screw it into the socket without using a stepladder. Now Peter had a full view of the through-line from the front door to the kitchen. The fight had flowed from front to back. Still near the vestibule, he knelt down on the plastic and leaned close to the corner where the plaster met the baseboard. He stood again and peered up at the junction of the wall and the ceiling. No dust had accumulated at the lower corner; no cobwebs at the top of the wall. He sighted along the surface halfway up and, aside from the blood spatter and several traumatic gouges, the wall was smooth.

The wavy bar of blood down the corridor had been made by someone trailing their hand along the wall. The track faded out halfway down as the blood ran out; the gruesome painter had dipped his hand — the right hand, he could tell — in a pool of blood again and begun a new line, which ended at the kitchen door jamb.

Peter left the hallway and explored the living room. The lighting remained subdued even though Willet had turned on the table lamps and a floor lamp behind the television. Peter at once noted differences in the blood patterning. There was plenty of it on the chesterfield and the stuffed chair, and even the ottoman, but it was thinly spread, and nowhere pooled. Anna hadn't made her last stand here. It appeared that she, or perhaps the husband, had sat in the blood on the footstool. *Did she retreat there and wait, sobbing and fearful? Would it be too much to ask the forensics wizards to test the carpet for salty tears?* The damage in the living room, aside from the blood, was oddly selective. On either side of the gas fireplace, the brocade curtains were bunched on the floor below their broken tracks. Someone had used an axe or cleaver to drive a ruinous gouge into the top of the mahogany sideboard, but neither the victim nor the attacker had upended chairs or the chesterfield.

"Constable," he called, "is there anything in the police inventory about an axe or a hatchet?"

Willet's form filled the entrance to the hall. "Not in the drawing room, sir, there wasn't. There's a cleaver in the rack in the kitchen, I can show you, but there was surprisingly little in the way of tools or blunt objects, given that Lasker was a car mechanic. We were looking out for a murder weapon."

25

"Has anything been moved from its original position?"

"No, sir, I can guarantee that. You see, sir, I was the one took the call. It was on my beat." Willet seemed bewildered; he remained wary of any challenge from Peter. "Kept it as it was, sir. Inspector Maris assigned me the key, as it were. No one has gone in and out without me."

"Thank you, Constable Willet." Indeed, the battlefield had been well preserved. Willet had not even rekiltered the furniture. But someone had moved the cleaver back to its slot in the kitchen, he was almost certain.

Willet was trying to be helpful but it was time to get rid of him. Peter Cammon's solitary habits were entrenched and, at the outset, always impressionistic. Here in the family home, emotions still hung in the air, and he hoped to latch on to their echoes. He didn't need the constable sucking the oxygen out of the rooms. But he reminded himself to be diplomatic.

"Constable, could you give me a half hour alone here? I want to get a feel for the movements of the wife."

Willet was offended, and he wasn't stupid. Peter's request was disdainful, if only because the Scotland Yard man wasn't taking him into his confidence.

"But I want to show you the kitchen," Willet said. "It's significant."

"Good. Give me a few minutes on my own, then we'll rendezvous in the kitchen."

Willet nodded and slouched outside, making sure to leave the front door unlatched.

Peter stood there for an additional minute, letting Willet's aura fade. The pace of his explorations was important. He wasn't reaching for some psychic resonance, and it was nothing so hackneyed as waiting for the dead to speak to him; he had known investigators who claimed to do that. It was more about order and disorder. Where had the fight started, and how had it progressed through the house? He saw that it had been a rampaging fight, leaving blood in every room. But where had it climaxed?

26

A wavering, finger-painted line of blood beckoned him up the stairs. It deteriorated to thick blotches at the top landing. The lavatory was right there and he almost stepped in a red stream that, trickling from over by the bathtub, had coagulated by the entry, where the tile transitioned to carpet. He took another step, trying not to slip in the blood, even though much of it had dried to an embedded crust. He scanned the room. The thickest concentration coated the rim of the tub. Peter thought it odd that nylons, at least ten pair (and not pantyhose), still hung from the shower bar, like Spanish moss.

In the sink, dried rivulets of blood, topped with fragments from the shattered medicine chest mirror above it, stained the porcelain. He would check the coroner's preliminary report to verify that Mrs. Lasker's head lacerations were consistent with having been rammed into the mirror. He bent over the sink. Even though the drain was open, there was an excessive amount of red liquid left, thickly marring the surface. Blood had jetted from a wound, leaving a feathered stain on the wall next to the cabinet. Experience told Peter that a gash would have to be deep, perhaps arterial, in order to account for such a spray pattern.

The lavatory deserved more investigation, but Peter decided to complete his tour of the upstairs. He walked straight across the landing to the bedroom. The fight hadn't started here. The shade was down and the curtains, of heavy velvet, remained drawn. Willet had turned on the two bedside lamps. There was no blood here, and no destruction. He turned off the lamps. He left the bedroom but immediately turned back and flicked the switch for the overhead. He stood at the foot of the king-size bed. Her side was on the left, from which a spicy perfume rose. A single earring lay on the bedside table. The rumpled sheets showed the turmoil of bad dreams. The husband's side, on the right, hadn't been slept in; the hospital corners were in place.

Peter started back downstairs but he stopped in mid-step, realizing two fresh truths about the crime scene. First, looking down the angle of the staircase, he understood that the blood trail had begun at the top of the steps, not the reverse line he had followed. It was clear that the violence hadn't begun in the bedroom. *But who begins to assault his spouse in the lavatory?* Also, in spite of the shambles, he discerned that in normal times the Laskers had valued order and conventionality; they had maintained a presentable house. The devastation was more than the by-product of anger: it stood out as a deliberate desecration of their pride of ownership.

He performed another loop, including the undamaged areas. He let the gloom, the hollowness, envelop him. If Tolstoy was right that every unhappy family is unhappy in its own way, then he could believe that every domestic quarrel was unique too. The blood pattern indicated desperation like he had seldom seen, yet André Lasker's escape had been reasoned out in every detail, he was becoming sure.

Peter decided to view the kitchen before calling Willet back in, but when he entered the back room, there was the constable on the porch peering in. He went directly to the door to let him in, as if he had intended to all along, but Willet saw the sham.

The damage in the kitchen was dramatic but limited. The two cupboards that had glass fronts had been poked in and the pieces had spilled onto the counter. A wooden knife rack stood next to the fridge; each slot was full, and the cleaver had been re-inserted into its leather pouch. Peter removed each blade in turn, finding no blood on any of them. The cleaver, about eight inches long and capable of making the gouge in the sideboard, was bloodless too.

"What do you think, Inspector?" Willet said.

"Hand me that torch on your belt, Constable."

Willet unhooked the torch and handed it over. Peter pulled the leather side pouch apart and illuminated the bottom of the opening. The fragments inside could have been merely dust, or possibly wood fragments.

"What do you think, Guv?" Willet said. Peter ignored him.

The out-of-synch item in the kitchen was the cooker, which was stained beyond redemption with tomato sauce and charred scraps of food. Spice smells mixed with carbon. A pot of clotting red liquid sat on a rear burner.

28

"Goulash," Willet said proudly. "I was here when the detectives first went through the place. They farted around with the pot there on the hob, started talking about was it blood, was it tomato sauce."

Peter sensed that Willet had more he wanted to tell him.

"Back and forth they went," Willet continued. "They weren't getting anywhere, so I leaned in, dipped my finger in the pot and settled it. Found out afterwards it was a Dutch stew, *goulash tomaat*, the kind wives leave on the back of the stove cooking for weeks."

"How did you find out what it was called?"

"Research. Obviously it was an ethnic recipe, by the taste. Thought at first it was Romanian, given the wife was from Bucharest. Then I jumped to the idea it maybe was Dutch stew, from his side of the family. I checked the Internet and found the ingredients."

Willet smiled broadly beneath his overflowing moustache. Peter was willing to grant the constable small victories, particularly when they were doomed to disappoint each other on other fronts. Peter glanced around the kitchen and let out his breath. He might as well get the next problem over with.

"Good work, Constable. I'm done for now but I want to come back tomorrow."

"Nobody'll be touching it as long as you need it, but . . ." Peter knew what he would say next. The constable mimicked the North Wind as he heaved a massive sigh and exhaled. "Gonna be a devil to clean. That blood is drying in and it'll all start to smell pretty soon. This kitchen . . ."

Peter wasn't concerned about the rehabilitation of the house. There were firms who did that kind of thing. What he needed was his own key. And so he did what he had to do to intimidate Willet: he invoked the Yard.

"The house cannot be released until we review the forensics, see what else needs to be done. If I have to call in London for additional tests, I will. We'll see. Thank you for your help, Constable. Can you provide me with a door key?"

He had tried for a firm tone, but not too harsh, and he watched the calculations roll over in Willet's brain. His face betrayed the lumpen resentment of a man who had spent a lifetime obeying orders from better paid officers. Peter edged towards the hallway and the front door. Willet was pondering his supervisor's reaction to Scotland Yard's request. Peter turned and looked expectantly at him.

"All right, Inspector, take the spare," Willet responded. "I found it out back under a flower pot. You're welcome to it."

"Leave it there," Peter said. "I'll retrieve it as needed."

Willet locked the front and they stepped down to the empty street. They agreed that the yellow tape and the *Keep Out* notice only attracted snoops and vandals and they removed the warning; a chunk of the green lacquer came off with the notice. Willet looked up and down the bare street and shifted from one heavy foot to the other. He picked up on Peter's comment from five minutes ago. "I dunno, Guv'nor. The scanners over in the local lab are pretty good."

"I have no doubt." Peter had confidence in the Regional Forensics Laboratory, which served all of southwest Britain, and the Whittlesun Force was proud to have the facility on the edge of their town. But they did not have Stan Bracher from the London lab, whom Peter liked to think of as his personal haematology expert. He'd make the call from the street once the constable went his own way.

Willet remained sullen and stoic. He'd done nothing wrong, Peter reminded himself. His tone was conciliatory as he said, "Constable, if you were André Lasker, how would you disappear?"

Willet rubbed his beefy hands together as if he had been waiting for someone to ask him this very question.

"I'd stash some clothes and a disguise in one of the caves up the coast and hide out there for a night. The next morning I'd hitchhike the short hop to Plymouth, buy a ticket on the ferry to Cherbourg."

"Why that ferry?"

"Well, it only takes three hours."

"Have you done it?"

"What, Cherbourg? What business do I have in Normandy?"

CHAPTER 4

It was now mid-afternoon and Peter was scheduled to meet Detective Hamm at the Crown at 5:00 p.m.; he intended to be on time. But he was restless. To some, though not to Bartleben, he was known as a plodder, yet he understood momentum, the momentum *he* needed in order to gain perspective and push the investigation along to the next stage.

And he already sensed that some things were wrong.

There was time for a quick interview with André Lasker's mother, who, according to the file material, lived nearby. Peter was still gathering general impressions, and she might be a good source of information about her son's marriage. He needed Willet to introduce him to the mother, but not to stay around. As it turned out, Willet was quite open to Peter's suggestion that he see Mrs. Lasker alone, and led him to the front door without ceremony, and certainly without griping. Peter chose not to over-interpret the gesture.

Having made sure that Peter had his mobile number, Willet waved goodbye and walked off. Of course, in the exchange, the constable now had his number.

The old lady occupied a typical terrace house on a quiet street. She had resided there for fifty years and had given birth to two sons in it, the first boy dying in infancy. All this he knew from the file, although oddly there was no record of her being interviewed by the Whittlesun Police. She answered the door when he buzzed, and smiled warmly when he apologized for interrupting her afternoon. She was grey and birdlike; her left eye wandered as she tried to focus.

"Officer Wilmot?" And Peter understood that not only had she been interviewed by the police, Willet had done it. He'd failed to mention that.

"Come in, please," she continued. "Are you here for Mrs. Pease or for Mrs. Lasker?"

"To see you, Madam," Peter said, for he recognized her from a family portrait in her son's bedroom. She spoke with a wisp of Dutch inflection.

The mother shuffled towards the interior of the house, assuming he would follow. The living room was populated by an excess of doilies, Toby jugs and teapots, but had been beautifully maintained. He estimated the place to be worth one and a half times the selling price of her son's home (if and when someone repainted it). The basswood trim around the doors had been refinished recently, and the paint on the walls was fresh and tasteful. Was André an attentive son wanting to comfort his mother, or had he been preparing for the day when she would be gone? Or the day when he would go.

The other lady, Mrs. Pease, came down the stairs and introduced herself in a hovering, protective manner, and waved him to a large stuffed chair. Her height gave her a mannish look. She begrudged him a smile. "Hello. I am Mrs. Pease and I live here."

Bully for you, Peter wanted to say, but he sat down anyway. "Chief Inspector Cammon."

Mrs. Lasker took what looked to be her habitual spot on the chesterfield opposite him, and before Mrs. Pease could speak, demanded: "Tea!"

It was apparent that the conversation wouldn't begin until the tea ritual was set in motion, and so Peter waited with the old woman while Mrs. Pease went to the kitchen. When they were settled, Mrs. Pease, who wore heavy pearls and whose hair had been permed that very day, took on the role of interpreter for her companion.

"Mr. Cammon is from the police, dear," she said, putting her hand over her friend's.

Senile dementia, in Peter's experience, varied widely case by case, and Mrs. Lasker's disease had rendered her a benign, happy figure. Still, he wasn't sure that an interlocutor was useful. He would have wagered that she had forgotten the distant years as a War refugee, and the death of her husband. Nothing he asked could revive any deeper truths from that era.

"Collecting?" Mrs. Lasker said.

"Collecting?" Peter said. "I'm here to ask you about your son, André."

Mrs. Pease placed her left hand over Peter's right, as if completing a séance circle, and frowned.

"My son," said Mrs. Lasker, "is dead. Buried in Marchmount Cemetery."

"André."

"He is my second son."

"Yes, and when did you last see him?"

"Sunday. He always visits then."

"That is accurate," Mrs. Pease said, withdrawing her hand from Peter's. Her duty, it seemed, as she saw it, was not to amplify but only to verify.

But Mrs. Lasker wanted to talk. She bounced from snippets of André's childhood to comments on current politics at Whitehall to memories of sunny days along the cliffs, when she and André would picnic and take in the views of the Channel. Peter gave up asking sequential questions and remained content with minutiae. Her rambling anecdotes by no means coalesced into a clear picture of the mother–son relationship but he learned that old Mrs. Lasker was on good terms with her daughter-in-law. Her son had remained devoted over the years and had kept up the house for both ladies. Peter had hoped for general impressions of the Lasker clan, and that was about all he got.

At the door, Peter turned to Mrs. Pease, who was three inches taller.

"Did André visit every Sunday?"

"Yes. She knows nothing of what happened. We've had the police here before. Now yourself." She looked worried, defiant. "Will you be executing a search warrant?"

"No, Mrs. Pease. But I may need to come back."

As he moved to the doorway he suddenly understood about the sauce. It hadn't been "research" at all; Willet had identified the Dutch goulash from the mother. Mrs. Lasker had taught Anna the recipe and she had kept a pot boiling on the stove to please her husband. Peter tolerated Willet's effort to exalt his police work. His unconfessed restoration of the cleaver to its slot in the kitchen was another matter.

Peter hastened back to the high street, not because he was late for the pub but to try to fit in a quick call to London before meeting Hamm. The air in the Lasker place had been rancid, in the kitchen in particular, and the atmosphere in the mother's house not much fresher. As he walked, he took in whiffs of tomato sauce, oregano and lavender. He should have dropped by the hotel to take a shower and change into his tweed jacket, but he didn't really mind. He carried part of the killing floor with him, and that was a memory he needed to sustain. He considered returning to the house now. He would like to sit in the hallway, or the kitchen, or the blood-painted lavatory, until Anna finished telling him her secrets.

He reached the Crown sooner than he expected. He guessed that Hamm would be early, probably already inside. Streams of young couples crossed in front of him on the pavement, celebrating the fading of their work day. Passersby seemed startled by the sight of the elderly man in the black suit standing in front of the pub window, trying to make himself heard through his mobile phone. Peter was lucky and reached Bartleben on the first ring, but it was almost impossible to hear through the din on the street. He shouted.

"Stephen, are you there? I've just visited the Lasker home. I have no time now but I wanted to make sure you'll be around later."

Sir Stephen had read the call display and picked up before his secretary outside could reach her phone. He was eating a very late lunch, take-away sushi from the place on the corner. He considered Cammon's statement doubly inane. If Peter needed to talk to him later, he need only ring up later. If he had to talk now, make the time. Bartleben didn't mind a bit. He understood the rhythms here, the momentum that Cammon must create at the start of a case, and if it sounded to the layman like neurosis, he knew that Peter was the most rational of operatives. His first thought when Peter made these calls was always: better him in the field than me. Bartleben's role, at this stage, was to man the cheering section. He was amused by the ambient shouts of the pub patrons on the street, and thought of baiting Peter with a comment about hanging out with a non-octogenarian crowd; but you didn't tweak Peter Cammon at this point in an assignment.

There was only one thing to say: "Christ on a crutch, Peter! Call whenever it suits you, and if I'm asleep, have a chat with the wife."

"Okay," Peter said. If Bartleben heard the unease in his colleague's voice, he didn't over-analyze it. It was the fact he had called that was important. He knew from talking to that pompous Inspector Maris that the Lasker place was a slaughterhouse. That was precisely why he sent Cammon. He now grasped that something in the house had set Peter off. It was a bit early, but, he guessed, Cammon was about to cause some trouble.

The Crown was nearly filled with after-work patrons but Hamm, whether thanks to his police credentials or because he was a regular, had commandeered a booth at the back. It was away from the swinging door to the kitchen, and Peter was grateful not to have warm grease added to the veneer of smells on his suit. Hamm looked as unkempt as ever, that white shirt never staying tucked in. His face carried the stains of a hard day and he had given up combing his hair. So much for trying to impress the man from the Yard. Yet he was openly glad to see Peter and pumped his hand with a dry grip. He gestured for Peter to take the bench opposite.

"I presumed to order you a pint," the young man said, but then he looked doubtful.

Peter smiled and sat down. He was suddenly happy to be drinking in a pub, and at once raised his stein. He loved beer, a little too much perhaps, and seldom touched wine or the hard stuff. The beer tasted wonderful.

"To your health. How has your day been, Mr. Hamm?"

"That's Hamm, short for Hamster, as in running in place on a wheel all day. I've been getting to know the coastline more than I wanted. Villages I never heard of, like Glenfanning, New Dominion and Dunstaffnage. Did you see the Lasker place?"

"A first time through, yes."

"And what did you think, Guv?"

"Ah, the watchful Constable Willet. I appreciate his preserving the crime scene, but I would rather he didn't seal it off against me."

Hamm laughed politely and swigged his beer. "While we're on the subject . . ."

He fished a thick envelope from under the table and handed it over. "This is the balance of the Lasker file, the interview notes and so on."

Peter took the two-inch packet of documents and tucked it under his coat on the banquette. He decided not to reveal his talk with Mrs. Lasker and Mrs. Pease, at least for the moment. He wasn't sure why he demurred. It had something to do with the cleaver, the possibility that Hamm himself had moved it.

"Thank you."

Hamm leaned closer. "Also in there is what we have on the Rover, the Task Force summaries. That's what they've shared with us."

"But aren't you officially on the Task Force?"

"As of today, yes. Before now we were ex officio members. Liaison status, if you will."

"Bureaucracy," Peter sympathized. He knew Jack McElroy and couldn't see a reason for him to exclude Maris. But McElroy was cautious by nature, and maybe the inspector had somehow overplayed his game — clearly he had career ambitions. Peter reminded himself not to speculate; it wasn't his case.

But then he immediately violated his own admonition. "Let me guess. Maris thinks the predator will move into Dorset soon, and McElroy won't yet concede the point."

Hamm raised his mug. "Exactly. You see, the predator has committed four murders in Devon, but he's definitely moving this way."

"I thought I heard three."

"Three confirmed murders. Girls about the same age. All local teenagers. A fourth girl, Molly Jonas, hasn't been found, but, you know . . ."

"Do they think the killer's local?"

"They won't speculate — the Task Force people, that is. But he leaves the bodies in obscure places along the cliffs, which indicates that our man knows the area. The curious part is, they were abducted from well-known walking trails, of which there are hundreds near the Channel, but left in odd caves or places that are hard to get to. The second girl was abandoned, dead, on a big rock overlooking the Channel."

"Ritualistic?"

"Yes. Laid out for sacrifice, you might say."

"Any indication that he knew the women?" Peter asked.

Hamm offered a puzzled look whenever Peter asked a question. He seemed to think there was a secret Scotland Yard technique in play each time, when it was just Peter's blunt style of inquiry doing battle with his resolve not to chime in too hastily on the Rover investigation.

"No indications either way. The women were taken from trails close to villages or their own farms. We're out there questioning everyone we can find. Alert them without panicking them."

Peter finished his pint a bit too fast and leaned back against the bench. The bar echoed with shouts and clattering glasses. McElroy seemed convinced that the Rover would limit himself to Devon, but the pattern clearly was linear, eastward. Investigators always looked for patterns, but this one — a measured geographical sequence — made little sense to Peter. For one thing, rapists are opportunists, as well as impulsive. He leaned forward.

"Just musing here, but could the spacing of the killings indicate that the Rover *doesn't* know his surroundings? That perhaps it's less risky for him to find a new killing ground and not revisit old venues?"

"But he would have to explore each new path and set up new observation posts, new lines of sight," Hamm replied. "Risky, I think."

The greatest fear from the Task Force's viewpoint, Peter knew, was that the serial killer would suspend activity for the winter and pick up again in the spring. Meanwhile, anxiety among residents along the coast wouldn't lie dormant. The political pressures, from village officials and women's groups, you name it, were already growing, he was sure.

Hamm was right with him. "Know who's squawking the loudest? The tourist authorities. Say they're losing business. From whom? Bird watchers? Boat spotters? Crikey, it's September! Soon be winter and nobody on the cliffs."

Hamm drew a line down the sweat on his beer glass. "There's something else in play, but Maris doesn't want us talking about it."

"Okay, I won't talk about it." Peter tried to look neutral.

"London just won its bid for the 2012 Summer Olympics. The organizers want the sailing events to happen on the Jurassic Coast. They don't need a scandal. Don't be surprised if J.J. McElroy gets nervous about publicity."

Peter understood that the pressure would be on to nab this Rover quickly. He grimaced at the likely fortunes of Scotland Yard in all this. For a while, Jack McElroy would resist calling on the Yard, hoping for quick clearance of the case; but if it dragged on, a way would be found to shift responsibility to London. Peter stopped before downing the dregs of his beer. He should give Jack McElroy more credit as a pro — cynicism had crept in with the booze.

Hamm fetched another round. He and Peter knew no one could overhear them, but they kept their voices low anyway. Peter hefted the envelope containing the Lasker and Rover material, held it aloft in acknowledgment, and placed it under his coat once more.

"Thanks for the briefing, Ron," he said. "I'll read the file through tonight. By the way, has there been talk of calling in Scotland Yard's profilers?"

"It came up at Maris's staff meeting," Hamm said. "McElroy has indicated that the Task Force can handle it, maybe with a bit of help from the Regional Lab. Maris strongly agrees."

"They're within their authority to refuse. You can be sure, however, London's already made the offer."

For some reason the pub began to empty out. It was midweek and perhaps the after-work drinkers were due home for supper; fewer than a dozen patrons remained, and the bar fell into near silence. The quiet seemed to change the air pressure in the bar, leaving Peter and Hamm light-headed. Hamm gave no signal that he was expected at home; Maris must be pushing his staff hard to put in long days, Peter reasoned. The young man persisted in treating Peter with excessive deference. His was the Scotland Yard of Lestrade and Gregson, and better yet the independent preoccupations of Sherlock. There was a certain belatedness in Hamm's attitude, as if he felt he was living a detective's career a hundred years too late.

Peter bought another round, which neither needed.

Hamm drifted off for a minute; Peter let him doze. He forced his thoughts back to Anna Lasker and pondered the case in its skeleton form. André had fled for good, Peter was certain. Interpol, Europol and the Yard were actively pursuing the international angle, the offshore investigation as it were, and with a bit of luck a customs official or an alert tourist would catch sight of him. If he had drowned himself, then he would wash up on shore somewhere along the Jurassic Coast in his own sweet time. But Peter knew that both these resolutions depended far too much on serendipity. If he was to determine where André had diverted from the plan, he had to move fast. He might still be close by; but within days he would flee England, remorse fading with his memories of his Romanian wife.

"I'm going back into the Lasker house tomorrow," he said, leaning close. Hamm roused himself. "Their computer is still in the house, I noticed. Has it been examined?"

Hamm smiled and straightened in his seat. "I was the first in the door," he declared. "Well, after Constable Willet. We have a very good computer man in the shop and I immediately had him dupli-cate the hard drive and the discs. It seemed to me that Lasker was pretty adept with computers."

"So the hard drive is intact and still in the home?"

"Oh, yes."

"Would you mind getting the necessary passwords from your colleague?"

Hamm paused again, but gave a firm nod. Peter didn't know how to read this constant hesitation. He decided to barge ahead.

"I also want to take a look at the cliffs where Anna took her fall." Hamm arched an eyebrow at this phrasing. "Could we meet here again tomorrow afterwards?"

"Maris wants me to go to Heffingdon in the morning. Another town official to brief. But I'll call you once I'm through. Let's try for the same time. Here's my mobile."

They exchanged business cards. Hamm looked ready to have Peter's card, embossed with the Yard's crest, framed immediately. He smiled broadly.

They stopped outside the bar. Peter was about to step into the sharp wind when Hamm called to him. "The cleaver?"

"Yes?"

"If you were wondering, I was the one who put it back in the kitchen. Couldn't stand the sight of it buried in the sideboard. Just thought I'd clear that up."

Peter, exhausted, retreated to his hotel room, placed the *Please Do Not Disturb* sign on the outer knob, and locked the door. He hung up his suit and lay down on the bed in his underwear. He no longer had any wish to interact with Bartleben; he only wanted to sleep.

Bartleben answered on the first ring. He seemed to have retained his jolly mood.

"Peter! Yes, I'm still at the office."

Peter massaged his stiff neck. "Thought I'd give you a progress report."

"Before we get to the Lasker business," Sir Stephen said, "what about the attacks in Devon?"

"I understood we were to dodge that whole mess," Peter rejoined.

"Well, it got play in the tabloids this morning. Communications has fielded eight calls, not counting those from little old ladies, who always seem to find *my* number. Just thought I'd check, Peter."

"We've nothing to tell them. Who's the Comm person on this? Markman?"

"Yeah."

"Tell her to tell everyone we're staying out of it. Avoid calling him 'the Rover.' So far, it remains a local matter. That's the line I'd choose."

"Peter, I can figure that much out. The question is, where's it heading? What options should the Yard be keeping open?"

The call had been a bad idea, Peter saw. They both had reason to be embarrassed. Peter had already indulged himself, snooping into the Task Force dossier, and evidently Bartleben wouldn't be able to stay out of it either. All he meant to suggest was that the Yard continue to play reluctant bridegroom with the Task Force for now, knowing that McElroy would eventually be calling for help. Bartleben should let it go for tonight. The Comm people would fudge everything anyway,

41

keeping all options open. And it would be nice if Bartleben acknowledged his primary — *and only* — assignment in Whittlesun.

"I don't know where it's headed," Peter finally said, "but McElroy doesn't want our help, so let's wait."

Sir Stephen was determined to stretch this out. "I'm a bit surprised at that. Three victims. The pressure must be building. Why do you think that is? Regional defensiveness?"

Peter wouldn't engage further, other than to snipe: "By the way, there are *four* girls."

"Is there a threshold for declaring someone a serial killer?"

"If there is," Peter said dismissively, "the press sets it."

"Okay," Bartleben said, "now what about Mrs. Lasker? Was she killed in the house or pushed from the cliff?"

"I'm leaning towards his knocking her unconscious and dumping her off the cliff, gruesome as that sounds. There's a lot of blood but no sign of a major arterial spill. I don't think she died in the house. I've got a few more days."

"Keep on with it, then." This bland vote of confidence was code; it meant that Sir Stephen was unable to judge the degree of progress Peter was or was not making, but he wasn't yet concerned.

"Regarding the house, I'd like Stan Bracher to take a look," Peter said. "And the vehicle too."

"Okay, but he's in Lyon at the moment, taking a course. Or maybe giving one."

"Anything from the French or Interpol?"

"No. We covered all the ferry ports on both sides of the Channel. No one fitting Lasker's description crossed at Plymouth, Poole or Newhaven, or any of the other southern embarkation ports. Passport Services and the Border Agency had no incidents reported. How hard do you want me to push it?"

The subtext of Bartleben's update was that Scotland Yard was willing to assert its natural role in pursuing international inquiries about the fugitive, but that an expanded international manhunt could get expensive and could take on some diplomatic sensitivity.

While the Lasker drama was fresh there would be no problem gaining full, active cooperation.

"Very hard," Peter replied. "I'd say it's more than even chances he planned his escape to the last detail. That's not to say he didn't drown in the process. And it's possible he's in the neighbourhood still. One officer here suggested he might be hiding in a cave up the coast."

Bartleben sighed at the end of the line. Peter was falling asleep. "Okay, Peter. Call me the day after next, or earlier if you need to. One final question."

Peter knew what was coming. Bartleben knew that he knew.

"Are you getting along with the locals, Peter?"

"Maris was unhelpful but I'm cultivating other sources. It will become intolerable if and when we start stepping on each other's toes, when we're both tramping up and down the coast of England. I might want to look into those caves, if they exist."

Bartleben was satisfied for the moment. His last thought before hanging up was that Peter Cammon was the oddest detective he had ever worked with, and that he had complete faith in him.

Peter hit the off button on his phone and lay back in the soft pillows. He immediately fell asleep, having forgotten to phone his wife.

CHAPTER 5

Peter had left an hour ago. Joan hadn't seen Verden arrive, but that was normal; she and Peter were too old to worry about his schedule, about short-term goodbyes. If waiting at the end of the lane was one of his idiosyncrasies, and there were many of them, it didn't bother her a whit.

She positioned herself at the window of the kitchen of the cottage so that she could see to the far end of the property. They owned about an acre, not all of it groomed, and the ninety yards or so out to the property's limit — she could barely make out the fence posts — had been left to grow wild. The grass grew to four feet at the untended property line and moss now coated the hillocks of stone and concrete the landscapers had discarded. The previous owner had once tried to raise flowers in this section, and red and orange gladioli continued to poke up here and there, even after three decades. But it wasn't glads she was looking for, rather the new quartet of pheasants that had invaded last week. Two pairs were now installed in the high grass. One at a time they would pop up unexpectedly, look around and then drop out of sight again. It was like a video game.

She expected Peter to call sometime that day. That was one of their agreed-upon courtesies, but it was only a matter of his checking in, and he might call anytime before midnight, and so she did not worry. She took the phone out of its cradle near the microwave and went outside to the front of the house. She could still see to the end of the yard.

The long shed, the biggest by far of their four outbuildings, framed the right-hand side of her view. The pheasants were hiding somewhere in the grass just beyond, probably basking in the increasingly warm day. Eventually the regular activity in the yard would flush out the birds for good; they would turn neurotic and fly away. For now, she had work to do in the shed and she hoped to catch sight of one or more of them out back as she fussed with her plants.

Phone in hand, she walked to the far end of the shed. The last owner had moved from flowers to chickens and had invested in this huge building as a coop. Like all his ventures, that operation never made money, but the building was solid and Joan and Peter had each had visions of ways to use it. After days of washing out the chicken droppings and repairing the cracked windows, they had sat down and negotiated. She wanted a potting shed and he wanted a hobby room and sanctuary. The shed was big enough to accommodate both. Her gardening gear now took up two-thirds of the length of the structure. His smaller domain became a sort of study-workroom, complete with teak shelving for his books, indoor-outdoor carpeting and a workbench for his projects.

She had dubbed it Hispaniola: his portion was Haiti and hers the Dominican Republic, with the wall between serving as the border. They agreed not to cut a door through the wall; one had to go outside to get to the other's space. She used her portion of the shed every day, but Peter, since beginning his semi-retirement three years ago, had been busier than they had expected and, in Joan's summation, had used his part of the shed only sporadically. But Peter evolved slowly and she sensed that more and more he regarded it as an important place to ruminate on cases, old and new — a sanctum. The question in her mind was: what had happened to retirement? At first he had claimed he was bored and cynical after so many years of police work, yet he had taken multiple assignments each year since.

45

She entered the potting room by its only door and went to one of the small, square windows that looked out on the unmowed section of the yard. She was pleased to see a female pheasant stick her head up and look around, retreating after only a few seconds. Joan inspected the stacks of pots and the pegboard of tools. Her gardening season was winding down. The flowers were flourishing in late summer glory but everything was overripe, almost ready to drop petals and wither, though it was too soon to cap the old blooms or dig anything up. There was work she could do but, perhaps because Peter had just left, she felt the need to take a moment and settle into her day of solitude. She paused to appreciate the absolute silence.

She told herself she wasn't worried about him.

Joan left the hut and walked around to Peter's side, entering the unlocked door. He wouldn't mind her going in; this was not a marriage where either spouse would accuse the other of snooping. The room had burgeoned into an Englishman's study, lacking the wood panelling but replete with dozens of books (they would have to be moved inside for the extreme part of the winter) and two green-globed reading lamps. A rocking chair added to the atmosphere and a wood-burning stove, an iron potbelly, completed it, although the stove hadn't been lit in months. Along one wall they had installed a low table, where Peter worked on his projects.

A tilting stack of old peach crates leaned out from the same wall; several more lay on the table. About two years ago, Peter had started making shadow boxes. Yet another scheme of the previous owner, his most misguided, had been the planting of peach trees. This was an unprecedented agricultural venture — unprecedented for a reason, the brutal cycle of English weather — and it had failed quickly. The trees had rotted out and he had left behind the stained, often rancid peach crates. At that point, Peter, still not knowing what he would do with the crates, hosed them down and set them to drying in the summer sun. He salvaged two hundred of them and by the time they were dried out, they no longer stank. It would take another twenty-five years for him to find a use for them.

"I have no evident talent," he had confessed to her, "but does assembling collages require much artistic flair?" He wasn't looking to her for an answer. In forty-some years of marriage he had seldom asked a question that wasn't rhetorical. But he took all his projects seriously. He did the necessary research on the Web and learned that the Surrealists, such as Ernst and Cornell, had often made collages and shadow boxes from found objects. Peter's lack of training didn't discourage him. He noticed that the Surrealists and Dadaists used collages to express dream states, and if there was one thing that Peter Cammon grasped as an operating principle in his professional method, it was the use of instinct and free association to lead him onto fresh pathways of thought. He decided to use found objects from the countryside around the cottage to assemble montages, and then see what resulted. His method was almost the reverse of Freudian dream symbolism. Rather than remember his dreams and then represent them inside a box, he randomly juxtaposed the objects, letting them tell him something about his own psychology. He was really more Dada than Surreal, more Arp than Ernst.

Joan picked up an empty peach crate and chuckled. When Peter started making his shadow boxes, he sometimes wandered into the house, or around the side of the shed to where she was adjusting some potted flower, and held up a crate, turning it from side to side to point to the purply ink pattern left on the bottom by rotting peaches. "Here's another miracle!" he would announce, inviting her to make out the face of Jesus in the stain. Perhaps, Joan mused, it would have been funnier had her husband been a practising Christian.

She examined several finished boxes lined up on the shelf over the workbench. Removing her bifocals, she stuck her face almost inside one of them; she wanted to absorb all the detail he had put into the tableau. The first one had a bird theme, with cut-out pictures of doves in midair and a black angel peering out from behind yellow clouds, which were fashioned from a mouse's nest. The clouds and birds hovered over pictures of incongruous items, including a pomegranate, a cricket bat and a chariot. These were part of what Joan had dubbed his "bird series," although he had frowned when she said it. From the very first box he had made she had thought them beautiful.

She had seen others before, such as the collage of glued-on watch mechanisms. But farther down the row she found peach boxes on a different theme. She saw that they were incomplete, awaiting important additions. In general the iconography was religious, with an angel in every scene and often the Virgin Mary or a male figure in robes. Joan was Church of England, and so was Peter to the extent he would admit an affiliation, but these images felt Roman Catholic in their depiction of Bible themes. She looked closer and saw that the cut-outs were all from pre-Reformation medieval art. They didn't own any books of medieval art.

And herein, she thought, lay the struggle that Peter was going through with his artistic efforts. He sustained jarring contrasts in these new boxes. There was a racehorse, the Millennium Bridge, a stub from the Tube, a Lucifer match and other contemporary objects in the mix. Religious imagery offers a rich vein of surrealistic references on its own, but each time a readily cubbyholed icon such as a lily or a garden or a beam of holy light popped up in a box, it begged the viewer to interpret the odder, modern items in context. Was he mocking religion or trying to shake up the viewer's perception?

She resisted the idea that Peter was moving towards religion. But then she regarded the next four boxes and began to wonder. She now recognized the thematic thread in each of them: the Annunciation of Mary. There was the Archangel Gabriel, on his knees but nonetheless exuding great power. There was Mary, head bowed, but just as powerful a figure. Clippings of cherubs, doves and fountains inhabited some of the boxes. There were still incongruous items — a lawnmower? — yet the overall tone in every box was reverent. The Annunciation boxes invited interpretation, as Peter probably intended, but she knew they were incomplete, not ready for viewing. It also felt disrespectful invading his privacy so casually. Finally, she admitted to herself that maybe she didn't want to imbibe the darkness in some of the assemblages: knives coming from a cloud, tears of blood and a tree on fire.

She turned from the workbench and decided that vacuuming the room, so soon after her husband had left for the week, would be finicky and slightly impertinent. She looked around the space appreciatively. She came in once in a while to dust the books on the wide shelves, not that she harassed him on the matter; but there were a few on a special shelf that she never disturbed. They weren't secret volumes but rather some of his favourites: a first edition of the full-scale *Seven Pillars of Wisdom*, a signed tome of Wordsworth poems, a history of New Scotland Yard, an out-of-date *Who's Who*, and a set of *Complete Sherlock Holmes Stories*. They gathered dust most of the time, the exception being the Holmes collection. Peter had adored the Conan Doyle series since his teenage years. They were bound in leather and were worn at the corners of the covers. Joan was unsure whether the three-volume edition on the shelf dated back to his youth, but she had often seen him in the middle of a stressful case pick out a volume and flip to a story at random, for relaxation. She had never read the stories herself, although she felt that she knew the red-headed man and the dog who didn't bark.

She leaned closer to the shelf and was surprised to see that dust had settled thickly into the top grooves of the three Holmes volumes. They hadn't been taken out in six months or more; she knew dust. Her first instinct was to take the books out one by one and clean them off with a rag, but she merely removed Volume One and blew the dust off as best she could. Then she opened the tome and read the table of contents. She flipped back and was surprised that there was no dedication on the flyleaf; she had imagined that the set had been a gift from Peter's father. She returned to the table of contents and read the list of story titles, some of them familiar. She opened *A Study in Scarlet* near the middle and sampled the story, as a shopper in a bookstore might. Checking that the phone was nearby, she sat down in the rocking chair, turned to the start of the novel and began to read.

She finished *A Study in Scarlet* by noon. She loved it. She had noticed that Peter hadn't been reading much lately. At some point in the midmorning she glanced up at the shadow boxes and wondered if there was a correlation between the increase in Peter's interest in the boxes over the last year and the decline in his reading, which usually was voracious. Or did the decline correlate with a growing curiosity about religion? She realized that this was unfair speculation about her husband, yet Sherlock had put her in the mood to hypothesize. Ever since Peter and Tommy had departed, she had felt odd about his current case, even though she knew few of the facts. She intuited, with no salient evidence, that she, or they, were on the brink of something different. It was no more specific than that.

When she went inside to grab a tuna sandwich for lunch she found that she couldn't concentrate at the kitchen table, and so she took her sandwich, bag of crisps and glass of milk out to the shed, and cuddled up in Peter's chair. She read the first three Holmes short stories but then, for reasons she didn't understand, began to read the very last ones, taking Watson and Holmes back in time and experience, tale by tale.

About 4:00 p.m., she glanced up from her reading. She hadn't seen the pheasants all afternoon. The fading sun bathed the workbench in yellow. She remembered one of the original characteristics of a shadow box; it was designed to let light inside from one, calculated angle. The afternoon rays at that moment slanted through the chicken coop window and angled onto the Annunciation tableau that stood on its edge a few feet from her, landing on the face of the Virgin Mary and setting it aglow.

CHAPTER 6

Peter woke up early the next morning with too much to do and considerable doubt about the order in which to do it.

He planned to walk, not drive, up to the cliffs but wasn't sure how long that would take. He hoped to meet Hamm in the afternoon, although he wouldn't be surprised to find that Maris had thought up some new assignment to keep the young detective away from him. Along the way he would try to reach Stan Bracher in Lyon; he wondered how the mobile reception would be up on the heights. Finally, he really should call his wife.

A hot shower cleared his head. He dressed in his tweed jacket, wool trousers and walking shoes, looking every measure the country squire, which wasn't necessarily the impression he wanted to make. Like every man who has turned sixty-seven, and is thinking about sixty-eight, he looked in the mirror and wondered how the hell he had got to this moment in time. "How the *devil* did I end up looking like this?" he said to the mirror.

The pudding-faced concierge idling in the lobby implied that Peter must be crazy to hike all the way to the clifftop in the early morning, when there would still be fog and high winds. So much for tourism promotion, Peter thought. He would have wagered that the man had never visited the cliffs; Peter didn't expect fog. He was in an energetic, feisty mood. If the winds were strong, they would dispel any fog, and the rising sun would complete the job; and if it rained he would turn back. When Peter stepped into the street, the morning was already emerging clear and dry. The few Whittlesun commuters who were up this early coursed towards him along Daubney Street, but once he turned uphill, the pavement out of the town centre was empty. A traveller's map from the front desk showed him the logical walking route out of town; the final mile or so was posted with *Abbey* signs.

The uphill road, which soon deteriorated to a poorly paved two-lane, took a radical left turn at the edge of the city, curved around the hill, and then continued straight up the hillside again on an even narrower lane. Many a transmission had been tested by the surveyor's stubbornness, Peter was sure. A stone staircase worthy of a Mexican pyramid ran parallel to the road. Peter, who often walked ten miles a day, climbed at an unintimidated pace. One level short of a grassy plateau, but already fifty yards above the sea, he paused for breath and sat down on a step. Not a car had passed him from either direction. He had a fine view of the Channel on his left. He took out his phone, suspecting that the battery had run down; he had fallen asleep before charging it. Whether through lack of juice or a blackout gap along the cliffs, Joan's phone rang only intermittently at the other end. She answered; he heard a distinct "Hello?" but then only a choppy word here and there. He shouted into the line. He thought he might have conveyed an "okay" and "later." Even with this disappointing sequence, he detected no worry from her end. She understood that he would call back an hour or several later, though he'd best not let another full day go by before calling.

Peter climbed the final section and found himself on a green plain that slanted inexorably up to the top level of the cliffs. Now he was able to catch a sweeping view of the Channel in both directions. Like every arriving tourist, he paused to attempt the impossible task of absorbing that overwhelming seascape and, like every visitor, imagined that he could see to France. This vista was Whittlesun's greatest asset, a destination to be preserved and promoted. But as he gained the top he immediately grasped the problem. He peered along the wavering rim of the land, several miles down the eastern coast, and understood the devastating impact of erosion. The cliffs were receding as if a monster had taken mouthfuls out of the shore. He was no expert in geology, but some of the landslides looked recent, creating scooped bays in the rock and leaving a crumbled moraine down to sea level. An observer instinctively sought out stability along the perspective of the shoreline and Peter did take comfort in the defiant promontories here and there. Some of the massifs were reinforced with granite and, without being able to see their base, he estimated that the collapsing rock itself created a barrier to further erosion by the pounding waves. Yet the land, often chalk or limestone, was in retreat on a broad front.

The road curved across the plain and narrowed to a rutted track, ending in a paved parking area, now empty, that pushed close to the edge of the near cliff. Anna had died here. Signs and cement barriers every twelve feet warned against climbing out farther. *Could the husband have surmounted them carrying his wife's body?* Lasker's car had been found about halfway along the asphalt pad, pointing out to sea. He would have found the access to the rim easier at the far end of the cement obstructions, but it would have been a clumsy manoeuvre even there, requiring him to roll the body down the precipice with enough momentum to clear a three-foot ledge. Had she lodged there, he would have had to shinny down and kick her over the shelf and into the void. According to the preliminary autopsy, Anna's injuries were massive, but it was proving a challenge to distinguish those caused by the fall onto the Channel rocks from earlier wounds inflicted, presumably, by her husband.

Peter noted that the light must have been subdued that night; there was one high light standard, with a Triffid-like fog bulb, set in the middle of the parking area, and it would have given off a sulphurous glow at best. The cliff face had been barely visible, if at all, under the quarter moon.

But Peter had no firm basis for any particular scenario. He couldn't tell precisely where Anna Lasker had tumbled over and it was naive to think that he would find any blood or clothing traces. Yet that was an important detail. How had she fallen? He was certain that no one had yet been over the edge to take a look, and he considered asking for an in-depth search. Skilled rappellers, probably military, would be required, and he could just envision Bartleben reviewing the voucher transfer from the SAS for the hundreds of pounds it would cost. Maris would make a dozen objections. And, not least of everyone's concerns, the press would be watching through telephoto lenses, helping to escalate panic in the tabloids.

At the far end of the car park, he took in the view eastward up the Channel. The problem of erosion appeared worse the farther he tracked the coastline. Nature's power seemed to be teaching civilized man a lesson, pushing back the race who took pride in calling themselves a seafaring nation. Now he saw that nothing could stop the eventual collapse of several of the promontories. Fortunately, there were few buildings close to the re-established edges of the cliffs, although some of the farmers, their white houses shimmering in the morning sun, must be worried.

But the obvious concern was the array of stone buildings about three hundred yards down the coast. This was the ruin of Whittlesun Abbey, which some of the brochures in his hotel room had described as a tourist must-see. Peter couldn't determine the condition of the Abbey from this vantage point. He knew that it had been pillaged in the 16th century when Henry VIII went after the Catholic monasteries, and weather and time must have added to the destruction. He could see red plastic flags and orange ribbon placed protectively around the main church. Even at this distance, the Abbey did not appear to welcome visitors.

Peter lacked binoculars, but he could make out a figure moving in and out of the church, sometimes going around the back of the structure but then emerging on Peter's side, and once walking to the edge of the cliff. The figure's movements were masculine, but otherwise

Peter could only tell that he was dressed entirely in black. It was like watching an ant walking upright, and not being able to discern its purpose. If he had been forced to characterize the movements of the man, Peter would have described them as fussy or compulsive, or, more generously, busy-making. The sharp morning sun made Peter dizzy and he closed his eyes against the delirium. When he opened them, the black figure was nowhere in view.

Exactly at this moment of concentration his mobile chimed. He turned it on and found that he could hear Detective Hamm clearly.

"Chief Inspector, it's Ronald Hamm here. Where are you?"

Peter wasn't sure why he lied. "I'm about to climb up to the cliffs."

"Well, I was hoping to join you at the Lasker house after lunch but I won't be able to do it. I've been assigned to go to a village to interview a lady who says she saw something."

"Is it anywhere near the Abbey?"

"Only if you're a crow. I'd have to double back to town to get to you."

"I'm sorry to hear that," Peter said. "Perhaps we can meet later."

But Hamm seemed not to have heard. The detective shouted into the phone, although Peter was having no trouble with reception at his end. "I can't fathom the need to take these call-ins seriously. There hasn't been an attack in our jurisdiction. But . . ." The line faded for a moment, and then Hamm's voice returned, quavering and distorted. "Chief Inspector, could we meet at the same time this afternoon, the Crown?"

"Yes," he managed to say, before Hamm cut off the call.

There was no paved route from the parking pad to the Abbey, although a Land Rover could have made it along the single grooved track. Even though the plastic flags indicated closure of the church to tourists, inevitably a few of them would persevere on foot just to take a closer look. The path dipped down so low that he soon lost the view of the Abbey, but as he began the upslope portion, the damaged tower began to grow out of the hilltop. He hoped that the mysterious man in black maintained a cache of bottled water. He rounded a curve and climbed the last five steps to the heights. There, limned against the bluing sky, was the black figure himself, seeming too tall for a human, thin as a cross. A Gothic wraith waiting on his visitor, Peter thought. The man reached down a wiry arm, half in welcome and half to help Peter to the final plateau of the churchyard.

"Good morning, friend!"

"Hello," Peter huffed, taking the proffered hand. He paused on the fringe next to the church to gain his bearings.

"I'm Father John Salvez," the black figure said. "I'm guessing that you are a morning person out for a walk, as opposed to an organized *randonée*."

"Peter Cammon. I guess I came for the sunrise but missed by a good bit." He wasn't sure why he had thrown out this tortuous justification. But he did appreciate conviviality at this fresh hour. The brilliant sun backlit the stark form of the priest. Peter still couldn't make out the man's face.

"I propose tea!" Salvez said, sounding a bit like old Mrs. Lasker. While Peter caught his breath and took in his first sight of the church, Salvez turned and went to a small stack of supplies by the west wall. He rummaged for a vacuum flask and two handleless cups and then turned back to Peter. Salvez wore the workaday cassock of a Catholic priest, flat black and buttoned down the middle. He was sickly thin, the monochrome garment making him appear even leaner. His elongated face was cadaverous; his jutting chin and long forehead reminded Peter of illustrations of the Man in the Quarter Moon. Yet all in all, he projected amiability.

Salvez unscrewed the thermos lid, letting out the smell of tea. He poured it ritually and they silently raised a toast to the rising sun. Peter soon learned that the priest moved compulsively, with the manic confidence of — there was no other way to put it, Peter thought — a man on a mission. In this regard, his centredness was real. Putting down his tea, Father Salvez beckoned for Peter to follow him around to the front of the church, which faced the sea. Peter scrambled to keep up.

The Abbey was in serious disrepair; only one of the low outbuildings had been fully restored. The stones of the main church were coarsened by sea winds, leaving the corners rounded and scored, adding to the feeling that the remaining walls were about to give in and tumble. From this angle, the west side, he saw that at least three fifty-foot-high walls still stood, but the slate roof shingles and window glass were entirely missing. The attraction of the church was the main tower, which, though crumbling, endured with historic pride over the entrance. Rounding the facade to the sea frontage, Peter saw that an oak door with iron hinges (not the original) had been installed in the entrance below the tower. From that one perspective, the Abbey looked almost intact.

Behind Peter, face to the sky, Father Salvez stood on the cliff about six hundred feet from the brink. Peter could see how vulnerable to erosion the Abbey and its attendant buildings were. One or two more major rock falls, and the remains of the church would slide into the surf.

Salvez pointed to the horizon. "On a clear day you can see France, but since I don't think Napoleon is looking back at us, no worries."

Peter had no intention of fooling the priest; he would tell him right off he was a police detective — on his own mission. There was a chance Salvez had seen Lasker reconnoitring the cliffs in recent weeks. The evidence summary hadn't mentioned an interview with any clergymen connected to the Abbey, and no one resided there, he could be sure, but he was otherwise hopeful.

"Would you show me your church?" Peter said.

"Be glad to. Of course, it's technically not my church, since it was deconsecrated years ago. Can't have people claiming to be parishioners of a church that no longer has an altar. Similarly, I'm not officially its prelate or its abbot. I hang my shingle at St. Elegias in Whittlesun."

They entered not through the big doors but around the farther side, the eastern exposure, where breaches in the outer wall allowed the determined explorer to gain the east wing of the transept safely.

They picked their way through ancient stones, but the trail was easy to find. The floor inside had been cleared and was intact; the nave, chapels and sacristy were demarcated by low, ruined walls. One typically Tudor window frame remained, with its pleasing parabolic arch proving the magnificence of the original architecture. Three oak beams ran the breadth of the church and served to support the remaining walls. If there was a crypt, Peter had missed the stairs, but he supposed the entrance would be nearer the front of the building.

"Welcome to St. Walthram's Abbey." Salvez looked around in a sweeping half-circle, inviting Peter's approbation. "The name is a variation of St. Walter, originally a Benedictine monk in the 11th century. But this is a Cistercian monastery, built no earlier than 1191. All very confusing."

"And suppressed by Henry VIII, I would guess," Peter said.

"Very good." Salvez smiled openly and heartily. "Most tourists think the wind and salt caused its destruction, but it was Henry in 1536 who sent out his agents, called railers, to find cause to take over and destroy the abbeys. Following the King's bidding, Parliament seized the assets of the Catholic churches and dispersed the monks, and along the way the railers, the King's men, pillaged the windows and the furniture, and any art that was not nailed to the walls. This was one of the smaller monastic churches, but Sir Thomas Pope, treasurer of the so-called Augmentation Office, wanted to set an example on the south coast, a hotbed of papism at the time, and managed to have the Abbot of St. Walthram's burnt at the stake. Sir Thomas simply coveted the wealth of the monastery, of course."

Peter was enjoying the tourist lecture, but he didn't understand why Salvez was here so early in the morning. *Frankly, there's nothing to do,* he thought. "I noticed that there's no sign on the path," he ventured.

A look of chagrin passed over the priest's pallid face. "We had to close it to the public. There was a collapse, about thirty feet, at the Front Rim, we call it. About six months ago. Heavy spring rains seeped into the siltstone and clay, creating hydraulic pressure . . ."

Peter wasn't particularly impatient but it was a long walk back to the Lasker house and he anticipated a heavy day of it. He should pose his policeman's queries and start back, but first he wanted to learn more about the priest.

"May I be so bold as to ask why you come up here so early? Believe me, Father, I do have a reason for asking."

A benign — or was it patronizing? — look passed across Salvez's cleric's mask. Peter's initial instinct was to trust him, but in his experience, the reaction of priests to unbelievers was unpredictable.

"Come with me, please." They left the church and went around to the green sward that ended at the cliff. "You're a police officer, aren't you?"

"Good guess, Father."

"Oh, you look like a policeman, Mr. Cammon. You move like one. Tweed coat notwithstanding."

"I confess."

Salvez laughed. "You get to know people in my line of work. Besides, I've been expecting the police."

"The murder."

"Yes. Mrs. Lasker."

"Did you know her?"

"No. She was Eastern Orthodox. There's a Romanian Orthodox church in Weymouth, but none in Whittlesun. I believe she was a member there. As for the husband, I didn't know him. A terrible, terrible thing. A sin."

They were twenty yards from the cliff edge, and the view was panoramic. Peter noticed a curious habit of Salvez's, almost a twitch. Whenever the priest dealt with a serious question, he paused and turned his face to the sky, as if in defiance of God or the sun deity, or whatever. No, Peter rethought, watching the man more closely; rather, Father Salvez is somehow declaring himself to the heavens. This is a serious man, he concluded, struggling with some larger force, though perhaps not a crisis of faith. Salvez was worth listening to and Peter decided not to rush his questioning. The priest held his pose for a full minute, letting the sun flood across his pale skin, then breathed the deepest of sighs.

"I don't suppose . . ." Peter finally said.

"No," Salvez said, firmly. "I wasn't up here that night. Sometimes I do take a walk up and down the goat track at sundown, but not that night. Nor was I around the next morning. The reporters said he parked his car on the rise."

Peter remained unsure of Salvez's schedule of visits to his beloved Abbey. *And did Salvez ever stay overnight? Had he seen Lasker on the cliffs before?*

Salvez gestured to the precipice directly before them and pointed a bony finger along the eastern rim. "Would you care to see over the edge?"

Peter hesitated. Approaching the rim, he grasped that the clifftop was a powerful place, captivating and breathtaking. How cold-hearted a man was André Lasker? He had followed through on his plan, had faced the blood and panic — hers, and perhaps his — without compunction. There was a strong chance that he had dragged her, still very much alive, to the lip of the promontory. There were so many things that could have gone wrong, including being observed by an insomniac priest. Yet Lasker, undeterred, had maintained his cockiness at every stage of his plan.

They padded to the stone outcropping and the priest guided them to a solid ledge that, although windswept, was set back a few feet. It seemed safe enough, but Peter worried that the wind would send Salvez sailing over; yet the priest's cassock was a tight sheath around his emaciated body, and Peter in his flapping coat was more at risk. He peered down and saw that the latest rockfall had accumulated on the shore directly beneath them. The tidal sea was already crashing against the stones, pebbling them and drawing them out with the ebb tide. He glanced up to the right, where the promontory that held up the parking platform, and from which Anna Lasker had fallen, projected over the waves. He had a better angle now and saw the risk the husband must have taken to ensure that she flew out from the farthest point without hanging up on a ledge or fissure. Still, it was impossible to tell whether or not Anna had plummeted straight into the water. If so, the waves would have lifted her corpse and thrown it against the rock face. He resolved to take a closer look at the autopsy report in conjunction with the tidal charts for that night.

The limestone, which had seemed solid, gave way under the foot on which Peter was leaning. Salvez happened to be gazing the other way. Peter tried to shift all his weight backwards; better to fall on the harsh limestone than pitch forward. The ground turned to shifting layers of shale that splattered out over the edge of the cliff like cards dealt from a deck. Peter began to slide helplessly along the same vector. He prepared to land on his bum; it was going to hurt, but worse was the likelihood of his following the shards of rock outward. He placed his arms behind his torso in the hope of planting his hands on the embankment and gripping something, anything. Maybe if he turned onto his right side, though that risked torquing him backwards off the cliff. The twisting failed to halt his skid and he moved by inches to the brim.

The priest's narrow arms slipped under Peter's armpits and hoisted him straight up, like a forklift would carry a pallet. He heaved Peter backwards, to the left and onto the safety of the grass. Peter reflexively rolled onto his front as if to grasp the earth. He immediately rolled back to face the sea and found Father Salvez grinning down at him. Peter's first thought was that the priest remained remarkably strong, whatever his illness.

"Thank you, Father."

"Let's not re-enact the crime, shall we?"

Peter was shaken but unhurt; a bruise would soon rise on his left elbow. He took two deep breaths to calm his heartbeat and lay on his back on the grass for a full minute more. Salvez bustled over to his cache of provisions and poured more tea into their cups. He called Peter over and laid out a blanket in picnic fashion. Peter moved flat-footed and flexed his arm; his tweed coat would require a patch.

"Thank you. That was stupid of me," he said. Salvez smiled; he wasn't interested in using the situation to gain advantage.

61

They stayed silent for several minutes, then Salvez asked, "How would you describe me, Inspector Cammon?"

What opened doors for Peter as a detective was his equanimity with witnesses, but what won answers was his professional demeanour. Until Peter figured Salvez out, the prudent approach would be to dodge leading questions, while staying friendly; but he found it easy to relax with the humble priest.

"I beg your pardon?"

"Say, three adjectives to describe my appearance."

So the priest likes games, Peter thought. He considered how frank he should be. The man looked deathly. But priests, in his limited experience, were like psychiatric therapists, always turning questions around in order to reveal more about the questioner than the therapist. *"Should I leave my wife, Doctor?" "Do you think you should leave your wife, Patient?"*

Peter rolled over onto his right elbow. He remained slightly dizzy. "Dignified. Ascetic. Gaunt."

Peter's list came across as fatuous, he thought, like plucking adjectives from columns A, B and C. Yet, Salvez wasn't offended, he could tell. Junior colleagues often said that Peter was a good judge of character. Bartleben, and those who worked with him most, understood that a lot was going on when he approached a suspect or a witness. He was adept at sizing up their fears, their desires, their needs. Now, at the beginning of a parlour game in the company of a black-wrapped priest who presented a melancholy smile to the sky and sea, he perceived that here was a man trapped in crisis. He was dying. He was working on his acceptance of the world and it was testing the anchor of his deepest faith. He was seeking moments of grace in a ruined church of which he was not even the prelate, and he wasn't playing games.

But for the moment there was a puzzle to play out. It was Peter's companion's turn to be silly. "Gaunt. John of Gaunt. Father of Henry VIII. Henry, destroyer of monasteries. Monasteries, St. Walthram's Abbey."

"Word games?"

"To keep the mind alive. Flex the grey muscle," Salvez responded.

After all, the man had saved his life, Peter reasoned. He played his turn. "Okay. John of Gaunt. England, bound in with the triumphant sea, whose rocky shore beats back the endless siege of watery Neptune. The Neptune Water Slide at Whittlesun Beach. Whittlesun Abbey."

Salvez shouted, "Very good!"

They both smiled. Peter could feel him building to something more revealing than word associations. Here was an opening to draw out the priest's insights into the town of Whittlesun and the strange cliffs that loomed over it. He would probe a little more. He would take the time to befriend Salvez. And, he realized, he was no longer in a hurry to re-enter the death house in town.

The priest's echoing laugh was undercut by the rising sound of a motor in the distance. They both turned and saw a thundering motorcycle breast the hilltop parking lot and continue down the goat track towards the Abbey. They both felt a twinge of regret at the interruption. Salvez stood and brushed dry grass from his trim and pristine cassock. He helped Peter to his feet. Peter's sore left elbow made him wince.

"May I visit you again, Father?" Peter asked quickly as the motorcycle bore down the path.

"By all means." But there was doubt in his face. His smile grew more determined.

"You're not well," Peter said.

"Prostate cancer."

"I'm sorry. But Father, I am more sorry that we didn't have a chance to talk about it." The motorcycle, sputtering and chugging, was just below the church hill. Peter had to shout to be heard. "I'll give you a call. I'm trying to understand the town better. You've been very helpful." This was feeble, Peter knew, but he hoped he had started a bridge to future conversations.

Salvez raised his face again to the sky, but only for few seconds.

He turned to look Peter in the eye, favouring him with the stern concentration of a sermonizing Catholic priest. "Inspector, do you know the one thing I have missed, experience-wise?" *Experience-wise?* Salvez was shouting now as the motorbike approached.

"What, Father?"

"Worldliness."

CHAPTER 7

The motorcycle's rattling roar flared as the driver rode over the last hillock and came to a stop on the church lawn. Relieved of his helmet and goggles, the driver turned out to be Constable Willet.

"Mr. Hamm thought you might need a lift back to town."

Peter found himself especially irritated. His conversation with Salvez had hardly begun. That he had been telling himself that he had to get back to town, and Willet was saving him a long hike, did not alter his mood. He stared at Willet, a buffoonish figure in his goggles, buttoned-up jacket and gauntlets. He realized that he wanted to stay the day with Father Salvez and learn about the town through him.

Peter turned to say goodbye to Salvez but the priest had disappeared. Just as well, he thought, since Willet in his uniform and with that ruddy face was a mood destroyer. He could make another visit. He looked in amazement at the sidecar attached to the bike; his spine ached already. Willet helped him into the pod and gave him a helmet to wear.

"He's a mysterious one, that priest," Willet said, unhelpfully. He started the motor.

Peter had Willet drive to the hotel so that he could retrieve his notes and the stack of forensics reports. At the front desk at the Delphine, the manager came out from a back office and handed him a thick envelope with Detective Hamm's stamp on it. A glance showed that the bundle contained more transcripts of interviews with neighbours and acquaintances of the Laskers. At least Hamm was on the ball this morning, he thought. Outside, he suggested that Willet let him walk to the Lasker house, and the constable responded with an indifferent nod. Peter guessed that Maris had told him to back off, for the moment. The constable lit a cigarette and Peter stood with him while he puffed.

"Managed retreat."

"What?" Peter said.

"That's what they call it. All along the coasts, and not just the Channel coast. The landslides are increasing, taking down the cliffs farther and farther inland. Call it climate change, whatever, it's getting worse. There's no easy solutions, Guv. Actually, managed retreat refers to places down closer to sea level that're vulnerable to the waves, but the principle is the same for the tall cliffs. They've proposed everything. Take sea walls, for example. Cost a fortune, and some argue they just shift the problem farther down the shore. The sea won't cooperate. Merciless, it is."

"So, managed retreat?"

"Managed excuse for doing nothing."

"So do they move houses back from the vulnerable sites?"

"They try."

But not St. Walthram's Abbey, Peter was about to say. Willet read his thought.

"Won't be able to move the Abbey, no. It will be a sad day when that grand bit of architecture falls into the ocean. And I'm not even Catholic. Of course, that's what your man in black is up there all the time doing."

"Doing what?"

"Worrying the problem like a terrier with a bone, as my mother used to say. I've seen him many times going to and fro, like that would keep the waves away from his church."

Neither of them bothered to repeat the obvious metaphors and ironies of God's house returning to the primal sea.

Peter reached the Lasker home in ten minutes. He entered quickly, hoping that the residents along the street wouldn't spy him, and he was grateful not to be trailed by the Great War flying ace. He turned on the hall lights. The interior had taken on a musty odour, and the lower hallway exuded a sharp, metallic smell where the bloodstains were thickest. It was plain that the next owner would have to gut the downstairs.

Peter was content to have this hermetic slaughterhouse to himself. Ignoring the blood pattern for the moment, he went down the corridor to the back room and seated himself in front of the computer. Hamm's colleague had done his job. He found a yellow sticky note on the monitor, which told him that no password was required to access any of the system's databases, and that there appeared to be no buried files. The CPU warmed up quickly; the logo of the Whittlesun service provider flashed onto the screen. In his first scan, Peter chose to believe the note, while recognizing that encryption was getting sneakier all the time and that he might have to ask the experts to delve deeper into the hard drive. The setup of files appeared to be routine. A second sticky note from Hamm's I.T. fellow suggested that he examine the history listing next to the Laskers' homepage, in order to get a feel for the kinds of sites the couple had called up recently. Smart man, Peter thought: it was notoriously difficult to get Internet service providers to cooperate in disclosing webpage records. Hamm's computer expert had realized that the history inventory would provide the next-best footprint. Perhaps Lasker had done his exit planning here, Peter speculated, seeking out places of refuge around the world. Of course, he might just as easily have deleted all daily records of site searches.

The files disappointed. They formed the record of two bland lives. No love notes on the email record, no orders placed to Harrods for caviar, no explorations of porn sites. So far, Peter had gained no feel at all for André Lasker's hopes and dreams. Yet, as he scrolled through the files he sensed carefully constructed deception in the very absence of human interest inside the computer. The record was too anodyne. Lasker kept no office or personal accounts on the home machine. Peter learned a little about the marriage from Anna's email traffic, and her participation in chat rooms, even though most of it was carried on in Romanian. There was a record of two flights to Bucharest, both pre-booked roundtrips on Ryanair, an indication that she had all the while intended to return to Britain at the end of each of her visits. Trash folders had been emptied. The screensaver showed lambs in a field; they might have been Romanian sheep for all Peter could tell.

Elsewhere in the electronic maze Peter found several video games: Masterplayer, Myst, Crusades, Life Construct — he would have to look into that one — and Urban War Challenge. There were surprisingly few word-processed documents, although the Laskers had the latest version of Microsoft Word. One spreadsheet file inventoried the household contents, probably to meet insurance company requirements. Peter turned on the printer and ordered two copies of the file. Then he shut everything down.

The blood. With Willet absent, he was free to roam the house and replicate the sequence of Anna's movements. He walked slowly upstairs, conscious of the fact that he was reversing her trail. In the lavatory, careful not to step in the blood on the tiled floor, although it had dried by now, he looked at each red blotch in turn and tried to estimate the trajectory of the blood spurt. He turned to the forensic and investigator reports, such as they were, to compare his preliminary impressions with theirs. There was nowhere to spread them out in the hallway or in the lavatory; he went into the bedroom and laid the reports out on the bedspread, and shuttled back and forth to the bathroom.

Anna Lasker's head had been driven into the medicine cabinet door, that was clear; shards had been found in her scalp. The preliminary autopsy estimated that the blood that had pooled in the bath came from slashes to both arms and perhaps from her mouth, given the quantity. At his first go, the coroner had been unable to distinguish injuries inflicted in the marital fight from the many wounds caused by the fall from Whittlesun Cliff and the further battering of the tide. He had also been unable to decide whether or not she had been alive when she tumbled over the edge. It was clear to Peter that he needed someone like Stan Bracher. Peter also comprehended that the Regional Lab, with three murdered girls in its cooler, was under more pressure than it could handle, and possibly had refused to rush the Anna Lasker results. As far as Peter knew, the Lasker automobile was also languishing in the garage at the lab.

Peter thought he had the sequence of the battle straight, from lavatory to downstairs corridor, with the destruction in the kitchen a sideshow. But the varying *quantities* of blood stymied him. The pooling was heaviest in the bath, but he was sure that the duel between husband and wife had moved from upstairs to down. He stood in the vestibule on the main floor and pressed himself against the door, hoping to gain a new perspective on the wainscoting of blood. He padded to the kitchen doorway and repeated the process from the reverse perspective. Yes, he was sure that the bloody hand — for now it was a disembodied hand, since he wasn't sure whether the husband or the wife had painted the walls — had moved from the bottom of the stairs to the back kitchen.

And then he was sure. Anna Lasker had painted those stains. The preliminary report ruled that it was her blood. But André simply couldn't have "carried" that much of it down the stairs, nor was he so perverse as to kill her and continually dip his hand into her wounds like a pot of ink. Anna, desperately injured, had resolved to desecrate her home, which should have been her refuge but, as she suddenly knew in her panic, was becoming her coffin. She had passed along the hallway, stopping three times to paw her fingers through her own seeping veins.

Peter returned to the upper bedroom and gathered the file from the bed. He entered the lavatory once again and stared at the carnage. Despite his conclusions about the source of the blood downstairs, the destruction there remained a mystery. There was simply too much blood. The nylons drooped from the shower bar. The house was silent, and he tried but failed to identify any sounds from the street. Before he could decide what to do next, his phone chimed.

"Inspector! There's a girl who's seen the Rover. Can you come with me to interview her?" Ron Hamm said.

"Have you already talked to her?"

"Yes. Well, no. I've talked to the mother."

"What does that mean?"

"She needs to be approached carefully. The girl. I need your . . . experience."

The Rover was supposedly none of Peter's affair, but he couldn't resist. Why did he always rise to the bait? Would Maris soon be calling Bartleben and calling him a troublemaker? He sighed, but it was his only hesitation. "Pick me up at the Lasker house. I'll be ready whenever you get here."

He immediately understood that Hamm was taken aback by his quick response, and so he put the query the detective had been expecting. "Does Maris know that we're doing this?"

"No."

"Let's be careful about mixing the two cases," Peter said.

"Inspector?"

"Yes."

"Something was mentioned about Lasker as well."

Peter had a few minutes before Hamm was due to pick him up. He was almost sure now that he understood how Anna had haunted her way through the house, certain of the end of her marriage and her life in England. She was with him in the house now, beckoning him to follow. Her ghost gave him permission to take possession of the crime scene; now the house resonated differently. He did a final, lambent tour of the bloodied rooms and corridors to imprint the overall scene on his memory. He made sure that the computer and printer had shut down, and pocketed the yellow sticky notes. Then he waited out front on the stone step. He didn't care if the residents of the street saw him.

Ron Hamm drove up no more than five minutes later. The wind along the street had picked up, a hint of coming winter. Peter got into the nondescript Vauxhall and sank into the battered and sprung passenger seat. Hamm was too big for the vehicle and had to hunch over the steering wheel; this pose made him appear even more in a hurry. Peter reached around and dumped his files on the back seat. The sedan lurched ahead and they were off down the cobbled street, headed for the outskirts of Whittlesun.

"Where are we going?" Peter asked.

"Still in Dorset but not very far from the Devon line. It's isolated."

"Good thing. In Dorset, I mean. Devon is out of your jurisdiction, I believe."

"But not out of yours," the detective joked.

"What were you doing over there in the first place?"

Peter wormed in his seat, trying to get comfortable. Hamm shifted his bulk in sympathy and squared his shoulders. "The Task Force is short of manpower, and so Maris volunteered me and a couple of other lads to help out with contacting people along the county line. Create goodwill and all that. The place we're going is only four miles inside the border. But hell and gone as far as driving there is concerned."

Maris was smart to keep it low-profile. Peter understood that Maris was officially on the Rover Task Force but by no means the co-chair — yet. The legwork had been done so far by Devon officers, and they would resent any duplication of effort. McElroy would be sensitive to levels of public paranoia, and it took little to provoke false sightings and letters to the editor demanding a massive manhunt. Peter thought it significant that Jack hadn't yet invited the Yard to attach anyone to the Task Force, even as liaison. McElroy intended to keep London separate from local, Devon distinct from Dorset, and — the primary concern for Peter — Lasker divided from the Rover. The only remaining question was why Hamm was risking Maris's ire by dragging Scotland Yard into both.

Hamm was talking. "The mother's name is Ellen Ransell. The daughter is called Guinevere. She's a drinker — the mother, that is. She rang up the Task Force and spoke to one of the investigating detectives. He judged that she was full of crap. Jack McElroy and his detectives wouldn't normally have hesitated to cross into Dorset and do the interview themselves but, as Maris put it to me, they think this is a low-grade witness. The mother was born in Finland, in Helsinki, I presume."

"You've never seen either witness?"

"No. It's confused. I talked to the mother. She says the daughter saw something, and mentioned Lasker, but the old woman only wanted to talk about the Rover."

The journey took an hour and a half, and Detective Hamm had trouble finding the house amid the twisting trails and rolling hills. Once in a while, Peter caught sight of a jutting cliff several hundred yards off, but then they seemed to be descending much closer to sea level. When Hamm finally parked the Vauxhall, still some distance from the house, Peter was completely disoriented. The countryside was particularly bleak here, with long grass obscuring the pathways and the wind strong enough to knock a hiker over. The sea wasn't visible from the Ransell property, but he could hear the distant breakers and taste the lingering salt spray. Turning a bend in the path, he caught sight of the ocean some five hundred yards down a steep slope; but then the path took them away from the overlook. The cottage had a thatched roof and was stuck in a cleft between two hills. As a result, it was always in shadow, except when the sun was overhead. At this point in the afternoon, the vale was rapidly losing the light.

Panting, Ronald Hamm led the way down a fieldstone path to the front door. Befitting a cottage for dwarfs or hobbits, the main door was made of oak and was held by black iron hinges; Peter would have sworn the same craftsman who had replaced the portals he had just seen at St. Walthram's had made this one too.

Ellen Ransell answered the door before they could knock. A smell of lime and sour alcohol wafted from her, and from the house itself. She appeared careworn and partly drunk. Her white hair, streaked with sickly yellow, as if stained with nicotine, was uncombed, and the deep lines in her face were vertical and sad, reminding Peter of the eroded fissures in the coastal rocks. On her face, the defensiveness of the recluse fought with the rare stimulus of having visitors who might draw her out of her boredom. She opened the door wide. The hinges creaked crazily, just like in a fairy tale.

"Welcome, Officers. You can come into the parlour." The voice was confident, only slightly defensive. She likely wasn't a witch, Peter mused, but a crystal ball would fit the scene.

Hamm and Cammon entered and found themselves in the one main room, which served as the kitchen and parlour. The two bedrooms off the back of the cottage had solid oak doors like the one at the entrance; that is, they were outside doors used as inside ones. Both were closed. The ceilings in the main room were low, and Hamm had to tilt his head slightly; after ninety minutes in a similar contorted position in the car, his neck would soon be creaking like the door hinges, Peter thought. The woman held a glass of clear liquid in her left hand; she did not offer them a drink. Peter noted the tall bottle of Koskenkorva vodka on the kitchen counter; the more popular Finnish vodka, he knew, was Finlandia. He didn't care to estimate her daily intake, before she passed out.

"I don't remember your name."

"It's Hamm, and this is Chief Inspector Cammon from Scotland Yard."

She looked at Peter. "I phoned it in, you see. My daughter saw the Rover. Maybe she did. She has special abilities. Comes from an expensive education combined with good genes. Her father was Finnish, you know. A strong people, they are."

Peter understood witnesses like these: lonely, pent-up people who, when finally given an audience, cram so much into one outburst that it's hard to pare down to the truth.

"Mrs. Ransell," Peter began gently. They were still standing near the door. "I imagine that you and your daughter know this region well. It would be valuable to talk to her about what she may have seen out on the heights."

He struggled for an opening to mention André Lasker's name. Mrs. Ransell shrugged, turning the burden towards the detectives, as if Peter, not she, had fixed on the daughter's roaming habits. "She wanders, you know. Leaves at first light, comes back after sunset. But she always stays safe." Peter and Hamm exchanged looks; the woman was apprehensive about something. "She knows the terrain, the cliffs, the caves, the dunes. Now this Rover fiend, making it unsafe for every woman in Britain."

"Could we have a word with her, Mrs. Ransell?" Peter persisted. The old woman would eventually let them speak with the daughter, Peter understood, but something was bothering her.

"She's strong and tough, stronger than me, Inspector, but she's unwell." She leaned close and whispered, through rancid breaths. "Astatic seizures."

Hamm looked over at Peter.

"Epilepsy," Peter said. He turned to Mrs. Ransell. "We'll be very careful. She can tell us in her own fashion. We won't take long." Peter spoke in earnest; the interrogation wouldn't be a long one. In his experience, there were some witnesses who would simply refuse to open up at the first conversation and had to be seen several times, and coaxed through a succession of short interviews. Unfortunately, this was likely to be one of them.

"Her name is Guinevere. G-w-e-n-e-v-e-e-r. She has reached the age of twenty-five," she declared.

The old lady went to one of the bedrooms and tapped on the oak door. Within half a minute it opened and Miss Ransell came into the main room.

Peter was standing on the far edge of the room when she entered, but the girl's aura electrified the entire space. Her radiance stunned Peter and caused Hamm to wilt and step back a pace. Her manner

74

and presence begged comparison with the great icons of beauty and idealized female grace. She was the Gothic paragon wandering the heath, but with a worldly understanding beyond the self-absorbed heroines of the Brontës. She was the Pre-Raphaelite ideal, but without the whiff of consumptive weakness. She had the alabaster head of a Greek maiden, but was a girl for modern times. He could tell all this before she spoke.

Her long hair was brick red, parted in the middle; it sprayed out in thick waves, naturally kinked and voluptuous. Her skin was flawless and there was a Scandinavian strength to her facial bones. She stood taller than Cammon and held herself like an artist's model, although there was nothing arch or artificial in her positioning. She smiled, though it was not a particularly welcoming look; it didn't seem right to offer to shake her hand.

She positioned herself at the end of the chesterfield, and this movement seemed to signal to the two men that they should sit too. She wore a long, layered dress that almost touched the floor and that now spread out across the cushions. A blue sash, firmly tied around her waist, showed her leanness. The gaping cuffs of her dress and suede vest gave her a renaissance-fair look. She was entirely comfortable in herself. She neither stared nor recoiled from the presence of the two dowdy policemen, who sat down on the two-seater across from her. Their visit could have been the most natural occurrence in the world.

"Hello. My name is Guinevere, spelt like the *Morte d'Arthur*, despite what my mother says. Call me Gwen."

Hamm croaked out: "I'm Detective Ronald Hamm and this is Chief Inspector Peter Cammon of Scotland Yard."

Guinevere suddenly looked concerned, as if something were misplaced in the room. Had she heard a disturbance outside? She gazed into the middle distance, but then turned full-face to Peter.

"Do you care to speak to me, Inspector?"

Her eyes were entirely upon him at that moment; Hamm might well have disappeared. Peter felt it urgent to establish a trust between them, and to do that he had to be alone with her. He couldn't hope to discover her secrets by treating her as just another witness. She would tell him what she knew, but only in her own time, on her own terms. He looked around the cottage. A fire blazed in the stone hearth.

"Is this your favourite place in the world, Miss Ransell?"

Her eyes flickered. She gave no response, as if waiting. Old Mrs. Ransell was already fading towards the other bedroom; Peter noticed that she had the vodka bottle in her hand. Even she was intimidated by her daughter's penumbra. She slipped into the second bedroom and closed the door.

Guinevere Ransell was keyed into different rhythms of thought and logic than most humans, Peter understood. He rarely encountered this sort of mind, and he cherished it when he did (as long as the conversation didn't veer into craziness, which he was sure it wouldn't). People like Guinevere tended to place themselves at a distance, befitting an oracle, and Guinevere did so now, moving to the farthest end of the chesterfield and crouching with her knees to her chin. This was the natural conversational distance for the two of them. He sensed her sizing him up.

The girl smiled at Peter's question. She turned to Detective Hamm. "Mr. Hamm, would you leave Mr. Cammon and me for a few minutes. Please?"

Hamm looked to Cammon for support and found none. He heaved himself up. "Well, maybe I'll take up smoking again. I'll be outside." He buttoned up his coat and prepared to leave. Just then Mrs. Ransell came out of her bedroom and palmed him a pack of Benson & Hedges. She retreated and Hamm went outside.

Peter waited for the girl to speak. She straightened her legs and paused for another full minute. "Have you always had a moustache?" she said.

"I grew it when I was thirty."

"To make yourself look older?"

"The phrase I used was 'more mature.'"

"You're older now. Why don't you shave it off?"

"Habit. My wife likes it."

"She says it makes you look distinguished."

"Yes, that's right."

"What's the worst thing anyone ever said to you about your moustache?"

"That it made me look like Hitler."

"Do you know why I want to talk about this?"

This was parry and thrust, but of the most benign kind. It was also her way of sliding into the conversation that she wanted to have. Honesty and directness were the only workable responses.

"You're interested in the way people present themselves to the world," he said.

"Yes. The phrase I would use is: I want you to know that I notice the appearance of things. Do you believe in appearances?"

"You mean the outward appearance of things?"

"Yes."

"Yes. It's often the way policemen uncover crimes, working from observation."

"The way people present themselves to the world is important," she agreed in a dreamy voice. "They create an impression that is different than the one they intend. Maybe that's why Dracula couldn't abide mirrors. Do you know why I gave up my studies?"

"I didn't know that you had. At university?"

"I was reading English literature and psychology. At Leeds."

"I majored in English lit too."

Peter, not being much of a risk-taker himself, was fascinated by people with a heightened awareness of the decisions in their lives and of the risks that they entailed. Her biggest risk, he imagined, was retreating to the edge of civilization with an alcoholic mother.

"I took an extra course in Freudian psychology. Freudian symbolism is a crock. If I dream of a ship in full sail, does that represent a fertile woman, as Freud says it does?"

"I never studied psychology," Peter said, "but I confess that after a while literature raised the same issue for me. Literary symbolism seemed too pat; it got in the way of seeing the real world. And there began to be an inverse correlation between my love of romantic literature and my exposure to the foibles of human beings. As a police officer."

Suddenly melancholy, she shifted to his end of the chesterfield and placed a comforting hand on his arm. It wasn't necessary, or even appropriate, but he didn't mind. He tried to appear relaxed, less the formal interrogator. For a brief moment, the atmosphere in the room was confessional. He was almost desperate to sustain that mood, to persuade her to open up to him.

"You're saying that we should get beyond easy symbols?" Peter babbled. He tried to convince himself that he would get back to his interrogation soon.

She sat back. "Yes. My point is that people are always putting on masks. They take on personae quite consciously. They're yearning to do it, but if they adopt a mask without controlling it, then they're in trouble."

He might have said the same to Guinevere herself, and she to him, though his would always be the policeman's mask.

"Yes. If I decided to put on a deerstalker and sport a meerschaum, that would be a personal crisis," he said.

She laughed. A line of perspiration had formed along her brow. It served to turn Peter more serious. He could talk to her all day about everything and nothing, but her circumlocution had to get to the point — her apparent sighting of the Rover — sooner rather than later. And so he said: "I have to ask you about the people you've seen along the cliffs. Do they wear masks? Have you seen strange people on the shore?"

Guinevere remained utterly calm in reaction to his new tack. He waited; he could tell that she would answer at her own pace. He wanted to talk with her all afternoon. He wanted to get rid of Hamm and exile the mother, so that he could remain alone with her.

"The Rover. Such a stupid label. It doesn't suit the mask he's put on. I bet he doesn't call himself that, either."

"Have you seen him?"

Her eyes glazed over as if she were going into a trance; then she refocused.

"I have seen someone different."

"Can you describe him to me?"

Peter's mundane query was not what triggered her epileptic seizure. She appeared calm, then for one second catatonic, then she spasmed. Her back went rigid but at first she stayed on the cushions. He saw that she was at risk of losing control of her body and tipping over. But, oddly, the seizure began as a very real trance.

"I have seen the Black Man, the Floating Man, the Cloaked Man," she rasped.

"Which one is the Rover?" Peter asked, bluntly, not sure that she would be able to reply before he lost her.

"He is the Electric Man."

He moved to catch her as she toppled. He called for Mrs. Ransell.

"And who is the man who went into the sea?" he whispered, the girl tightly held in his arms to limit her convulsions.

"He is the Cloaked Man."

The mother must have known something; she rushed out of her bedroom before Peter called out again. Hamm, too, heard something, for he charged in from the front step. The two officers placed her on the settee. The seizure ended in five minutes. Mrs. Ransell swabbed her child's forehead with a wet cloth.

When Guinevere came to, she smiled at the two police officers and said, "Do you know that epilepsy used to be called 'mater puerorum'? 'Mother of Children'?" Then she closed her eyes and slept.

Peter had no idea why André Lasker should be the Cloaked Man, but he was sure who the Floating Man was. Despite the gender switch, the Floating Man was Anna Lasker.

CHAPTER 8

The ride back to Peter's hotel was tense. The young detective deserved some comfort, some explanation from his colleague about what had happened in the cottage parlour, but Peter was slow to give it. It was understandable that Hamm might blame him for Guinevere's epileptic fit. He dissembled when Hamm asked about the girl's revelations; he said there was nothing useful. When Hamm grunted in doubt, Peter offered that the seizure had started before they got very far. In truth, Peter had been shaken up by the girl. She presented a reflecting surface for his own sense of where he should be going in the Lasker investigation.

At the hotel, Peter apologized for his inattention. They agreed to cancel their late-day rendezvous at the Crown but decided to meet the next afternoon, same time. Peter knew that Hamm would have to debrief Maris. He thought of asking him to hold off but decided that this would be unfair. Peter himself would try to dodge Maris for a day or two more.

He lay on the bed in his room for a few minutes. Chambermaids were gossiping in the hall, but otherwise the hotel was peaceful. He had planned to visit Lasker's Garage, and there was still time before closing. The most promising angle might be the money, he reasoned.

Lasker was in a perfect business to skim cash regularly from the till, and who knew where he might have stowed it. Peter had also planned to drop by the Whittlesun Community Theatre before day's end; it was within walking distance of the Delphine. He got out the packet of reports Hamm had left at the front desk and flipped through the interview notes. The theatre's director was a local named Symington. The perfunctory interview indicated that André had been "active" in the annual season of plays.

Peter tried Bartleben, who, as usual, was in his office. His secretary put Peter through immediately.

"Peter?"

"Stephen, just a quick one. It's going slowly, minor progress. One vague indication of a Lasker sighting in the dunes along the coast . . ."

"Do you trust it?"

Peter delayed his answer, knowing that whatever he said about Guinevere Ransell would sound ambiguous, evasive. "I trust the witness but I haven't been able to confirm what she saw. I have a few more interviewees to cover. The garage. The local theatre where André volunteered."

"Maybe he played Jesus in the Passion play," Sir Stephen offered.

"Come again?"

"Walking on water . . . ? What about the blood in the house? Still need the Canadian?" Stan Bracher, from Saskatchewan, was known as "the Canadian."

Peter ignored that part of the question. "The forensics are disturbing."

Bartleben moved on, uncertain why Peter had called. "Nothing new from Interpol or the French. Ferry authorities, coastal patrols, Border Agency — nothing."

Bartleben felt the hollowness at the other end of the line. He leaned back in his swivel chair and contemplated the abstract metal sculpture his wife had insisted he hang on the far wall. He had always hated that thing. He knew when Peter was absorbed by the evidence spinning around in his mind. He recognized the pattern, and he smiled to himself. Yes, something was coming with Peter. He didn't bother asking about the state of relations with Inspector Maris.

"Okay, I'll be in touch," Peter said.

"Yes, Peter. Hang in there," said Sir Stephen, still smiling.

Joan was reading Sherlock Holmes when he called, but she didn't tell him. The sun was going down and she had been thinking of moving in from the veranda. She had had a lazy day and was glad to hear from him. Her own slackness, which she would have admitted to if asked, attuned her to the preoccupation in her husband's voice.

"Are you making progress?" she asked. The words were deliberately vague; she wanted him to say as much or as little as he wanted.

"It's slow but that's to be expected. It's the kind of case where a bit of serendipity will solve it." She didn't quite believe that, but she murmured agreement.

Touching base with her was important to him at times like these, when the mists weren't yet clearing and, indeed, seemed to be growing denser, but he was almost falling asleep on the bed. Also, Guinevere ruled his mind for the moment and he wasn't going to discuss her with Joan. Not yet. "What have you been up to?"

"I talked to Sarah. She's over at the Graveney Marshes taking samples."

Their daughter was a marine biologist, recently launched on a promising career. Graveney was over in Kent. A little too close to Whittlesun, he thought. Images of the Rover — the Electric Man? — flashed in Peter's mind, but he suppressed them.

"Lord, aren't all the animals getting ready to hibernate about now?"

"Peter, that's the kind of comment that gets you in trouble with her. And I don't think 'hibernate' is the right word for it."

Peter was in the grip of what she termed his distillation process. She wasn't his confidante at these times. She didn't resent his moods during an active case, and knew when to offer a supportive word and when to say nothing. When he was at home he would refer to evolving cases obliquely, and he often retreated to his study in the shed in order to think through his preliminary theories. She didn't resent that habit either. She had looked up the Lasker reports on the Internet, as well as the tabloid details about the Rover, and she understood the basics of the crimes. She wasn't about to get much more out of him today. The fact that she had spent much of the previous two days reading Conan Doyle made her smile at the end of the line; perhaps that was why she'd gone exploring on the computer. She would tell him all about it when she next saw him. He would be amused.

For now, she wasn't going to try to drag him out of his mood. Her husband could be, as she put it, "a bit of a mystic" but, like everything else, they had negotiated this part of their married life long ago.

That was it. He said he loved her, she echoed him, and they hung up without any discussion of when he would be home.

Peter went into the hotel bathroom and brushed his teeth. He stared into the mirror without focusing on his own face, but imagined Anna's head smashing into the medicine cabinet; he blinked the image away. Returning to the main room, he decided to postpone his visit to Lasker's Garage, and instead spent two hours reviewing all the material on the case, laying out loose pages across the bed and the floor, until the space was coated with paper. His room overlooked an alley and a brick wall, but he peered out to verify that night had descended; as best he could tell, a storm was building. Deciding that he needed a pint, he went down to the hotel bar.

Peter thought it paradoxical that he usually found it more useful to chat up the locals rather than travellers in the lounges of commercial hotels. This breed of drinker was naturally opinionated and willing to embrace queries about home-bred crimes-of-the-week; perhaps the locals fancied themselves defenders of parochial honour, the reverse of a welcoming committee. But entering the chiaroscuro gloom of the Delphine bar, Peter saw that his anticipations were moot. It wasn't particularly busy on this weekday evening. Several solitary men occupied tables at the sides of the bar; these were salesmen, eating pub food and downing their second or third glass. Peter sat at the bar itself, where it was more likely that the indigenous Whittlesunites would be sitting, except that tonight there was merely one grizzled denizen who had placed himself at the extreme end of the bar; next to him, although there were plenty of other seats, sat a woman with too much rouge who refused to focus anywhere but on the bright liqueur bottles behind the bartender.

Peter ignored them and ordered his pint from the pump. The television over the bar was tuned to a regional news channel. The volume was set low but, since there were no conversations happening in the room and the two lounge lizards at the far end were not on speaking terms with the world, he could hear parts of the newscast. The screen jumped to a blond woman with a microphone. She stood in front of the cliffs, the grey English Channel behind her. *Wendie Merwyn reporting* appeared at the bottom of the screen. Peter grasped right away that she wasn't announcing another Rover attack. She spoke with intensity, using the throwaway words "take precautions" and "fear," but there was something tepid about the report. There was nothing really new about the Rover, and Peter had the impression that the woman had been told to damp down her language. There was no reference at all to Lasker.

The picture went staticky. The scene cut abruptly to another angle on the sea, although there was no way to tell if this was the same stretch of cliffs. It seemed to be a live report. A handsome young man fought to keep his hair in place as the winds buffeted him and the camera jiggled. The picture was so shaky that Peter could not make out his name on the screen. He and the female reporter had been created from the same bland, and blond, template. Peter couldn't hear his spiel, although he was employing the same solemn look as the blond woman. Apparently the weather along the south coast was turning nasty. An inserted graphic showed grey clouds roiling across Dorset and Devon. The blond fellow wrapped up. The overall impression was of the intrepid weatherman braving the elements to bring ordinary citizens the latest news of nature's wrath. The TV image blurred in pathetic fallacy. Peter wondered if the locals would take much interest in the reporter's forewarnings of storm clouds, or the presence of a human killer.

Peter fell asleep on the coverlet of the bed before he could review his list of tasks for the next day. As he faded, he reflected that what he really needed to do was go back to see if Guinevere had recovered. He understood the identity of the Floating Man: it was surely Anna Lasker. No, he admonished himself, he needed to see her again to talk about the Cloaked Man.

The Whittlesun Community Theatre occupied a former abattoir. Peter found the cement building, a perfectly respectable if utilitarian structure, in an older district of the town where gentrification had only recently started. Small theatres worried a lot about real estate and if the WCT — its logo was stamped on the front door in curlicue letters — owned this spot free and clear, it was sitting pretty.

A pencilled note on the door directed inquiries to Mr. F.R. Symington at the Middle Secondary School up the street. Peter had arisen at 7:30, late by his regimen, and had worked on the Lasker file most of the early morning, and it was now about 10:45. A separate, typed notice instructed those wanting tickets to call a local number or go to the theatre's webpage. He wondered how many ticket buyers went in search of Symington by mistake, thinking he was the ticket agent; or perhaps he did double duty. A poster advertised an unadventurous winter season, consisting of *Charlie's Aunt*, *Oliver!* and a *Christmas Panto*, billed as "an old-fashioned family delight." He couldn't help parsing that promise: to which word did the adjective belong?

A short walk took him uphill to the school. He could see his breath in the fall air. A sudden flood of students exiting the building onto the cobbled street made him a fish swimming upstream. Most of the children gripped pieces of paper, probably test sheets, and they all rushed out like escapees from prison. They wore blue wool uniforms, but most had on green trainers, their only bit of sartorial protest. He reached the front door and went inside in search of the main office; in this age of child predators it wouldn't do to wander the halls unannounced. A secretary directed him to a room on the second floor.

Symington was eating a bagel at his teaching desk and two students, a boy and a girl, lolled at the back of the room. He looked up when Peter knocked. His expression didn't change.

"Mr. Symington. The name is Cammon."

The teacher turned to the children. "Mr. Sharf, Ms. Jaynes, you can go."

"Really?" the boy said, tossing a cowlick back from his forehead. He ran his fingers through his straw-gold hair and smiled at the girl; a blond Byron, he was. The boy stood and gathered his books.

"I can't even remember what you did," Symington said, wearily, "but whatever it was, don't do it again."

The students bustled out. Symington stood and at once waved Peter to his own chair. At least he didn't make Peter sit at a student's desk, where he would have been in a ludicrously inferior placement. Peter saw that Symington had already made him for a copper. Was he that obvious to all the citizens of Whittlesun?

Symington was over sixty and underweight. His shaggy hair was equal amounts grey and yellowy-white and his face was strained by past distress; ropy veins ran across the tops of his hands. He seemed to be recovering from some disease, or possibly he was fighting alcoholism, yet the eyes were bright and the voice had been trained — in the theatre, no doubt.

"Representing the police?"

"Yes."

"The André Lasker matter?"

"That's right."

"Let's walk. Fancy a snack?"

Peter glanced at the buttered bagel on Symington's desk. "Not on

my account. Not particularly hungry, but take your bagel with you."
He had eaten a sticky bun with his two morning coffees.

"Then let's go over to the theatre. I'll show you around. My next
class isn't until one." He left the bagel where it was.

For some reason, Symington led him out the rear exit of the
school. They ambled downhill along a series of twisting streets.

"I'm not psychic," Symington said as they went. Peter didn't react
to this. He had met lots of people who were mildly psychic, but that
wasn't what Symington meant; he was merely breaking the ice. The
teacher, angular and with his long arms hanging loose, was in no
hurry. Peter instinctively liked him; he came across as a fellow who
knew his mind.

Symington continued. "I expected the local police to be around
again sooner or later, since André participated in the WCT. I knew
you would show up."

"I'm with New Scotland Yard, but yes, I am on the Lasker case."

"Then I can tell you a lot about André." In fact, the police notes,
which Peter had read an hour earlier, showed that Symington had
disclosed very little to Ron Hamm the first time around. Peter
had been looking for someone to offer a full portrait of Lasker. He
remained an indistinct figure at the emotional level — that is, his
motivations and yearnings. None of the witnesses had provided real
insight into the mechanic's secret ambitions. The family home had
been an advertisement for banal existence in modern England. What
had made André Lasker so desperate that he befouled his old life with
blood and rage? Any coherent story, whether melodrama or farce,
would be refreshing.

Symington unlocked the front door of the theatre and led Peter
through the lobby. The performance space contained about three
hundred seats, recently upholstered in scarlet fabric. The two men
walked up to the proscenium stage and Symington took a seat on the
edge of the apron, the red seats arrayed before them.

"Here we are," he said, a small note of pride in his voice. There
was a bit of an echo in the big room.

Peter Cammon parked his old bones beside the teacher and shared his actor's perspective. The space was ideal for a small regional theatre. The playbill for the winter season was mundane, but he could already tell that the man worked hard to make the program a local success.

"I like your theatre."

"Thank you. The WCT survives and sometimes thrives, I frequently tell people. Summer season does better than winter, due to tourists. We've been around since World War II. Of course, we never get too ambitious. I suppose if the town grew appreciably we would raise our game and might try Pinter or Brecht. Our city fathers have generalized notions of reviving the waterfront and creating a tourist Neverland. Doubtful."

Peter looked around the room and up at the grid holding the lights while Symington finished his introduction. "We get a lot of abattoir jokes and, yes, suggestions that we mount a *Slaughterhouse Five* production. But I think we used our subsidy well."

Symington realized that his speech had taken on a singsong quality. "I'm sorry. I sound as if I were debating with myself."

"The acoustics seem good," Peter said.

Symington sang out in a resonant baritone:

If music be the food of love, play on,
Give me excess of it, that, surfeiting,
The appetite may sicken and so die.

Peter, surprising himself, tried to match his projection:

That strain again! It had a dying fall:
It came o'er my ear like the sweet sound
That breathes upon a bank of violets.

"Very nice. We could use a good Fagin in our January *Oliver!*

By the way, did you know that some scholars say it's 'south,' not 'sound'?"

In fact Peter did know this. On the other hand, he had forgotten it. "Are you sure?"

Symington laughed out loud at this pedantic trivia and Peter laughed with him.

"English major?"

"Absolutely. But a long time ago."

"What do you want to know about André Lasker?"

"I feel that I lack a clear picture of him. Of what made him do what he allegedly did. Did you know him well?"

Symington didn't so much hesitate as ponder the question for a long moment. "I knew him and we did have a few talks, but I never guessed at his motivations, his deeper feelings."

"Was he active in the theatre?"

"He's been a regular in our productions over the last three years. We're an amateur operation relying on the good graces of the towns-people. I cultivate local talent whenever I find it."

"Lasker?"

"He was an excellent Perchik in *Fiddler*. Worked hard on his lines and his lyrics and made his own, very authentic costume. I think his wife helped. She's Romanian."

"She never took part?"

"No. Not her thing. I could see her in *Mother Courage* or *Les Miz*. Kind of a gypsy look, perfect for climbing the ramparts. But she wasn't the type for the stage."

"Did he ever get the lead in a production?"

Symington became thoughtful, wanting to be precise. "No, he always had self-doubts. Though I would have welcomed a tryout. In a place this size, rarely do you find anyone who can fly over the cuckoo's nest successfully or climb every mountain. The biggest role he ever had was in *Our Town*, I guess."

"Did he ever miss a rehearsal?"

"No." Symington seemed amused, overly so. "Is it Detective or Inspector?"

"Chief Inspector, but you can call me Peter."

"Okay. Didn't you discover that? André is a diagnosed insomniac. He'd often show up here at odd hours. I gave him a key to the theatre at one point, although I recall that he gave it back before . . . you know."

"When exactly did he give it back?"

"Six months ago."

"I'm surprised that, if he liked being here that much, he didn't go out for bigger parts."

"Amateur actors who come out for these things often have a fixed view of what they are suited for. André thought he should only play serious roles but I wanted to see him try comedy. He wasn't there yet."

"Did he have a good sense of humour?"

Symington hesitated. No one had asked him this question before. "No. He was serious."

"Did his participation decline over the last year?"

"He was active, did some backstage work, but yes, I think his interest was waning."

"What do you think of him? What motive would he have had for disappearing?"

Symington understood that Peter wasn't asking about extramarital affairs or financial woes. "I liked André. He had an intellectual, cultured streak and that was part of what led him to the theatre. In my opinion there was nothing seriously wrong with his life, his job, his marriage, and I told him that, but he aspired to something more."

It was Peter's turn to take care to be precise. "In my experience, men who go on the run, who try to disappear, have a very specific image in mind of their new life. It's the reason so many fugitives are found in Thailand living on the beach, or in placid villages in the Andes."

Symington frowned and folded his arms; a mildly defensive posture, Peter thought. "Well, whenever I see *The Tempest*, I think every man in the audience probably secretly wishes he could flee to that island."

But Peter was no longer discussing theatre; he wasn't seeking an assessment of a stage character. Something in Symington's mood and tone made him suspicious. He pressed on. "It amazes me that more men don't leave home."

"I suppose," Symington said, noncommittally. "But don't you live in the same place, perhaps the same house, you've inhabited for years?" The director was guessing here but Peter didn't mind.

"Twenty-eight, in fact."

"So, then?"

Peter often drew out witnesses by revealing a bit about himself — but not on this point. In effect, Chief Inspector Cammon, semi-retired, who lived so much of his life inside the lives of others, "left home" every time he took on a case. In his way of thinking, this was the perfect template for an adventurous life, and indeed it had been. But he wasn't about to betray this to Symington and he was too experienced, never mind dogged, an investigator to let a witness take over a conversation.

"It's my view that Lasker already had a plan," Peter said. "The fight with Mrs. Lasker may have been spontaneous, but that doesn't mean the escape was equally spur-of-the-moment."

"I'm not so sure," Symington said. "We may be talking about the impulsive reaction of a generally unspontaneous man."

"I don't think so," Peter said. He recognized that he risked sounding argumentative, and he liked Symington. He converted to a mildly confessional tone. "The battle with Anna may have been spontaneous, but not the overall scheme of it. I believe we're talking about a man with a detailed scheme who invoked it when prompted by events. Was he visibly unhappy?"

"Yes, I'll concede that much. In the sense of frustration, sure. But I never believed his unhappiness with Anna would have led him to kill her. Sometimes he came here at night to think. I'd drop in and find him drowsing, or pacing the stage at other times. We talked occasionally. He said he wanted to travel. I told him there was little stopping him. He had enough money, I knew. But he would go silent when I said that."

"Was there an image on the horizon? The impossible dream, if you will?"

"God, Peter, don't you start talking in show tunes. He said he'd like to see Tahiti. He was reading the journals of Captain Cook at the time, so take it with a speck of salt."

"His father was in the Dutch Navy. Did André ever want to be a sailor?"

"I don't imagine. His father was never in the picture. I never met him, though his mother came to a few productions. And *she* never idolized André's father, that's certain." Symington stepped down to the orchestra pit and walked up the ramped centre aisle to one of the rear rows. He was bothered by one seat that had been left down. He straightened it and came back.

"I think André wanted to find some intellectual pursuit that would carry him into middle age. And, even more important, that would gain him respect. He said that he lived a dull life. The theatre was an aspect of that need."

Peter shrugged. "But people who want to be respected for their intellect believe that they're already intellectual. Did Lasker expound on any particular areas?"

"Funny you should say that. The answer is yes and no. André was interested in geography, British history, the weather, all kinds of things. He may have taken a university course or two in one of those disciplines. But, no, he never engaged in any academic debates with me. When we did *Fiddler on the Roof*, he immediately began researching the pogroms. He was like that. He would begin to experience something and then dive into the topic. Yet I don't think he ever allowed curiosity to lead him towards radical changes in his humdrum life. He wasn't a man of action. Sorry to be harsh."

They both understood that André had taken action to effect the biggest change possible in his life.

"Is there anyone else you would call a close friend of his?"

"No. That's important, I think. André did not have close friends. But you should probably talk to the priest at the Romanian church in Weymouth. He knew Anna."

"The secrets of the confessional?"

"Yes. 'Say but the word, and I will be his priest.'"

Peter recognized *Henry VI*. "Thank you. You've been very helpful." He prepared to go.

Symington smiled. "If we do *Twelfth Night*, I'll be calling."

They walked back up to the main door, and Peter said goodbye on the pavement. Symington took out his dog-eared address book and flipped to the back.

"You won't find the Romanian church easily in Weymouth. Here's the number of the priest. Best to call him. Father Vogans."

Symington wrote down the number on a theatre programme and handed it over. As he was walking away, Peter turned.

"By the way, do you know Father Salvez?"

"Yes, we met once."

Symington closed the theatre door. Peter left unsure whether or not he had begun a friendship here. A few minutes later, it occurred to him that he had never learned Symington's Christian name.

CHAPTER 9

Peter kept a leisurely pace as he headed downhill. He had decided to hire a car to visit Father Vogans in Weymouth, and he would drop by Lasker's Garage on the way. He recalled several car hire places not far from the Lasker house itself. Within a few blocks, he realized that he wasn't feeling all that well. His stomach had knotted and he was perspiring. On Daubney Street, he encountered a decent restaurant and, since it was noonish anyway, he decided to grab lunch and a pint before proceeding to the car outlets. All he needed was a short rest.

The place was empty, except for a salesman sitting at the front. He took a table in the back and the waitress brought the lunch menu and, he was pleased to see, a lengthy beer list. She graciously offered to bring him a St. Peter's; it was a traditional ale and it was a long time since he had had one. The special was fish and chips and he ordered it. He was a little out of breath. He forced himself to relax, and thought about home, the garden, his children, and everything except murder and mutilation. Let the evil rhythms of Lasker and the Rover vibrate in the back of his brain, unarticulated.

The food pacified his stomach but the pint made him mildly woozy. He beckoned to the waitress for his bill. When she arrived he said, "Are the car hire places much farther down the hill?"

She considered the question. "Yeah, they're mostly there. But you can get a much better deal at Sam's."

"Where's that?"

"That's the bonus. He's only two streets down, one over. You can't miss it. It's where the IRA let off its bomb."

A bit light-headed from the beer, Peter strolled down the hillside and did an automatic left turn where the waitress had indicated, although she might have been pointing to the right, he thought. He was bad with maps, worse with verbal directions. As he walked, he said to himself: *I need a SatNav in order to find the place where I can hire a car with a SatNav.* It reminded him of the old joke that defined existentialism. Existentialism is going to the shops, buying a rubbish bin, putting it into a paper sack, taking it home, taking it out of the bag, crumpling up the bag and tossing it into the bin. Then again, the joke wasn't hilarious to anyone but Jean-Paul Sartre.

He found the garage pocketed between two ancient brick buildings. The IRA might have bombed the structure that had been there before, but Peter doubted it. Now, a one-storey shed-like office stood back from the street, and cars of varying age were slotted at conflicting angles in front of it. By Peter's estimate, most of the cars would have to be moved in order to free any of the others. The simple sign, *Sam's*, which was bolted to the roof of the shed, was as weathered as everything else. Peter entered the office. Behind the desk, the eponymous owner-manager of Sam's Auto For Hire — Peter guessed that the full corporate name didn't fit on the outside sign — a fleshy Armenian with the profile of a barrel, looked up and arched an eyebrow at Peter's official ID, half impressed by, and half suspicious of, any police-derived document. He came out from behind the battered desk and made a point of shaking Peter's hand. "Greetings, Inspector. Welcome to Whittlesun. More importantly, welcome to Sam's."

Peter thanked him. He felt a bit nauseated. His tweed coat felt heavy and hot; he had already loosened his collar.

"You are here for the Rover? Not the car the Rover!"

Peter, confounded, could only manage: "Not really."

"We hope the Rover soon will be over."

Peter looked at him blankly but Sam, undeterred, continued. "You have the Rover covered." "Rover" and "covered" rhymed, and Peter understood that the man was practicing his English.

"This here is Mayta," he continued, moving to unblock Peter's view. He wondered how he had missed Mayta in the confines of the shed. She was the definition of a bombshell. Five-foot-ten, add a foot for the black bouffant, with a tight dress of some satin substitute, high heels and a necklace of beads, the thirty-something woman towered above the two men. She must be the bookkeeper, but if Sam were smart, Peter thought, he would add front desk duties to her job description. Mayta smiled, nodded and said nothing. She didn't need to speak.

"So," said Sam, "You want a car for the week? Three days? See the sights?"

"Only until tomorrow afternoon. Something with a SatNav?"

"I have a Subaru with the latest SatNav. It's preprogrammed with the longitude and latitude for the spot we're standing on. Like a housing pigeon."

"Homing pigeon."

"Whatever. In Armenia we eat pigeons. Just have to cook them right."

"Not the pigeons from around here," Mayta said in a silky voice, as Sam and Peter went out to the yard. She watched from the doorway.

Sam walked directly to a black late-model sedan. It shone propitiously in the only ray of sun that had managed to reach the yard between the brick buildings. The Armenian kept his vehicles clean, Peter remarked. Sam tossed him the keys, which Peter dropped; he bent down and picked them up. Since Peter hadn't seen him take the keys down from the punch-board in the office, he supposed that Sam had somehow chosen the for-hire vehicle before Peter even entered the office. He was still bothered by the man's instant deduction that he was involved with the Rover case; the murders had a broader public profile than he had imagined.

"While you get the feel for the Subaru, I will move everything else." Peter then understood that Sam had simply brought the keys for *all* the cars on that side of the yard; there was bound to be one of whatever kind of vehicle a customer desired.

"Mayta will do the paperwork. She is fine with paperwork. You don't look like a man who wants extra insurance. You want extra insurance?"

"No." Peter peered into the car. It seemed clean, acceptable. The SatNav was built into the instrument console. Sam started to walk away.

"Excuse me, Sam, but could you include a road map? I need to get to Weymouth, the Romanian church."

Sam turned. "Belt-and-suspenders. I include the map and a SatNav."

"And do you know André Lasker's garage?"

This time the Armenian offered a sharp look. He halted, rattling the ring of keys like worry beads.

"Lasker is dead. That's sad."

"But his shop is still open. Is it an honest place?"

Sam held up a finger. "Give me a minute to free up your car."

There followed a stop-and-start conversation as Sam moved a vehicle, paused to offer a comment, then moved another. The street was soon lined with rental cars. Only the Subaru remained on the left side of the space. The two men stood by the driver's-side door.

"Put it this way, Inspector," he said. "It was an honest business before and even more honest now. Do you want directions there?"

"Did you know Lasker?"

"Met him one time. We competed in the hire business, I suppose, but I deal in quality motorcars. He rented more, what do you call it?"

"Down-market?"

"Exactly. Cheaper cars. Bought them, repaired them, put them out to let." He jangled his ring of keys, waiting. How do you ask the owner of a cash business how to skim the till? Peter wondered. He was having trouble finding diplomatic words. He could find no way to gloss over it, and so he said to Sam: "Don't get the wrong impression, but if you wanted to keep your cash off the books, how would you conceal it?"

Sam shrugged like a man quite comfortable with the magical properties of cash. "My advice is, hire an honest bookkeeper. It's, what do they call it?"

"A contradiction in terms?" Where did that come from, Peter thought? He was sweating through his shirt now, and felt a weakness in his chest.

"Here is what I am trying to say," Sam continued. He tilted back against the Subaru. "The woman you want to see is Sally, who runs the office at the front, the books, and so on. She is honest, if honest means keeping accurate ledgers. Now that the boss, Lasker, has disappeared, she is even more honest. You understand?"

Peter merely nodded.

Mayta glided out from the office with the papers. She seemed even taller in outdoor daylight. He signed where she had X-ed. She ripped out the second copy of each form, clipped them to the SatNav manual, and made sure that Sam had handed over the right keys. She favoured him with a sly smile. *Did she hear the discussion about Sally, the bookkeeper, roughly her counterpart at Lasker's shop?* Both men watched her walk back to the office.

"Right," Sam continued. "An honest accountant does what you tell him with what you give him. He's stupid, and that is good. You want to skim, you never let the cash come near the books in the first place. That way the honest accountant stays honest and everybody is convinced by the books he, or she, keeps."

Not that he needed the lecture, but Peter had never heard such a succinct explanation of the challenge facing forensic accounting.

Mayta had paused at the entrance to the shed, and now turned to face Peter. She walked directly back to him, looming above, and peered into his eyes, like a censorious hypnotist.

"You look unhealthy, Inspector."

She moved in even closer and held up a flat palm to within an inch of his right cheek. For him, it was as if the fever in his face was extruded into her hand. She looked into her palm as if it were a mirror reflecting his shining, perspiring aura.

"You're running a fever, Inspector. Come with me."

Peter was unwilling to be led — he had a schedule to follow. But that didn't matter, for he followed her magnetically, despite the turmoil in his head. He fought his delirium. He thought of Gwen, of Symington. He imagined a single murderer of both Anna Lasker and the four girls. He conjured up huge crows, harpies, flying out over the Whittlesun Cliffs.

Mayta herded him into the office. As he entered, she whirled and stared into his face again, like a mesmerist anxious to get started. A filthy coffeemaker stood on a cabinet against the wall. She began to root in the cupboard underneath. *This is ridiculous*, Peter told himself. He leaned back on the desk, even though he dislodged a stack of papers in the process, and grimaced from the bruise on his elbow where he had fallen; his left shoulder ached too. Mayta had her back to him but somehow sensed his pain. She paused in her search for her elixir and turned to dart him a look of motherly disapproval. She returned to her search.

Peter closed his eyes against the dizziness. *How did I end up in a smelly car-hire shed with the owner's voluptuous girlfriend preparing to pour some homemade formula down my throat? The small portents are the same as the big ones*, Peter mantra-ed, and tried to relax. *No-matter-where-you-go-there-you-are.* He found himself hoping that there would be real magic in that elixir.

She emptied the coffee in the sink attached to the lavatory and filled the flask with water. She poured in black tea, flipped the switch on the coffee machine and stood back to watch it boil. She joined Peter in leaning against the desk, either in some kind of covenly solidarity or to catch him if he toppled. Taking a towel from behind the desk, she wiped the sweat from his forehead and neck, at once making him her patient. He didn't resist. He was dysfunctionally delirious. He thought of women. Guinevere. Joan. His daughter Sarah. And then he had a fevered premonition: Sarah would somehow be drawn into the investigation. The image was clear: Sarah, her shell collector's rucksack over her shoulder, walking on the Channel strand.

Satisfied with her necromancy, Mayta poured a cup of the chai and added sugar to it. "It's hot, but drink it as soon as you can stand it."

Peter, barely confident that he wasn't ingesting poison, downed the tea in a series of small sips. The heat and the steamy spices — he identified cardamom and cinnamon — broke through his fever like a compact tidal wave, seeming to flush the sweat right out the top of his head. Mayta rubbed his head again with the towel, like a hairdresser or a swimming coach would. His temperature dropped within seconds. His vision cleared and he found himself staring at Sam, who stood in the doorway grinning. By this time, Mayta was brushing Peter's tweed coat. She even looked down to check the polish on his brogues.

"You're better," she pronounced. And he was. He thanked her and walked out to the parked vehicles.

"How about I drop you off at Lasker's, then you take the car?" Sam said.

Peter rubbed his eyes, and shook his head to clear it. "Then how will you get back?"

"Don't worry, don't worry about that." He got in the driver's side. Peter gratefully occupied the other.

Sam slalomed through the streets of Whittlesun, with no need for the SatNav. In five minutes they were in the neighbourhood of Lasker's Garage, but then Sam halted in an empty lane and began tapping new coordinates into the very device. "Here, I'll leave that for you, the Romanian church in Weymouth. An hour and a bit away."

Peter looked at the vacant cobblestones ahead. "Forgive me," Sam said. "It's probably better I don't show my face at Lasker's." They got out of the Subaru and Sam tossed the keys to Peter. "Keep the car as long as you need it." He walked away before Peter could comment. There must be some Armenian sales practices he didn't understand, he mused.

Lasker's Garage lay a half street along and around one corner, on a dead end stretch. Like Sam's, the office was a shed set back from the road, but it was also bigger than the Armenian's operation, with a closed-in garage to one side, from which the sounds of mallets and drills reverberated. Cars were brought into the work bay area from a square portal out at the street; a typical pull-down garage door controlled access. A sign had been posted: *Honk to Enter*. He knew from the files that before André Lasker's desertion, the business employed four full-time mechanics. Judging from the traffic, the garage seemed to have moved along nicely. But there was no Mayta, only an elderly bookkeeper-receptionist in the office, with copper-wire hair and glasses suited to a bored librarian. She looked up as Peter entered. He flipped open his Scotland Yard credentials, which utterly failed to impress her. A doorway led from the office into the repair zone and the banging and grinding formed a constant backdrop to conversation in the office. This was Sally.

"The police have already questioned me," she affirmed, implying that she had been detained in shackles, or worse.

"I would like to see the company books," he stated. The shop's black-spined ledgers stood in a neat row on the shelf behind her head.

"The books? Whatever for?"

Peter looked around the office. There were testimonial letters from customers on the wall and a couple of gold-stamped parchments of commendation from the local business council. The most recent award was two years old.

"Those," he said.

This was the moment when a witness either mentioned warrants or she did not. Sally seemed to believe that she was the Defender of the Faith, preserving an empire and a legacy even after the founder had fled.

"Them's only the last six months."

But she handed over one of them. The pages were filled in with her neat penmanship.

"We do a cash business, eighty per cent," Sally said. "Majority of customers with insurance settlements deposit their cheque and pay us in cash. But I record everything."

"Do you take the cash to the bank yourself?"

Her tone turned even more defensive, for a number of bad reasons, Peter thought. "I do now. Mr. Lasker always did it before. Took the bag to the night deposit at the Barclays branch."

"Is that near his home?"

"Might be. I've never been invited along, myself."

So André Lasker likely used the same bank to handle his family and business accounts, and that branch was closer to his home than to the garage. Why was it more convenient to use a bank near to his house? Perhaps someone at the bank was in on Lasker's scheme.

"That was before all that business happened," Sally continued.

It seemed evident that the business was continuing without let-up, as it should, he supposed. But he asked anyway.

"Is the business still prospering?"

"Prospering? Oh, we're doing fine. Revenue stream's flowing nicely, even above the usual, I might say. Are you really with Scotland Yard? Can I see your identification again?"

"No." He went behind the desk and took down the most recent volume. He scanned the last three months of entries, including the week of André's flight; the pattern of cash payments appeared to remain steady in the days leading up to his disappearance. Lasker had maintained his habits to the end, at least at the office. The entries in the ledger had halted the Sunday after the incident.

"Was Mr. Lasker well liked?"

"Well liked? Oh, he was a reasonable boss. Everybody misses him."

"Did he socialize with the staff?" Peter understood that he was reaching his point of marginal return with Sally. He glanced at her desk and noted that a fresh volume had been started for the post–André Lasker regime, although this one was blue rather than black.

He refrained from taking it; instead, he would ask Ron Hamm to impound the lot of them.

"Socialize? No, mechanics aren't the kind to socialize with the boss after hours. But he always bought three bottles of Bailey's at Christmas. He was well liked, Mr. Lasker."

Her comments fell into the category of not speaking ill of the dead. Peter pointed to several items in the credit column of the last month's account book.

"These seem different. What are they?"

"We run a car hire business on the side. Very profitable but not that big an operation, you understand."

"A cash operation?"

"Fifty-fifty. Because it's mostly business types that rent, they need receipts, and that makes them think they might as well put the hire charges on a credit card."

"But less than half the customers."

"Mr. Lasker tended to offer them a better deal for cash." While old Sally remained wary, she was enjoying the attention, so long as she could continue to educate the ignorant policeman from London.

He had only one more important question. He would interview the mechanics later. "Sally," he said, with ersatz intimacy, "who's managing the garage now?"

"Albrecht Zoren, our chief mechanic," she replied.

Peter took down another ledger, merely for general comparison. He replaced the two volumes in their proper order and left the office.

"But don't you want to talk to the men?" Her tone was plaintive, but he didn't turn around.

CHAPTER 10

"The 'open road'?" Stan Bracher, the Saskatchewanian, had once said while they were rolling down the A5. "Try three hundred miles of nothing but grain elevators and frozen wheat stalks." Peter had once driven the I-70 across the State of Kansas in mid-January and knew what Stan meant. The drive to Weymouth from Whittlesun hardly compared but Peter realized, as he swung the Subaru onto the dual carriageway, that he was in the mood to drive. The SatNav brought him to the front of a tall church near the centre of Weymouth. The trip took precisely an hour. The church overfilled the small backstreet square on which it stood. Its narrow footprint, and its grim steeple, recalled a rocket ship. The front steps ran right to the edge of the pavement, and exiting parishioners were expected to move immediately to the grassy quadrangle across the way.

The neighbourhood was dead quiet at this time of day; shadows from the looming buildings turned the air damp. Peter parked the car in the sexton's spot at the side and walked to the front of the building. He stopped at the bottom of the broad stone steps. Etched into granite above the main door were the words *Saint George's Anglican Church.*

He walked around to the common entrance, where a sign advertised:

St. George's Anglican Church
Office of the Bishop Anglican Diocese
Office of the Patriarchate Romanian Orthodox Church
A separate hanging sign had been turned to *Open*.

The door was unlocked. He entered without hesitation and descended a level. Modern churches in Britain did not have crypts; they had basements decorated with linoleum flooring. The place was as silent as a tomb, though. He explored the rooms along the musty hallway, but neither the Anglican Bishop nor the officiating priest of the Romanian contingent in Weymouth appeared to be anywhere downstairs. The door to the Administration Office had been left ajar and a desk lamp was on, but no one was home. A ceiling light provided a beacon to the winding stairway at the end of the hall, and Peter traced his way up to the main church.

The building, in Peter's quick, almost dismissive judgment, was like many other houses of worship built since World War II. It had a late-sixties or early-seventies feel. Holy fathers, complicit with church architects of the era, forgot that modern styles, in this case with a bias towards pastel colours and teak trim, dated quickly, leaving their inventions oddly retrograde and unimpressive three or more decades on. St. Walthram's Abbey, even in its crumbling state, projected more warmth than this edifice.

A man was sitting at the large pipe organ in the alcove created by the left branch of the transept. He sat high up, the keyboard in a crescent embracing his body, the pipes like a jungle of reeds facing him. Peter could imagine F.R. Symington staging *The Phantom of the Opera* in this space. But he had another sharp sensation, namely, that the man at the organ was waiting for him. It wasn't true, but nonetheless he paused and waited. The priest, who wore a black suit, turned to look at his visitor, even though Peter had not made a sound. Father Vogans was in his early seventies, with a grooved face and bushy eyebrows; he had a heavy, Slavic jaw and the shoulders of a middleweight boxer.

"Do you play?" The voice was warm, with only a hint of an Eastern

European accent. It carried clearly through the cool air beneath the hollow of the cupola.

"I'm not in the least musical," Peter admitted. His voice carried distinctly; he was glad he hadn't shouted.

"Then there is no point in your coming up here. I will come down."

The priest descended and met Peter by the rail in front of the altar.

"Nicolai Vogans."

They shook hands. Peter identified himself as a Yard chief inspector. The information didn't faze Vogans, just as it had not surprised Father Salvez or F.R. Symington. Vogans only nodded and led the way down to the passageway and staircase that Peter had just used.

"Have a seat," the priest said, in the Administration Office. Immediately, Vogans began the elaborate ritual of making coffee. He had all the accoutrements — filters, ground coffee, a jug of water and a shiny, copper-piped machine. "What can I do for you, Chief Inspector?"

"I'm here about Anna Lasker."

"I thought you might be."

"Why is that, Father?"

Father Vogans turned, a teaspoonful of coffee poised in one hand. He peered over the top of his glasses, at the classic ironic angle. "I'm pushing seventy. So are you, I'm guessing. Let's see what else we have in common, Inspector Cammon, as men of a certain experience, able to cut through the niceties."

"Okay. Was she was a member of your congregation?"

"Yes."

"An active member?"

"Let me get this coffee going before we talk. It is too important for distractions." He finished his preparations and left the coffeemaker to bubble and steam. He took the chair behind the desk, across from Peter.

"'Active' is not the right word. She lived in Whittlesun, not an easy commute every Sunday when you have no car."

Peter had been unaware that she couldn't drive. Apparently, André did not see fit to drive her.

"And we are a small parish. No, again I am not being precise. We serve the Romanian community across all of southern England, but the Weymouth contingent is not large. And this is not wholly our church. It's owned by the Anglicans."

"I see that. What's the connection?"

Vogans got up and turned back to his machine, recalibrating a knob. "The connection of Christian to Christian, I hope. This was established first as an Anglican church, St. George's. He's the patron saint of our church as well. So it was appropriate that they offered us space. Moreover, the Romanian Orthodox church in London, a beautiful church, is also a joint operation with the Anglicans. It is called St. Dunstan's. You should visit it when you are next in London."

"I see. Isn't that unusual?"

"Not at all. Have you been to St. Patrick's in Dublin? There is a whole Protestant section within that important Catholic cathedral."

Peter tried to take the analogy at face value. To compare the Romanian church's experience to that of the Huguenots was a stretch. He took a closer look at Vogans. At almost seventy the man remained physically strong, his face hardened by outdoor work. Peter was not even tempted to patronize him as peasant stock; there was something of the trained athlete in his dignified strength.

"What did you think of Anna?" Peter said.

"A sad death. An unhappy life. But she had faith in God."

"Was it her marriage that made her unhappy?"

Peter was choosing his words carefully but the priest was having none of it. "Don't worry, Chief Inspector, I will not be disclosing confidences from the confessional. But I don't mind telling you, she was unhappy. She still had ties to her family in Bucharest. Or Iasi, to be exact. She was bored with life in Dorset, and very frustrated."

Great, Peter thought. *Two people who hacked each other up out of boredom. They sent me down here for this?* His sudden irritation took him by surprise; perhaps his fever was returning. Condescension towards the victim was not his habit. He still ached from his near-fall up on the cliffs.

"Was she . . . volatile? Dramatic in nature? Emotional?" he asked.

"I would say so. Loved passionately. Hated passionately."

"Whom did she hate?"

"No one, in effect. No one she told me about."

"Did she talk about leaving her husband?"

"I can firmly say no to that, Chief Inspector. Anna wanted what every immigrant, and every young woman, wants."

"Did she try to get pregnant?"

Father Vogans hesitated. He had poured the coffee and completed the sub-ritual of adding cream and sugar. Peter wondered about Romanian Orthodox rules on contraception. Vogans proceeded.

"She wanted children. He did not. But I want to say, Inspector, that they loved each other. Sometimes people cannot see the way forward." Vogans crossed himself. "What they think will be inevitable progress in their lives turns out to be the same old thing. I feel guilty about Anna. If she had lived in this city, I am sure I could have involved her in the church more than I did. It would have given her a life."

That was a pretty harsh summation of the woman's failures, Peter thought, even if the priest was eager to take on her sadness. "But what did she want, Father? What did she tell you she wanted?"

The priest looked at Peter. He discerned no pleading in the visiting policeman's tone. Vogans peered into his coffee cup, watching the steam curl across the surface, and understood that he'd best give a direct answer this time. Thus far the priest had let their common generation shape his answers, but this last question was a police officer's firm query.

Peter noticed for the first time that the cleric's eyes did not shine, that the irises were flat black, giving him an intimidating stare. A sermon from the pulpit by this priest would be something to experience. But his words were sincere and measured. "She wanted to bring her mother over from Bucharest."

"And that wasn't possible?"

"The mother didn't want to come. Anna pleaded and wept, and she flew there several times, but the mother refused. My church is under the direct supervision of the Patriarch of Bucharest but my efforts were also in vain."

"I have to ask, Father: did she seriously think of going back to Romania herself?"

Vogans went quiet but Peter was sure that he would answer. "Once, she talked about it. But I told her that her loyalty was to her husband, who had given her a good life in England. I'm afraid that we both pinned some hopes on her persuading him to have a family — a child, I mean."

Peter flashed on Anna's blood spread across the corridor walls. He said nothing as Vogans sipped his coffee from a small cup. He noticed that the cleric's black cassock, very similar to Salvez's, hung on a man-ikin-like rack at the side of the room. Vogans saw him staring.

"I usually wear this suit in the daytime," he said, glad to shift the subject of conversation. "The cassock runs down to the ankle and the hem drags on the floor too much. I wear it for liturgical occasions, of course."

Draped over the shoulders of the cassock was a red cape, implying an elevated status. Peter recognized it as the chasuble. He wondered if Salvez owned one.

"The cape? That's the chasuble. Frankly, a nuisance to put on."

In Peter's experience, when a priest started joking, he was trying to end the conversation. He had enough for the moment, anyway. The portrait of Anna was forming. The caffeine zinged through him; he stood and prepared to go. And then he had a revelation. He was in a church, and so why not? But it wasn't a specific revelation resulting from prayer; it arrived more obliquely than that. It was subsurface, something to do with Anna, with the pattern of the blood. He let his eyes go out of focus and he remained still an extra minute, even though Father Vogans must have been staring at him (Peter bet that the Romanian had seen his share of mystics). Something to do with the way Anna moved. In his reverie, he saw her sweep an arm across a wall that seemed to stretch into infinity. His lightheadedness had no connection with his dizzy spell in Sam's office, though it might have had something to do with the coffee.

Vogans broke in. "Let me show you something upstairs before you leave."

He came around the desk but paused at the manikin and reflexively smoothed the front of the cassock. "Did you know that there are thirty-three buttons on the cassock, one for each year of Christ's life?"

Vogans led him back up the stairs to the main church. Peter was all right now. The priest turned to the wing of the transept opposite the pipe organ and gestured to a large wooden panel; Peter hadn't noticed it earlier. It resembled a rood screen in a Protestant church. The wood was intricately carved into frames, each of which housed a painted scene from the Bible. Peter naturally looked for the Annunciation and found it near the bottom of the panel. Gabriel knelt, as always, in front of the radiant Virgin, while God, the Holy Spirit in the form of a dove, and various cherubs looked down on the archangel's audience with Mary.

"That is called the iconostasis," Vogans whispered. "It's an altar screen of great age and value from Romania. The Archbishop of Canterbury himself, in 1964, paid for its transport and installation. So you see, the ecumenical spirit is alive in southern England." Peter accepted the devotion behind Vogans's explanation, even if he sounded like a boy who had been forced to move into his rich relative's house. Peter agreed that it was beautiful.

"Do you know Father Salvez?" Vogans asked.

"Yes. We have met. You know that he has cancer?"

The priest seemed startled by the question, but there was real sympathy in his response. "I've been told."

Peter said his goodbyes and Vogans let him out the front door of the church so that he could see the stonework lining the entrance. He had the distinct feeling that Father Vogans didn't want to talk about Father Salvez. And it was interesting that the Romanian congregation, housed within this temple to Anglicanism, was large enough to deserve its own SatNav entry.

Paper covered every square inch of the desktop. More documents of various sizes, tagged and corner-turned, trailed across the carpet from the desk to the door and back again like some Ourobouros loop, in a sequence laid out by Chief Inspector Peter Cammon that only he understood. It was as if some bureaucratic Theseus had trickled out a path of paper in order to find his way out of the maze but hadn't succeeded. Other reports and photographs were stacked next to his chair, or perched on the settee in the corner; he had taped folio-size maps of the coast on the wall next to the television. This was the second time he had laid out the Lasker material, but he was no happier with this configuration. He had closed the curtains, but now it was about five o'clock, and he opened them again. He would have stood on the desk and looked at the evidence that way, if that would have helped. There was still a gaping hole awaiting the detailed autopsy. In Stan Bracher's absence, he would have to drive out to the Regional Lab and introduce himself to the presiding pathologist.

The husband would either float to the surface near Whittlesun Beach, his body bloated and nibbled away by small fish, or he would be found with a new moustache and beard in Kathmandu. Neither scenario pleased Peter. It was becoming personal, and he wanted to be the one to make the arrest or, if it came down to it, identify the etiolated corpse.

There was a third possibility, but Cammon couldn't see Lasker just walking up to Inspector Maris and turning himself over to the Queen's judgment. Maris wasn't destined for that much luck.

Peter needed a way to force the issue.

There had been other disappearances into the ocean: Lord Lucan in 1974 and the Australian prime minister Harold Holt in 1967 came to mind. Lord Lucan, a minor aristocrat, had walked into the sea after killing the family nanny and attacking his wife with murderous intent. Peter had been peripherally involved in the investigation in the early part of his career, although the feckless Lucan was never found and reports of his reappearance had been rife ever since. Holt's drowning had generated similar conspiracy theories; he had served as PM for less than three years, and he was an experienced swimmer. Peter's favourite paranoid story was that a Chinese submarine had been waiting for him offshore.

Peter was familiar with both files. Tragic as they might be — Holt's vanishing was certainly an accident — these were lurid anecdotes whose features only appeared remarkable to the tabloid-credulous. Peter understood the purpose of the sea in the popular imagination — oblivion for the ingenuous, the jettisoning of identity and rebirth for the egoist. But Peter knew that the disappearing man, whatever his motive, fears the tide washing him back to his departure point. That is his definition of defeat. He shivers at the prospective scene as his bloodless corpse is loaded into the unhurried ambulance, his pale rictus photographed by police and by broadsheet stringers.

He flipped the cap of the second bottle of ale he had commanded from room service. He sat back in the armchair and frowned at the ragged display of paper. He didn't like hotels much, and he considered moving to a new one. Of course, that would also require him to clean up the mess. He took out his police notepad and drew up a list. He was an inveterate maker of lists. He wrote:

1. Too much blood — why?

2. The second beach

3. Mechanic kills wife — no weapon? no wheel wrench?

4.

He didn't fill in the *4*. On a second scrap torn from his notebook, he wrote and underlined: *where do I want to go next with this?* He crumpled the page and tossed it into the basket.

He felt the lack of progress in his day. A confrontation with Maris was coming, probably tomorrow. He still needed local guidance, perhaps from Willet but better from Hamm, in order to efficiently explore the coastline. A search of the caves east of Whittlesun was more appealing than ever.

He lay down on the bed, not intending to sleep, and shifted some of the papers aside. He got out his mobile and flipped it open, but then left it lying beside him. He'd see how it felt in the morning. His penultimate thought before dozing off was that Lasker would not be found in Kathmandu: it had no beaches.

And then he asked, as he floated into the twilight: *Who is the Black Man? If the Cloaked Man is Lasker, has Gwen seen him? Watched him? Tracked him? Above all, who is the Electric Man?* He'd find that out tomorrow, too.

Stephen Bartleben lay abed with the woman to whom he had been married for forty years. He loved her, he supposed, but after what he considered a geological epoch, the best he could articulate was that they were companionable. Time's companions — endurance, habit, acceptance — overwhelmed love and you settled for the terms of the contract you made with the Church looking down on you. That was the rule, especially applicable to the privileged class. It was 5:30 a.m., and he was not in a generous mood. He struggled, unmoving next to her, to clear the mists with a happy thought. *What is the best aspect of marriage?* he considered. *Why the hell am I looking to my marriage for a happy thought? This woman is snoring, ruining my rest! No chance of getting back to sleep. Merde! No, no;* he chastened himself for using an expletive, even if unspoken. *So, what is the best part of our marriage?* he persisted. *What romantic parallel applies?* They were faithful to each other. She supported his ambition, even if only by leaving him alone to pursue it. Eloise and Abelard? *Shit, didn't they castrate him?* No more expletives. He tried to drift on the pre-dawn mists, but she, a mountain next to him, kept on with her snoring. Christ, it was like sleeping next to an active volcano. He tried for a classical analogy. He settled for "faithful companion." He was like Long John Silver, with his parrot always riding on his shoulder. Of course, at the moment she was a hippo on his shoulder. She had gained weight. He'd been losing weight. He was Deputy Commissioner, New Scotland Yard. A serious bureaucrat. Stephen determinedly gave up this train of fantasy, but suddenly Cammon visited his brain. *Where did he arrive from? The conventional little man in the black suit. I love him. How many days has it been? Four? No, only three. A few days on the south coast of England, in some Brighton-wannabe town, fighting against all kinds of tides. Better him than me.* Three or four days. The frustration would be building now; it always happened this way. Cammon ready to burst, rummaging around for the final pieces of the puzzle. Waiting for the breakthrough. The image comforted Bartleben and he immediately fell back to sleep. His wife, he supposed, loved him. She certainly appreciated his knighthood.

CHAPTER 11

Sherlock Holmes once said: "You have a grand gift of silence, Watson . . . It makes you quite invaluable as a companion."

The phone rang at 7:30 a.m. and Joan answered before the second ring. She was sitting on the side veranda of the house, which gave a direct view down the lane, although she couldn't see the main road. A neighbour was due to pick her up at any minute to drive her to the railway station to catch the midmorning train to Leeds. She sat in a deep wooden chair called an Adirondack; Peter had seen them in New England the time he worked on that case with the FBI, and had had one shipped home. (The idea for the snake-rail fence had come from Peter's sojourn to Quantico, Virginia, and points south.) A satchel sat next to her. She was happy to be going to visit Michael and his girl, and she was reading the tail end of "The Man With the Twisted Lip," the story that referred to Watson's "grand gift."

She wouldn't bring the Holmes collection with her, since this was one of Peter's valued books, and so she wanted to finish the story before she left. Although she was absorbed in it, she kept an eye out for the pheasant in the tall grass at the end of the property. There was only one now, a male, and Joan worried that the other three had abandoned it. Pheasant pairs bonded for life. She didn't see him and hoped he had joined the others for their migration.

"Hello?" she answered, thinking it must be Sarah or the neighbour.

"Hello, dear," Peter said.

"Hello, Peter. Is everything all right?" With Peter, it could be anything, but she wasn't prepared for what he said next.

"Yes, perfectly fine, but I have a big favour to ask you. Can you come down to Whittlesun?"

In forty years, Peter had never directly involved her in an investigation. That he did so now wasn't a sign of panic — and there was none in his voice — so much as it told her that the Lasker case had reached a significant obstacle. His request wasn't exactly flattering; she wasn't Sherlock, Mycroft, Irene Adler or even Watson himself. Still, he had never called for help before. She didn't overreact. Even so, as she absorbed the surprise of her husband's call, she rushed to figure out what he wanted. Her usual role was to be supportive of his moods and to nod at his occasional oblique musings, but they were hardly sharing the same harness. She understood the stages that he worked through and she estimated that by now Peter had formed a theory of what might have happened that tempestuous night in the Lasker home.

And then she understood. He was telling her that he needed a special resource in order to untangle the knot. He needed the perspective of a woman.

"If you could see your way to coming down, I'd like you to visit the Lasker home with me," he said, rather formally. "It will only take the morning. You can stay on at the hotel, if you like. It's very comfortable."

Of course she would accept; she could always visit Michael another time. She was excited but wondered about a number of things. She understood his efforts to reassure her; she had never been through a crime scene. On the other side of the coin, she thought, I'm a nurse and I've seen as much, if not more, blood and guts than he has, including knife and gunshot trauma. The visit probably would be strange. Her husband would be preoccupied, and stay that way even if she gave him what he wanted. He often retreated to the shed, muttering to himself for long periods; she suspected that he did the same in hotel rooms too. How far was he drawing her into his complicated world now? Nevertheless, because she had the greatest faith in her husband's skills, she remained unruffled.

"Okay. What's the arrangement?" She wasn't heading to the coastal town for a frolic, yet, although she didn't tell him this, she thought: this is going to be thrilling. Conan Doyle had scored a convert.

"I'm sending Verden. He'll be there at nine o'clock, if that's okay."

Joan understood that Peter had summoned Tommy Verden already, and therefore he had been confident that she would acquiesce. She didn't bother telling him of her scheduled trip to see Michael. Instead, she said, "Okay," in the softest, gentlest voice.

She was no longer in the mood to finish the Conan Doyle tale. She closed up the house, made her calls to postpone her trip to Leeds and waited on the veranda.

Joan arrived in Whittlesun well before noon. Tommy Verden drove fast, but not so fast as to alarm her. They had always liked each other, since she regarded him as her husband's devoted protector through many an investigation. Today they travelled in silence, both aware that something unprecedented was happening. Tommy let her off in front of the Delphine. Peter was there to greet them, and Tommy handed her over safe and sound, along with a pile of reports from Bartleben. Peter couldn't resist glancing at a few pages there in the driveway; they were missives from Interpol and the ferry authorities. Tommy offered to pick up Joan the next morning but she insisted that the train would do fine. It was all so reasonable and normal, as if Joan participated in their investigations all the time.

Tommy left and Peter conducted her to his room, now cleaned up. She placed her satchel on the bed.

"Do you want lunch first?" he asked, deferentially.

"No, I'm not especially hungry. Let's eat after. Can you tell me what I'm going to see?" She smiled as she said this, not in the least apprehensive, though she was tingling. She already knew that she would be exposed to evidence of extreme brutality.

"Let's walk. It's not far."

They followed his route through the central streets of the town and down the sloping road to the Lasker residence. He was solicitous, placing his hand against her back to make sure she didn't trip on the cobbles. He explained about the excess of blood and the odd pattern of destruction that she would see in the house. He gave her a brief biography of Anna and the information he had gained from Father Vogans. "There's something I'm missing," he said. "I want your overall reaction to the scene. Unbiased by what I bring to it."

She had taken his hand on the last stretch before the house. Now she gave it an affectionate squeeze and smiled. Peter was not the man to lose his objectivity, no matter what she said, and this very fact, her husband's solidity, somehow freed her to make independent judgments. This was going to be interesting.

On his second visit, Peter had used the key under the flowerpot by the back steps. He employed it now to open the front door, from which the police tape had been removed. He hoped to avoid alerting the neighbours, but he had no doubt that curtains were shifting somewhere nearby. He asked Joan to wait in the vestibule while he turned on all the overhead lights downstairs.

Joan entered the house gingerly. She didn't want to brush against the walls, or step on any evidence. She stood in the hall for a minute facing the bloody wall, just as Peter had done the first day. She kept in mind Peter's admonition that understanding would come from maintaining a healthy distance from the violence, yet the first thing that grabbed her as she caught sight of the blood trail along the hallway was the kinetic flow of this marital battle. She was instinctively attuned to Anna's fear. Someone had run in terror down this hall, probably from the upper bedroom, trailing blood and seeking sanctuary in the back of the house.

"Let's look at the other rooms first," Peter instructed. "We'll come back."

She wanted her hands unencumbered. Usually she carried her purse everywhere, like the Queen, but now she left it by the front door. Peter guided her ahead of him. She entered the living room and catalogued the mayhem wreaked on the furnishings. A bloody palm print covered the light switch. A glass vase lay shattered on the carpet, and she knelt down to examine it. She surveyed the arrangement of furniture. She ran her hand over the obscene gouge in the sideboard and guessed that a kitchen cleaver had done it. To keep her composure in the midst of this sadness, she took herself back to her days as a hospital nurse; she became all business. The triptych on the sideboard interested her more than the ruined mahogany surface. The icon had been left undamaged. Peter watched as she closely examined the curtains puddled on either side of the fireplace. With a look, she indicated to him that she wanted to go on by herself to complete her first pass of the house.

Alone, she followed the track of blood back into the kitchen and immediately saw the anomaly. Yes, the two glass-fronted cupboards had been poked in, and broken crockery, pans and utensils lay all about, but the pot of tomato sauce stood upright on the back burner of the cooker, right where it belonged. It was semi-solid and cracking now. She looked from the pot to the doorway opposite. It should have been the first weapon Mrs. Lasker reached for when she fled to the kitchen. She rotated, trance-like, in the middle of the kitchen, and faced the stove once more. She sensed Peter coming up behind her.

"The pot," she asked, "is just sitting there. Wouldn't she have hurled it at him?"

"I noticed that too. It's a tomato sauce with all kinds of spices in it. The saucepan was cold when the police arrived. There are only minor blood traces, hers, around the stove; the rest is tomato paste."

"What's the name of the haematologist you often sing the praises of? The Canadian?"

"Stan Bracher."

"It might be worthwhile getting him down to look for blood-stains on the stove. I can tell that Mrs. Lasker loved to cook. She was a messy one at the best of times, you can see, but does that matter? Exactly how much blood is there here, do you think?"

Peter shook his head. "I don't know. But I need him for a number of tests anyway. I'm not sure about the amount of blood."

"Were there burn marks anywhere on Anna's body?"

"One double mark, shaped like bars, on her outer arm near the right elbow. She was right-handed."

"I'm guessing she wasn't cooking at the stove when he attacked her," said Joan. "But I'd like to know how recent the burns were. Could she have burned herself deliberately, either that day or in the days before? If it was self-inflicted, that might coincide with the day she found out his plan. And that would show her desperation."

Joan heaved a deep sigh. Despite the overhead lights, the gloom in the house overwhelmed her. The rancid tomato sauce added to the closeness. Bypassing the hall stains, she went up to the lavatory. Seeing right away that there was more blood there than in any other room, she surprised Peter by abruptly turning and entering the bedroom. Like Peter, she wanted to leave the worst for last. He waited on the upper landing. She was back in less than a minute, having grasped that the fight hadn't played out in the bedroom, and there hadn't been a rape. Frowning (in puzzlement, Peter thought), she re-entered the room across the way. She took in the gauzy stockings hanging limply on the shower bar. The blood in the sink had crusted, ruining the porcelain, and had begun to crack. She peered in the bath and then leaned carefully into it, taking special interest in the wavy blood pattern around the drain. She sniffed at the blood in the tub area, and did the same at the sink. Then she squatted, making sure her coat didn't swish on the tiles, and examined the stains on the floor.

She opened the vanity doors, as if looking for a particular item.

"Can we open the medicine chest without spilling glass everywhere?"

"The room has been well photographed. With a little care . . ." Peter swung the shattered panel open to reveal the array of medicines on the narrow shelves. Joan leaned into the space and took her time checking each vial and bottle with a nurse's acumen.

"The contents have been inventoried," he said, trying to be helpful. He was amazed by his wife's instinct for itemization and detail, a talent all good detectives need.

Joan left the room, took a final look along the walls of the upstairs landing and went down again. She sniffed at the blood in the corridor. She paid another visit to the kitchen and marked where the few bloodstains were. Back in the hall she turned to him and put her hand on his shoulder. The gesture was to reassure him that she was okay.

"How does blood spattering work?" she said.

"A slashed artery will spray like a garden hose fully open. But it's rare that a major opening of a blood vessel will involve the victim standing still. Therefore, traumatic cutting, namely an attack, will have the victim turning away from the danger and thus the fan-like effect you see in the loo in places and at the bottom of the stairs, here." He pointed to the wall next to her.

"Often," he continued, "you'll see thicker deposits of blood on the floor, not just from the gravity effect, but because the victim soon becomes dizzy and naturally, or unnaturally if you like, falls down. That applies to a major severing. Smaller veins or surface cuts may actually bleed a lot, and for a long time, but not with the spray impact. Don't be deceived by the quantity of blood in any one spot. There's a lot of blood in one body."

"What about the patterns along each of the hallways?" she said.

"Ah, yes, that's more complicated. Evidently, in some spots, where you see handprints, Mrs. Lasker held herself up, perhaps to avoid fainting. But she also trailed her hand along the walls in that wavy rhythm."

"Was it all her blood?"

"Yes. According to the first-round report."

"Was any of the husband's blood found anywhere?"

"Not in the house. There was an old bloodstain on a carving blade in the kitchen," he said.

"He had plenty of blades to choose from and you'd think he might nick himself at some point in the assault. For that matter, *she* could be expected to defend herself with a knife, but none of his blood was spilled, and nobody resorted to the knife rack. Strange."

Joan went into the living room area again, crossing immediately to one of the fallen curtains. She knelt and rooted through the piles of cloth.

"Tell me about her again."

"Born in Romania, a city called Iasi. She was close to her mother, also called Anna, and flew back occasionally to see her. Father Vogans, her priest, said she was discouraged by her inability to persuade the mother to emigrate."

Joan judged that she had seen enough for a first go and needed time to retrench. She wasn't sure why. Even if she decided to tour the house again, she wanted to digest what she had just seen. She now appreciated what her husband went through on an average murder case. She paused in the hall again.

"Was she very religious?"

"I think religion helped keep the connection with Romania real for her. But when she visited St. George's, the Romanian church, it wasn't so much for Sunday services as to see the priest."

They went out to the back steps for a break, both glad of some fresh air. She could tell that he was waiting for her to gather her thoughts. She leaned against the wall and turned to him.

"Three comments, Peter. First, assuming they were both after each other in the fight, that they were taking the battle *to each other*, they were oddly selective in what they trashed. Wouldn't you have flung that pot of sauce at him, or vice versa? She's running through the rooms, eventually into the kitchen, and she sees the pot? Irresistible. Then the living room: someone pulls down the curtains. You're the one with experience of these domestic fights, but why would they yank down the curtains yet leave the pictures on the walls, undamaged?"

"That bothered me too. The good vase was shattered. I thought at first that he was out to hurt her by destroying her prized objects, but there were other things left untouched. The icon, for example."

"That's my point. Here's what I think." She held up a hand, trying to hold onto the logic and keep everything straight, in effect telling him to bear with her while she explained her theory of the fight. "The drapes were pulled down but not otherwise harmed. The broken vase was nearby, and one of them could have taken a piece of glass and slashed the curtains. They didn't. The same with the icon. Why didn't he break it, and really batter her feelings? It was a link for her to the old country, a link that I bet irked him. The same with the bedroom and the kitchen. Why not trash everything? And frankly, angry spouses like to throw pots and pans."

She paused and they looked at the dismal back garden. He wanted to keep her in her zone.

"Tell me your thinking, Joan. Where does all this lead you?"

"Horrible as it is to even think it, I think she was responsible for almost all of the destruction. I think she pulled down the curtains but valued them enough not to cut them up. The glass vase? That was a wedding present, I'm confident, and I bet it came from the 'other' side of the marriage, depending which one of them broke it."

"And the second thing?"

"The second thing somehow connects to the first thing. If this was truly a room-to-room, back-and-forth war, it's incredible to me that there wasn't a drop of the husband's blood. Glass was flying. Blades cutting. I don't have an explanation."

Joan looked out at the shabby back garden, overgrown with weeds.

"I wonder how it worked for him," Peter said. "If she hurt him, physically, she still didn't manage to stop him from going. If he wasn't hurt, he remained a cold-hearted bastard, unmoved by her panic and her wounds." He paused, letting her get to her final point at her own pace.

"The officers who went through the house, were they all men?"

"Yes, as far as I know."

"The medical people, the person who signed the death certificate, the coroner I suppose, men too?"

"I believe so," he replied.

"Peter, I agree with your feeling that something is very wrong with this house. It gives me the shivers."

"I'm sorry."

"No, that's not what I mean. The woman was desperate for something. And the husband obviously was desperate to leave her."

Joan was surprised at how exhausted she was. She heard a clock chime one o'clock in the distance. Focusing on the back of the property, she thought it odd (as Constable Willet had) that, given André Lasker's profession, there was no work shed, and no car parts anywhere in the garden.

"The most blood was in the lavatory," she finally stated, as if confirming the most salient fact about the killing ground.

"That's right. In the sink and the bath."

"Were the cuts on her arms deep?"

"Yes. The worst were two slashes across her left forearm, and a third lengthwise. There were other cuts on her left shoulder and her right wrist, but not as deep. Some of the blood in the sink and around it came from the head wound, when she was slammed into the mirror."

"On TV they talk about defensive wounds. Was the cut on her arm a defensive wound?"

Peter smiled. For a moment there her speech rhythms sounded like his. "If they were fighting at close quarters, then anything could have happened in a messy situation like that. The gashes were to the inside of the arm. Maybe defensive, but I kind of doubt it. And they weren't caused by the fall from the cliff."

"Peter," Joan said, looking directly at him, "you know the blood on the upstairs walls and in the bath?"

"Yes."

"It was menstrual blood."

They heard a sound from the front part of the house. Peter silently motioned for her to stay put. He went back into the kitchen. For the next couple of minutes, Joan made out only a few sounds, but then heard voices from the kitchen.

Peter emerged onto the back porch followed by a constable. Joan didn't flinch at the sight of the police officer but knew that this was trouble. Still, she smiled as if all were normal.

"Joan," Peter said, "I'd like to introduce Constable Willet. He's been very helpful to me in Whittlesun."

"Madam," Willet said, barely making eye contact. It was somewhat farcical, Joan thought, the three of them crowded onto the back porch of a dead stranger's home, Willet's stomach threatening to bump someone down the stairs.

"Shouldn't be here," Willet said, bluntly. "Neighbour called in an alert. That's why I'm come out."

"Yes, well," Peter said. "I had to do a final check on the computer files. Something I forgot to do yesterday. My wife's in town so we stopped by on our way back to the hotel."

Willet must know, Joan thought, that they had no vehicle and therefore their visit was deliberate. Still, she sensed that Willet was too much the deferential gentleman to raise the point. She avoided looking at her husband; otherwise she would have giggled. For his part, Willet didn't know what to say. There would be a report back to Maris forthwith, they all knew. Peter decided to go in for a pound and raised the door key.

"I got this under the flower pot back here. I was just putting it back."

This lie allowed Willet to save face. They traipsed into the house and right out the front door. Willet went first but paused to make sure that Peter and Joan locked everything up. Peter could think of nothing to say in the face of this mother-hen treatment, and so they all exchanged a perfunctory "goodbye."

Willet walked down the wet cobbles to his motorcycle, which he charged up with a great roar that must have jolted all the neighbours.

Peter and Joan headed with no particular haste back along the street. They didn't speak at first. The tragedy they had just viewed outweighed the farce with Constable Willet. These were common enough sights in a crime zone, Joan knew, but domestic violence brought its special, targeted forms of hurt.

As they turned off the cobbled streets into the commercial district, she turned to Peter. "Do you think he had *everything* planned?"

Peter hesitated. Joan could see that he was gathering his thoughts in order to be precise. "Most of it, yes, but not all. I think he set the exact night that he would disappear. He worked out the details, like abandoning his clothes in a neat pile on the beach. This was the night, yes. You don't alter such a plan easily."

Joan knew that it was so much worse. This form of desertion, without a word of warning or a scintilla of caring, was the nastiest thing André could have done. She was uncertain still about one thing.

"Did he plan all along to kill Anna?"

Peter paused again, but eventually let out his theory. "No. That wasn't his plan. I think she somehow found out and confronted him, just when he was almost away and clear." He squeezed her hand.

And then Joan realized that there were some facts that her husband wasn't going to disclose — not now and maybe not later. It wasn't to save her from the ugly truth — he had just exposed her to the saddest realities imaginable. It wasn't because professional codes prohibited disclosure of the bottom-line truth — he had opened a secret door to her that, she knew, he could not close completely. No, she had helped him, but Peter was already moving on to the next stage of the case. Her mind might be full of horrid images of broken mirrors, blood-drenched sinks and a dying woman's handprints, but his head contained whole floating universes where she held no domain. She grasped ruefully that she would not likely be present when the planets aligned.

They found a comfortable pub along the route. A couple of lagers lightened their mood. All things considered, she was happy.

"Thank you again, dear," he said, leaning across the table to give her a kiss.

She laughed. "Stop, Peter! That's the fifth time you've thanked me. You're welcome. But I have a confession to make."

Peter noted her wry smile. Sensing that she had the advantage, he simply said, "I'm listening."

"I've been sneaking into your Conan Doyle out in your side of the shed." She saw that he was amused, but waiting for her to continue. "Okay."

Joan recalled that the Holmes set had been layered with dust, a sign that Peter hadn't been reading any of the stories lately.

"I know your *Complete Sherlock* is one of your prized books."

Peter laughed out loud, something he didn't do often. "That's your confession? Which stories do you like best?"

"I love them all. I read *A Study in Scarlet* first but then, for some reason, I've been reading the stories in reverse order, back to front. Holmes and Watson are getting younger."

Peter laughed again. Joan was content. For the next two hours, they were both detectives, equal, as they discussed their favourite stories. By the time they returned to the hotel, they were both tipsy.

Hotel sex is as good at sixty-seven as it is at twenty-seven. Afterwards, still in the waning daylight hours, they lay side-by-side, she feeling very much appreciated. She turned to him and said, "Do you think he told her about the details of his plan before he killed her?"

He continued to watch the shadows on the ceiling above the bed. For some reason he glanced at the door, knowing quite well that the chain was on. He rolled towards her on the mattress. "Yes, Anna Lasker knew before she died that he was planning to leave. Forever."

They talked for a few more minutes about the children. She didn't mention that he had called her a few minutes before her scheduled departure to see Michael, but now she told him that she would take the train in the morning from Whittlesun Station to London to shop for the day, and would go on to Leeds for a quick visit.

"I'm pretty sure I'll be home in a day, two days at most," he said, "although I'll have to come back here sooner rather than later."

They lay there a while longer. She didn't dare ask how he thought the case was going. She knew that she had helped him, yet she could feel him slipping away. But after another moment, he said precisely what she needed to hear: "I will tell you every detail of the case as soon as I can, dear."

Since their schedule was out of whack anyway, they napped for two more hours and then went for a walk just as the lights along the high street were coming on. There was a nip in the air, and they agreed that the weather along the coast was more changeable than they were used to, and the morning would probably be warm again. They returned to the hotel and ordered sandwiches and beer to their room. They sat on the bed, cross-legged like campers around a fire, and got crumbs on the duvet. They discussed the Rover investigation. Peter told her most of what he knew.

"Can I ask you something?" she said.

"Anything."

"I'm not asking you to speculate about this Rover, but how do you think he'll be found, ultimately?"

Joan had observed that Peter was disturbed as much by the Rover case as by Lasker. Perhaps for the first time in their marriage, he was seeking — though in an unspoken way — her reassurance about a case. During the Yorkshire Ripper manhunt he had become depressed, but then, everybody who worked on that calamity was haunted by the serial killer. At the time, Peter's solitary methods had ceded to the endless meetings and the team effort. He had pulled out of his funk eventually. Now, Joan worried, was he back in that zone?

"Put it this way," Peter replied. "We don't know enough about the Rover. The file provided by the Task Force is general stuff, most of it public anyway. Thin on the forensics and no witnesses. The Task Force thinks it has pinned down a pattern. Four girls now. They think he's moving in a straight line down the coast, closer to Dorset with each abduction. McElroy's team doesn't get it."

"Get what?"

"There's no pattern at all. He's toying with them."

Joan stroked his cheek. "Well then, dear, you'll have to join the Task Force."

In the morning, Peter stood in front of the hotel as Joan got into the taxi that would take her to the station. "Stay safe. I'll call tonight."

She said to him, "watch out for the Rover."

A pang of loneliness hit her as her taxi pulled away but she smiled and waved. She didn't know that he felt a similar moment of loneliness as he watched her go. The morning was bright and warm. He turned into the hotel. It was time to get back to the files and then start on his appointments. He wondered if he could put off Maris for another day. There was going to be hell to pay on that front once Willet reported back.

Couples and families were checking out as Peter re-entered. The Delphine had a wide-open lobby that took up the entire ground level except for the reception desk and a small office behind it. There were several groupings of armchairs and settees, and a rack of daily newspapers. As he crossed to the lift, Peter turned to the bitter sound of a mother berating a child on the far side of the room; every parent knows the tone, a combination of weariness and bursting frustration. He looked just as the woman swatted the child, who was about five years old, with the back of her hand. She did it only once but the blow landed flatly on the boy's left cheek, and he howled with indignation and pain. Peter considered intervening but, like everyone else, he held back and watched. The drama ended and the tension in the lobby dissipated as the guests went about their business. All except Peter. He continued to look at the woman, although he was no longer focused on her movements. Tumblers were slipping into place. He saw clearly. Anna Lasker had died from the fall from Upper Whittlesun Cliff. She had despaired at the shattered pieces of her marriage — of her marriage, her childlessness, her shopworn faith.

She had tried to pull down her house about her. She had avenged herself on her husband with a final act.

Anna Lasker had committed suicide.

CHAPTER **12**

What made Peter Cammon a good detective was that he never stopped at one idea. He had read philosophy in school and knew the famous saying of Archilochus: the fox knows many things, but the hedgehog knows one big thing. Peter identified with the fox, if in fact a fox was capable of stacking one thing on top of another to reach a logical, definitive conclusion.

He went to the desk, now cleared of documents, and took out a blank sheet of paper. At the top he wrote Anna Lasker's name and underlined it. Below it he jotted three summary conclusions and numbered them:

1. André Lasker is a master of deception.

2. He is alive.

3. To find him I may have to find the Rover first.

He crumpled the note and threw it at the overflowing waste basket. For reasons he was unsure of, he took it out of the basket and flushed it down the loo.

He could see how the next few days would play out, and none of it would be pleasant. He was destined, of course, to be summarily dismissed and sent home the moment Willet reported back to Maris.

Although he would soon be back in Whittlesun, he would have preferred to stay on and, above all, visit Guinevere Ransell again.

He poured the last cup of the room-service coffee and called Ron Hamm on the hotel phone. The detective's answerphone responded. Rapid fire, before the tape could run out, Peter asked him to have all documents, indeed all paper of any kind found in the Lasker home, shipped to the Forensics Centre for him to study.

"And Ron," he concluded, "could you give some priority to a production order application to access Lasker's accounts at Barclays, both business and personal? I think Maris is the one to do it, rather than the Yard."

There was a good chance that Lasker's banking habits, including the way money flowed in and out of his accounts, would reveal any skimming of profits from his garage operation. A man intent on abandoning everything for his new life must accumulate a large nest egg.

"Oh, one very last thing, Ron. The Yard will be sending someone down to photograph the entire house."

Peter sighed. Sometimes he couldn't resist employing guerrilla tactics. Let Maris absorb all that.

"I don't need to get into the house today," he finished off, blithely.

As soon as Hamm heard the message, he would feel compelled to see Maris within seconds. Peter wanted to be on the phone when the young detective called the hotel. He hung up but immediately picked up the receiver and punched Bartleben's London number. Sir Stephen answered on the second ring. Did the man ever leave the office, Peter wondered? There was a clipped impatience in Bartleben's voice this time, as if he were late for something.

"Good morning, Peter. What can you tell me?"

"Stephen, you're going to get a call from Inspector Maris in, I'd say, as soon as we hang up. He won't be happy."

"You seem serene enough about it." Sir Stephen tilted back in his chair and put his feet up on his massive Victorian desk.

Peter ignored the ironic tone. "I'm neither serene nor sanguine about it. The call will amount to a demand for my withdrawal from his jurisdiction forthwith."

Bartleben exhaled, loud enough for Peter to hear. "Maris is an idiot. What progress have you made?"

"I think Lasker is still alive, if he didn't unintentionally drown. I'm also pretty sure that he stole a lot of money and we need to verify that."

"Can you be more clear on that point, Peter?"

"We don't have definite information on where he went, how he got away from the British Isles or his destination once he pulled this off. Getting his bank records would be a good starting point."

"Maris?"

"It would be better if Maris applied for the warrant. Barclays Bank. Bull in a china shop if we show up with it."

"So it was all for the money?" Bartleben said.

This was the kind of question that revealed Bartleben as an armchair strategist. Peter wasn't ready to draw that conclusion, nor had he implied it.

"No, it's more complicated than that. But knowing how much money he absconded with will give us a better picture, not to mention clues about where he may have relocated to."

"I still don't see why Inspector Maris should be calling me with pietistic indignation in his voice."

"In part because I asked Joan to take a look at the house."

"*Inside* the house?"

"Yes."

"Good Lord, Cammon, you don't mean . . . ? This isn't because I didn't call Stan Bracher back to help you out?"

"No, but I want him down here soon. And I want to tell Maris today that the Yard needs to retest all the blood samples and shoot the whole house under lights."

Bartleben took a very, very long two minutes to ponder his situation. Peter was used to these silences and waited patiently. He had no doubt that Stephen would back him up.

"There's something I have to update you on, Peter," he eventually said.

"Tell me."

This was worse than a public line. The operator could be listening in. Sir Stephen spoke anyway.

"Jack McElroy has been trying to keep a low profile on this 'Rover' problem. For example, not using the inflammatory moniker itself. Not publicizing the Task Force, no press briefings, and so on. Well, Jack's afraid the predator is moving into Dorset. Did you see the Olympics announcement in July?"

"Olympics? I heard London was awarded the 2012 Summer Games."

"Peter, don't underestimate it," Bartleben chided. "This is big. Maximum publicity. The PM's called it a 'momentous day,' not to mention we beat out Paris for the rights. They're talking about an Olympic economic boom for locales that nab the various events. There are strong indications that the sailing events will be held in the south, Weymouth and Portland. If the Rover attacks inside the Dorset line, the publicity could kill their chances. There are other places they could hold the sailing."

"You make it sound like we were called in on Lasker to create a distraction."

Bartleben regretted his snap reaction before he gave it. "Only if we solved it."

"Christ, Stephen! Maris is incompetent, so he calls us in, but if we find Lasker, he'll take the credit, publicize the arrest and draw attention away from the killings."

"More ominous than that. If we *don't* find Lasker, he can publicly blame the Yard. Same impact."

Peter wanted Lasker, and Bartleben knew it, but Bartleben would have to take some static for his manipulations.

"So, you've been under pressure from the Home Secretary to throw a line to the county administration. Isn't that getting a bit political?" Peter said.

"Maybe, but in fact the pressure comes from even higher up.

Anyway, Peter, we'll look good if we solve Lasker using Yard resources, over and above the other matter."

It was Peter's turn to deaden the phone line. He thought it through. Bartleben had sent him down as a token resource, a tepid concession to local anxieties. This was insulting but, bottom line, Peter was hooked. He wanted Lasker. "Okay, here's what I want," he finally said. "I want you to get me assigned to the Task Force."

Bartleben groaned. "Lord, Peter, you do play it to the bone. Why the Task Force? Aren't we trying to keep the cases separate?"

Peter persevered. "Lasker may still be hiding somewhere along the coast. We'll both be searching the same geography."

"Maris and McElroy will see it as an intrusion on their bailiwick, maybe a prelude to taking over the case, and that's something we don't aspire to."

"You'll be meeting with Maris anyway. Tell him we want to improve coordination but we need to avoid overlap if I'm out there exploring the cliffs."

"And *will* you be out there rooting around on the cliffs?"

It was Peter's turn to be evasive. He planned to enlist Guinevere Ransell to help him look for André Lasker out there, but he wasn't about to tell Bartleben. "Yes, but with no duplication of effort with McElroy's people."

"All right, Peter. Come clean. What's the plan?"

"I can't avoid Maris, and that will mean he'll kick me out of his jurisdiction. I'll have to leave temporarily."

"Meanwhile, I'll call him and agree to meet."

"As fast as possible, please. There's something else, Stephen. But you can't tell Maris."

"What?"

"Anna Lasker committed suicide."

"What? Wait a minute. Shouldn't that make Maris happy? Case partly solved?"

Peter let the question fade into the ether. Bartleben finally understood. "You mean you're not planning to tell him? Jesus, Peter."

"Anna's suicide doesn't hold a lot of meaning for us without the other half of the case, namely, what happened to the husband. We won't get any more public cooperation if we reveal there *wasn't* a murder, probably less. Or think of it this way. It'll be as difficult to explain the suicide to the press as the murder. We'll just be forced to come up with a lot of speculative theories. And finally, if we spook Lasker too much, he'll go to ground even more deeply than he has."

"So why not confide in Maris alone? He can keep a confidence, I presume."

"He'll just make it public, drive Lasker to ground," Peter said. "Why don't we try this? Maris will call you in a few minutes. Tell him that if he ejects me from the case, he'll carry the burden of doing the financial forensics, the photographing of the house, the new serology testing and so on. I'll meanwhile promise him full cooperation. You can also argue that I'm a convenient liaison for the Yard on the Task Force and can mobilize HQ resources. And if we're stepping all over each other searching the coast of England, we'll be more at odds than if we work together."

At this point, Bartleben took mild offence. He hated to be told how to handle the Yard's allocation of resources. He loved his budget — keeping it intact, that is. There wouldn't be any Yard men, other than Peter, wandering the Channel cliffs if he had anything to say about it.

"Peter, I can handle this end. When are you meeting Maris?"

"I haven't set it up, but by noon would suit me. Get it over with. I can work from the cottage for a bit, but not more than a couple of days."

Bartleben picked up his desk book and checked his schedule for the next two days.

"All right then, I'll put off answering his call until . . . 2:00 p.m. Is that okay?"

"Yup."

"And Peter, leave Joan at home from now on."

Peter, of course, could not see Sir Stephen, back at Headquarters, smiling as he hung up.

Peter Cammon wasn't smiling at 11:00 a.m. when he walked into the odd building that housed the Whittlesun Police Service. He was ushered directly to the glass office in the corner. He expected this to be a hopeless effort that would lead to his banishment, whatever arguments he pitched to Inspector Maris.

And so it proved. Any progress that he might have reported was peripheral to the two principal topics he could not report on, the conclusion that Anna had taken her own life and his scheme to launch a search of the cliffs for André. Nor could he raise Maris's failure to accelerate the full autopsy at the Regional Lab; that was one of Bartleben's trump cards. They talked at cross purposes for half an hour. Maris focused on the lack of progress in the investigation but he soon got around to his main grievance.

"I understand that you invited your wife to enter the crime scene."

"Yes."

"Why the devil would you do such a thing? It makes a mockery of the investigation."

"It does nothing of the sort. I handled it discreetly."

"I have to provide the media with a briefing later this week. If they find out that your spouse has been inside the house where Lasker slaughtered his wife . . ."

"Allegedly killed his wife."

"Oh, is that what I should tell the press?"

"You shouldn't hold a press conference at all."

"Never?"

"Give me one more week, but for now there's no need to respond to their pressure."

"No, I'm sorry, Chief Inspector. I'm taking back the investigation. Detective Hamm will pick up the thread."

Peter had already phoned Tommy Verden early that morning to arrange for a lift home. He walked out of the police station, managing to avoid running into Willet or Hamm, and made his way back to the Delphine. Verden was waiting with the car at the same spot where he had delivered Joan a day earlier. Peter's Gladstone and the two boxes of evidence were stowed in the boot. Peter got in the front seat and they were off.

"Did it not go well, then?" Tommy said.

It was only a conversational gambit on Tommy's part. He knew that Peter didn't categorize his investigations as going well or going badly; he simply persevered at inquiries until they broke open. Peter's sitting in the front seat signalled that he was in the mood to talk. This was a good thing, Tommy mused: Peter had a habit of keeping his theories to himself.

"As well as I have any right to expect," Peter replied.

"Lasker taking shape yet?" This was merely another way of posing the question.

"Put it this way, Tommy. I'm about halfway there but only the easy half. Mrs. Lasker killed herself, I'm sure. But how that dovetails with the husband's plan, or doesn't, is unclear."

"Do you think he's alive?"

"Probably. And he's likely long gone from England, but I'm not even sure of that. Did you get that inventory of ferry services for the south coast?"

"I have the schedules for the whole country. All I can say is there are a lot of ways to get to the Continent. Sir Stephen is in regular touch with the French and Dutch authorities but so far nothing beyond what you saw in yesterday's package."

They proceeded in silence for a few miles. Peter undid his collar button and massaged his stiff neck.

"You getting enough help down here?" Tommy said.

"There's one good detective on the Whittlesun force I've been cultivating. Reasonable type but I don't want to get him in a vise between me and the good Inspector. I have to be careful." Peter reflected that he hadn't seen Hamm for two days. He would remedy his neglect when he returned to Whittlesun. When the time came, Peter would need his special talents, and his friendship.

"I can come down if you need backup," Tommy said. Peter was well aware of Tommy's plodding way of saying things twice. In this instance, the second mention meant that Tommy wouldn't mind at all getting out of London for something more lively than chauffeuring, and whatever else Bartleben had him doing.

"Thank you. I'll likely take you up on that. I don't know, Tommy, there's something off-kilter here."

"Run me the scenarios."

Peter leaned back in the seat. "André had been planning his disappearance for a long time. He wasn't going to tell her he was leaving."

"They seldom do."

"She found out about it, or maybe he told her that night. They argued. She started smashing things but nothing she said stopped him. He stormed out. One way or another, he left."

"By the way," Tommy interjected, "do you think she attacked him, left any scars?"

"No. There were no epithelials under her fingernails, none of his blood in the house. But then she looked out the window and saw that he hadn't taken the family car. She would have noticed that he didn't leave with a suitcase, or anything at all. Maybe then she understood that he had this schemed out for a long time. She grasped that if he didn't need to pack a bag, every other part of his escape must have been in place. She rampaged through the house, cut herself in the lavatory and smeared menstrual blood on the walls."

"So the husband didn't smash her head into the medicine cabinet?"

"It's hard to know in what order it happened but I'd say it was part of her frenzy once he left. If we find him, it will be my first question."

"And she took the car and went looking for him, right?"

"Right. Except that she didn't know which way he'd gone. He was on foot, so how far could he have gotten? She guessed wrong. In fact he'd begun walking, maybe running, down to the lower strand while she struggled uphill to the Upper Cliffs. She parked the car in the tourist pad, got out and scanned the horizon for signs of him. I tried to duplicate her line of sight. There was no way she could have seen her husband below."

"Did Mrs. Lasker even have a driver's licence?"

Peter thought back to his discussion with Father Vogans. "No, she didn't. But I still think she drove up there."

Peter tried to imagine Anna getting out of the automobile, walking to the edge and peering into the obsidian night. Did she see a light offshore, the vessel waiting to pick up her husband?

"Did she fall or did she jump?" Verden singsonged.

"One thing's clear. Why would she drive to the cliffs instead of the shore? Because she feared that André was about to commit suicide. She still loved him." Peter thought for a minute. "She jumped."

They batted about the idea for the rest of the journey. Only a few miles from the cottage turning, Peter said, "I expect to call you in a couple of days to take me back."

"I understand," Tommy said.

"It's nice to be home," Peter said. "Michael and Sarah are up. Can you join us for dinner?"

"Thanks very much, Peter, but I have to see my sister and her three children, with the seven grandchildren. Command performance for me, you might say."

"And you are the presiding uncle?"

"More the presiding horsey. Did you ever get demands to play horsey from your two? It's exhausting being a horse." Tommy turned into the cottage lane.

Peter laughed, the mention of children calling up a picture of his home, just ahead.

CHAPTER 13

Tommy drove all the way up the lane to the front of the house. Sarah and Michael had already arrived and they came out on the porch with Joan as the car pulled in. Peter shook hands with Michael, who took the Gladstone bag and placed it on the porch. Sarah embraced her dad but made a bigger fuss over Tommy, who had known her since infancy. He was like an uncle, or even more — a protector of the entire Cammon clan. He easily lifted Peter's slim daughter off her feet. She pecked him on both cheeks and implored him to stay for dinner. Verden begged off for the reason he had given Peter and, with a kiss for Joan and a cheery wave to the others, drove away.

Peter sized up his two children. Michael was older than Sarah by seven years, and had a much quieter nature. It wasn't so much reticence, Peter thought, but a confidence in how he lived his life; he always made firm decisions and never felt the need to justify or explain himself. In a group, people would turn to him, and they listened to him when he finally entered the conversation. This was helpful in the parole trade, as Michael called it. Acquaintances remarked that Michael had followed his father into a criminal justice career, but that wasn't it at all. Michael had found his calling early. A summer job with the county probation department had set him on a career path quite different in focus from his dad's. He had once told his mother that his experience that summer had opened his eyes to society. Where others saw human failure, he saw the possibility of redemption. It was the people part of the job that attracted him, and as soon as he finished his degree in criminology he joined the Parole Office in Leeds. Four years later he had gone back for his master's, and now he was moving steadily up the ranks in the regional operation. As a parole officer, Michael saw more people in a day than Peter saw during an average investigation. Peter felt a mutual respect with his son, although, like every parent, he wondered which parts of his son's character came from him, and which from Joan.

Sarah was a different matter. She grew up feisty, independent by nature and constantly moving. Marine biology was a perfect fit. She travelled to every shore and cove around the Isles, from the Orkneys to Guernsey. She was on call at the Ocean Institute in Oxford and was always being summoned to the far corners of Britain. Peter had no idea how her career would unfurl, but Sarah, at the age of twenty-nine, seemed happy.

Peter took his suitcase up to the bedroom while Michael hauled the boxes of papers to the shed. Peter was glad to be home. He tossed his laundry in the wicker hamper in the hall. Normally upon returning from the road he would change into old clothes and go for a walk in the garden or up the lane. Joan called this one of his tools of decompression and, in truth, after a short walk he was usually able to banish thoughts of the job.

Since both his children were present, a rare occurrence these days, he decided to skip the walk and changed into flannel trousers and one of his best shirts, a Christmas gift from Sarah. He sat on the edge of the bed and gathered his thoughts. Investigations proceeded at their own pace, and he sensed that this one had a long way to go. The clash, though violent, could be regarded as nothing more than a domestic dispute taken to extremes by both the husband and the wife; his cruel plot to abandon his marriage was matched by her self-destruction, and the tragedy had closed in on itself. He had no doubt that he would be back in Whittlesun within the week.

He thought of Gwen Ransell. He had to see her again. To this point, the Lasker case was a criminological puzzle, but she had implied that it was something more, that real evil was involved. He was willing to discount her spectral visions, but he needed to know what she meant. The image of Gwen made him think of Sarah. They had a strained relationship sometimes, and he was unsure of the cause. He had trouble sustaining a conversation with his daughter. But both his children were downstairs now and he had no complaints about life, and so he determined to avoid any kind of friction that night.

He needn't have worried, for Sarah and Michael were giddy from the start.

And it was Michael who delivered the inadvertent clue about the Lasker case that helped Peter sleep.

He came down to the dining room to find the wine already poured and his family waiting for him to propose the toast. Memories of Whittlesun faded away as he raised his glass. The sun was setting beyond the linden tree at the far end of their property, past the tangled hedgerow, and orange light flooded the room.

Peter was about to improvise his toast when Joan interrupted.

"There he is!"

They turned and followed Joan's pointing finger. The last pheasant, his bottle-green head iridescent in the declining sun, had reappeared in a space in the tall grass. He looked around and then froze, as if on alert.

"*Phasianus colchicus*," Sarah said.

They watched for a full minute. Joan slowly waved her hand.

"Mum," Michael chided, "you realize that you just waved at a bird?"

"Why not, you insensitive nit," Sarah retorted. "I wave at birds all the time."

"You do? Does that work well?"

"I worry about him," Joan said. "He's the last of the group."

Michael and Sarah engaged in raillery that sometimes struck their parents as too aggressive. Perhaps it was the seven-year age difference, which made them almost of separate generations. Michael's devotion to Sarah was unquestioned, since he had been her defender throughout childhood, but part of her emergence on her own was a need to assert her views by correcting him. He didn't mind, but sometimes he went too far with his banter. Peter could see that he was about to toss a cutting comment at Sarah. But both men understood that the moment had shifted to Joan, who was looking wistfully out to where the pheasant had been sighted.

Sarah added, just a little pedantically, "The ring-necked pheasant is the official bird of the American State of South Dakota."

Michael had a dozen quips ready for this non sequitur, but it was Peter who surprised everyone, including himself, by blurting out, "Damn, he's a long way from home!"

Sarah collapsed in helpless laughter. Her recovery wasn't aided by her blowing wine out her nose, nor by her brother's admonishing: "Please. A daughter should not make fun of her mother's pet bird."

The tone was set for the dinner itself. Through the sibling teasing, Joan and Peter were updated on the lives of their children. It turned out that Sarah was on the verge of a promotion that would send her on a major project to wetland areas around Britain. Her success was paralleled by Michael's elevation to a project of his own called "unit management," which targeted high-risk offenders coming out of top-security prisons. He had pioneered the strategy and it was already showing promise in Leeds.

Joan had set out the fine silver for dinner along with her best linen tablecloth. Sunday fare, which now encompassed most occasions when all four of them gathered at the cottage, never varied: roast beef, Yorkshire pudding, roast potatoes, cauliflower with white sauce, trifle for dessert. Peter wielded the carving set that he had inherited from Joan's father. He finished his artistry with the roast while the family watched, and then rested the iron blade of the knife and the

144

pronged carving fork on two tiny silver peacocks that were one of the favourite heirlooms passed on to him by his mother.

Joan, in his absence that week, had bought the wines. Peter, still standing after carving the meat, made sure that everyone's glass was full, or in the case of voracious Michael, always half full, and raised his glass.

"I never did get to propose that toast before being interrupted by wildfowl."

"Just a second, Dad," Michael said.

"Will I ever get to make this toast?"

"Yes," Michael said, "at the wedding in April."

Sarah was around the table and kissing Michael before the veteran chief inspector of Scotland Yard absorbed the message. Michael had been seeing the same girl for four years, although Joan and Peter weren't sure whether they were living together. Her name was Maddy and she coordinated women's shelter services in Leeds.

"It's a shame that Maddy couldn't make it tonight," Joan said, after the whooping died down.

"Yes, she had to work," Michael said. He pulled his mobile phone from below the linen tablecloth, having just speed-dialled a number. "But she's waiting to take your call, Madam!"

They each had a turn congratulating Maddy over the line, even if technically you weren't supposed to congratulate the bride-to-be. Peter opened champagne and the meal got seriously cold. No one minded.

After the call and the good wishes, Joan stated: "You know, the garden can get quite cold in April."

This struck everyone as hilarious and led to more pheasant jokes. The conversation turned to reminiscences of Michael and Sarah's childhoods. She had grown up here, but Michael remembered the move from London. He reminded his father of the times they had taken Sunday strolls so that Peter could show off the old Headquarters edifice on the Embankment. Thinking that such memories might make Peter, whose semi-retirement seemed problematic to Michael, long for the days at the old Headquarters, he changed the subject, instead toasting Sarah's meteoric career as a marine biologist.

"To my sister, love and success." They were all getting tipsy now.

Sarah swirled the last ounce of claret in her glass. She looked at Peter. "Do you know the exact moment I decided to become a zoologist?" She gave him a shy smile; she'd never told this story before, at least not to him.

"No," he said. "Tell us."

"One day you were taking me through the garden, pointing things out, and we saw a snail. There were dragonflies and robins and creepy-crawlies all about, but it was the snail you pointed to. You picked him up and said, 'Do you know why the snail is the cleverest animal? Because he carries his house on his back.' From then on, I was hooked."

Peter and Joan smiled with pride. Michael Cammon, who respected his sister's profession but had gone into a much darker occupation, one in which he dealt with drug addicts and career criminals, raised his glass yet again. He had drunk too much but his words were gently delivered. "Speaking professionally, I would say that the monkey is the cleverest animal, for he gets others to carry him on their backs."

It was then that Peter understood that he had to adopt a new angle on the guilt of André Lasker.

After dinner, Peter strolled out to the back of the garden. It was an uncommonly warm evening. He lifted the lid of the old air raid shelter and descended the chiselled stone steps to the small room. A previous owner had built the subterranean chamber during the Blitz, but if buzz bombs had in fact ever rained down on the cottage, Peter was unaware of it; he had never found any shells or unexploded detonators in the garden. The shelter was useful as a root cellar because it was the driest place on their property.

He stored his gun in the bottom of the heavy steel cabinet that stood in the corner against the three-foot-thick cement walls and beside a crate of turnips. A simple wood chair and a square table completed the spartan décor of the bunker. Before they renovated the shed, he had taken guilty pleasure in coming down here once in a while to review his old files. Now he took out the Smith & Wesson pistol from the lower drawer and hefted it in his hand. There were newer guns, and newer models of the S & W, but this one fit his hand and he was comfortable using it.

None of the six men Peter had shot in the line of duty had gone quietly. He killed three men in a single bank robbery in Durham over a period of a mere three hours, and employed two different weapons to do it. The fourth dead man was a Moroccan immigrant, a self-styled jihadist, back before the term was in wide use; he had pinned his plan for an Underground apocalypse to the wall of his flat in Brixton and failed to get the thumb tacks out before Peter, checking door-to-door for witnesses to a completely unrelated assault, had walked in, but then decided to shoot it out with Scotland Yard. His pursuit of martyrdom ended in a minor key, with a whimper in a puddle of blood. The saddest was the fifth, a domestic dispute that never should have happened; a heart-rent husband, a dead wife and suicide-by-cop. It entailed a decision (on Peter's part) and a termination so quick that for a week Peter wasn't certain it had happened.

But the five deaths at his hands during the early days had an impact that could be considered politically incorrect: each death made him a better policeman. He had learned something about professionalism from each incident.

The bank heist saga was pervaded with the death wish of armed thieves on a high, and no one at the time took much pride in the outcome, in spite of the boost it gave to Peter's career. He had ever after been amazed by how it went down.

All inspectors are required to undergo firearms training. That particular week, Peter had been allowed, at his own request, to join an advanced course up in Durham, having taken to long-range rifle shooting in his basic training session. He had a talent for it, the trainers all agreed, and he won a certificate of "Marksman" to put on his wall. He remained at the first-plus-one level of accredited firearms officer, however, since full accreditation required even more training, as well as defensive driving courses and psychological testing. But, for winning Top of the Class, Peter was invited by the chief constable of Durham, who provided occasional teachers to the rifle program, to lunch at Headquarters; from time to time, the chief constable succeeded in hiring away Yard up-and-comers to his regional force. The lunch never happened. The bank robbery in downtown Durham turned deadly from the start, with a security guard killed in the first five minutes and the getaway vehicle surrounded and seized by police officers in the following minutes. Every county in England possessed a flying squad, and the chief constable called out his in full force. He also understood how to organize a perimeter, and he had one in place in record time; he also had the siege weapons to enforce it. What he didn't have at that moment was trained snipers on duty, and that was where fate entered the equation. It seemed both routine and exciting to Peter at the time — and that accounted for his willing enlistment — but the chief, who carried inspector rank, immediately assigned him to what turned out to be the pivotal observation point. The bank formed one wing of a retail shopping complex and while Durham sharpshooters manned the front entrance, Peter was positioned across a pedestrian mall from a secondary exit of the bank. This turned out to be the door through which the first hostage-taker emerged.

A constable on the Durham force delivered a rifle to Peter at his post across the arcade; until then, he hadn't even a service revolver on his person. The weapon was a Heckler & Koch carbine, a semi-automatic that later became standard issue for police tacticians in Britain, but Peter had never used one before. His station remained quiet, at first. He hefted the sleek rifle, double-checked the sighting and loaded a full ammunition clip. He let the crosshairs play over the side entrance to the bank and estimated the distance at one hundred and fifty yards. A sergeant with the flying squad, in full body armour and carrying a full-scale sniper rifle, entered the store where Peter had set up. At the very second that he was about to introduce himself, and as Peter was locking onto the bank doorway for practice, one of the robbers, high on heroin, came out with a hostage gripped in front of him. The robber had been mightily impressed by *Dog Day Afternoon* but had learned nothing from it. He waved his gun in an arc, apparently and needlessly to gain everyone's attention, and then held the woman forward and raised his pistol to her temple.

"Shoot!" the sergeant barked.

Peter took the addict's head off. The recoil set him back at least a half-yard but he fought to restabilize, moving back into the triangle posture of a sniper. When he re-sighted, he saw the body crumpled on the mall terrace, blood soaking into the pavers. The sergeant, standing, held his own rifle in a parallel line to Peter's. The constable who had delivered the carbine came back into the store. He held a light pistol. He took up a position and used a small pair of binoculars to monitor the bank, while Peter continued to sight through the scope.

A minute passed. "Won't they be in retreat, at least for a bit?" the constable ventured.

Five more thieves burst out of the bank door. Peter, always prone to one-off thoughts, wondered how they had expected to fit six armed men into one getaway car. Subsequent ballistics testing verified that Peter killed another hostage-taker before his gun jammed. It was an individual shot; the Sergeant eliminated three more with his weapon set on semi-auto. The young constable got off one shot before a bullet from across the concourse slammed into his shoulder. The phalanx of robbers hadn't advanced more than fifty yards before disintegrating. The last of them turned from his intended escape route and rushed directly at the three officers. Peter picked up the constable's pistol and emptied it in the general direction of the final man.

Peter went back to work the next day. He never saw the flying squad officer or the constable again. Even at the inquest into the death of the bank guard, and the internal police investigations that followed, he was lightly questioned; he received no medals, but no reprimands either. The Durham chief had played fast and loose with the rules. Only an inspector was permitted to deploy firearms at a crime scene; while both he and Peter were technically of inspector rank, Peter wasn't under Durham's supervision. Despite his training, Peter was certainly not qualified as a specialist firearms officer for hostage-taking sieges, though the flying squad centurion was. Nothing was said of it, and what might have ended his career instead made his whispered reputation in the early days.

Peter had slain six men in four decades, and five of the deaths occurred when he was young. He had learned from each tragedy, and dispassionate as it might have sounded (had he recounted his war stories to anyone, which he never did, not to Joan, not to his shrink), they stood as milestones in his career. The bloodbath in Durham, three corpses bleeding into the street, had impelled him to a watershed decision about policing, and set his compass: the cold rule was that you embraced whatever destiny hurled at you; it was the detective's lot. After that, violence could never surprise him. As of that moment, he knew that he would stay a detective. The Moroccan, the fanatic with the blueprint, demonstrated that violence could be a form of vainglory, all-consuming of a human soul and impenetrable to reason. The distraught husband, provoking him to open fire, had exposed the sadness at the core of every death. Peter looked for that sadness in every assignment after that, even in his quest for the Rover.

The sixth death was different.

Greydon Wellington Kershaw, degenerate gambler, son of a minion of the Krays, untalented entrepreneur in crime, and bad shot, was asking for it that day. Kershaw ran a poker game on the fifth floor of a boxy office building in Bethnal Green. Unknown to the gatherers of police intelligence, he also offered two blackjack tables on the third floor; this was a central factor in the subsequent mayhem. He managed a few prostitutes and hijacked a lorry once in a while, but remained a dabbler, until the day that the more important hoods in the East End noticed that Kershaw's operation was a fine little money-maker. They forced a partnership on Greydon Kershaw. They moved in a roulette wheel, expanded the poker game to five tables, and added a massage cubicle down the hall. The building known as the Cube became an anthill of vice. The silent partners allowed Kershaw to believe that he remained in control, and he continued to run the games on the fifth and third; they didn't object when he made the dealers wear velvet vests and green eyeshades. He entreated everyone to call him by a nickname, suggesting High Roller Kershaw, Big Slick or the Dice, but nothing stuck, and he remained small-time.

As Tommy Verden later said, "They weren't harming anybody until the nobs complained." He had it essentially right: neighbours are unlikely to be disturbed by tapped-out poker players and exiting massage-parlour patrons. But it only took a few calls from prurient landowners in the area before the Metropolitan organized crime unit decided that this criminal activity was sufficiently organized to investigate. It was a short step, almost inevitable, from authorized wiretaps to transcribed, persuasive and probative evidence of money-laundering. But it was still small stuff and Peter was always sure that the driving force behind the raid was Stephen Bartleben. It was widely thought that he owed his knighthood, at least in part, to his work in busting the Kray gang for gambling offences and tax evasion (Peter himself had once interviewed Reggie Kray up at Wayland Prison in Norfolk; there had been no point in questioning Ronnie Kray at Broadmoor, since paranoid schizophrenia had taken over his brain). For Bartleben, Kershaw was unfinished business.

Peter and Tommy resisted going in the first place. A dozen London officers could handle a routine scoop, collecting Kershaw as the kingpin and any found-ins luck might drop in their net. But Bartleben insisted they be there to represent the Yard, and compromised by allowing them to hang back, and merely observe. "Leave weapons at home, if you prefer." Thus, they entered the fiasco relatively underprepared. But, however casual Sir Stephen might be about field operations, Peter and Tommy never participated in a police raid without a gun each; Tommy brought along a SIG Sauer pistol and planned to borrow a shotgun at the scene. Peter intended to rely on a .38 carried in an armpit holster, but he threw an empty shotgun into the back seat of the car for insurance.

Unknown to the police team, it turned out that Greydon Kershaw owned the whole Cube, and was able to shift from floor to floor as the police worked their way through the building. Kershaw knew it was the police when their unmarked vehicles were left in the Handicapped Parking spaces. The squad's second error was to ride the elevators directly to the fifth, where they arrested five dealers and a cluster of late afternoon touts, while letting others exit by the stairwells. But there was no Kershaw to be found; at that point, he was monitoring the blackjack tables on the third floor. A dozen officers proved insufficient to explore and hold down all six levels of the Cube and to serve the fistful of search warrants. There was also confusion about whether the warrants encompassed every floor and any legitimate businesses they might confront.

Peter and Tommy had been assigned the alley next to the Cube, and were ordered by the Commander to prevent the escape of any gamblers or staff from that side of the building. They regarded "escape" as a nebulous term, since there was no uniform worn by poker players, nor a way to tell gamblers from ordinary customers of legitimate businesses. They let a dozen pedestrians pass merely based on their banal and unconcerned appearance.

Graydon Kershaw, however, did sport a uniform. An admirer of Western movies, he required his dealers to wear glittering vests and long frock coats on the job. The drink servers at the tables were tarted up as dance-hall girls; embarrassed, they always changed clothes before going outside. And so, when Kershaw slipped into the alley, the Scotland Yard detectives recognized him right off, for he liked to emulate his staff's outfits.

"Management," Verden announced.

The alley stretched two hundred and fifty yards from where they stood. Kershaw had reflexively turned right out of the building, having seen from inside that the raid was underway and he was the likely target. He strode away from them but had forgotten that the alley led to a cul-de-sac, with the only exit lying behind the approaching detectives. He turned when he reached the blocked end of the row.

The alleyway served as a junkyard, with every kind of pitiful detritus leaking out of the buildings along its fringe. Old motors, packing cases, broken furniture and mattresses were embanked against the walls. Although they had Kershaw trapped, the path down the centre line was a deadly zone for the policemen. In normal circumstances, it allowed Roma scavengers to search the junk piles for scrap metal and such, but now it offered a succession of hiding places to anyone with a gun and an inclination to shoot it out. The detectives entered the cul-de-sac expecting an ambush.

It never played out that way. Kershaw's devotion to Hollywood myths unfortunately extended to fantasies about Wyatt Earp. The gunfighter from Tombstone never carried an FN FAL semi-automatic with a load of thirty cartridges, but Kershaw had brought one along in anticipation of a Mexican standoff. He still might have been discouraged into surrendering, had he not seen one of his assistants coming out for a smoke at that second. The underling had aspirations in Kershaw's little empire, and accordingly chose to wear the dealer's flashy uniform; he also saw fit to carry a gun at all times. Kershaw waved him down his way.

One of the things that Peter had learned was not to fear looking ridiculous in a crisis where guns were involved. The image of two demented gunfighters in shiny vests and long coats striding through mounds of baby carriages and shattered televisions might have induced caution in other policemen, but Peter and Tommy, both at the age of fifty-plus at the time, had reached a common view of these idiots. It was best described as disgust. They were tired of weak men using guns to indulge immature fantasies about tough guys. Peter had lost his romantic, literary template in the shootout in Durham City. As Kershaw and his helper approached in tandem, with Kershaw, whom Peter later learned was calling himself the Gambler, levelling his rifle to shoot from hip position, Peter and Tommy matched them stride for stride in mirror opposition. Peter was neither mocking their bravado, nor validating their posturing. It was just that it was the shortest way between two points.

Peter had the unloaded shotgun exposed and angled towards the ground. Tommy carried his borrowed shotgun loaded and at the ready. He tossed a single cartridge to his partner, since there was no time to load more than one; Peter chambered it. By this time, Kershaw was firing in bursts, sending eruptions of garbage out the top of the junk piles to the left and right of the detectives. Peter and Tommy were soon covered in filth. The Gambler changed tactics, fanning a horizontal spray of bullets, none of which scored hits. His subaltern pulled out *two* pistols, one a small pocket gun and the other a .357, which he had trouble aiming. The Scotland Yard men, without changing their vector towards the shooters, waited, knowing that they needed to be closer to make their shotguns effective, as well as to put Peter's concealed .38 in range; the SIG in Tommy's belt would take care of the pistolero when the time came.

Calamitously for the young fellow, his pistols were of different weights and threw off different recoils. Firing both at once torqued him to the right and sent a shot dangerously close to Peter. Dresden or Coventry must have been like this, Peter thought blithely, as the fragments of junk swirled in a cloud around them. The FN never seemed to exhaust itself, the bursts of fire thundering in the tunnel formed by the buildings on either side. The shotguns, fired in unison, changed the soundscape: Tommy's shot obliterated the right half of the landscape ahead, and presumably Kershaw's flunky with it. If Peter's single round ended the rifle bursts from Kershaw, it may have been merely the shockwave effect of the blast, since the autopsy showed no pellets hitting him. Peter discarded the shotgun. The two sides were no more than ten yards apart. Kershaw, his sparkling vest bloodied and his long coat shredded, retrieved the long gun from the pavement and struggled to raise it to his eye; had he done that at the outset, the detectives would have been dead. Peter reached in a smooth motion into his holster, drew the .38 and shot Graydon Kershaw through the heart.

The clean-up crew logged in one hundred and eighty bullets. None of them had hit Peter Cammon.

He told Joan about this one, whereas they never discussed the other five deaths. He narrated it to her factually — it was, after all, a melodrama with a clear start and end — as a way of sorting it out. His own survival struck him as a miracle. It was a puzzle to him. Kershaw chose to die, to play out his foolish gunfighter fantasy to the end, and Peter obliged him. No blame attached to Peter; everyone said so. Yet, he knew that he had had options, that he had made decisions at every step of that confrontation. For one thing, he might have walked away, let Kershaw survive (the lad had died too). Yes, it took courage to keep walking into that hail of fire, but had it been *necessary*? Something else had kept him moving forward. He hadn't flinched. He knew that he would do it again, aim straight for the heart. In sum, this one was like all the others, a test of obedience, another dimension of his commitment measured. Yet it still nagged him. Sometimes being in the right shouldn't be enough for a killing, but for a police officer it had to be, when evil, perversity and sometimes stupidity were arrayed against him. It was against his nature to obey without question, but he did so with Greydon Kershaw. He would do the same with the Rover and with André Lasker, if it came to that.

CHAPTER 14

Stephen Bartleben looked forward to his jaunt down to Whittlesun, in part for the bureaucratic fun of it. Maris was predictable, and Sir Stephen had no doubt who would win the internecine argument between police agencies. He knew exactly how he would play it with the inspector, the forces he would bring to bear. He was too long in the tooth to feel guilty about this.

But his own view of the situation had evolved since talking to Cammon, and now he wanted something more from the arrangement: a piece of the Rover investigation. The decision flowered from instinct: the serial killings were already preoccupying two counties and could soon become the Yard's problem. He had requested a press scan from Media. There were degrees of media frenzy, and so far press sensationalism had yet to foment general panic, but his people had judged public awareness as "growing rapidly." As such things went, localized concern was approaching a threshold where it would only take one more incident to make the Rover a national story, with the attendant distortions and recriminations for the Yard. That event, in Bartleben's experienced view, was likely to be the taking of another young victim, at which time the serial killer would enter Sutcliffe territory. He remembered the Sutcliffe serial killings all too well, when

"Yorkshire Ripper" appeared in every newspaper headline, and not just in the rags. Bartleben hoped that this madman wasn't about to attack again soon but he wanted the Yard to be well placed if and when the Ripper struck a fifth time.

The problem with asserting a major role on the Task Force would be Maris; hence the lunch on his home ground. J.J. McElroy would grasp the larger picture and, if not welcome a liaison person from the Yard, at least concede the advantages. Maris, on the other hand, was preoccupied with Peter's abrasive and unorthodox methods and would do everything he could to deny Peter's appointment. He had his orders from the local council to do whatever was necessary to advance Dorset's bid for the Olympic sailing events by preserving the image of the Jurassic Coast as a bucolic, crime-free zone.

But Stephen himself saw the larger image problem, even though he had never been in Dorset. For much of the public these days, mention of coastal ports of entry called up concerns about immigration and terrorism. The Rover's predations along the coast could easily grow to echo both issues.

As the sleek Mercedes crossed into the county of Dorset, Sir Stephen Bartleben gazed out the window at the rolling countryside. He leaned forward and said to Tommy Verden, who was driving, "This is pretty country."

Tommy, who understood that the statement meant "how much longer," replied, "Even prettier along the coast. Should be there soon."

Since Tommy Verden knew the way and was available, it made sense for him to drive Bartleben down to the coast. Both men were intimates of Peter Cammon, but Verden was not about to presume to discuss his old friend with the DC. But the two men fell into intense conversation about both Lasker and the Rover, and as the E-class Mercedes pulled up to their destination, Tommy concluded that he had contributed to his boss's appreciation of what Peter was dealing with in Whittlesun.

Sir Stephen's secretary had reserved a private room in the restaurant at the best hotel in Whittlesun, the Carfax; it was two cuts above the hotel where Cammon had been staying. Bartleben made sure to arrive before Maris. He ordered a bottle of Chardonnay, and, glancing at the menu, he speculated on whether the haddock was locally caught.

When Maris arrived — Bartleben had known he would be early — and was shown to the table, Bartleben stood and shook his hand with disingenuous bonhomie. Maris nonetheless looked startled; he was thrown off by Bartleben's booking of a separate room, for he was not aware that one could do that at the Carfax, even though he and Mrs. Maris had dined there several times. He had put on a good suit and a rep tie to give himself an executive look, but leaving the station he cringed when Detective Hamm, trying to cosy up to him, commented, too loudly: "Going about in mufti today, sir?" Maris was coming to despise Hamm.

"I thought a bit of privacy was a good idea," said Bartleben. "We may be discussing some security matters. I took the liberty of ordering a bottle."

Maris said, ineffectually, "Thank you for driving all this way."

Bartleben waved him off. The London man pretended to scrutinize the menu. Maris decided on the haddock and felt better when Sir Stephen ordered it first.

The pleasantries did not last long, as Maris was eager to get to his strongest point, his denunciation of Cammon. "I feel compelled to formally register my complaint regarding Chief Inspector Cammon. Drawing a civilian, his own wife, into the investigation is unprecedented and unwise, I would suggest."

Bartleben somehow managed to look sympathetic even though his expression did not change. "Yes, Peter Cammon is sometimes capable of unusual behaviour. I've known him for forty years. He hasn't done that before, and I'm not defending his conduct. But I do know that if he does something dramatic in a case, he's not trying to be melodramatic. He will have his reasons."

"In this case, what were his reasons?" Maris persisted. "If he needed expertise, he need only have asked. I had already established formal liaison between him and my force."

"I take some responsibility for what he did. Please mark that I'm not condoning it. But Peter asked me twice over the phone to send down our serology expert, Lieutenant Bracher. He was unavailable. Peter wanted a fresh perspective."

Maris walked into Bartleben's trap. To compare a serologist with Cammon's wife was absurd, so ridiculous that Maris approached his retort obliquely. "Regional Forensics has done a pretty thorough work-up. They were also effectively on call."

"Their report identified the bloodstains in the bath and the upper landing of the home as Mrs. Lasker's. It did not identify them as menstrual blood."

"Menstrual blood? What is the significance of that?"

Sir Stephen had no choice but to lie. Anna's suicide would not be on the table. "I don't know. But Cammon must know. And keep in mind that he was pursuing a hunch and he felt the need to move fast. Ergo, calling in his wife."

However much he needed to manipulate Maris, Deputy Commissioner Bartleben ultimately didn't want to fully alienate him. He adopted an upbeat tone.

"I would like Chief Inspector Cammon to have a chance to complete his work."

Maris set down his glass. His look offered no concession. He had arrived in high dudgeon and remained that way, but he was intimidated enough by Bartleben to back off a bit. "Is there anything he can do that my people cannot? I mean, given his lack of progress to date?"

"I don't agree. There has been progress, but Cammon is like that. He plays it close to the vest."

"That doesn't help me. What good is it to know that the blood was menstrual blood? I'm the one who stands up in front of the media and has to explain where we are in the case. And he needed his wife to tell him that?"

Bartleben had mastered the ploy of talking as if the world had moved beyond the other man's grievances, thus making him feel petty, and in this situation, parochial. "I'm asking your indulgence for a bit. I would like Bracher to come down, photograph the house and then spend a few days with Regional Forensics. We understand that the full autopsy on Anna Lasker is a work in progress. Cammon thinks the blood patterns are significant. I would also like to arrange space for Cammon to review all the material taken from the Lasker house. I understand that Mr. Willet and Detective Hamm are more and more in demand for this other case. By the way, Peter speaks highly of both of them."

Bartleben could tell that Maris was willing to move into a negotiation mode. That was fine with him.

"I need some good news," Maris said. "Some progress that I can offer the media. Cammon won't even hazard an opinion on whether Lasker is alive or dead."

Bartleben savoured the Chardonnay, though he was indifferent to the poached haddock, which certainly wasn't fresh. From the moment Verden had dropped him at the hotel, and he'd stepped onto the cobblestone street and smelled the sea salt, he had felt fully confident in his strategy with the local man. He hesitated for only a few seconds.

"I will say that Cammon believes that Lasker is likely alive," he disclosed. "Sixty-forty."

"He told me fifty-fifty, for all the use that estimate is."

"Consider this. I fully agree that we must throw something to the media. But not until we're sure that what we announce will constitute 'progress' in the eyes of the press."

"I don't understand where that leaves us."

Bartleben held him with a look. "It means, give it one more week. If we haven't collectively solved Lasker, I pull Cammon in. Meanwhile, I promise a big push with our international friends at Interpol and the EU. We remain the supporting partner."

Maris looked unconvinced. Bartleben saw that he was still thinking in terms of getting the upper hand, telling the man from

London how it was going to be in his domain, and so he moved to lock in the larger deal.

"That brings me to another matter," he intoned. "It is, in part, why I wanted this meeting. I sense that we're entering a new phase in Lasker but also this Rover business, and I want to offer you our resources as needed. I was talking to J.J. McElroy the other day . . ."

"You know McElroy?" Maris said.

"Oh, yes. We've worked together over the years — last year on that Moroccan immigrant smuggling case. I believe he would welcome our help."

"Well, so would I — in appropriate ways." Maris felt there was nothing else he could say.

"I know Peter mentioned to you that he wants to search the coast, some caves or other."

"The Task Force is now mobilizing to do exactly that. Including my people. I think we can handle it locally for now."

"Yes, but you two discussed the search in the context of avoiding overlap between the two cases, Lasker and this Rover problem. My broader concern is stepping on the toes of various national operations."

The corner of Maris's left eye twitched. "Which would be?"

"Terrorism and immigration." These were trigger words for the media, both men understood. Maris envisioned TV-20, the Whittlesun affiliate of a national network, running endless features on the spectre of an invasion of Muslim suicide bombers.

"Will the terrorism people want to get involved?" Maris said.

"They won't, as long as we're careful. With all the focus on infiltration threats, our colleagues on the terrorism desk, and a big desk it is these days, can pre-empt any other investigation whenever they want. As you know, we've worked with that side of the Home Office on the Underground bombings and everything else with a tinge of terrorism. You know their outrageous demands too. If we're all rummaging around the cliffs at the same time, there will be friction."

"What do you suggest?" Bartleben noted that the Inspector finally seemed to see the advantages of an alliance with the Yard.

"Can we keep it low key?" Bartleben replied. "Let me assign Bracher and Cammon to the Task Force as Scotland Yard's formal liaison. Jack McElroy and yourself can manage the Rover process, while you also retain the lead on Lasker. You thus continue to make the key decisions on the management of Lasker in terms of media."

Bartleben was telling him that he could shift the blame to the Yard whenever he wanted. It was an acceptable risk, Bartleben could see.

"Why Bracher? Isn't he a technical expert?"

"Yes, but he's a good man. A veteran investigator with the Ontario Provincial Police. Handled a serial killing problem over there, I recall. He's a character, a very flamboyant Canadian, if that isn't an oxymoron. He'll balance off Cammon."

He polished off the Chardonnay. He decided not to suggest liqueurs. He wanted to end the lunch, but Maris still seemed obsessed with Cammon's actions, and so Sir Stephen went to another tangent. Sometimes the simplest thing was to keep talking.

"Meanwhile," Bartleben continued, "Stan and Peter will finish up with this phase of Lasker. You can be sure they'll be meticulous in laying an evidentiary base for eventual prosecution when he shows his face."

"If he didn't drown." Maris wondered how it was that he had only drunk one glass of the wine but the bottle now stood empty.

"One way or another, he'll surface," said Bartleben. "Oh, yes. There's something else I can try." Maris leaned forward. They were allies now. "I can have my minister have a word with the Minister for Sport. We all love sailing and we all want Dorset to keep the Games."

Bartleben knew without looking at his watch that Verden was waiting at the front entrance to the hotel. He certainly didn't hear the Mercedes; the engine on the Executive series hummed so discreetly.

The deal — all the understandings — went off the rails immediately.

Inspector Verden transported Cammon back to the coast on Tuesday morning, the day after Bartleben's lunch with Maris. They drove generally southeast, with the sun beaming through the windscreen most of the way. They shared the front seat, but neither found much to say. A few miles from Whittlesun, cerulean clouds in a solid, defensive bank took over the sky, threatening a storm.

The very moment Tommy turned off the A35, Peter's phone chimed.

"Peter! It's Stan. How's it going?"

"Stan," Peter responded, startled. "Where are you?"

"Whittlesun. Just following orders, Peter."

"That was fast. I thought you were in Lyon."

"I was. You tried to reach me, I know. Sorry I didn't get back to you. I was planning on getting to London tomorrow anyhow. I thought that would be soon enough. Then Bartleben called two days ago, said you needed help at the Regional Lab — I know those boys well — and said to hurry it up. Okay, I had a flight booked to London from Lyon, but then he called yesterday . . ."

"Stan, slow down . . ."

"The good part's coming," Stan bellowed into the phone. "He, Stephen, said I had to attend the briefing today. Guy called Maris called my number and confirmed."

"Confirmed what?" Peter said.

"Some kind of inter-agency briefing at noon."

"Today?" Peter struggled to sort it out. Bartleben had confirmed his and Stan's appointment to the Task Force. Now Maris was already playing games. He'd notified Stan of the briefing session and ignored Peter.

"Where are you staying, Peter?"

"Sunset Arms," Peter replied. He had decided, for reasons he couldn't explain, to change lodgings.

"Me too."

"Where are you now?"

"In a cab on my way to the Whittlesun police station."

"I may be late," Peter said.

Stan always had to have the final word. "Save you a seat. See you." *Click.*

Tommy Verden looked over at his friend. "You want me to wait?"

Peter hesitated. Tommy was the one he trusted, more than Stan. At some point, he would summon Tommy back to Whittlesun, but not yet.

"No," Peter finally said. "But I don't like the games they're playing."

Tommy eased the car into the central zone of Whittlesun.

"Just call, Peter."

"Soon."

Shiny official vehicles clogged the front and side car parks of the Whittlesun station. Peter went inside as a distant church bell chimed noon. He was let through security by the same woman guard behind her Plexiglas window. Entering the open area, he met clusters of lower- to mid-level police officers, most of them in uniform, coming out of the big conference room. He seemed to have missed the entire briefing, although Stan had clearly said noon.

Detective Hamm tapped Peter on the shoulder from behind. As Peter faced him, he smiled broadly. Peter saw that once again his shirt was rumpled, and he was generally unkempt and sweating.

"Chief Inspector, I'm glad you made it back. I'd like a chance to follow up with you on a couple of things. The pub at 1600 hours?" Peter wondered what Maris might have said about Hamm's continuing working relationship with him.

"I'd like that, but could we make it five? Better yet, 5:30?"

"Done!" Hamm seemed anxious to return to the conference room.

"I've moved to the Sunset Arms, but the Crown is still convenient. Did I miss the meeting?"

"No, sir. Our fellows just got an overview briefing on the Task

Force's work. The Task Force itself, of which you are a member, I'm glad to hear, is meeting now. Most of them are already in the room."

Detectives were crowding into the conference room and Peter assumed they were from both the Dorset and Devon Forces, although only official members were allowed in this time. He hung back at the doorway and noted that a head table had been set up at the far end; he wondered if he was expected to sit up front. He spied McElroy conferring with Maris in a corner; the Devon chief inspector, his back turned, failed to see him. It seemed to Peter that his old colleague looked sickly. Peter threaded his way through the groupings of detectives. On the wall behind the wide table someone had tacked a map of the coastline, a satellite photograph blown up to panoramic proportions. Peter recognized the Whittlesun Cliffs and the two beaches. St. Walthram's Abbey was a rectangular speck on the map. The car park up on the hill was visible as a grey smudge.

He scanned the crowd and nodded to several veteran detectives he had worked with before. He stopped at the sight of Stan Bracher sitting quietly at one side of the room, his legs crossed at the ankles in an insouciant pose, directing a wry smile at Peter. Stan was tall, round-faced and thick across the shoulders, reportedly from a youth spent tossing bales of hay on farms in Saskatchewan. When he stood up he seemed to be all upper body, almost triangular. But for now, he was lounging in his chair, his long legs stretched out; he didn't care if he tripped several people. He projected affability and informality. He was a nice guy, everyone agreed, but Peter knew that his sociability was also a policeman's persona crafted to win over witnesses and other strangers; Peter's own formal politeness served the same function. Stan could be combative, and he loved to defend — and endlessly debate and recast — evidence that fell within his domain of scientific expertise. With his open demeanour and his uninflected speech, he was often mistaken for an American, which Peter supposed was the curse of all Canadians abroad. But inevitably when Stan grinned and corrected inquiries about his nationality, the questioner smiled with relief that he wasn't American, and became friendlier. He had a sardonic sense of humour too. He had pasted an OPP logo, a black-and-yellow badge, on the side panel of his attaché case and liked to leave it exposed during meetings. Often as not, British officers would puzzle over the acronym, which stood for Ontario Provincial Police. Their usual gambit was: *That badge looks familiar. Where have I seen it before?* Stan would answer: *The Beatles were members of the OPP. You saw it on the* Sgt. Pepper *album cover. Paul's wearing it in the picture.* He would then pull out a copy of the album jacket and point to the shoulder patch worn by Paul McCartney. Many a meeting veered off topic as aging police officers revisited their Carnaby years.

Stan had been reserving the chair next to him. Peter came up and they shook hands.

"Who's he made the official liaison, you or me?"

"Peter, you know I hate that bureaucratic stuff. I'm a techie. Why don't you be the official rep?"

"What did Bartleben indicate to you?" Peter said.

"Nothing. You know him, always jockeying for position, using you and the likes of me as pawns. That's a mixed metaphor, isn't it?"

Now *there's* a good reason for not making Stan our spokesperson, Peter mused: he can't stay on topic. But he liked Stan.

"I'm in the doghouse with the locals," Peter noted.

"And how's Joan?" Stan said, with what he would call a shit-eating grin on his face. Peter ignored the provocation.

"You available to see the Lasker house at two?"

"Absolutely. I hear it's quite something. I'm looking forward to it."

The meeting was about to start. "It's quite something," Peter whispered.

Maris called the briefing to order by tapping a drinking glass with his pen. As the group, twenty men and four women, settled down, Peter caught Jerry Plaskow waving at him. Jerry, Royal Navy, resplendent in his uniform, was an old colleague. He gestured to two empty seats at the head table. Stan took the chair on Jerry's right, while Peter occupied the last spot at the table, farthest from McElroy.

Maris kept his introduction short, conscious that this session was an extension of the briefing earlier. There was a good reason for two sessions, however: this one was for Task Force members only, and thus would cover inside information on the Rover. Or, as Bartleben would have summed it up, it would be about optics and politics. As Jack McElroy rose, Peter understood what had happened. Maris had told McElroy that Peter wouldn't be in the room; Maris had to invite one of the Yard men, per his commitment to Sir Stephen, and thus the phone call to Stan. The only remaining question was why McElroy was so hostile to Peter.

McElroy had the build of an old football centre-half. He boasted a full head of completely white hair, which he kept flamboyantly long, and he wore impeccably cut suits — unusual, to say the least, among police officers in County Devon. He liked facts, a tad like Mr. Gradgrind in *Hard Times*, Peter thought, and had a declamatory style when discussing case files. Peter preferred a more free-flowing manner in briefings, but McElroy, he admitted, was the right man for a disparate group like this, most of whom had never confronted a serial killer.

Except that he wasn't. Today his shirt collar was frayed and his suit coat shifted off one shoulder when he stood. The group of detectives sensed the change. Their first, forgiving reaction was that McElroy was under the weather, but Peter felt that something else was going on.

"Gentlemen," — the four women went unacknowledged — "this is not this morning's briefing. We are here to talk strategy, and here is the first strategic decision you need to make. Any member of this Task Force who talks to the media will be sacked. The watchword for all of us must be containment. I am not just referring to our media strategy, though talking to reporters would serve no useful purpose. I mean, this tragedy must be contained. There is no need for the public to panic and we will avoid doing anything to feed paranoia. The tourist season is over; we're into October. The predator is working the cliffs of Devon, and possibly moving into Dorset, but he has shown no signs of working the tourist beaches in the area. The victims are local girls, the children of farmers. He hasn't taken anyone from the beach huts, or hikers from the paths higher up. We can contain this, with solid police work."

Peter watched Maris frown. McElroy was veering off script. He should have done introductions, or passed the podium on to Maris himself to do them. Peter dreaded what might be coming next. But then McElroy appeared to settle down; at least, his voice became calmer.

"I want to point out several people who are new to our group. Let me welcome Jerry Plaskow from Ports Security. If you have ever dipped your toe in the English Channel, you undoubtedly know Jerry." Plaskow nodded.

"I also welcome two members from New Scotland Yard to our team, Detective Stan Bracher, late of Canada, and Chief Inspector Peter Cammon. They will provide liaison with the Yard and — we in the regions are always hopeful — access to 'central' resources."

There was chuckling around the table and Stan, who seemed oblivious to McElroy's earlier distress, joined the banter. "Mr. Chairman!" he called out. "For the record, my 'Detective' is a Canadian designation, so that I am not officially a Yard employee."

"Duly noted. In the event, we welcome the Detective, despite being lost in the mid-Atlantic."

But then McElroy's face darkened and he seemed to lose energy. Bitterness entered his voice. "Dorset men are full partners in our Task Force effort. Out on the pitch . . . out on the field . . . in the field . . . our regional forces will triumph, without the need of meddling from London." He faltered, and turned his uncertainty into an acceptable pause by pretending to refer to some papers. "Our evaluators, and by that I mean experts attached to my force, and people at the Regional Lab, believe that he will move up or down the coast in a linear pattern. Admittedly, that brings him anywhere from Land's End to where we are now." His voice faded, as if he had just delivered a non sequitur.

Jerry Plaskow, two down from Peter, put up his hand. "Jack, can you tell us why your profilers say he'll keep moving that way?"

"I'll let Martin Finter answer that." McElroy finally sank into his chair. He wiped sweat from his forehead. Attention turned to the young man sitting next to the head table. Peter recognized the executive assistant type. Finter stood up; he spoke without notes.

"Thank you, Chief Inspector McElroy. Our behaviouralists have assessed his psychological makeup as well as his geographic pattern." The tone was slightly patronizing, as though this group might not understand how rapists established their territory.

Finter went on. "The first two crimes occurred exactly six kilometres apart, bodies found in a rocky cave or grotto, both in Devon County. The third girl was discovered lying on a rock on the clifftop even farther east. The fourth girl, Molly Jonas, vanished close to six kilometres eastward, towards Dorset, but still inside the Devon line. We've searched every cavern and inlet in the area but we haven't discovered her body."

Not a person in the room believed that Molly Jonas was still alive.

Finter proceeded. "This is a pattern, make no mistake. His method is meticulous. He lays out the body neatly, like the corpse at a funeral. Cleans off the faces, puts a handkerchief over their eyes. In the first two murders, he threw the girls' shoes into the sea. The first body was left on a sandy, silted area inside a cave, yet there were no footprints."

Peter hoped that Stan wouldn't be the one to challenge the theory that the Rover was moving up or down the coast in regularly spaced intervals. He wanted someone less amiable to confront Finter, to bring him down a notch.

Jerry Plaskow, who knew the sea cliffs like a pirate, raised his hand again.

"A follow-up. I was here this morning and you mentioned the need to keep a watch on the whole south coast. That's a real manpower challenge. Aside from the views of my colleagues within Ports Security on the feasibility of doing that, are there reasons to believe that he *won't* follow the same pattern? Or that he'll even kill again?"

Peter saw McElroy give Finter the go-ahead, even as he grasped that Jerry might be baiting the slick young man.

"The killer won't be satisfied until he's stopped. Now, he might stop killing for the time being because of winter setting in, but our profilers are sure that he'll simply start up again in the spring."

This wasn't a popular answer. Peter, like every police professional in the room, wanted to stop the Rover fast. Nor did it fully address the killer's modus operandi and geographic patterns.

Plaskow spoke again, not bothering to put up his hand this time. "I checked the charts for the days the first three victims disappeared. On two nights there were four-foot seas in the Channel and cold, driving spray along the shore. He may not be deterred by winter."

Yes, thought Peter, who had read the Task Force summaries, but there was also fog on all three days, he seemed to recall.

Stan Bracher put up his hand. "Forgive me, but I will ask the obvious next question if no one else is going to." Peter looked over at McElroy, who was looking anxious. "If we measure six more kilometres down the coast towards us, does that put the Rover in Dorset County?"

Finter looked around the room, obviously reluctant to answer definitively. "No, but it puts him awfully close."

Large meetings have a lifespan, after which the talk becomes repetitive and the increase in useful knowledge marginal. McElroy continued to look pale. As Finter went on to lay out a communications strategy (in effect, a non-communication plan), Peter scribbled a note, folded it in half and passed it down to Maris via Stan and Jerry. Maris read it; turning to Peter, he nodded assent. When Finter was done, Maris quickly stood up.

"Ladies and gentlemen, I think we have reached our productive limit for the day. On behalf of Chief Inspector McElroy, I can promise we will convene another meeting of this group in two weeks, earlier as events require. Let me thank you on behalf of Dorset Region and Whittlesun Police Services. We will do our part in this investigation."

CHAPTER 15

Exiting the police station proved difficult as old colleagues impor-
tuned Peter to say hello and ask his guess at the identity of the
Rover, as if forty-plus years with the Yard had earned him divination
powers. Hoping to avoid Maris and Jack McElroy, he worked his
way through the Plexiglas gauntlet and out to the pillared entrance.
He hoped to buttonhole Jerry Plaskow before joining Bracher at the
house, but just as he hailed Jerry out on the driveway, Stan vectored
in from the side.

"Are we on for two?" the Canadian asked, all in a rush. "I haven't
encountered your Constable Willet."

"You don't need him," Peter said. "There's a house key under the
flower pot around back."

Peter edged him towards Jerry, who was waiting for them by his
Land Rover. Jerry did everything in style, and his spiffy vehicle complemented his flawless uniform; he might have been posing for an
advert.

Stan continued. "Well, I'd like to get out to Regional by the end
of the day. Let's see, two hours at the scene, get your Constable to
drive me out after . . ."

Bracher's addled state confused Peter. He had explained to Stan

171

that the Lasker home was painted in blood, up and down, and he must have understood that photographing the blood patterns would take the full afternoon, perhaps longer. He knew that Stan would get so into it that he would end up travelling inside Anna's bloodstream.

"On second thought, Stan, Willet would be helpful. Do me a favour? Could you go back in and track him down? You can't miss him; biggest fellow in the room. I'll join you at two."

"Yeah, yeah, that's good," Stan said, like a New York gangster. "Do you think he likes samosas?"

"What?"

"I'm in the mood for samosas and ginger beer. Late lunch on the fly."

"That's the way to Willet's heart."

Stan trundled off with his bags of photography equipment. Peter turned his attention to Jerry, who was waiting patiently.

"What the devil was that about?" Jerry said, not meaning Bracher. His smooth voice complemented his leading man looks.

"Has Jack McElroy been showing signs of . . . instability?" Peter said.

"I haven't seen him in six months, not since this Rover thing developed. In fact, this is my first contact with the Task Force at all. He's changed and I don't understand it. How have you been, Peter, and what was that all about in there? Passing notes in school?"

"Bartleben appointed me and Stan as liaison with the Task Force. Maris doesn't like me, for any of a dozen imagined slights. He was about to call on me to brief the group on Lasker, but the way Jack McElroy was acting, I suggested to Maris that we hold off. Frankly, I thought it might push Jack over the edge."

"So to speak," Jerry said. "Lasker interests me, Peter. You think he might be hiding in a cave somewhere?"

"Possibly. I don't know. It's a bit complicated."

Jerry smiled and jiggled his key ring. "Same old CI Cammon. Works alone, solves it alone."

Peter liked Jerry Plaskow, but he almost took offence. He believed he collaborated generously with his colleagues most of the time. Was that his reputation? Plaskow noticed his reaction and, to compensate, became even more cheery and changed the subject back to the Rover.

"Listen, Peter, we should discuss a plan for searching the cliffs. Personally, I don't see this Rover's pattern. He has to be an opportunist, kidnapping young girls wherever he can pull it off, but even if there are hundreds of hiding places up there, it's hard to imagine him discovering a rock cave precisely every six kilometres. I trust your judgment more than ninety per cent of these coppers." Plaskow was not beholden to the Police Service and could choose how he spent his time as a Task Force member. He smiled, almost as if he wanted to find a way to tweak McElroy's nose. There was a history there — Peter didn't know it, but Jerry had a reputation for independence that rivalled Peter's own.

"I was thinking the same thing," Peter replied. He looked around to see if Maris or McElroy were in earshot. Peter hoped that Stan wouldn't return too soon. Two bantering gadflies would be hard to take.

"Did you know that the Jurassic Coast is designated a World Heritage Site?" Jerry continued.

"Yes. It's in the brochures."

Jerry smiled. He looked up at the sky, judging the grey clouds. "Yeah, that's all we need. Tourists gambolling down the path, holding onto the handrails and tripping over dead girls and phantoms who've just murdered their wives."

Peter arched an eyebrow. Jerry had a sly look. "Could it be that we're thinking the same thing, Jerry?" Peter said. He paused for only a second. "Molly Jonas?"

"Exactly," Plaskow said. They both instinctively walked away from the traffic at the entrance towards the far end of the parking area, where there was more privacy.

"So," Peter said, "have you been over the area where the Jonas girl disappeared?"

"The sixth kilometre?"

"Yes, if you like."

"I wasn't part of the land search for the girl and we weren't asked to scan the coast from the sea angle. But I know the area well. You buying into the 'Six-K' theory?"

"Not necessarily," Peter answered.

"Let's play this straight, Peter. You think you know where to look for Molly?"

"I have an idea or two. Listen, Jerry, I'm not prepared to invoke a massive search for Lasker, yet. I need to have a valid trigger before we go to that expense. But a quick reconnoitre would help to gain some familiarity with the cliffs. Could you take me and Stan Bracher there? How far is it?"

"The young fellow, Finter, was right about the location. Six kilometres puts it just across McElroy's side of the county border. As for Molly, the unfortunate girl comes from a sheep farm in the zone. It's reachable in an hour from Whittlesun by boat, but I don't know of any convenient coves or sandbars along that stretch."

"I'd like to try. Get a feel for the territory anyway." If Jerry was surprised that Peter was injecting himself into the Rover investigation in this way, he didn't show it. The friction with McElroy and Maris — Jerry evidently disliked Maris — made them conspirators. But they understood each other. Peter didn't believe in the Six-K pattern for the future, but who knew what games the killer would play. As Jerry had asserted, the predator had to remain an opportunist, and conforming to a rigid sequence of attacks was like a poker player's tell. The Rover, he was sure, was about to change tactics. But for now, there was every reason to conclude that Molly would be the fourth in a measured row. It would be instructive to find that she was the latest in the pattern, or maybe the last.

Even more important, to the family and the Task Force process as a whole, retrieval of her corpse would move everyone to the next stage.

"How about tomorrow morning? Meet me at the slip by 8:00 a.m., we'll ferry you up the coast and put you ashore at a place I know. Less than a kilometre or two from ground zero."

"Done!" Peter said. "We'll be there. But actually there was another reason I wanted to find you. Are you free for lunch?"

"Sorry, no. We've been assigned to patrol for a boatload of Somalis somewhere in the Channel. Rumoured to be escapees from a refugee camp in Brittany. But I've got a few more minutes."

"Jerry, it's the Lasker case. I wanted to ask you about Whittlesun Beach, both the Upper and Lower Beaches."

Plaskow nodded in anticipation of the question. "Thought you'd raise that."

"The conventional scenario is that André Lasker dumped his wife off the cliffs onto the Upper Beach, which is where she washed up. Then Lasker abandoned his car in the parking area, walked down the hill and committed suicide by walking into the sea."

"How do we know that?"

"For one thing, he left his clothes neatly stacked on the pebbles at Lower Beach."

"Methodical bastard, wasn't he?"

"So if he wanted to kill himself, why not follow his wife over the cliff?"

"I'm not being facetious here, Peter, but maybe he was afraid of heights."

Peter regretted taking the conversation off on a meaningless tangent — meaningless since Peter knew that Lasker didn't know about his wife's demise; he had fled before she decided to throw herself onto the rocks. "I don't mean to be speculative, Jerry, but Lasker didn't commit suicide, I'm sure. I think he planned all along to disappear off Lower Whittlesun."

Plaskow shrugged and tried to look sympathetic, even though he was reluctant to be Cammon's sounding board much longer. "So, what's the question?"

"I've read the weather reports for that night, and for the days before and after. The forecast was for calm conditions all week. But how calm is calm? Would it have been difficult for him to walk straight out into the Channel?"

"That was ten days back?"

"On a Tuesday. Sometime after midnight."

"As I recall, the Channel was tranquil all that week. Don't forget, the sea is completely tidal here. He likely could've walked out a long way that time of night. Would have been a piece of cake to reach a hundred metres out before it was even at the top of his noggin. And the water would have been cold, enough to seize up the joints."

"Okay." Peter had never mastered the links between moon phases and tidal flows.

"The wind would have been the big risk. It can whip up inshore waves without warning, even when the sky is clear. The wind stayed low that night, I recall, but I'll pin it down for you."

"What about the conditions on the Upper Whittlesun Cliffs?"

"Once again, the wind could have been an issue. The waves are always strong against the cliffs at high tide, no matter what the other conditions. But even when the sea's backing out, a gust of wind could have carried them both over in a blink. Unpredictable."

"Thanks for all that, Jerry."

"One more thing occurs to me," Jerry said. "We should check for fog conditions at both beaches."

"I was thinking of that. You record the data?"

Jerry put his hands behind his back, a Duke of Edinburgh pose. The naval uniform contributed to the effect. "Have since Elizabethan times. A sailing nation needs to know the habits of fog. I'll check. Are you thinking that Lasker was waiting for the right moment to get rid of the wife? If it suddenly got foggy, and knowing the beaches as I bet he did, he might've seized his opportunity."

"Maybe. Okay, Jerry, thanks again for all this. I'll see you tomorrow at eight."

"You know where to find me." Peter didn't know, but Plaskow handed him a plastic-coated card with a map of the harbour. He smiled. "Listen, Peter, I didn't mean to insult you before. It's always fun working with you. Look forward to tomorrow."

Peter counted Jerry Plaskow as a friend, even more so now that

Jerry had tolerated his jumping from one case file to the other, and back again. In essence, Peter had been thinking out loud and Jerry had listened. All that talk served as justification, and perhaps even evasion, of Peter's challenge if he found Molly: how to explain his meddling in Task Force business.

Just as Plaskow started up the Land Rover, Detective Hamm rushed around the corner of the station. He was carrying Peter's satchel.

"Chief Inspector! Glad I caught you. You forgot your bag."

"Thank you, Detective." The sight of Ron Hamm somehow sparked a recollection of what Jerry Plaskow had said about André Lasker being methodical. "Mr. Hamm, what are you doing now?"

"Thought I'd have lunch."

"You were the first investigator at Lower Whittlesun Beach, weren't you?"

"Second. Constable Willet took the call and arrived first, and he called me."

"Could you run me there? I'm due to meet up with Willet and Stan Bracher at the Lasker house at two. You can join us, if that's convenient." Peter missed Sam's Subaru, which the Armenian had kindly retrieved from the Delphine two days ago, when Peter had been ostracized from Whittlesun.

Hamm brightened. Peter was sure that Maris had instructed him to keep an eye on the Yard men. "Excellent! I'll fetch the car."

Peter got in the familiar Vauxhall and they set off. Hamm shared the sandwiches his wife had made; there were four of them. They picked up bottles of lemonade at a take-away, and just before entering the preserve of the beach, Hamm stopped again and they bought coffee, a brace against the cold wind along the exposed shore.

Peter held the coffees, one in each hand, as Hamm worked the sprung Vauxhall along a rutted path to the strand. It was somehow a different route than Peter and Tommy had followed on their first visit. The path ended at a sand dune, and they had to walk up the rise to gain the shore. Peter stopped at the top of the dune as the grey panorama came into view. Hamm paused a few feet away and slurped his coffee.

"Back to where it all started, sir?"

"Or where it ended," Peter mused, staring out to sea. He hoped to interpret Lasker's escape route with fresh eyes. Instead, he once again cringed at the shabby view before him. The sea faded into the horizon and promised a cold grave to the reckless swimmer. He reasoned that only a man with the arrogance to attempt to walk on water could have made the escape. Yet at that instant he was convinced that André had made it out alive.

As before, the beach was almost deserted. A teenage girl and boy huddled together way down the shoreline; even from that distance he could tell they were there because they had nowhere else to go. The breeze was picking up, riffling through the long grass at the top of the pebbly shore. The waves were steady but the tide was moving out. Both men shivered in the relentless wind.

"Show me exactly where Lasker's clothes were found," Peter said.

Hamm pointed to a wiry bush down the shore. "We put a spike in the sand over there. In case someone moved it, we set a reference point. You see that stubborn gorse bush closer to the waterline? We took a measurement from there, thirty yards at a thirty-five degree angle. It sounds silly, but gorse bushes don't move."

Someone had absconded with the spike, and so they had to estimate the location. They were able to confirm that the clothes had been piled just above the high-water line. Lasker must have been familiar with the tides, or perhaps he simply observed the discoloration of the land where the inflow reached its limit. Peter crouched down on the pebbled strand and stared out at the horizon at an acute angle.

"You say that two boys found the items and reported it?"

"Yes. They thought it strange that a complete suit of clothes had been left in a mound, neatly stacked like their ma's laundry. They were sniggering when they came in, because the man's trollies were folded like a crepe on top, they said."

"Logical that one would take them off last. Did you meet either of the kids?"

"Yes. Constable Willet knows one of them casually. Son of a cousin of his wife's, he says. Decent kids, really."

"You trust them to tell the truth?"

"As far as it goes, sir."

The first time Cammon had visited the beach, before knowing any details of the sins of André Lasker, he had felt right off that something was odd about the case. The motives of any man who chose this form of escape from his old life needed careful parsing. Now he had the same uneasy feeling, something to do with the incompleteness of the picture. In his mind, Peter addressed André Lasker. *You planned every bit of it, didn't you? But not her suicide. Didn't see the menstrual blood, did you? So unneat.* Peter now understood that Lasker had operated within a classical mode: leaving his clothes neatly stacked behind him had been important to the image of a tidy, organized departure. The Inspector gazed out to sea once again, turned to the sandy ridge that formed the horizon behind him, and rotated back to the receding waves.

So, André, what did you leave behind that signalled closure with your old life? A wedding ring, of course.

"I'd like to meet with the boys, if that's feasible."

"Of course," Hamm said. "We can do it this afternoon."

"Good," Peter said. "After we visit our colleagues at the house."

His schedule was filling up — Stan, who had a compulsion to stuff every minute of his day with busywork, would say that his dance card was full — and at such moments Peter liked to take a step back and reassess his priorities. In this instance, an idea, a tweak of his agenda, occurred to him.

"Detective, I've arranged with Jerry Plaskow to visit the area along the shore where Molly Jonas disappeared. Would you care to join me tomorrow morning?"

He felt Hamm's immediate excitement and suppressed a smile. "Absolutely." Reality arrived just as quickly. "Oh, wait a minute,

Maris won't like it. No, he wants to take charge of any moves we make regarding the Rover."

"So, we ask him," Peter said, as ingenuously as possible.

"You mean, make it seem like your idea? That's what I'm talking about, Chief Inspector. He won't like it especially if it comes from you."

"No, Detective, you make it seem like *your* idea."

"I'll try, but . . ."

The chime of his mobile interrupted his demurral. Ten seconds later Peter's own mobile rang, and he knew there was new trouble.

Peter could tell that Constable Willet was calling Hamm. Stan Bracher was at the end of his own line. The two policemen — were they getting along, Peter wondered idly. They were probably standing inches apart in the Laskers' main hallway. Hamm looked up at Peter as they listened to parallel messages.

Peter moved a few yards inland to get away from the wind. "The Rover has struck again," Stan said. Peter could barely hear him. "Someplace up the coast, in McElroy's jurisdiction. Never heard of the place. But this time he left his victim alive. Maris just called Willet at the house and demanded that all his people repatriate to the Whittlesun station."

Only the salient points had to be absorbed for now. Peter told Stan to stay at the house and complete his inspections of the blood-stains; let Willet go, and arrange to lock up the place yourself, Peter instructed. Stan seemed grateful. Peter turned off his phone just as Hamm completed his call.

In the car, Peter and Ron compared notes. The Rover had attacked near the Devon border, apparently more than six kilometres from where they thought Molly Jonas had been taken. Other than that, little had been confirmed. Peter's instincts moved towards the perverse: could he argue with Maris that the latest assault should free up Hamm to join him tomorrow on the expedition along the cliffs? Then again, if the Six-K theory had been debunked, Maris could maintain that the effort would be useless.

"Tell me, Ron," Peter said, "any personal theories about this Rover, the kind of predator who could pull off these attacks?"

It at once became clear that Hamm considered these assaults an affront to his hometown.

"Well, Peter, I'm guessing that this fiend is likely an interloper." Peter had learned over the years that ordinary citizens — Hamm was a practised investigator but his outrage as a local trumped his uniform — often resorted to florid language to explain crimes close to home. His response was born of indignation. "If he's someone from the area, then he must be young."

"Why do you suppose that?"

"He has to be mighty strong to wrestle those three girls, the ones we're sure of, off their feet and into the rock field. Those were village girls, bred strong. And to carry a dead or unconscious body along those paths to the cliffs, that takes strength."

"Good point."

"But a native to the area would certainly be noticed if he acted out of the main. Small, traditional places notice change."

This was all conjecture, but Peter encouraged it, as long as it kept Hamm thinking of the cliffs.

They weren't the first to show up in Maris's glass office. Three other detectives, unknown to Peter but assuredly part of the Whittlesun Force, had gathered in the confined space. Maris was shaking his head when Peter and Ron Hamm entered.

"I can't reach Jack McElroy, so let's proceed. If he wants our help over in Devon, he'll contact me. Here's what we know. Daniella Garvena is a girl of nineteen. Unlike the other victims so far, she's an urban girl. She was unfamiliar with the coastal walkways in the area of East Devon, where her family moved a year ago. Her mother says she feared a tumble from the cliffs if she got too close, and in fact she was assaulted on a well-travelled road in sight of the family house, which lies on the edge of the village of Combfield."

One of the detectives, obviously a veteran, asked: "The road wasn't the main coastal road known as the Jurassic Trail, I'm assuming?"

181

"No," Maris said, "but it was a popular road, nonetheless. Took a risk, our chap."

"Excuse me, Inspector," Hamm said, "but the girl was afraid of the cliffs. Does that mean she was on the outs with the local teenagers, the lover's lane group?"

"Yes, you might say that," Maris said. "She refused to go with kids on their picnics along the heights. She had only lived there a year and a bit but she's popular, apparently doesn't have a loner's attitude. Okay? Anyway, she took a wrong turn last night. No moon. He attacked her from behind, silently. The girl is conscious but in shock. He knocked her down with some kind of club, or a bar, maybe a tyre iron. Then, when he had her down, he slashed her back with a knife, and left her."

"Sexual assault?" someone said.

"Not rape. But he did undo her brassiere and he stole her knickers."

"What was she doing there?" the third detective asked.

"She liked to go out and look at the stars, she told the interviewing officer. The family is Italian, first generation, so there's real shame in having her knickers taken. We can all agree she's lucky to be alive."

There was an uncomfortable, unexpressed feeling among the detectives in the office that this assault was distinctly unlike the others. Peter was content to listen; he tried not to lean too hard against the glass wall. Comment on the Six-K theory was premature, almost unseemly, but the Task Force's strategy would have to be revisited. The detectives would regroup after Maris contacted J.J. McElroy.

Peter fled the room in order to dodge Maris, and to avoid any hallway chats with Hamm that could set off the inspector. He wanted Hamm with him tomorrow, but it was the wrong time to approach Maris with the proposition, while the Inspector was fixed on the Garvena attack. The Rover had screwed up, and not for the first time. The assault on Daniella Garvena bore a whiff of panic — no kill, no follow-through, no ritualistic disposal. But Molly Jonas had been his first misstep, Peter was sure. Daniella had been lucky. Molly's body probably lay full fathom five beneath the Channel.

Peter took out a business card and scribbled *The Crown at 5:30* on the back. *Please ask Maris about tomorrow.* He placed the card in the centre of Hamm's cluttered desk and left the station. Around the corner, he paused to call Stan who, Peter had no doubt, was still at the Lasker house. He answered on the third ring.

"Hello, Peter." He has to be concentrating on something, Peter thought.

"Stan, how's it going?"

"This is fascinating, Peter. Like the work of a demented artist. Like she made sure to mark every wall."

Peter didn't want to get into an analysis of the blood pattern, and neither did Bracher, he could tell. Let the man finish his job. Stan was like himself in this regard, often unwilling to discuss the bottom line until sure of his evidence.

"Listen, Stan, I have a suggestion. You need time to finish up."

"And go to the lab," Bracher interjected.

"That too. How about you skip our journey along the shore tomorrow? I'll take Detective Hamm with me instead."

"Oh, sure," Stan said. "I'd almost forgotten anyway. Are we still on for the Crown at 5:30?" Stan never forgot assignations in pubs.

"Yes, sure. It's along the way from the police offices, off Daubney Street."

They hung up at the same moment and Peter immediately called Sam's Auto.

"Inspector!" the Armenian shouted into the line. "Where are you?"

"Back in Whittlesun. Can I get the Subaru again?"

"Of course. Where do you want me to drop it off?"

"I'm staying at the Sunset Arms this time. But I can come by your shop."

"I insist, no. I will drop it off now at the hotel. I know it."

"There's no rush, Sam. I won't be there for a while."

"I'll leave the car in the hotel lot, the keys at the desk. Mayta says hello."

CHAPTER 16

The Crown did a roaring business on a Friday evening, with dart players and weekend drinkers crowding the aisles, but Detective Hamm, as usual, had managed to snag a quiet booth for four. Peter arrived early, only to find that Stan was already there, a stack of nylon camera cases piled on the spare seat of the booth. He had staggered over directly from the Lasker house. Now he was demonstrating the f-stop setting of a camera to a captivated Detective Hamm. A large pitcher of draught ale stood between them.

Peter removed his jacket. Stan poured him a full glass of the ale and said nothing until Peter had drawn a long swallow, but he had been waiting to deliver his line.

"Peter! Where did you stash Joan?"

Peter rolled his eyes; Hamm blushed. "I only call her in when I don't have your expertise, Stan."

"Now that was either the smartest or the dumbest strategy I've ever seen. Bringing your wife into a case." He turned to Hamm. "Detective Hamm, you need to understand that this fellow always has a reason for what he does. Always."

"Method in his madness?" Hamm replied jovially.

Peter had warned Stan not to allude to his suicide theory in front of the young detective. He knew that the camera sitting on the table contained dozens, probably hundreds of shots of the bloodstains that proved the theory, and Stan would start speculating after a couple of drinks. Peter decided to steer the talk in another direction, while reminding himself that Ron Hamm deserved a briefing on Anna's death within the week.

He turned to Hamm. "Detective, what's the verdict from Inspector Maris about tomorrow?"

Hamm perked up. "It's a go. Inspector Maris told me to work hand-in-glove with you."

Stan raised his glass and the others followed. "Here's to inter-agency cooperation!"

"No," Hamm said. "He just wants me to keep an eye on the chief inspector."

The waitress brought a plate of something unrecognizably deep-fried, but Peter ate it anyway. The conversation quieted for a few minutes as they dipped into the appetizers. Peter fetched another round.

Stan switched directions again, back to the Task Force. "Peter, I suppose we noticed the same flaw in their game plan?"

"The watch-and-warn strategy?"

Hamm nodded; they all understood. There had been a consensus in the morning meeting that the aligned police forces of the two counties should attempt to monitor a large swath of the English Channel. That, self-evidently, required a huge workforce, and the Garvena incident only expanded the active search zone. McElroy and Maris further assumed that the Rover would continue his attacks all the way to Whittlesun, in rough six-kilometre increments. The attack on poor Daniella should have fractured that theory, but there had been no sign of a change of plan in the brief caucus with Inspector Maris.

"Maris says the strategy hasn't changed," Hamm said. "But maybe he's reconsidering it. We need to be consistent about setting threat levels in various sections of the Coast."

"But he hasn't dispatched you to Devon to help out?" Peter said.

"Nope."

Stan spoke. "There must be a hundred miles of rocks and bays, a lot of them near impossible to monitor from the ocean, or even from the land side."

"I collared Jerry Plaskow afterwards to discuss it," Peter added. "He doesn't think it's feasible either."

"Jerry should know," Hamm added. "Lived here all his life."

It may have been the beer, but Peter was in the mood to do some theorizing of his own. Normally he wouldn't have speculated like this, and not in a raucous pub over pints with two fellow officers who had never met before, but he was excited about his adventure tomorrow. It would be his first chance to see the rocky shoreline up close, and perhaps he would obtain insight into André Lasker's thinking.

"Gentlemen," he began, "let me put it on the table. What about the Six-K theory?"

"To start with," Ron said, "we've already offended the locals by using 'Six K.' Everyone down here hates the metric system."

"Statistically," Stan proceeded, "if you have two criminal incidents, then the six-kilometre spacing is discrete evidence. But add a third, it's a pattern that begs verification. Add a fourth and fifth, that's a definite trend. That assumes — statistically — that Garvena's an anomaly."

"Do you believe it, Chief Inspector?" Hamm said.

"I do and I don't. Unlike Mr. Finter, I don't believe the past is prologue. This Rover is toying with us. Just because he strikes every six kilometres over a space of twenty-four — or even thirty or thirty-six — he's capable of stopping, even reversing direction. There's no inherent logic in 'six kilometres.' I'd put more faith in the phases of the moon. He thought he was being clever with Daniella, but it was a mistake, because he let us know he's a player of silly games. The Task Force, depending on whether Jack McElroy takes the bait," — Peter and Stan exchanged glances — "now shifts direction, and he keeps us wondering where he'll strike next. It's all a game."

"So, Peter," Hamm said, "why exactly are we looking for Molly?"

"Finding Molly Jonas wouldn't prove that he'll keep the pattern in the future, but it will tell us several things about him. Say we find her at the six-kilometre measure. Supports the theory, right? But, why was he inconsistent regarding the body? Did something go wrong? The Rover left the first three girls in places where they could be found by a not-too-intensive search. They were laid out in formal poses that were meant to be seen. Recover Molly and we learn a lot about our man."

"The first three were like bodies in a funeral pyre along the Ganges," Hamm added.

"Why didn't he leave Molly in the same kind of location?" Peter asked.

"For that matter," said Bracher, "why bother with the Six-K intervals at all? It just exposes him to surveillance."

Peter knew the answer, but it was Hamm who responded. "There's a broader question. What kind of publicity does he want? What's the point in just killing women? If you see yourself as an avenging angel, or if you want to be famous and notorious, you'll want something more. He wants to be known for his murdering *style*. The Six-K thing provides a template, but I agree with Peter: he thinks he's invincible and he'll ditch the old pattern when he feels like playing silly buggers."

Peter smiled. Bracher looked stunned. "Brilliant! I'd like to buy this man a beer."

"I wonder if he likes his nickname, the Rover?" Hamm said.

"Better than the Six Kilometre Man," Bracher said. "Sounds like *The Loneliness of the Long Distance Runner*." The Canadian was a fanatic for British films.

Peter turned to Hamm. "Jerry Plaskow committed to taking us anywhere we want along the coast. I propose we cruise the section about three kilometres either side of the Six-K mark where Molly Jonas logically would have been found. Ron, did they leave up that huge aerial map in your boardroom?"

"Yes. I'll go back and do the calculation."

"Then we'll meet at the harbour tomorrow morning."

"Yes. And I don't get seasick."

Hamm headed back to the station while Peter and Bracher, laden with equipment, took a taxi to the Sunset Arms. Stan excused himself and rushed to the lift. Peter knew that he would be up all night with his slides, feeding a stream of digital photos into his plug-in viewer.

Peter registered and reclaimed the Subaru keys left by Sam. His new room was perfectly adequate, and the in-room computer connection was a bonus; this time he had brought along his laptop. The cool evening air had sobered him up; it was still early and he was restless. He felt like driving somewhere. He left the hotel and walked around to the parking area. Booting up his mobile, he selected the stored phone number for Father Vogans in Weymouth. The priest showed no surprise at the call.

"Drop by if you don't mind sitting through a late christening."

When Peter arrived, the door to the downstairs was open, as before, and he simply followed the light to the admin office. Vogans stood at a lectern thumbing through a sheaf of correspondence. Peter saw that he was working standing up to avoid wrinkling his impeccable cassock. Vogans was wearing the full chasuble, with its dramatic white panels and woven gold trim. It made Peter feel seedy.

The priest looked up. "Good evening, Chief Inspector. Please come in."

"Am I interrupting, Father?"

"Not at all. But I have a christening at 8:15." That was forty minutes off.

The two men were old enough to cherish comfortable pauses (and both in professions that demanded patience). Peter took off his rumpled coat but remained standing while Vogans finished with a handwritten letter, taken from a stack of similar correspondence.

"Constituency business," he said, not looking Peter's way.

"Mm." Peter looked at the walls. There were numerous plaques, attestations; some were in Romanian. Vogans appeared to be wrapping up and so Peter said, "My two were christened on a Sunday morning." He was making conversation but it sounded slightly inane to him.

"Ah, Peter, so you have a religious streak after all."

"I'm a little outside the tent, Father."

"Why don't you stay for the service? It might bring back fond memories. Frankly, we don't have many evening christenings, but young parents have such schedules these days." He moved away from the lectern and eyed the coffeemaker, then thought better of it. Guests would be arriving any minute.

"It's a family occasion," Peter said.

"I'll say you're the policeman we've brought in for security. That's a joke, Peter. Christenings are joyous occasions. People are so busy these days that we do them when we can. And, yes, people do wander in to enjoy them."

"Thank you anyway, Father."

Vogans leaned against the back wall of the office and folded his arms. "Is it about Anna?"

"Yes." Peter paused to shape his question. The room was silent, the atmosphere expectant. "I need to know one more thing about her. Please understand that I'm in no way asking you to violate the confessional. This conversation is not about the legal protection of her privacy. I don't think what I'm asking is a Church secret, but if you can't tell me, don't tell me."

Vogans held up his hand. Ninety per cent of parishioners who sought confidential advice from him were worried about sex, infidelity or conception. Like the Church of Rome or the Anglican faith, Eastern Orthodox priests performed their duties against a backdrop of complex edicts and doctrine. They acted a role, fatherly, stern or comforting, as needed, but always sympathetic to wives and mothers in distress. The doctrinal rules affecting women might shift up and down over the years, into and out of view, like the scrims behind the actors on a proscenium stage, but the edifice still exerted the same powerful force. Peter sensed the heavy presence of the altar above them.

"Let me be clear," Vogans finally said. "I'll tell you as much as I know, and I do so because I feel guilty. I didn't help Anna when she was in agony."

"Are you sure she could be helped?"

"Do you, Chief Inspector, tell yourself that you could have prevented any given death?"

"Not for many years. But I understand regrets."

"She did come to me. She wanted children, several she said, but her husband did not. Is that your question?"

"That's helpful, but no. My question is this: did she ever tell you that she had ever been pregnant?"

"Was she pregnant at the time of her death?" Vogans said.

"No, she wasn't."

"I've been bothered by the possibility. That she died pregnant."

Peter, more firmly now, said, "Could you answer my question?"

"No, she had never conceived, I am certain, but she said she was going to try to get pregnant, drop her birth control without telling André." Vogans avoided a direct look. "Do you want to know what I told her?"

"It's not absolutely necessary."

"Perhaps *I* need to confess. Ironic, isn't it? But I want to tell you. I told her that the Church does not approve of birth control pills, but she should talk to her husband, not give up all precautions using Church doctrine as an excuse."

"Thank you."

"Does that answer your question?"

"Yes."

"You're still trying to figure out her state of mind that night."

"Yes." Peter didn't tell him that his inquiry into her mind and heart would suddenly end when he determined once and for all how she died. It was a cruel truth of his profession.

"Are you sure that she wasn't pregnant?" Vogans said.

"Positive."

"Well, I don't know if I could have deterred her death. But I could have tried harder."

They stood in sad silence while the new parents waited for Father Vogans upstairs.

"I'm doing a communion before the christening, to catch people on their way home from work. Why don't you stay for the service, Peter?"

Peter left the church as the last light was vanishing over the rooftops. As he passed the staircase that led up to the main floor, he smelled cool air and flowers. The olfactory memory stayed with him as he started the car and drove below the speed limit back to Whittlesun.

All the way he wondered why he was tempted to go back to St. George's for the evening ceremony.

CHAPTER 17

"We're landing *there*," Jerry Plaskow announced from the railing of the Ports Security craft.

Peter and Ron Hamm followed the line of his outstretched arm towards a distant bay. It was a fine landing spot, if they could reach it. They had been on the water for about an hour since leaving the Ports jetty in Whittlesun. Jerry had advised them before departing that he would try to drop them in the centre of the "Zone," the so-called Six-K spot on his marine charts, but it had become evident at once that none of the coves marked on the maps for that stretch was accessible, and they had been forced to sail well beyond Jerry's target. Peter was not a sailor but the sea appeared rough to him, diminishing his hopes of landing anywhere close. Even at mid-tide, waves crashed against the bluffs, intimidating anyone who would dare infiltrate the rocks from below.

At least, in Peter's view, they had the right boat for the job. At fifty feet long, the tri-hull steel craft spoke of speed and stability. Its two 420-horsepower turbo diesel engines were enough for every kind of sea. Ports Security not only provided general monitoring of coastal zones and safety enforcement in the harbours, it also supported scoops of illegal immigrants and seizure operations by the

Border Agency. Since 9/11, its list of duties had doubled. Peter could well imagine a further doubling as the Olympic sailing schedule advanced. For Peter and Ron, the Ports Security boat guaranteed that none of the many agencies mandated with shoreline security would question their snooping along the inlets and caves of the Jurassic Coast.

The crew were an odd collection. While Jerry claimed the post of captain, the real sailing was done by Lieutenant Hogart, introduced as a Royal Navy secondment and an expert in inshore navigation. He sported a George V spade beard and wore military flashes on his pea jacket. Hogart stayed inside at the controls while the others gazed at the shoreline.

The landing place chosen by Plaskow and Hogart lay behind a crumbling breakwater of stone and cracked cement, and Peter could see that they would have to go around the far end in order to achieve the calm water of the bay.

Jerry called above the idling engines, "There's an engineering marvel bequeathed to us by the Victorians. A hundred and fifty years old, probably. The Victorians loved their engineering projects, and you know what? They dealt with coastal erosion in perhaps the best way possible. Look how the rock face up from the beach is still intact, almost fully protected. Now every town along the Coast wants their own sea barrier."

Jerry turned towards the wheelhouse, looking for someone. A tall, lean figure emerged from the entrance. Peter had not seen him before, and Jerry did not introduce him now. He wore a ribbed sweater that displayed a shoulder patch that Peter did not recognize, but he was sure this man was SAS. He and Jerry consulted while Hogart, exercising his own judgment, eased the boat farther along the breakwater to the opening.

Jerry turned to the detectives and spoke again. "The first victim was found in a niche in the rocks pretty near the rim. The second girl was laid out in a rock cave halfway along a defile that continued to the shore. The third girl was found much closer to sea level. Our man, we're agreed, most likely would have come down from the top with Molly Jonas. But we don't know how far. You're going to have to use your judgment to identify the killing grounds."

Peter agreed with Jerry's analysis, as far as it went. The Rover had been very picky, and had roamed far and wide to find just the right chapel-like setting where he could pose a body. That didn't mean that he hadn't searched them out *before* abducting the girls. It was Hamm who amplified Peter's thoughts.

"The killer has been consistent. In the first three, he worked hard to put the bodies on show, in ritualistic settings. He would have tried it with the Jonas girl as well. Even if he fouled it up, we should look for a distinct, unique spot."

"Okay then, what we're looking for initially is any substantial path up from the shore," Plaskow stated.

They nodded. They had a rough plan to follow.

Hogart piloted them around the artificial point and into the tranquil bay. Without hesitation, two sailors lowered a Zodiac dinghy with a small motor attached. Peter regarded the benign shore, green and gently sloped, and protected from the tide. A farmhouse, really a crofter's cottage, sat at the top of the rise; there was no smoke or other sign of life, but the day was exceptionally warm and the farmer was probably trying to save fuel. Even from this distance, Peter could feel the loneliness of this spot, which hadn't been altered in a century. He was reminded of the UNESCO designation protecting this area; it was one more effort to stave off change. He had briefly seen sections of a walkway on the heights west of Whittlesun Harbour as they passed, but not since. This locale seemed too rugged and distant for strolling tourists or anyone other than extreme hikers. He wondered what he had gotten them into. He looked at Hamm, who appeared to be having the same thoughts.

The detectives, assisted by the crew, eased down into the Zodiac. Jerry joined them in the front. Peter hadn't seen them load the pile of equipment, but two yellow rain slickers, sou'wester hats, rubber-coated torches and coils of nylon rope were now stacked around the motor in the back. Three walkie-talkies poked out of a gym bag at Plaskow's feet. The dinghy roared across the bay and the SAS man (if that's what he was) at the throttle homed in on the sandy landing spot ahead. With a last acceleration, the rubber boat raised its bow and they were home and dry, literally. They eased over the rounded gunwale and the helmsman began to unload the gear. The three passengers walked up the beach like arriving explorers. Hamm saw the path first and pointed.

"There, leading uphill to the east. That must be the route everyone uses."

Peter, Hamm and Jerry Plaskow gathered by the small pyramid of equipment.

"Here's what I suggest," Jerry said, and gestured to the filament of a trail, evidently the only way up from the beach, aside from the route that led to the cottage. "The path you're looking for isn't on any of our maps, so look sharp and think logically. Molly Jonas was riding her bicycle that night, so she could have ridden to this area even though it's a long way from home. She liked to admire the views, her mother said, so she probably knew the cliffs in detail. They never found her bike. Watch your descent. You'll come across tracks that end suddenly at a sheer face. These are fisherman's stoops: a man stands on the crag with a rod and three hundred feet of line, and fishes for sea bream. The only other place I've seen this is Portugal, down in the Algarve. Why they do it, I can't imagine. We lose one or two each season. I'm allowing you four hours. We've loaded a rucksack for each of you: a food packet, water bottle, gloves, climber's rope and a walkie-talkie. Stay hydrated. Call us on the walkie-talkies an hour before your arrival back here at the beach. Report to me on your weather. It may be different on the clifftop than it is down here. Any storm that moves in shouldn't block your signal, but big rocks will. Now, let's get you dressed."

He held up a bright yellow rain slicker, surprisingly light given its rubber coating and dense weave. Peter took off his old jacket and handed it to the SAS officer; he wore an Irish wool sweater underneath.

Plaskow examined his gumboots and pronounced them acceptable. Underneath his coat, Hamm sported a red wool pullover, as well as canvas trousers and work boots; they weren't climbing boots but Hamm was secretly proud that they contained a steel shank: protection against nails and, hopefully, sharp rocks. Jerry frowned at them but let it go. He handed a slicker to the younger detective. Hamm and Peter resembled SAS commandos who had bungled the dress code.

With a wave to Plaskow, the two policemen began to trudge up the windy trail, heading due east. Near the crest of the first hill, Peter looked over his shoulder and noted that the dinghy had already moved out into the bay.

Peter had his own ideas of where to look. If Molly had cycled to the cliffs, she would have started on familiar paths, the established ones, and then jettisoned the bike in a regular hiding place before exploring on foot. Of course, it was possible that she had a rendezvous with the rapist, and that might have altered her route. All the principal tracks had been searched, the fringes and the lay-bys too, but no bicycle had turned up.

Inland from their current vantage point, the police officers could see that the promontories were treeless, cleared over the centuries for firewood and replanted with grass for sheep. Peter saw no herds or flocks, and the fences that had once kept livestock from the rim were gone entirely. Nor could he see any human beings, or even houses. The point was: the heights extending inland in this subsection of the Zone were passable for a girl on a bike but too exposed for the Rover to risk seizing her there. Peter was certain he had waited until she came closer to the water.

But not here. The fields and ridges to the north led nowhere. Ahead about a kilometre the terrain changed. The forbidding cliffs began — he could hear the grind of the crashing surf — and the plateaus, which ran back from the brink several hundred yards, supported copses of windswept, stunted trees interspersed with piles of boulders. Anyone might hide there.

They would need two hours or so to reach what seemed to be the most promising area. Peter guessed that they would end up one to two kilometres inside the Zone. Even so, he was doubtful that Molly would have penetrated this far into their search area. He looked at Hamm, who gave him a thumbs-up, and they continued.

The temperature rose. They were tempted to dump the yellow raincoats but decided to strap them to the tops of their packs with pieces of the rope. The walk took the full two hours. They came across narrow pathways here and there, actual goat tracks, and followed a couple, but soon realized that these routes didn't connect to the sea lower down. Hamm conjectured that the Rover could have pushed the body over the cliff at the end of any one of the tracks. "In that case," he said, "there's nothing we can do up here. This would become a search for a bicycle."

"Which likely is at the bottom of the sea with her," Peter said, with a hint of exasperation. In his estimation, the Rover had sought a location closer to the water where he could operate undisturbed and leave the body on display. If so, why hadn't it been found?

They tramped on. Stoicism changed to anticipation as they explored all the possibilities of the rugged plateau. The sightlines were good here, and the scooped bay was laid out before them. Hamm rooted through his rucksack and came up with a pair of compact military-issue binoculars. From a high boulder, he scanned the inland horizon and counted the trails.

"One. Two. Three. Maybe four."

The problem was that no single path was self-evidently more promising than any other. None showed frequent use. Only by following one or more of them seaward would they figure it out, and that strategy presented its own challenges.

The binoculars proved useful as they negotiated the bay from up top. They found themselves on one side of a U, a vertiginous rock face across from them, a crashing sea below. Peter borrowed the binoculars and scrutinized the cliff sides opposite and to his left. He found only forbidding caves, unreachable by humans. But he was starting to understand the geology of the Zone. Shelves of black rock, with domed indentations disappearing into darkness behind them, had been formed naturally at the lowest levels of the gorge. Some would be engulfed at high tide, but others stayed above the water, though not always clear of the highest waves. Many of the indentations were cut off from the plateau above. Peter searched carefully for caverns at the bottom of a path, however narrow the access route.

They circled around the rim of the U to obtain a clear view of all sides below. The sea was opaque from this height. It funnelled into the bay from several angles and sent up a grim bass note as it assaulted the rocks. At this dizzying distance, the battle fought by stone and water seemed abstract, like a computer-generated effect.

They found a flat rock and paused to get their breath. Ron Hamm brought out crackers and cheese and they snacked like picnickers taking the sun.

"You realize that there may be a dozen fjords like this one?" Hamm said.

"Then the Task Force can send out teams to check the others."

The prospect was discouraging; they had hoped to make a discovery themselves. Over the past week, Cammon and Detective Hamm had grown to trust each other on professional matters. Each was tuned into the other's rhythms; they found they could talk without too much explicitness, or over-explanation. Peter was starting to rely on the younger man's instincts.

"What's your view, Detective?" he continued.

"I think we're on the right track, in general terms. The Rover's a creature of habit and knows the terrain. He'll try to find the ideal cave or sacrificial stone. If he could find a spot, we can find it, too. The Six-K rule may be his downfall after all."

Hamm aimed the binoculars up the coastline, vaguely in the direction of Dover and Calais.

"Hard to figure where we are," Hamm stated.

"Let's see if Plaskow can help us out," Peter said.

With Plaskow out at sea and Peter and Hamm poised on a

platform in the sky, the connection was direct, even though the PS boat was out of sight. Jerry answered promptly, his voice coming across clearly enough.

"Peter, where are you?"

The rushing static on Peter's device was no louder than the surf in the cove below. "Jerry, that's why I'm calling you. We figure that we walked two kilometres inside the Zone, maybe less, but it would be helpful to know exactly."

"You still think he found a killing ground precisely at the Six-K mark?" There was scepticism in his voice. Peter wasn't about to debate the theory over a walkie-talkie.

"Not necessarily. It's just that we can see a series of cliffs and bays, one after another, like fingers on a hand. Ron calls them fjords and that seems pretty accurate. But we're only at the first one and our time is running out. If this one's too far away from the mark, we'll go around to the next instead of descending here."

"You see the blue bulb on the side of your walkie-talkie?"

Peter held the device away from his ear, then returned to the line. "Yes, Jerry."

"Is the light on?"

"No."

"Then depress the button above the bulb."

Peter again examined the side of the walkie-talkie and pressed the round pad. The bulb flashed blue. "Got it."

"Okay, Peter, wait while we lock you in." Peter could hear the hollow voice of Lieutenant Hogart in the background. The reception was so good that he could detect the boat's engines. Plaskow came back on the line.

"The walkie-talkie contains a locator, like a SatNav. We have your latitude and longitude and Mr. Hogart is comparing it to the map . . . Good news. You're right in the mid-point of the Six-K Zone."

"Are you sure?"

"Yes. You walked farther than you thought."

"We'll keep looking here," Peter said. "If we find a path down to the sea, we'll test it out. We'll probably be back at the beach an hour or so later than we planned."

"Keep an eye on the weather."

Encouraged, Peter and Hamm were determined to find every pathway the Rover could have used. It occurred to Peter that the predator might have employed an entirely different system, identifying trails, coves or other hiding places in advance from old maps, or perhaps by asking local farmers about secret landing sites used by smugglers. On the other hand, the locals distrusted idle inquiries from outsiders, which meant anyone who hadn't lived there for three generations. Peter sensed a cockiness in the Rover that had him making it up on the fly.

In practical terms, the only approach was to back away from the rim of the fjord. It was dangerous there anyway, and they could discern no promising trails from above, even with the binoculars. They moved inland several hundred yards — Peter reminded himself to think in metres, given the Six-K convention they were following — to a point where the barren rock began to give way to forest and views of the pastures to the north. None of the ground was level here; gullies and piles of glacial rock forced them to take frequent detours. They were able to rule out most of the footpaths by walking a short way downhill until they dead-ended. Peter guessed that they had arrived at the base of the U but had strayed too far from the sea. They were about to confront the far side of the first bay, having inscribed a great half-circle. He was about to suggest they make a sharp right turn to get them reoriented to the rim of the inlet when Hamm found it.

There was one category of secret place that Peter hadn't thought of: the cliff-edge equivalent of a lover's lane. Out of Peter's view a hundred yards ahead, Hamm called out, his voice echoing: "Stonehenge!"

Peter followed the voice. Hamm was waiting twelve feet below him on a sloping path. Peter himself was standing, in effect, on a stone roof that concealed the lower trail, which was worn smooth by foot traffic and was lined with cigarette butts and crisps wrappers.

"Stonehenge?" Peter called down. There were no standing stones here.

"My wife and I went to Stonehenge this summer," Hamm called up. "We were disappointed that we couldn't walk in amongst the stones themselves; they were roped off." For some reason, Hamm was eating the last of the cheese as he stared down the trail. "In any event, the way you get to the display is to park at the visitors' centre, then walk along the access path *under* the road and come up the other side."

Obviously, Hamm could see farther than Peter could. He scrambled down the embankment and met Hamm on the path. He could now tell that it ran straight ahead, under the rock roof, on a downward slant for a hundred yards, after which it curved off to the left. They followed the track for several minutes until it abruptly split at an opening in the rocks. Both men were surprised at how far they had descended. The sea was a mere thirty yards below them. They were also faced with a choice. The left access seemed the easier; it was well used and there was more garbage lining the edges. Chalked graffiti of the adolescent kind marked the passage of teenage lovers.

"Let's start with the easy one," Hamm called out, animated by their discovery.

The track enlarged into an overlook at the centre of the U. Sheer walls of stone flanked their position, while the sea roiled below them, dangerously close. The lover's leap offered the perfect dumping spot for a body. Back from the edge was a caveman's dwelling with a flat stone floor; bonfires had been built in the recesses of the chamber, and stones were lined up across the rim to provide a safety barrier. A fall from the edge would likely break an ankle or an arm but wouldn't be fatal, Peter judged, for there was another wide ledge three feet down. The site was promising: an intrepid killer would have all the privacy he needed.

Except that there was no bicycle, no clothing and no body.

Peter hadn't expected such convenient discoveries, but somehow he knew that the spot wasn't right.

"Let's try the other fork," he said to Hamm, who looked doubtful but gave a thumbs-up.

Even if this tentative foray onto the cliffs proved unsuccessful, Peter was gaining a better understanding of the killer. He had greater hopes for the more precarious route, for obviously the Rover was a risk taker. He wouldn't want to make the sacrificial altar too easy to find. Peter also suspected that the killer was flirting with greater danger with each successive crime.

The other path was daunting in every respect. Even the rock differed from the first hideaway, becoming blacker and more shale-like as they descended. Somehow the sea spray reached this high, and it rendered the narrow path slick and treacherous. Peter had forgotten to ask Plaskow for a tide schedule, but he guessed that it was three-quarters in by now. *What had been the sea's level when the Rover had carried Molly Jonas's body down here?* The steps were like rotten, black teeth, and the pair took a full ten minutes to descend the twelve yards to the cavern. It offered less space to move around than the other one had, and they were nudged to the precipice at every step. Peter led the way as best he could, and they were careful not to bump against each other. The salt spray greased the pockmarked platform of black rock forming the base of the small cave. Peter had trouble imagining the Rover carrying out his depredations in this tight space, but he did note that the single slab of sea-blasted limestone resembled an altar, the scene of an oblation to evil gods, that a Druid or an Inca priest might have found alluring.

Ron Hamm pressed himself against the back of the cave so that he could look out to the Channel without succumbing to vertigo. Peter, too, kept to the rear wall. In the few minutes they had stood there, the sea appeared to have risen. That was an illusion, but the fans of spray came up beyond the stone floor like kinetic water sculpture; it could only get worse as the tide rose over the next hour.

Hamm was the one who thought to check in with Plaskow on the walkie-talkie. He connected with the boat as quickly as before but either the noise at his end drowned out Plaskow's voice, or the walls of the fjord created too much interference to make out anything.

Peter moved around by the cavern wall. There was no obvious sign that the Rover had worked his evil here. "The man doesn't leave clues, he leaves bodies," Hamm had said during the march along the cliffs, with some accuracy. Peter focused on the shallow space. *Where is Molly?* Teenage explorers had visited this unromantic outpost; there were cigarettes and condoms, although only at the very back of the cave. The men were rapidly becoming soaked and there wasn't much more to see, but Peter remained patient. Even with the sharp spray in his face and the reverberating din from below, his instincts were heightened.

They put on their yellow rain slickers and broad-brimmed hats, becoming ridiculous parodies of fishermen. Peter had once been forced to dress like this on a boat tour of Niagara Falls. But that had been fresh water; now he was grateful for the protection from the salt, though the coats made any movement awkward.

Sarah would find plenty of professional stimuli in this sodden cave, he thought. Clusters of limpets hung from the dark ceiling of the cavern. What he knew — from the bowl of shells in the front hallway of the cottage — to be helmet and trumpet shells clung to the outer rock ledge that bolstered the stone floor. Spray from the repeating waves bathed the floor every thirty seconds. Stubborn moss coated the ceiling stones.

Hamm tried the walkie-talkie again, with the same result. Peter noted that the blue light was pulsing on the side of the device. He didn't know whether this happened regularly or only when someone at the other end was trying to locate them.

The search of the small space was proving fruitless. The sea was mesmerizing and Peter wanted to move away from its siren stare. But he intended to search every nook of the cave, if only so that no one else would have to later. He took a quick minute to adjust to his surroundings, for he felt the inherent instability in this etched-out dome (like the inside of someone's cranium), no matter that the rock formations had stood for thousands of years. The arches just above his head and the pilasters at the sides of the chamber seemed to be constructed of rounded, molten stone, although Peter knew that this was merely the honing of sea and wind. He realized what a tame person he was at heart. Sarah wouldn't hesitate to explore the grotto from front to back. Of course, the Rover was the boldest, the one who sought out these hiding places with deadly purpose. Peter stood still a minute longer and, like the practised investigator he was, mentally stepped back and attempted to make sense of this chaotic room. But for once, his reasoning didn't plod in short steps; rather, it jumped to a precise conclusion.

The Rover had been here. And he had underestimated the risk.

The killer had exhausted himself carrying Molly Jonas's body down the crooked stairs, all the while thinking how clever he was. He laid out the body, arms by her sides, inevitably to be found by the police when local teenagers revealed their *Cabinet of Dr. Caligari* lovers lane (except that no one had told). In those moments, exhilarated, the Rover congratulated himself, right up to the second when he tried and failed to climb out of the trap. The sea rose, or it started to rain — *or did he injure himself?* — and the water rendered the steps impassable. He panicked. He had already thrown the bicycle down the steps and over the edge. Now he decided to jettison the body as well, in case he couldn't get out. He was forced to wait for the drying sunrise, even though it might also bring those snotty kids and their marijuana joints.

Or maybe the prospect of a night with his victim was too ghoulish even for him.

Peter got down on his hands and knees — salt spray had already soaked his trousers and crept under the collar of his wool sweater — and began crawling around the back perimeter of the chamber. Amid the rubbish he noted strands of seaweed, filigreed coral, blue heather and bright, pink anemone washed up from the sea floor. Except that anemone are not made of pink wool. The sad, saturated lump had lodged itself in a crevice at the far border of the cave. It was a pink toque, definitely a girl's item. *Had the Rover forgotten it there?* It would be a simple matter to verify Molly's standard wardrobe on these solitary bike rides of hers. What Peter would never know, he understood, was: *had the toque been his calling card, or had he left it inadvertently?* Either way, the Rover had shown a weakness. The flamboyant predator had made a pitiful statement in leaving the sodden piece of wool behind. *Do serial killers get bored with their own patterns?*

He turned to Hamm, who huddled against the back wall. Peter held up the cap and Hamm slowly comprehended what it was, whose it was. The realization seemed to freeze him in place with horror.

Peter stuffed the toque in his slicker pocket and moved towards the brim of the rock platform. He felt a compulsion to look over the edge. Sarah would do it in a second. Hamm tried to restrain him but he pulled his yellow coat sleeve from the younger man's grip. Hamm took the coil of rope from his pack but Peter shook his head. He approached the rim on his knees, like a timid, small boy would. The wind had picked up, causing an increase in the spray, but he sensed that the tide was reaching its zenith. He wasn't so naive as to expect to see a body when he peeked over the edge of the platform. A hollowed ledge just over the brink stretched out another yard or so before the rock finally ended and the open sky began. It was a mini-ecosystem of its own. With the sun reaching its zenith, the self-contained aquarium on the lower shelf glowed with prismatic light. Oxides in the rock lit up red and indigo. Mitre shells poked straight up from sandy spots, and a meadow of living moss coated the floor of the etched trough. It bewitched him. He yearned to see a ring, a bracelet or Molly's necklace gleaming in this garden. It would have been perfect.

One movement, one shift to the left was all it took. The boulder that had looked so firm on top of its ageless pillar gave under the weight of his arm, and he was over. He tumbled fifty feet in the air, his arms open, pleading to Hamm, and he was instantly out of his partner's sight, beyond redemption.

Unseen by Peter, Hamm seemed to react faster than gravity. It was almost as if this was his moment to find the heroic, the unequivocal within himself. People do impossible things in a crisis. He took the end of the rope coil, already in his hands, and threaded it through his rucksack, tying it with a startlingly correct sheetbend knot that he had learned in the Boy Scouts. He jammed the walkie-talkie deep in the pack to give it weight, pulled the drawstring tight and tossed the whole thing into the void.

It is retrospection that makes it seem that time slows at a moment like this but it did for Peter. He fell backwards, the yellow raincoat flaring out but not really retarding his fall. He waited for his back to slam into the sea and it took an eternity. Colours — the sea foam, the cliff side, the evocative clump of pink wool — gained sharp relief as the foam engulfed him, and he smacked backwards onto the surface.

He was asked later if his life passed before his eyes (these were barroom conversations; Joan would never ask such a question). It was not so much his life but rather the truth about the life and death of Anna Lasker that came out in three involuntary words as he tumbled back. He might have been speaking in tongues. He splashed into the water, the raincoat preventing him from immediately sinking. An incoming swell raised him up and he cried:

"Anna! The boys!"

In the cave, Ron Hamm might have peeked over the edge to find his partner or he could have braced himself waiting for his colleague to grab the lifeline, but he couldn't do both. Confident that the line would reach the sea, he chose to hold back for at least a minute, waiting for the tug. There was precious little footing and nowhere to affix the rope but he tied it around his waist and dug his heels as best he could into depressions in the rock floor. After a full minute of terrible waiting, he crept forward to the edge.

Below, Peter floated on his back in a relatively calm eddy, a false vortex created by the cross-running waves. The rain slicker would soon drag him under and he worked to shed it. It was easy enough in the calm pool. The heavy boots were more difficult and he gave up after a feeble attempt. He looked up but the spray obscured any view of the ledge. Dangers encircled him. The tidal flow would soon press him back against the canyon walls, where there was no place to hold on, let alone climb out. The currents shifted erratically. Sea spray plumed and blanked out his view of the cliff. In the temporary tranquillity of the pool he looked down for a second and saw forests of kelp. He took this as a positive sign: perhaps the sea along here covered an accessible beach where he could find his footing.

Peter saw the rucksack fall. It landed in a surge ten feet from his pool and was soon followed by Hamm himself. The detective slapped leadenly into the swell. He rose to the surface just as the wave carried him towards the stone walls. Peter could see that he would be battered to a pulp. The rescued became the rescuer. Hamm was still attached to the rope. Peter took it and pulled hand over hand until he grasped his partner. He held him like a buoy at the end of a line. He pulled hard on the rope. Hamm's raincoat, billowing out like a flotation device, was both a help and a hindrance. He was awake but not struggling and Peter turned to retrieve the pack, which was sodden but still floating despite the walkie-talkies inside. He hoped that it would provide some buoyancy; when he felt its unnatural weight, he reached inside and pulled out the walkie-talkies. For a moment he thought of trying to call Plaskow and he pressed all the buttons on one of the devices, but then comprehended they were useless, and he regretfully let them sink.

Within a few minutes the light began to fade, much faster than Peter thought possible. What had been a sparkling mist turned to an oppressive fog as contradictory waves funnelled into the gorge at high tide, sending up blades of water that became a permanent rain. They moved back to the rock face, problematic as that strategy was. Hamm remained semi-conscious. The rucksack, freed of the radios, allowed them, one at a time, to float and rest; but it wouldn't last long. The second man had to tread water, and Hamm's strength was fading. The sea was surprisingly warm but temperature wasn't the biggest problem. The canyon walls provided only crevices and finger holds, and Peter couldn't see any ledges or inlets to either his left or right. Hamm was bleeding from both nostrils but claimed that he was all right. An errant wave twisted Peter's hand where it was lodged in a niche in the rock face and he heard his little finger snap. The sea water washed away any immediate pain and he reached for a purchase with his other hand.

It appeared as the eye of Moby Dick. And it was an eye, a monster's orb. The iris of bright yellow came up from the depths and the glassy lens diffused its beam. It moved as a confident sea creature should, floating up, waiting out the wavering current, bound straight for the surface. Peter stared at the eye. It was everything Melville or Verne or the Old Testament had forecast, he thought. The creature was somehow knotted to Hamm's nylon rope. Except that Hamm's line was blue and white, while this one bore red stripes. Peter reached out and pulled the electric eye towards him.

The bulbous torch was a clever contraption; it floated like a top and put out a bright, piercing light that might have been seen in France. Peter had the torch now. He had no idea where it came from. He couldn't trace the other end of the line in the churning water; he pulled as hard as he could, simultaneously wrapping his end, torch and all, around Ron Hamm. The young man was losing consciousness. In his effort to shelter him, Peter was slammed into the rock face by a wave.

The far end of the rope, still obscured to Peter, went taut, and Hamm's body went flying away from him, like a surfer's body on the crest of the pulsating waves. Peter was growing delirious. Pushed to the rock wall, he bobbed, alone, abandoned. If his life was to end, he prayed for one last sight of the eye. He would swear to his grave — not far now — that it truly was a Leviathan's eye.

The rescue arrived by boat. A dinghy, perhaps the one that had landed them on the shore, careened out of the fog and bumped right into Peter. Steering the arm of a small motor at the back was one of the sailors from the ship. But in the front, leaning out with hand extended, was the sinewy man in black. If the helmsman seemed unconcerned, the SAS man — Peter in his reverie thought of him as his personal SAS guardian — was positively blank-faced. Just at the point of fingertip contact, God reaching to Adam, a swell caught them; his rescuer's arm sawed high into the air, sending Peter under the water.

He heard a shout. "For Christ's sake, Walterman."

Peter sank farther than he expected, and moved sideways under the water, too. He was tangled in ropes and clothing and his boots dragged at his tired legs. He panicked, thrashing at his bonds. He reached blindly forward and gripped the swimmer. As he surfaced, in the arms of the figure, the waves came into play and drove them against the cliff wall. Peter clasped the body and cringed for the impact of the rocks. He felt the nakedness of the form. He opened his eyes and saw the battered face of the naked girl, and the pink wool scarf that still choked her.

A long gaff with a blunted hook came over his shoulder and grappled onto the girl's scarf. He felt, rather than saw, a second gaff find his collar and he was quickly drawn back from the cliff.

Peter, broken and waterlogged, lay in the bottom of the dinghy. He was on the brink of hypothermia. The commando looking down at him was costumed in a black sweater, black trousers and a black watch cap, and amazingly had dabbed lamp black (Peter supposed) under his eyes. He held a gaff in each hand. *Imagine that*, Peter thought, and passed out.

Later when Peter told the story he left out the part about praying.

CHAPTER 18

Sometimes the chief inspector irritated himself. As he lounged in the bed in his private room in Whittlesun General Hospital, Peter wondered how he always managed to alienate everybody.

He was fully dressed, except for his tweed jacket, which hung in what passed for a cupboard, and he lay on top of the covers. Having patched his wounds, they were holding him "for observation." It was 6:30 a.m., and despite the hospital's efforts at climate control, zephyrs of fresh October air seeped into the room, beckoning to him to walk out of the place. He detected no movement out in the corridor, and this was another inducement to flee. They were holding him in a prison without bars. If they thought the drugs would pacify him — they were painkillers, but not sedatives — they had outsmarted themselves; the dregs of the medication served only to mask his residual aches and pains, and he was ready to go.

But he had to get the train of events clear in his mind; then he would leave. He plumped up his pillows, crossed his hands on his chest, sank back and began to work his way back in time. Jerry had driven him to the hospital in the Land Rover, while Hamm was transported in the ambulance that was waiting at the Whittlesun jetty. Peter's concussion was mild and he displayed no signs of shock or fevers. The presiding doctor at Whittlesun General had examined him all over, cleaned and patched his various abrasions and splinted his broken baby finger. The doctor, not a day over thirty, a Whittlesunite, annoyed Peter with repeated expressions of amazement at his survival in the sea. He blathered on about how his parents had warned him of the perils of the cliffs. Peter recalled hearing the words "heroic" and "admirable." What he had clearly understood through his haze was their condescension towards his sixty-seven years. His every word of resistance had confirmed his frailty.

He had made matters worse by batting at the nurse who tried to inject him with some fluid, unidentified but certainly a knock-out sedative. He knew perfectly well that he had the right to discharge himself. Two orderlies, two nurses and his doctor had surrounded him, all speaking in soothing terms. The matron, part of that no-nonsense breed, broke the standoff by pointing out that Peter had no clothes (and perhaps metaphorically too), and he should eat something. His stomach gurgled at the mention of food; he hadn't eaten since the picnic of cheese and crackers on the promontory overlooking the Channel. He had agreed to wait for the hospital meal cart but then had fallen asleep without the sedative.

He had awakened before sunrise, hungry, wrapped in a bleached-out blue hospital gown and wearing paper shoes. Since there were no staff about, he had decided to look in on Hamm; for some reason, he had known that Hamm was lodged in the room next door. He moved slowly into the hall. Swamped with grogginess, he paused against the corridor wall for a moment. Circumstances considered, he felt not too bad, he had told himself. He shuffled into the adjacent room and found Ron Hamm asleep on his side. Peter went around to the window side of the room and peered at the young man. Bruises coated his face like stains from a thrown plum, purply and deep. But there was none of the swelling typical of a facial fracture. A day-old dinner tray lay on the swing-out bedside tray and Peter stole a stale scone from it.

But this sequence, he now understood, was a fragmented memory.

He now recalled a series of telephone conversations — he had had to fight them for phone access too. He had reached London, instructing Bartleben to call Joan and tell her *not* to come down to Whittlesun, since "it was only a scratch or two," although evidently he had a concussion and a broken finger. He had cut the conversation short, only informing Stephen that Molly Jonas had been found, that she was certainly a victim of the Rover, and that he would provide a fuller briefing as soon as possible. Then he had rung off. In one quick step, he had offended both Bartleben and his wife.

He had slept again, getting up with the dawn light to find his clean clothes in the cupboard. He had dressed and sat back on the bed, plotting his escape from the eerily empty hospital. The quiet would end soon, he told himself, just as his bruised body dragged him back into sleep.

It was either the smell of coffee or the creaking hinges on the room door that woke him the second time. He opened his eyes to the hulking form of Constable Willet, who stood in the doorway with a huge coffee cup in his fist.

"Chief Inspector," Willet said. "You're up. How do you feel, sir?"

Without waiting for a reply, Willet came over to the bed and levered Peter to a sitting position. Willet caught him eying the coffee and poured half of it into a plastic cup. Though eager to talk, he had the sense to let Peter savour a few sips. By now the hospital was coming to life and Peter smelled food; a moment later, an orderly brought in a tray and set him up for his breakfast.

"Was it you who brought my clothes, Constable?" Peter said.

"Mr. Bartleben asked me to. I retrieved them from your hotel. Trust they're all right for present purposes."

"Yes. Thank you."

"But I forgot the shoes," Willet said.

"No matter," Peter said, and bit into the limp toast. "What are you doing here, Constable?"

"Keeping out the undesirables. The media have gotten wind that you and Mr. Hamm were instrumental in finding the Rover's latest, poor lass. They've shaped the story like you and the Detective are heroes."

"They've used that term?"

"Oh, yes, and a lot of people agree. It was quite the effort, sir."

The adoration of the media would be short-lived, as they refocused on the failure of the authorities to make an arrest.

"Do the press have my name?"

"Don't know that, but they do know that our second man was from Scotland Yard. Don't worry, sir, the chatterers won't get past me. I'll be watching over you and Mr. Hamm."

"How is he?" Peter said.

"They say he'll be all right. The concussion is receding, but he won't be getting out today. You neither, I expect. But they've put the press conference over until tomorrow."

"Lord," Peter said. He imagined the circus in the Whittlesun Police boardroom.

Bland as it was, the toast and coffee invigorated him. His impatience rose. His mind grew feverish and his thoughts jumped to the Lasker case. It was dragging on too long. For all the predictions of serendipitous breakthroughs, there had been no sighting of André Lasker and the trail was cold. Anna deserved better. Willet swung the tray table away from the bed. At that moment, Peter recalled the three words that had come into his mind as he fell from the cliff: "Anna. The boys."

His thoughts buzzed around a schedule for the day; it was his automatic way of moving beyond this confinement. He wanted to touch base with Stan about the bloodstained car, now lodged at the Regional Lab, and then contact Jerry Plaskow to fill in the end of the melodrama. His hire car must be sitting overdue on the Ports pier. He flashed again on the slow-motion fall backwards into the bay. *Anna. The boys.*

"Constable," Peter said, "before you get back to Detective Hamm, he told me that you're related to one of the boys who found the pile of clothes on Lower Whittlesun Beach."

"Oh, yes. Young Percy Callahan. Father's Fred Callahan. Good people."

"Could I pay them a quick visit?"

"Don't see why not. When you recover, of course. I'll ring up and alert them. Maybe tomorrow or the next, you'll be out?"

"I'd be grateful. Leave me the address. Tell them there's no problem. The boy isn't in any trouble."

Willet turned serious and leaned over Peter. "Inspector?"

"Yes?"

"Percy is a special boy. Very special, and everyone knows it in my family. He likes to collect shells. Knows the tidewaters like the back of his hand. That's why he was on the beach that day."

Peter understood that the boy's love of shells wasn't what made him exceptional.

"Thank you, Constable. Do you mind if I make a quick call?"

"Certainly, Chief Inspector. I'll check on Hamm next door." Willet wrote down the Callahans' address and went out.

Peter was lured by the telephone on the bedside table. It surprised him that the hospital had risked someone in the tabloids finding out the number.

He woke Stan up at the hotel. "Peter, why are you calling so early? Aren't you in pain?"

"Sounds like you're the one suffering," Peter said. "Are you finished at the house?"

"Finished at the house," Stan echoed. "Yes, I'm done except for a bit more spectrographic work on the blood. It tells the true story."

"Suicide."

"Peter, you know I can't officially go that far, since she died outside the confines of the house. But the wounds, the cuts were self-inflicted. I also took a look at the vehicle she drove up to the parking lot."

"Car park," Peter corrected.

"Right. No doubt she drove the car and he didn't. Stains on

the driver's side. That must have been the ride from hell, with her bleeding out and not being much of a driver. I went up there. Jumping wouldn't be for me."

Peter was amazed that Stan had bothered to go up to the cliffs, but he said nothing. "Are you going to the press conference, Stan?"

"Sure, wouldn't miss it. I bet they'll give you an award. The keys to the city or something. But it won't be until tomorrow afternoon, I hear. How is Detective Hamm, anyway?"

"Good. He's next door. Has a concussion but he's sleeping it off. They wouldn't let him sleep if it were still serious."

"Shall we announce Anna's suicide?" Stan said.

"No, and Maris doesn't know yet. But it's overdue that I tell Hamm. As soon as he wakes up. He's earned our trust, Stan."

"Don't do it, Peter." Stan's lighthearted voice had levelled.

"Do what?"

"Keep vital information to yourself. You're always doing this, hiding in some corner of the world with all the evidence spread around you, concealing the key facts until the last second, then making your wrapped-with-a-bow announcement."

"I don't make announcements," Peter said, in feeble defence.

"No, you hate the limelight. But it amounts to the same thing. You keep too much to yourself, for too long, then it bursts out. You have to learn to play nice with others, namely, your colleagues."

But the lecture seemed beside the point to both of them and, after agreeing to touch base later in the day, they rang off.

Peter tottered from the bed and walked around the room. It was going to be difficult to escape in paper shoes, he thought. He lay down again and dozed off. Two minutes later, he opened his eyes to the sight of Sarah's smiling face, inches above him.

Peter had killed men in his time, six of them. He renewed his weapons certification every year. He had seen bodies opened up on morgue tables and never flinched. He had argued with butchers and consoled the hopelessly violated. He had saved lives. But he had never learned to talk one-on-one with his own daughter.

But Sarah's open grin peering down on him promised a difference this time.

"How are you, Dad?" she whispered.

"Fine. Stiff." He ached more than before. He noticed that she had pinned back her hair. "You're here."

"We were all worried. Sir Stephen called Mum. Uncle Tommy wanted to come down. Turned out I was the closest, otherwise Mum and Michael would be on their way."

"Tell them not to bother."

They both laughed. Sarah was the worldly one and each knew what the other was thinking: what should Sarah, as family delegate, report back to the others about Peter's condition?

"I'm healthy," he proclaimed. She arched an eyebrow and looked at his broken finger.

The buoyant mood continued, carried by the family love of irony. "Haven't you sprained a finger before, on your expeditions? I recall . . ."

"Yes, Dad, twice in fact. Both times I was winkling out trilobites, not dead bodies," she said.

Peter shifted himself against the bedstead, rumpling his tweed jacket even more.

"What are you doing in Whittlesun?" he said.

"Not Whittlesun. We were taking our road show out to Land's End. Mum called me on my mobile so we turned slightly left, and here I am."

"Well, I'm okay."

"The matron says you have a concussion."

"Doubtful. The doctor's a local lad, can't stop talking about the hazards of the cliffs. Too histrionic."

"God forbid." She helped him get comfortable. "Why don't you come home for a few days? Let yourself heal."

"I have an assignment, can't leave it. Would you?"

"Sure. I do it all the time. The cottage is still home. I come back there to decompress. All the time."

Maybe Peter hadn't been there to notice all the visits, but he was sceptical. He didn't want to argue. Besides, although their conversation was playing out in typical father-becomes-the-child fashion, there was something different on this occasion. They were fellow plotters and he liked that she was as keen to leave as he was.

"What are you really doing out there?" he repeated.

There was more petulance in his voice than he intended. The painkillers had slowed him down. She smiled. She understood his worry but decided to keep it light. "Now that I'm on the Jurassic Coast for the first time, I may take the opportunity to do some fossil hunting."

Peter knew she was being provocative, but what struck him at that instant was the solitude that underpinned her profession. She ventured into remote wetlands and moors, camped out in the Highlands or on windswept islands; yet Sarah was the most gregarious of the Cammon clan, and the least prone to loneliness.

She smiled again. "You've never understood, Dad. I'm a detective like you, in my own way."

He had no retort, nor did he want a debate. She laughed.

"From what I hear, you want to turn the whole family into detectives. Mum won't stop talking about her little sojourn to Whittlesun. Nick and Nora Charles, I heard her say once."

Peter laughed aloud, causing his whole ribcage to ache. *Had Joan mentioned the blood-soaked lavatory?*

"I need to get going," he said. He looked at his feet and wiggled his toes.

"Yes," Sarah said, moving off the bed. "Let's get out of here."

She reached under the bed and retrieved a pair of shoes. "Now we can make our escape."

She helped Peter slip on his loafers. "Where did you find these?" he said.

"Just when I arrived, which is about an hour ago, Jerry Plaskow came in at the same time. He brought the shoes and left you this note. Handsome bloke." She handed him a lumpy, brown envelope. When Peter ripped it open, his car keys fell out, along with a scribbled note from Jerry and several lavender message forms bearing the logo of the Sunset Arms.

Your car is in the hospital lot. Other stuff is from your hotel as of this morning. We should talk. Glad you're OK. Call me.

The other squibs included call-back requests from Bartleben and Markman, the Director of Communications in London, and a call from Melissa Hamm, presumably Ron Hamm's wife. One note distressed him: Wendie Merwyn, the reporter from TV-20, whom he had seen on the television in the hotel lounge, asked him to call her back by 4:00 p.m., identified as her "deadline," whatever that meant. He preferred to avoid all reporters for now. Another was from Father Salvez, giving a phone number but no other information.

"Good, I have the car," Peter said.

"Where are we going?" Sarah said, and helped him to his feet. She slung a well-worn rucksack over her shoulder. Peter halted at the doorway. They both peeked into the hall conspiratorially.

"Sarah, I have a favour to ask you. I have to interview a young boy, one of the kids who found some evidence on the beach where André Lasker disappeared. Apparently he's interested in marine biology."

"You want me to meet him?"

"If you would. But only after I ask him what he saw. He may believe he's in trouble."

He could tell that Sarah wasn't making sense of this, for the simple reason that Peter was failing to explain his anxieties about a visit to the Callahans.

They walked to the lift at the far end of the corridor.

"Then it's official," she stated. "We're all in the detective trade now."

"They tell me this boy is very special," Peter said.

Sarah drove while Peter called ahead to the Callahans and simultaneously punched the address into the SatNav. Constable Willet's cousin lived inside the town's formal limits, in a district that Peter hadn't visited before. The neighbourhood offered a view of neither the sea nor the cliffs. The Callahan house was identical to the others in the row and Sarah found a parking space in front. This time the door was painted glossy kelly green, while the others along the row were orange, red, yellow and robin's egg blue. Peter saw no point in drawing comparisons between the Callahan and Lasker houses, even if the former was merely a smaller version of the latter. The Callahans likely were a happy family (from Willet's report), and the Laskers had not been, and that fact made all the difference.

Leaving Sarah in the car, Peter rapped on the lion's head knocker on the green door and waited for a minute. Willet's cousin, Fred Callahan, answered. He was tall, rake thin and wiry, and wore clean overalls. He had kind, deferential eyes and a handsome moustache. He was very much the artisan archetype.

"Good morning," he said to Peter, gauging him but showing no hostility. He peered out at the car with Sarah in it, but was too polite to do more than look.

"Good morning. I'm Chief Inspector Cammon." Peter might have appeared a bit rumpled, his face scraped, but he never doubted the impression of authority he conveyed. He tried to smile, though he ached.

"Oh, I didn't expect you so soon. Come in, Inspector. My wife has to be at work, but we're here."

Peter entered the cleanest front hallway he had ever seen. The wallpaper, a tasteful yellow stripe pattern, was perfectly applied. Peter noted that the runner on the oak floor was in top condition; there was no sign of wear or stain. It wasn't the typical home of a twelve-year-old working-class boy. The small table in the vestibule was a fine Queen Anne piece, and the lamp centred on it, with a lace doily underneath, was a Zolnay design, which he recognized from Joan's antiquing expeditions.

Fred brought him to the living room, which was as tidy as the hall and decorated with beautiful furniture. His host gestured to the chesterfield, and Peter gratefully took a seat. He tried to put the father at ease by appearing relaxed and informal, although his joints ached severely and there were multiple scrapes on his hands; his splinted finger invited questions, but Callahan was too well mannered to ask. The boy wasn't present, and Peter, from considerable experience with child witnesses, prepared himself for the usual parental preliminaries.

"So, Inspector Cammon, you are a Scotland Yard detective," Willet said on the phone."

Stan Bracher once said that he delayed as long as possible telling people that he represented the Yard, since they always thought that he was "putting on the high hat." Peter supposed that it was a Canadian expression, but it sounded New York City to him. Nevertheless, it summed up the risk of interviewing witnesses in their homes. This roundabout chain of musings brought him back to Fred's questioning look.

"And you, Mr. Callahan, are somehow in the furniture business."

It was a Holmesian moment. Callahan looked at him in surprise. A wave of queasiness washed over Peter and he fought to stay expressionless. Fred seemed not to notice. Peter refocused and fought the rising bile in his throat.

"The table?" Peter continued.

"Oh, yes!"

"It's a beautiful piece. The chairs and sideboard, my wife would love them."

"She'd pine for them."

"Pardon?"

"It's a family joke. I work in furniture refinishing. When I tell my wife about a particularly fine table or chair I'm working on, she says I'd better stop or she'll start to pine for it."

Fred went on to explain that he worked for a local company that brought in old pieces from Europe and refinished them for resale within the British Isles. Fred was a master finisher. The furniture arrived in small freighters at Whittlesun Harbour.

"Would you like some tea?"

Standard practice was to refuse hospitality. Peter was about to decline when he realized that he had eaten one piece of toast and half a hospital coffee that morning. "I'd love tea, be my first cup of the day."

"Coming up, then."

Before Fred could leave, Peter creaked to his feet. "Why don't I help you?"

Peter was trying hard to sound amiable and non-threatening. This was a first, Fred was likely thinking, a Scotland Yard copper in his kitchen. Fred immediately said, "First time I'll have had a Scotland Yard police officer in my pantry."

In the kitchen, Fred went through the ritual of preparing the tea. Peter looked around at the spotless room, so far from the Lasker devastation. He wouldn't have minded spending a couple of hours drinking tea in the Callahan living room, but he had a schedule, he reminded himself. It was also likely that Fred Callahan was expected for a noon shift, or maybe earlier. Peter got to the point.

"Thank you for seeing me."

"My wife's sorry she couldn't be here to meet you," Fred said. "Works in the town."

"Mr. Callahan, I won't take up your morning." Peter's promise came out insincere and stiff, a copper's euphemism. Percy wasn't in evidence and Fred had yet to mention him directly.

Peter tried again. "Constable Willet speaks highly of young Percy."

"Do you have children, Inspector Cammon?"

"Two. Could I have a very quick word with Percy?"

"He's a fine lad, sir. The best."

Peter had heard many fathers defend their sons, even boasting of non-existent virtues, but Fred's assertion was different. It was not a defence; it was an objective conclusion.

"Percy's done nothing wrong," Peter said. "He and his friend discovered a pile of clothes on Whittlesun Beach."

"This is the Anna Lasker murder?"

Peter nodded. He wondered how Sarah was doing out in the car; he had failed to indicate how long he would be. "There've been no charges of murder laid. But the case is complicated, and every detail helps."

Fred took a deep breath. "I'll call Percy." He went to the hall and gently called out: "Son?"

Peter listened to the steady footfalls on the stairs and in a moment the boy turned into the kitchen. Percy Callahan was angelic. His straight blond hair framed a flawless portrait of innocence. Though the child was on the verge of puberty, Peter understood that the charismatic purity would stay, with any luck, in balance with his heartthrob handsomeness. He was shy, a little fearful as Peter shook his hand — working around the splint on his finger — but he looked Peter in the eye and sized him up. He evidently sensed Peter's benign intent. Peter himself, for reasons he couldn't pin down, was anxious to know if Guinevere Ransell knew the boy. For the tenth time already that day, he felt the gut-level need to call her.

Percy helped his father with the tea, not self-consciously but with the quiet bond that they had, and waited for the adults to speak. They stayed in the kitchen, even though the living room would have been a more natural place to conduct a police interview.

"You're a detective, Mr. Cammon?" the boy said, in a soft voice.

"Chief Inspector," Fred corrected.

"I've been a detective for a long time, Percy."

"Do you like being a detective?" The question was open, ingenuous, like everything about Percy.

"It is what I do. It's inseparable from what I am."

"It is your vocation?"

Peter smiled, almost chuckling. "That's right. I can't do anything else."

"It's important to do what you like, Dad says. I want to be a marine biologist." His voice turned up; it was a half-question.

It was Peter's turn to measure his words. "Were you collecting shells on the beach that day?"

"How did you know?"

"The shells. There above the cupboards. There are hundreds of them."

Fred nodded. The boy nodded in the same way. "Martin and I are allowed to go to Lower Beach."

"Do you spend all your visits just looking for shells?"

Fred was growing concerned. "Why?"

Peter wasn't threatening the boy, and so he persisted. "Do you look out to sea sometimes? Just look?"

"Martin gets impatient." Percy was struggling for accuracy but Peter was still unsure what the child wanted to say.

"The man I'm looking for disappeared into the sea."

"He walked out into the salt water?"

"Percy, it will be difficult to find him. Sometimes I stand on the shore and try to imagine how he did it."

"You think Lasker is still alive?" Fred interjected. Peter stayed focused on the boy.

"Percy, Mr. Callahan, that is indeed my opinion, but please don't tell anyone. We haven't exactly publicized the theory. And Percy, please don't try to look for him along the beach. He's gone."

Percy nodded. "You want to know how he thinks so that you can understand where he went."

"That's exactly right."

Percy moved away from the counter — none of them had drunk their tea — and glanced at his father. He went out to the hallway. Peter caught Fred's eye and shook his head: let the boy go. They waited in silence. A moment later, Percy returned. He held something in his two cupped hands, as if he had trapped a grasshopper.

"Percy. Before you show me, you need to know that you did nothing wrong," Peter said.

The boy opened his hand to reveal a royal blue ring box. He opened the cube and showed his father and Peter a man's gold wedding ring.

"I wanted to give it to Mum," he whispered. "I found the velvet box upstairs and put the ring in it."

Fred put his arm around his son for comfort. Peter impulsively came over to the boy and patted him on the shoulder, a very unpolice-manlike gesture.

"It's fine, Percy," Peter said.

The boy handed over the ring without hesitation. "The man, he took off all his clothes. I could tell because the clothes were stacked in order, the way a person undresses. Martin laughed when he saw the man's underthings on top."

"Just to be clear," Peter asked, "The ring was on top. Was it in the centre of the clothes?"

"Yes."

"The very centre?"

"Yes. You see, Inspector, it was the last thing he took off. It made it sad. He put it carefully in the middle of the folded things. That's the sad part."

Peter had to smile. It had taken him a week to understand André Lasker's mood in his final moment, or at least his final moment on British soil. The boy had understood right away. Peter wanted to ask — another unprofessional thing to do — if the boy believed that André was still alive, but he held back.

It was the same question he wanted to ask Gwen Ransell.

Peter prepared to leave. They moved to the hallway. He turned and thanked father and son, then said: "My daughter is a marine biologist. If you would like to talk to her about her work, she's more than willing."

Percy smiled broadly, and looked at his father. "That would be super."

"She's outside in the car, as it happens."

Fred and Percy offered identical astonished looks.

"You take your daughter along on your investigations?" Percy said, hitting the issue dead on.

Peter stepped onto the pavement. Sarah was leaning against the car, rucksack on the bonnet.

"Your turn," Peter said. "This boy is something special, believe me."

Sarah grinned broadly and picked up the pack. She shook it and Peter heard the rattling seashells. "Half an hour," she said.

Peter drove this time. His splinted finger clacked on the steering wheel, making it difficult to make turns; his elbow still ached from his near-fall at the Abbey four days ago, and the abrasion on his cheek had grown angry. But, for all this, he was happier than he had been in a long while, with Sarah in the car, and with the echo of the Callahans' hospitality. His momentum had been re-established, his day's schedule laid out in sharp relief. He knew that he had to see Gwen: a hundred policemen might have theories about the Rover's habits, but she was the hedgehog working on a grand theory. There was also more to be gleaned from her about the Cloaked Man. He was in a mood to get organized. He would check in with Sam's Auto and extend the car for another two days. He'd call the hospital about Ron Hamm's condition, while doing everything possible to dodge the press before the media event the next afternoon.

Sarah lounged in the passenger seat, still in the glow of her conversation with Percy Callahan.

"What an exquisite child," she said. To Peter, it seemed she had Joan's speech rhythms. "I'm taking him on our wildfowl count out at Land's End this weekend. His dad's driving him down."

"That's kind of you," Peter said.

"He's so keen to learn. Knows what he wants, that boy."

Peter had been captivated too. He had known what he wanted to do since he turned fourteen. He had stood in the lobby of the old Headquarters on the Embankment and waited for the case officer, Mr. Cape, to come down the staircase, and he had known. Oh yes, he had known. Fifty-three years ago.

"Where can I drop you, Sarah?"

"The Ports pier."

"What? The harbour?"

"Actually, just about where you parked your car yesterday. Jerry Plaskow's taking me down the coast. Fossil hound country, he calls it."

"What does Jerry know about fossils?" Peter said, causing Sarah to raise that eyebrow again. Peter changed direction towards the seashore. They drove in silence for a minute. "Grass doesn't grow under you," he said.

Sarah laughed. "Well, he is dead handsome."

In less than twenty-four hours, Sarah had made a new friend in Percy Callahan and hooked up with Jerry Plaskow. She astonished Peter.

He let her off at the shed by the jetty where the Ports boat was moored. There was no sign of Jerry's mysterious SAS man. Jerry was probably inside. Peter could tell that Sarah was watching his reaction to returning to the sea but it didn't bother him; there was no flash of panic.

As Sarah retrieved her bag from the back seat, Peter wound down the window. "Can we meet for dinner tonight? Say, about six at the hotel."

"I'll be there." She leaned in and gave him a hug and a kiss on the cheek. "Dad, stay safe. I'll call Mum and tell her you're okay. You are okay, aren't you?"

"Yes. Tell Jerry thanks. I'll call him later."

Peter drove a few hundred yards through the harbour alleys and parked behind a warehouse made of corrugated steel, out of sight of the water. He opened his mobile and retrieved Gwen's number from the index. Mrs. Ransell answered.

"She's in her room," the old woman said. She sounded sober enough. "I'll get her."

There was a long pause. His back ached but none of his injuries from the day before was serious, he judged. There was that odd survivor's feeling that he had been given a second chance, and it energized him.

"Hello, Peter," Gwen said, in her smooth, calm voice.

"Hello, Gwen. Are you well?" He felt protective, a transference from Sarah.

"I am. But are you, after your fall into the sea?"

How does she know about that? Surely the press hadn't yet named him as one of the adventurers on the cliffs.

"Just curious, Gwen, but did the news reports mention my name specifically?"

"No," she at once replied. "But it was you, wasn't it?"

"Yes."

"The TV people know it was you. You couldn't conceal it anyway, though I'm sure you'd like to stay in the background, Peter."

"I want to see you about something. You mentioned the Cloaked Man, the Electric Man and the Black Man."

"And you want to talk about the Cloaked Man," Gwen said immediately.

"How did you know that?"

Guinevere gave no answer, but after another long pause said, "I'll be here this afternoon."

"I'll call first," he said, feebly, and rang off.

He closed his eyes and sat in silence in the car. He was swamped by a feeling that he had missed an opportunity to forge an alliance with Gwen that could propel him to the capture of André Lasker.

CHAPTER 19

He could have extended the Subaru rental by phone, but he had several reasons for visiting the Armenian in person. He drove up the hill to Sam's Auto and was astonished to find only three cars for hire in front of the shed. He could make no sense of it. *Where is his stable of cars, all out for hire?* There had been more than a dozen Mercedes, Subarus and BMWs lined up in the lot before. He decided then and there not to quibble: his visit was all about the intricacies of the auto-hire business, anyway.

There was no Sam, and no Mayta either. He placed the Subaru in a marked parking slot and walked over to the shed. The first sight on entering was Mayta's estimable behind. She stood on a tippy chair with a tack hammer in her right hand, the kind used by rock hunters, while Sam stood back from the chair, and the desk itself, and evaluated her installation of the Armenian flag on the office wall. Sam wasn't at all surprised to see Peter waiting in the doorway dangling the Subaru's keys. He seemed to be enjoying Mayta's struggle.

"What do you think, Inspector?"

What could he say? The Armenian flag came in red, blue and orange horizontal stripes. "Very patriotic, Sam."

"You are in a good mood today, Inspector?" Mayta got down from the chair and the three of them studied her handiwork. Satisfied, Sam guided Peter outside, where he ignored Peter's car.

"Was that you on the news, Inspector?"

"I sure hope not."

"Sure. They found the poor girl, Molly, in the sea. Two detectives, one with the funny name, a local copper."

"Mr. Hamm?"

"Yes, that one. Picture on the telly, taken from his driver's licence."

"More likely they got it from his police identification records."

"Same photographer. Anyway, they said a Scotland Yard detective was the second police officer involved. Those were the words. I have a photographic memory for words."

Mayta sidled out towards the Subaru. "Photographic memory. Then why do you keep losing your keys?"

Sam tried to smack her on the bum but she was too quick for him. She tossed him a vamp's look and went over to the sedan, where she slid a yellow invoice under the windscreen wipers. Peter nodded to her in acknowledgment, but she had already retreated to the office.

"Can I extend for another day, Sam?"

"That's what Mayta just did. But keep the car even longer, if you like. And, Inspector? No charge for the second day. I have been on those cliffs with my boys, doing the picnic, you know? I cannot imagine falling into the ocean. What you did was very good, *heros.*"

Peter didn't bother to tell him that filling out his expense claim to show a free day's rental was more of a hassle than paying the extra. Mayta emerged from the shed and came over. By the time she reached him she had sized up his health again. She tucked a steel vacuum flask under his arm. "Take this with you, Inspector. You look like you may need it. *Heros.*"

Sam waved her away and she returned to the office, but at her own pace. Sam wiped a blotch of dust from the roof of the Subaru. "You visited the garage, Lasker's?"

Peter nodded. "But I still need to interview the remaining staff."

Sam nodded back. "Albrecht Zoren is the boss for now, like I told you. Did you see him?"

"Not yet."

"He won't be friendly."

"Why not?"

"He's a Silesian, what can I say? No, seriously. They're working under some kind of receivership order until Lasker is ruled dead. It is a formal procedure, long time, and maybe the authorities will pry out the money story. Zoren will be nervous, no doubt."

"Is Zoren worried about the state of the books?"

"Maybe," Sam said. "Maybe he's just Zoren."

"I want to find any sales and leases André Lasker might have kept off the books. If he put away large amounts of cash somewhere, we may be able to trace it. You understand about money laundering?" It occurred to Peter that he had forgotten to ask Ron Hamm to collect the ledgers from the garage.

"Oh, yes," Sam said. "But if Zoren was in on the scam, there will be no accounts. You'll never find them, because they don't exist."

"That's right," Mayta chimed in. She had suddenly materialized next to them.

"Any suggestions?" Peter said.

Sam shrugged and looked at Mayta. She nodded her go-ahead.

"Lasker did a small business on the side selling used cars, right?" Sam began.

"Yes."

"In cash, no names. If he was desiring to keep his trade very quiet, he would probably sell them out of the country. Some places in Europe."

"Isn't there a lot of paperwork under the EU rules?" Peter said. "They have rules for everything."

Mayta spoke. "The point, Chief Inspector, is that it is easier to sell abroad, or at least within the European Community members, because there is a demand for so many categories of autos."

"Doesn't that just mean more rules, more signatures, and bureaucratic delays?"

"No," she continued. "It just means that countries will find ways to encourage the export trade, while taking their cut through fees and taxes. The British government doesn't care very much about the car, as long as it meets what the EU now requires. The more complicated the rules, the better for the seller, because it creates opportunities to cover up embarrassing details."

"The more complicated the rules, the less the British bureaucrats want to be bothered," Sam added. "They . . . ?"

"'Defer?'" Peter said.

"Yes, they defer to the European Community rules. It becomes a European problem. Isn't that a very British thing?"

"How does it help us?"

"Because the exporter will have to give a name," Mayta said.

"A fake name?"

"He has to give a *corporate* name, his company's name, if he wants his company to sell the car. The company is going to need an address and phone number. He could sell as one person and give a phoney name, but he may be selling the cars as non-drivable, so he doesn't have to bring them up to U.K. driving standards first. Only companies are going to do that in volume."

"Does 'non-drivable' mean they're scrap? Where's the money in that?"

"You'd be surprised," Mayta said. She brushed back her raven hair from her face. "We would never do this, but a lot of people are marketing these old cars under a bunch of different categories, and they show up in funny places in distant countries of the Union. And, guess what, they are being driven!"

"Oh, I wish Armenia would join the EU!" Sam said.

"I think I'll visit the garage, meet Mr. Zoren."

"Good idea," Sam said, "but may I suggest a strategy with Zoren. Ask to see the books. See if a new company name appears on any of the export documents. Then we will go and visit a friend of mine at Driver and Vehicle Licensing."

Peter had left the Subaru keys in the office and Mayta produced a set from somewhere — Peter could not imagine where she had pockets — and tossed them to Peter. "You want Sam to drive you?"

"I'm okay," Peter said. Mayta leaned forward and gave him a kiss on the cheek. She glared at Sam and retreated. The two men watched her disappear inside. "I'm just curious, Sam, but is there an Armenian church in Whittlesun?"

"No, we're too small a community. You have to go to St. Sarkis in London. But we Armenians are everywhere."

Peter promised to call Sam within a couple of hours.

The yard in front of Lasker's Garage was populated with five-year-old sedans of various makes. Peter idly wondered if ocean salt threatened their paint jobs if they were left too long in the open; these had stood a while in the lot, he estimated. He recalled that the work areas could be accessed through the corridor at the back of the office, but when he approached the shed, he found it dark and silent. The door was locked and the venetian blind in the window had been pulled down. He went back to the street and checked the access ramp: the corrugated door had been lowered and bolted. Back at the office, he found a scribbled note taped to the corner of the door window: "Closed for funeral." He tried to peer through the window and he jiggled the doorknob again. There was nothing overtly suspicious about the place, but every policeman's instinct told him that uninvited visitors should be careful. He tried a firm but not insistent knock.

He knocked twice more and still heard nothing from inside. But he had a feeling that someone was waiting for him to depart, standing stock still in the dark interior of the office, or more likely farther back in the work bays. Peter looked in through the slats in the blind but failed to discern any vehicles. He was unwilling to break in without a warrant, since the evidence he was seeking was documentary and the process had to be kosher if the paperwork was to do any good later in court. He waited a full minute and rapped a fourth time, a little more aggressively.

A piece of iron, probably a wrench, hit the floor. The door swung open, almost as if by itself, and Peter peered into the gloom. He could see a man's booted feet nearer the back of the room but couldn't make out the man's face; the tip of a wheel brace poked out from the shadows on the floor. He detected no oil or acetylene that would indicate a repair job in process.

A light flashed on, one of those floor-level lamps favoured by mechanics, and it lit up the man's face from below. The effect, as intended, was to startle Peter and drive him back to the exit; the face was very Boris Karloff, he immediately thought, the light emphasizing the deep grooves of the cheeks and the prominent Slavic nose.

"Who the hell are you?" Albrecht Zoren said.

"Chief Inspector Peter Cammon. I was here the other day."

"I haven't seen Lasker at all," he volunteered.

"I'm coming in," Peter ventured.

"No you're not!" Zoren said, picking up the brace and slamming it down on the corner of the office desk. The blow took off a sizeable chunk of the veneer and the plywood core. Peter recoiled, stepping back into the daylight, but only for a moment. He quickly judged that the man had expended his immediate anger; there was a cooling of the atmosphere in the office. Zoren wasn't the owner of the facility; he had limited authority to keep a policeman out. It also seemed to Peter that he hadn't been toiling on a repair, and he could see enough of the area behind the desk to grasp that Zoren hadn't been fussing over the account books or customer records either. Peter sized up the mechanic's potential for violence. He ought to know that police visits would continue until Lasker was found. Peter kept his hands in his pockets and edged forward. He decided to counter Zoren's aggressive posture with a bit of verbal melodrama.

"I'm not armed, Mr. Zoren." *Why would I be?* Zoren placed the wheel brace on the desk and backed further into the office. Peter

moved inside. He found the light switch and turned it on. Albrecht
Zoren had positioned himself against the side wall, his fists raised
like a defending boxer. But then his shoulders sagged and he looked
down at the linoleum floor. His coveralls were stained with oil, and
grease streaked his cheeks; redness and grimy sweat rimmed his eyes.

"Sally died," he said.

Peter recalled his one visit with the bookkeeper. He estimated that
she was only about sixty. "I'm sorry. What was the cause?"

"Heart attack. She was a smoker. I never smoked beyond the first
year of my apprenticeship. Can't do smoking working under the
chassis of the autos."

"You didn't go to the funeral?"

"I could not stand it," Zoren whined. "She taught me English."

Zoren didn't appear to be management material, yet Sam had
been sure that he was guiding Lasker's through this period of limbo.
Undoubtedly, Zoren felt betrayed by circumstances, his anchors of
Lasker, and now Sally, yanked away in the cruellest fashion.

"I'm sorry," he repeated. "I'll bet the rest of the staff appreciates
your efforts."

"My efforts to keep the place going?" Zoren said, his voice turning
harder. "I can get a job anywhere tomorrow. But Lasker left behind
a very good business. He promised me a share. Now there is no one,
nobody in charge, no owner. Not even a bookkeeper."

Zoren was right. It would take months to sort out the ownership.
The matter would shift from the criminal authorities to the bank-
ruptcy courts, and after interminable debate, the easiest thing for
everyone would be to wind up the company. There was little solace
that Peter could offer. Instead, he changed tack.

"What do you think André Lasker was trying to do?"

The twisty phrasing of the question was deliberate; let the
mechanic interpret it his own way. But Zoren wasn't interested. He
eyed the wheel brace, picked it up from the desk and disappeared into
the work bays without a word. Peter followed as far as the doorway.
He observed that there were only three cars under repair, a Mercedes,

a Vauxhall and a Morris. Zoren was standing over the bonnet of the Mercedes but merely stared down at the car, as if it were some alien beast. Peter recalled that there had been seven or eight vehicles when he first visited the shop. The unfortunate, and sudden, death of the bookkeeper shouldn't have forced Zoren, or whoever was handling the place, to reject business. It struck him that Lasker's Garage was in serious decline.

The sense of danger remained, but Peter was in a mood, the source of which he couldn't identify, to barge ahead. Perhaps, he thought, the incident along the cliffs has changed me, a reminder of mortality and all that. He dismissed the thought. More likely, he reasoned, I'm tired of parrying with the Whittlesunites. Everyone was vague about André Lasker. The man had disappeared like smoke, but few locals seemed to care, or have any curiosity about how he pulled it off. Intimate that he had absconded with a million pounds and the vicar's wife, and they would perk up, but for now they remained indifferent.

Peter had little concern that Zoren would come raging out of the recesses of the garage to crown him with the iron bar. He returned to the tiny office and stepped around the ruined desk and the splinters on the floor. While listening for any unusual sounds from Zoren's direction, he took down the ledger that, according to the label on the binding, covered the previous year of transactions. It was filled with yellow copies of invoices and summaries of repair work done. He found little correlation between repair jobs and the marketing of automobiles for sale. André Lasker's sales of fix-ups could only be described as occasional. He had kept this work off the books. Moreover, Sally, whose residual perfume clung to the pages of the binder like a memory, seemed indifferent to the repair-and-sale flow-throughs. Rarely were repair cost sheets stapled to the eventual sales invoices. Peter soon realized that Sally's binders covered only domestic sales. Foreign transactions had to be kept elsewhere, he surmised. Of course, it would have been easier for Lasker to abscond with a separate binder. But Sally hadn't mentioned the disappearance of any paperwork when Peter visited the first time. She had been a loyal and fastidious employee, clearly a linchpin in the operation. The gap in her precisely aligned shelf would have distressed her.

Peter took down several more binders and riffled the pages like a flip book. No foreign transactions were listed. He guessed that Lasker sold forty vehicles a year domestically, scarcely more. A quick scan of the sale prices showed modest profits on each transaction. The money would have been in the export traffic.

A stack of unfiled papers sat on the credenza against the back wall. He shuffled through them but found only more of the same. He opened the deep drawer at the left side of the crippled desk; it revealed personal items, hand cream and cigarettes. The middle drawer of the bank of three on the right gave him what he wanted. Three pale blue sheets bore the logo of the European Community; they were stapled to other forms displaying the title of the British DVLA, and were stamped *For Export*. Peter removed them, reviewed all three, closed the drawer and folded the pages twice so that they fit into the inner breast pocket of his jacket. He slipped away without looking for Zoren. It wasn't clear to him why the mechanic was at the garage at all. Probably he just couldn't think of anything else to do that would justify his evasion of Sally's funeral. He was unstable, and Peter pretty much dismissed the possibility that Zoren had been André's partner in crime.

Peter returned to Sam's and explained his adventure in full to the mechanic and Mayta. They pored over the three blue invoices, both of them nodding with apparent understanding. Once they were done, Sam punched the buttons of his mobile, which was answered at once. "Okay, Martin," Sam said into the line. "We have a name, we think." He handed the phone over to Peter. "My nephew at the DVLA."

Peter took the phone. Mayta held up a snapshot, one of those school portraits, of a young man with black hair. "Martin," she mouthed.

"This is Martin at the Driver and Vehicle Licensing Agency," a young, baritone voice said. It matched, in Peter's mind, the school portrait. "Sam tells me you have a name."

The tone was eager. Sam nodded encouragingly to Peter. Evidently the young man was ecstatic that anyone would want to talk intelligently about the manipulation of auto exports under European Community regulations.

"I have two names," Peter said. Sam held up one of the invoices, Mayta the other two. "There are three different cars covered by the forms. Each transaction is authorized by a blue EC form and a white U.K. carbon containing exactly the same data. Two were the property of Artistic Auto Reclaim and the third was exported by Western Auto Flow Sales."

"Give me the date stamp on the forms, and the model and vehicle identification number for each unit," the boy said.

Peter cited the data. Two of the exports were Mercedes and the third was a Saab. All had shipped within the previous six months.

"All right," the boy said, with undiminished enthusiasm. "I'll run these right away. If you come by the office in about an hour, I'll have a lot more facts about all three."

"Can you run a search for all the exports made by those two companies?"

"In a flash," the boy said. "In the past, the problem has been incompatibility of computer records. Now that Brussels has centralized computer registrations, it's a lot simpler to track the history of most vehicles."

"Does Britain have different rules for exporting vehicles?" Peter asked.

"Not so as to impair the export trade. No one wants to block used car sales within the EU. Half the taxi fleets east of Paris depend on the trade. No one much worries as long as the fees are collected."

"Is this the kind of business a garage owner could engage in profitably?"

"Certainly, but this is where a strategic decision has to be made.

He can sell a vehicle as a scrap item, for parts, and do virtually nothing to prepare it. Easy to do under both British and European rules."

"I don't want to jump the gun," Peter said, "but could that be what my guy was doing?"

"Maybe, but probably not. There's a lot more money in cars that can be resold as quality items. Not luxury cars, that's a whole different set of fiddles, but good used cars. For that you need full registration, verifiable engine numbers and cylinder capacity, chassis number and a British Changes to Current Vehicle Form. You don't want some customs official in Rotterdam reading *Scrap* on a ship's manifest while he's looking at a refurbished Mercedes 280SL.

"What if someone tries to use false corporate names throughout the export process?"

"Can be done, and it happens all the time, but at some point there's got to be an *individual* name stated as the contact person for the company, and that's where he may get tripped up. If your corporate name is phoney, and your signatory is invented, and the listed phone number doesn't check out, you run a big risk. Best to give a real name. Look, if you do this regularly . . ."

Peter's mobile phone chimed in his pocket and he jumped. He hated to cut off Martin's lecture, but the readout showed that it was Stan Bracher, and that meant something urgent. He did the usual juggle, telling Martin to hold, then asked Stan to hold while he dealt with the young man.

"Martin, I have a call I need to take. Can I meet you at the DVLA in, say, an hour and a half?" He could delay his rendezvous with Gwen by a half hour, and fit in lunch somewhere along the way.

"Sure," Martin said cheerfully, and Peter handed Sam back his phone.

"Stan," Peter said, "where are you?"

"At the lab."

"Find out anything new?"

"Still examining the car. But I also went through the papers collected from the home. Found a third Ryanair ticket stub for

London–Bucharest. Also, interestingly, a reverse ticket to London that was cancelled."

Peter was suddenly in the mood to make a guess. "I bet it was for the mother to come to Britain."

"Right," Stan replied. "Then she chickened out."

"How's the car?"

"A bloodbath to rival the lavatory scene. She was bleeding profusely. And the wind up on the cliffs that night. That's why I went up there this morning."

This was the second time Stan had tried to make sure that Peter knew about his visit to the cliffs. Was Stan making a point? But the silence that followed had little to do with Anna's trials and travels. Peter at once understood that Stan was calling about something else.

"Peter, that's not what I'm calling about. They've moved up the press conference to three o'clock."

"Today?"

"Yup. Hamm's feeling better, apparently. I talked to him briefly. He called me. Maris wants to keep the momentum going, whatever that means, and intends to catch the evening news cycle."

This could only mean that Maris didn't mind if Peter missed the news event entirely. Hamm had been instructed not to call Peter, and that was why he had called Bracher.

Peter sighed. "Will you be there, Stan?"

"Reluctantly. If I can get the blood off my pants. I'm a member of the Task Force, but you're the co-hero on this one. Good luck with that, buddy."

Peter stood in Sam's lot, the sun now spotlighting the three of them as it crossed between the tall buildings on either side. He held his mobile in one hand and Mayta's flask in the other. Stan and Peter had Maris pegged. He understood that Jack McElroy was losing it, and might soon step down as chair of the Task Force, leaving an opening for himself.

"Will Jack McElroy be there?" Peter said.

"Word is, he's not. There's a rumour of a nervous breakdown. I like Jack a lot, Peter, and I wish him well. Pressure's getting to him, I guess. Why don't you come out to Regional and pick me up. We've got time. I can show you the car."

"I don't think so, Stan," Peter said. "I'm going to try to get some rest before the media scrum."

"Looks like Pathology is doing the preliminary work-up on Molly Jonas. I may sit in, but I won't miss the press event. Just thought you should know."

"Right."

"Peter, something a bit funny happened. When I told Ron Hamm about the autopsy on the girl, he became agitated."

"In what way?"

"Keen to sit in, to observe the autopsy. I had the impression he's never done one."

Peter thought about Hamm's enthusiasm for all elements of the Lasker case, but this was different. Hamm had no need to attend the examination of Molly. Stan misinterpreted Peter's silence.

"You know, Peter, you could skip the press briefing if you're not up to it."

Peter flared. "I don't need a second wife, Stan."

"Good," the Canadian called out cheerfully. "I hate carrying the ball for the Yard. Can you pick me up at the lab at 2:30? We'll drive together."

Peter had Sam call Martin back and reschedule for 9:00 a.m. the next morning. Peter called Gwen again; the mother answered and passed the receiver on to the girl, and he apologized, suggesting he come by after the press conference. He interpreted her pause as indifference — she was not one to complain about a necessary rescheduling — but she finally said, "You know, Peter, you have to finish this."

"What? You mean Lasker?"

"I mean, anything." Her voice had turned hard. "You don't finish anything. You haven't completed the witness interviews. Do you know how André vanished? You don't understand Anna."

Peter was angry, and he didn't expect to be. "How do you know that? How do you know that I haven't finished interviewing the witnesses?"

"Peter, do you feel you're where you should be?"

"No," he admitted.

"You have to understand that time flows. A tragedy unfolds. It will try to get ahead of you, if you don't work to keep up. You have to master time, ride it like a wave."

They both held to a silence. He waited for her to say "Finish it. Finish it!" but instead she whispered, "Whenever you get free, Peter, call."

She hung up. Sam had moved away and was polishing the Subaru with a rag. Mayta stood in the office doorway with her face raised to the sun. Peter felt ill with a familiar fever, and wondered if he now held the elixir in the burnished steel container.

"I need to rest, Sam." He checked his watch: half past noon; time enough for a nap before picking Stan up. "I'll head back to the hotel."

Sam offered a shrug. "Take a nap here, Inspector."

"In the office?" Peter said.

"No, no. For a detective, you have to be more observant. We have an apartment behind the office. Very practical."

He pondered how many customers took a nap behind Sam's garage, and with what understandings. It would be smart to avoid the Sunset Arms before the press conference. Sam led him into the office, where Mayta took over, ushering him through what was effectively a dark tunnel, into a back room and yet another passageway. He found himself in a cosy bedroom with a cot made up with a puffy duvet; there was no window. A beaded curtain across the doorway completed the seraglio atmosphere. On a side table stood several liquor bottles, and Mayta poured a shot from one of them.

"More tea?" Peter said.

"No, just straight-up brandy."

He was asleep two minutes after she tucked him in.

CHAPTER 20

Mayta shook him awake at 2:10. He could have slept forever, having sunk into intense REM dreams, none of which he remembered. He awoke to the thrum of a motor outside, either a well-tuned car engine or an air conditioner. Mayta said nothing, but as he sat up, struggling to get his bearings, she handed him a wet cloth, with which he wiped his forehead. She tapped a large-faced Swatch wristwatch to show him that he should hurry. Nonetheless, as he stood up, she took the time to straighten his shirt collar and brush his hair; she helped him on with his coat and squared the shoulders so that he was presentable. He followed her through the tunnel and into the parking area of Sam's Auto. Sam himself heard their approach and slipped out from under a Mercedes parked across from the Subaru. The humming noise came from the German sedan.

"The SatNav is set," he reported.

Mayta handed him the Subaru keys. She had yet to speak, and now she merely helped him into the driver's seat. She did peer into his eyes, but only nodded her satisfaction. It seemed tacitly agreed that there was no need to say anything. He waved as he exited the lot.

Stan was waiting at the broad glass doors of the entrance to the Regional Forensics Laboratory when Peter arrived. The place had a deserted look, as morgues and pathology labs often do. The Canadian got in and put on his seat belt. He was dressed in a tie and jacket, rare for Stan, with no bloodstains on the trousers.

"Let's boot it," he said.

Peter was fully awake now. "Is McElroy still expected to be absent?"

"Don't know," Stan replied. "I've had no contact with them since we spoke. Looking forward to being on TV?"

"No." Peter wasn't sure how he would react, physically or mentally, to any queries from the press. The nap had revived him, but his elbow ached; he would have appreciated a quick workout at a gym.

"I'm satisfied about Anna's suicide," Stan said.

"She was alive when she went over the edge?"

"The car proves it. You really should see the mess inside. How she made it without passing out, I don't know."

"How *did* she make it?" Peter said.

"She was bleeding when she got into the car, and it kept up all the way to the parking pad up on the cliffs. Stains all around the top half of the steering wheel. Smudges on the seat from menstrual blood. Leakage from her arms and skull. The clincher is the near absence of blood elsewhere in the sedan. Anna's palm prints are on the right front door and hood — sorry, bonnet — but nothing in the back seat, and little on the passenger side. André Lasker did not dump his wife in the trunk, nor was Anna ever seated in the passenger seat."

"Boot," Peter said.

"Right."

"We really should go over this with Bartleben," Peter said. "What about toxicology?"

"Traces of sertraline. No other drugs. And no, no fertility drugs."

"Sertraline is Zoloft?"

"Yes, but I think her prescription ran out. There wasn't much in her system, and no pills in the home."

For the next twenty minutes, as Peter steered them towards the Whittlesun station, they built a likely scenario, strong enough so that both of them, speaking from somewhat different perspectives, could attest to it in court. Anna must have confronted her husband that night as he was preparing to leave the house for good. She might have surprised him with how much she knew. She pleaded with him to stay and didn't believe, at first, that he would abandon her. At some point, he stormed out into the street. There was nothing that didn't seem final, yet she struggled for solace, for a hint of compassion from him. He fled. She stood in the front hall and reflected on what to do. The neighbours hadn't reported any screaming or confrontation in the street in front of the house. This proved that when she emerged from the front door, he was gone, and when she saw that he had left the family car behind, it finally sank in that he had cast her off, and every other symbol of their life.

Her abandonment was complete. Stan believed, although he didn't claim to be certain, that she then retreated to the living room and pulled the curtains to the floor in her anger and desperation. It was the kind of halfway commitment to destroying her marriage that would still allow her to go back — if only he came back for her. But then she lashed out, smashing the vase that had been a valued wedding gift, and this transitional act shocked her. She went to the kitchen and stove in the panes in the two glass doors in the bank of cupboards. She drew blood, scarring the fleshy pad of her right hand. Stan pointed to a photograph showing a stain on a shard of glass. "She was right-handed," he said.

Anna went upstairs to the lavatory, likely intending to kill herself. But she wasn't yet beyond the call of sanity. Who was she? The mirror reflected the face of a wife who wasn't beautiful enough to keep her husband. She removed her clothes. She wasn't in the least beautiful in her own eyes. The nylons — she never liked pantyhose — hung on the shower rod, wafting in the air that came from the heat duct next to the bath and seductively mocking her. She decided to kill herself in the tub. But then the ultimate cruelty. She began to bleed, and that blood was a final affront. She got out of the bath and stared once again into the mirror above the sink. She butted the medicine cabinet mirror with the top of her head, generating more blood. The rampage continued into the upper corridor; she smeared blood in a wavy pattern along the wall, then trailed her hand downstairs — a bit of the mirror was found in the wall by the stairs — and continued her vengeful pattern, defacing the lower hallway. She somehow got dressed again and went out to the car.

Her despair increased as she forced the sedan up the hill to the Upper Cliffs. She couldn't find him. Had André told her that he was going to jump? She reached the concrete pad at the lookout and that's what she did: she looked out to the blackened Channel and saw . . . nothing. There was no way to tell how long she waited on the rim of the cliff.

As they rounded the last major turn into the downtown, Stan turned to him. "You know this Father Salvez, up at the Abbey?"

"Yes. Did you meet him?"

"Yeah. He was walking along a trail just below the parking area. Said he didn't know the Laskers, hadn't noticed a thing. Any chance he's bullshitting?"

"No. Salvez is a non-combatant." Peter remained sceptical about Bracher's reasons for venturing up to the cliffs, and didn't ask for Stan's impressions of the sick priest. He didn't want them.

Every imaginable rationalization had him avoiding the media spectacle. He considered arriving late, or sending Stan on ahead. He would try to slip into the back of the room and let Maris occupy the spotlight. Of course, there were good reasons to attend, aside from Bartleben insisting that he go — or he would have insisted, had either of them bothered to call him. Peter was curious about how much the press already knew, and whether they were ready to feed public panic regarding the dead girls. He suspected that regional politicians had pressured Maris to show restraint and generally underplay the crisis. Peter had absorbed the regional papers, read a couple of Reuters feeds and the Task Force media package, but in sum, the Task Force had revealed the facts in dribs and drabs, with scant detail about the Rover's pattern and profile. The reporters would push for particulars. Maris, controlling the show, might throw him and Stan to the pack, blaming them for the shortfall in behavioural analysis. And, for reasons he couldn't yet pinpoint, he wanted to see Wendie Merwyn, the blond from TV-20, in action.

The cluster of reporters and officials around the station forced Cammon and Bracher to park up the street. This time they entered through the back door, for once avoiding the Plexiglas guardroom. Peter squeezed by the crowd into the conference room without anyone marking him as Scotland Yard; even the local officers seemed to understand that he would be deferring to Hamm's moment of fame. Two cameras and a bank of microphones had been set up in makeshift fashion, with folding chairs for the press and two long tables across one end of the room for police officials. There was precious little space for the TV camera operators to position themselves; questioners would have to crane around one or the other camera and dodge cables strung across the floor. The microphones seemed inadequate to Peter; there were only three of them, and so speakers at the front would be awkwardly passing the mikes back and forth.

He knew that his placement at the front had been predetermined, and was inevitable. He reminded himself to stay cool and present a blank face to the cameras. He repeated his mantra: keep the two bloody cases separate.

The meeting was still minutes away, and so he retreated to the outer room. He couldn't find Wendie Merwyn, but he knew she would show. He spotted Maris huddled by one of the pillars, giving an interview to a newspaper columnist. Ron Hamm was nowhere in sight, although he could already have entered the conference room. A young policewoman announced that the "briefing" was about to start, and the stragglers in the anteroom began to filter inside.

He tried to be the last in. Even so, Inspector Maris, who had claimed the Chair's position at the head table, drew a bead on him from the far corner of the room and scowled. He almost seemed prepared to have one of his officers usher Peter out to the asphalt. Jerry Plaskow, also at the front, urgently gestured for Peter to take a seat beside him. Maris tracked him as he wound through the crowd and equipment.

The police contingent arrayed themselves in a line behind the draped tables: Hamm, Maris, Plaskow, Peter and Finter, the slick young assistant who had briefed the officers on the Rover and who evidently now represented McElroy and the Devon wing of the Task Force. The space was both oppressive and chaotic, boding poorly for controlled interaction with the press. Peter estimated that six reporters flanked the two cameras, which appeared to be in competition rather than pooled, resulting in double the illumination necessary. He identified — barely, in the blast of light — two technicians negotiating the stopping down of the camera lamps.

To start, Maris stood up, causing the two cameras to lurch to the right, like prison-tower searchlights, and everyone at the table winced in the glare. He set his voice an octave lower than normal and, after first testing his microphone, struck his theme. "Good afternoon. Thank you for coming. As chief of the Whittlesun Force and acting chairperson of the Joint Police Task Force, it is my sad duty to confirm that the body of Molly Jonas has been found. We will provide forensic details concerning the victim in due course, but assuredly within the next twenty-four hours. Today, we will respond to questions about the search for, and discovery of, Miss Jonas. I caution you not to be too speculative about this series of crimes, because I and my colleagues certainly won't be. My colleague, and chair of the Task Force, Chief Inspector J.J. McElroy, cannot be here today, but I will adhere to his policy of respecting the dignity of these young crime victims. We are intent on conducting a methodical and thorough investigation, drawing upon the police forces of Devon and Dorset Counties, and any additional police agencies that can help across Southwest Region. Finally, I wish to highlight the heroic efforts of Lieutenant Plaskow of the RN and Ports Security, Chief Inspector Cammon of New Scotland Yard and Detective Hamm of the Whittlesun Force."

He sat down; the lights remained on his stoic face. There was a momentary, stiff silence. Peter understood Maris's strategy. The conventional move would have been to anticipate their questions at the outset and talk out the clock, and thereby dictate the agenda. But Maris knew that he had few good answers yet to the basic questions about the Rover, particularly his identity, but also his predatory pattern. Filling up the time with details of the exciting hunt along the cliffs offered the better approach. Peter waited for the planted questions.

For twenty minutes, the session took on a tentative rhythm, with a reporter posing a deferential query, with a follow-up about progress made by the Task Force. Maris soon brought the discussion back to Hamm's bravery and doggedness, while Hamm himself modestly filled in a lightweight storyline. It was a shining moment for Ron; his gentle, factual answers, embedded in a tone of self-effacing professionalism, showed a maturity Peter hadn't seen before. Peter himself was grateful to avoid fielding any queries himself.

But all this was preliminary. The newspaper reporter Peter had seen outside caucusing with Maris stepped out to one side of the camera.

"Inspector, is the predator likely to kill again soon? It's been said that he's following a lunar cycle. And, doesn't his pattern of attacks, so far, prove that he's progressing in a straight line eastward into Dorset?"

It may have seemed at first to be a provocative question but it was another plant, setting up Maris to return the attention of the media to the work of the coordinated police agencies.

"That," Maris responded, "is speculative. The search we undertook yesterday — and remember that all those involved in that effort are members of the Task Force — is an example of cooperative, extensive mobilization of regional police agencies. Under Chief Inspector McElroy's leadership, we are trying to blanket the coastal zone with a large contingent of police personnel. This strikes the right balance."

Peter caught Jerry recoil at the term "coastal zone.'" The wild

Channel was never so self-contained. Jerry mischievously leaned over to Peter and whispered, "Can the three of us have dinner later, Peter?"

The three included Sarah, Peter understood, having already suggested dinner with her. He had no choice but to nod his assent.

The same reporter played along. "How many officers have been assigned?"

"Dozens," Maris stated, remaining seated. "Don't forget, we have access to the Regional Laboratory's resources, other county forces and New Scotland Yard."

This stratagem was a mistake. Maris had little to deliver on the criminal profiling front. If I were a reporter, Peter thought, I'd ask if the Yard was prepared to take over the investigation. The answer would be no, but . . .

The same reporter, a little too eagerly, jumped in: "Has Scotland Yard done a behavioural assessment of the killer?"

Maris saved Peter from having to dissemble. The cameras stayed on the Whittlesun chief. "We are developing our profile here. We believe the killer is a male, relatively young given that he carried two, possibly three of his victims some distance, and he's comfortable with the territory along the coast. Even so, we're not prepared to state that he is a local man. He seizes opportunities. We are watching."

Maris handled other questions artfully, sidestepping any inference that Dorset residents should panic. Peter thought it true cosmic luck that the Olympics were not mentioned at all. Several newswire and TV reporters tried to probe the issue of public fear as the Rover moved east, but Maris reiterated the tandem themes of public precaution and increased police surveillance of the cliffs. The lock-up-your-daughters refrain, in Peter's opinion, would wear itself out soon, but for now it bought the Task Force some time. It all depended on deterring the predator from further attacks on the high cliffs. It was also fortunate for Maris that the questioning by the press reps was poorly coordinated. But Peter was flabbergasted by the complete absence of questions concerning Daniella Garvena, until he realized that someone had put the screws to the media outlets across southern

Britain; they had agreed to respect the Italian family's privacy. But how long could this manipulation last, and what promises had been made to gain media cooperation?

Peter glanced at Maris's smug face. The inspector was doing a fine job of burning up the time, and was almost home, safe as houses.

Wendie Merwyn, whom Peter had failed to see lurking behind one of the cameras in the middle of the room, stepped forward. She focused on Peter. "Has New Scotland Yard been directly involved? Is there some thinking that the Yard should take over the Rover case?"

Peter knew where she was going with this, and so did Inspector Maris. Peter was tempted to shunt the question off to the Whittlesun chief, but he was saved by the failure of Merwyn's cameraman to follow her line of sight. The bright lights stayed on Maris, and he jumped in.

"At the risk of sounding bureaucratic, the Yard is providing cooperative liaison. They have volunteered all their capacity, as needed, but the Task Force remains a Regional operation, and that is sufficient for the moment."

It was apparent to both Peter and Maris that Merwyn, not surprisingly, was digging for a headline, and "cooperative liaison" wasn't it. But his non-reply left an opening for a supplementary from the blond news anchor — Why, then, haven't you made more progress? What, then, does Chief Inspector Cammon bring to the table, and why was he gallivanting around the Jurassic Cliffs yesterday morning? But she posed neither question. Peter found her intriguing.

Hamm's energy was flagging, and Maris moved to sum up. Peter saw the risk: they were hopeful of getting away unscathed, but Maris had been too vague. He had to give them something for the front page, yet his wrap-up was more of the same.

"We are doubling our police presence inside Dorset, but it makes sense for residents not to wander, not to let their children go off without supervision and, naturally, not to talk to strangers. You know each other and you know your community, and you are in the best position to notice the unusual . . ."

He thought he was safe, but Wendie Merwyn stepped forward again. This time Peter was staring into a lens and bright lights. She had been redirecting the camera, and that was the reason she hadn't launched a supplementary question. Now, she stood almost touching the head table. The camera swooped in on her, and Peter sensed that it would soon turn to his face for a close-up reaction.

"Chief Inspector Cammon," she began in her mezzo newsreader tone, "I understand that you are managing the investigation into the death of Anna Lasker, and the disappearance of her husband."

Peter stated calmly: "I am assisting, and . . ."

"Assisting when you are not leading searches along the cliffs for the predator known as the Rover. Which is Scotland Yard's priority?"

"Neither investigation is being led by New Scotland Yard."

"Chief Inspector, can you tell us where the Lasker case stands at this point? It has been two weeks or more. Do you know where André Lasker is?"

Maris stood up but the camera failed to move over his way. "The investigation of Mrs. Lasker is continuing and is making progress," he said, to hollow space.

"Has an arrest warrant been issued for Anna Lasker's murder?" she persisted, with the camera still on Peter.

"No."

"Why not?" she said.

"Because," said Peter, "Anna Lasker committed suicide."

CHAPTER 21

Why the hell had he done it? He didn't know. (Stan Bracher, later reporting back to Bartleben, said, "That's the kind of crap Cammon is always pulling.")

Perhaps only Merwyn, Maris and Peter immediately understood his revelation. Other reporters had been entirely focused on the Rover murders and resented her shifting attention to a local crime on which there had been little progress. Peter's answer certainly begged a follow-up, but Maris at once called the session to an end, and everyone stood up, eager to leave the stuffy room. For once, Peter was glad to be short, and he attempted to slip away through the out-flowing police detectives. He only succeeded in evading Maris by the quick assistance of Jerry Plaskow. He caught the eye of Bracher, who offered only what Peter's mother would have called a "watery" smile; there would be no rescue by the Canadian, and Peter decided that Stan would have to find his own way back to the hotel. Jerry took him by the elbow and hustled him out the back of the Whittlesun station and into the parking area. They paused, out of breath.

"I think we'd better run for it," Jerry said. Neither man was encumbered by files or briefcases, and so Jerry began to jog towards the back of the lot. Moving around cars and motorcycles, and a

TV-20 equipment van, they ran to the next street, and only a block later did they dare stop. They had distanced any pursuers and now, Peter gauged, they were two streets up and two over from his Subaru. Jerry made to leave in the other direction. Peter didn't worry about whether Jerry had transportation. He was one of those soldiers who disappeared into the night, like Peter's SAS guardian angel.

"What was that all about?" Jerry said.

"It happens sometimes," Peter replied, calm now. He looked up and down the street. He had stepped back from the drama in the briefing room, and was more or less philosophical about it now.

Plaskow reacted in the best possible way. He laughed. "Are you still up for dinner tonight?"

"Certainly," Peter said. "Let's eat in the hotel restaurant. As far as I can tell, it's decent. Do you know where Sarah is staying?"

"Not at the Sunset Arms. I've arranged to pick her up at seven at the Marine Institute. Is 7:30 good for you?"

"Sure. Gives me time to . . . recover." He was perspiring.

"How are you feeling?'

"Bruises are healing. Jerry . . . ?"

"Yup."

It was time to pay some dues. "Could you thank your colleague for me?"

"Smith."

"Your SAS man is named Smith?"

"No," Jerry laughed. "Better get out of here, Inspector."

When Peter retrieved his rental car, he sat looking straight ahead at the empty street. The crowd from the briefing had dispersed, but it was safer to abandon the area entirely. He turned the Subaru around and climbed randomly into an unfamiliar part of the grid until he found a deserted side avenue with a view of the sea.

The street was dead quiet. He wasn't in the mood he expected to be in. For one thing, he felt little interest in chewing over why he'd done it. He glanced down the hill at the Whittlesun rooftops and, although he spied no landmarks, he knew precisely where the Sunset Arms stood, and how to reach it by road. He had always been terrible with compass points, and this was some kind of progress, to have picked up a new spatial sensitivity at this late age. It gave him new confidence. He would drive back without employing the SatNav.

He thought about his mother, long buried in the democratic City of London Cemetery. She never suffered fools; to his knowledge, his father had managed to avoid conversing with fools entirely. His father had been a barrister, and he valued the finiteness of the law, the closure that the legal process brought to every case. His mother taught, and she was the one with the dreamier, epic view. She talked about "the stages of man." Humans passed through archetypal phases of awareness as they matured. (She taught adolescents English and biology, so Peter supposed she knew.) A boy started out optimistic, she said, with a faith that events were subsets of an epic mechanism, a rolling machine called society. Education was about placement of your experience in that epic context. Peter remembered her caution, though, that too many men and women gave up on the vision; their dreams stalled and dissipated with old age.

For a career policeman, the tension between the epic and the ordinary was never settled. It wasn't even a matter of balance. You lived with both or you went a bit crazy. You might tell yourself that the Rover was a grand villain, diabolical, a one-man schizophrenic cabal, who staged Arthurian farewells in the weathered stone fields of south Britain. But this predator, he believed, wouldn't know a Tennyson lament from a Viking ritual from a sunrise ceremony at Stonehenge. He might be all the more dangerous for his game-playing, but his classical sensibility was shoddy. Killers — especially the ones who toyed with the authorities — often believed they invented murder. All they did was reinvent clichés, inviting the pursuing detective to sink into his nightmare of the sordid, the mundane and the disappointing. The Rover would stay one step ahead, until suddenly he wasn't, and it would take the hard slogging of the police to set the trap.

He gave Maris some credit for understanding this. The inspector had refused to buy into the epic crime spree of the predator. Peter hadn't meant to undermine him with his sudden revelation; he wasn't spiteful. It was a pity that he had had to do it, but there was one fugitive out there who did think in epic terms of crime and just punishment, of guilt and free conscience, of death and the need to affirm life.

He had pronounced Anna's suicide in order to attract André Lasker's attention.

To his surprise, there were no messages for him at the desk at the Sunset Arms, nor was his phone blinking when he got to his room. He washed up but decided not to change his clothes. He was looking forward to dining with Jerry and Sarah and felt quite good, not at all feverish anymore. It would be nice to get back to the cottage — there was no doubt that he was washed up in Whittlesun — and he should probably call Tommy Verden to pick him up tonight, and then he could treat the evening as a farewell dinner. He rang Tommy on the mobile and requested a pickup at Sam's garage at noon the next day. He planned to fit in an appointment with Sam's nephew Martin before abandoning the town. He checked the pockets of his jacket for notes and messages that he might have forgotten, and came up with the purple chits of the calls from Salvez and Wendie Merwyn.

There was a knock on the door. At its worst, it would be Maris, at its best Sarah. He opened the door to confront a young man who looked distantly familiar. He had blond hair, not far off the colour of Wendie Merwyn's, and wore a maroon sports coat worthy of a game show host. He also sported an expensive Burberry raincoat. He smiled with even teeth and came across as overly sincere, but unthreatening.

"Excuse me, Inspector Cammon? Wendie Merwyn asked me to leave you this message?" His voice turned up with uncertainty. He held out a sealed envelope.

"And you are?"

255

"I'm Parnell Moss, reporter with TV-20. I'm known as Parny Moss."

Peter's immediate reaction was that the young fellow was likeable but wanted too much to be liked; well mannered, but on the superficial side. Peter recognized him now, though not the name. He was the weatherman on the television sitting beside Wendie Merwyn at the anchor desk. He was even more handsome in person than on the box. Peter reassessed him: he had the right kind of persuasive authority beneath the veneer, and would do well as a news reader.

"Why didn't she give it to me herself?"

"She's on air, like, now. She had to run from the press conference. I'm only about fifteen minutes behind her myself."

"But you're the weatherman?"

"Among other things. That's why I have to get back. Wendie's doing the news now, and I tag on at the end. I'm also a reporter and a news reader. We do a bit of everything at 20. We're a small staff."

Peter ripped open the envelope and read the note, which was what he expected: *Can we meet to follow up? Join forces? What is Kidd's Reach? Wendie M.* The third question mark was written with an elaborate curlicue. Parnell Moss stood waiting.

"I don't wish to be presumptuous, Mr. Moss, but were you hoping to interview me yourself?"

"Wendie says *she* needs to pose her questions to you." With that self-effacing reply — or was it self-effacing? — the fellow lost momentum and looked down at the carpet. Peter decided not to embarrass him further.

"So, does everyone ask you if your parents named you after Parnell, the Irish revolutionary?"

"No. My real name is 'Partnell.' A family thing. I thought it better sounding to adopt 'Parnell.' More dignified that way. Then I came down to this job, and the station manager suggested 'Parny' had a friendly feel."

Even with this slightly evasive answer, Peter still thought he detected an Irish lilt in the boy's chatter. He was mildly curious to hear his on-air voice, and speculated that the accent would emerge as BBC neutral; or, showing the talent for mimicry that ambitious TV personalities seemed to have, he might already have picked up the regional inflections. For that matter, Peter wanted to hear Wendie Merwyn's broadcast voice again; he needed a better fix on her.

"Tell Miss Merwyn that she can call me here, leave a message." ·

Parnell Moss thanked Peter and strode away down the corridor.

It was about time to meet Jerry and Sarah. He turned on the television, but for some reason could not find Wendie Merwyn's newscast; she had probably just finished. He took the elevator to the lobby, desperate for a drink. His daughter and Plaskow had already found a table at the back of the shadowed restaurant.

"Fancy meeting you," Jerry said, lightly.

Sarah sat to Jerry's right and jumped up from her seat to give her father a tight hug. She looked him up and down, assessing his health, and maybe his state of mind, he thought. In the recesses of the restaurant there was barely enough light to read faces, but the shadows allowed them to indulge in conspiratorial talk. Sarah was openly glad to be with her father, and Jerry knew it, and the two veterans of the crime wars were happy to be drinking at the end of this very long day. Plaskow commanded a rum and Coke from the waitress. Peter ordered beer, as usual, while Sarah already had a bottle of claret in front of her. They took a moment, sipped their drinks. Peter looked at Sarah, and her response showed that she didn't mind shop talk. She was completely relaxed and promised to interject when she felt like it. Jerry struck the right upbeat note immediately by mentioning what, on another night, might have been verboten.

"Mr. Smith thanks you," he said. Peter explained who his rescuer was, although Plaskow added few background details about the SAS commando.

"I'm afraid I lost both your walkie-talkies in the drink." ·

"That's okay. He went back for them."

"You mean he *dove* for them? Were they that valuable?"

"Well, Peter, Smith was diving for the bicycle anyway. Thought he might as well retrieve the radios as well."

"He found it?"

"Sure. Maris sent his people out to search the cave. We helped. But they found nothing beyond that wool hat belonging to the poor girl." Jerry made the sign of the cross. "So, Peter, what was that all about this afternoon?"

"I'm guessing that Lasker is alive. I wanted to goose him a little, make him feel guilty."

"Maris was pretty steamed."

Peter murmured his understanding, but there was no guilt in his voice. "I'm leaving tomorrow, ahead of the firestorm." He looked at Sarah. "Lasker's out there."

"I'll bet Maris's already been on the blower to Sir Stephen," Jerry said.

"We'll run it from London for a while," Peter said resignedly, but without going into detail.

He explained what Jerry would already know but Sarah would not. "Maris will shift the burden of non-success to the Yard anyway. It was already starting to happen. It's in the Yard's interest to find Lasker any way we can, either through Interpol or Passport Services."

"Or," Sarah said "at some point you come back and arrest him in Whittlesun."

"You figure he's alive, and in touch with events?" Jerry said.

Peter hesitated, and then looked at Sarah. "I was thinking about your grandmother today." He glanced over at Jerry to show that he was welcome in the conversation. "She used to say to me that people don't understand the balance between the epic and the ordinary, and they get worse at it as they age. You were talking the other night about the day you decided to become a marine biologist. Well, for me, it was that piece of philosophy from my mother."

"That, and Sherlock Holmes," Sarah said.

"Agreed. I've worked for years to figure out how crime works, the psyche behind it and how a policeman should react. Violent crime seems like a grand scheme at the beginning, full of calculating intent and detailed planning. But later, the criminal almost always disappoints you, his motives exposed as callous, his emotions overruling logic, his visionary clarity suddenly murky and not very impressive. It's a lot like life itself. But here's the thing."

Peter paused to give Jerry a chance to complete the analysis. The sailor glanced at Sarah before responding. It was clear to her that he was about to reveal a truth about her father.

"The thing is," Jerry said, "you have to go through the epic stuff before you can understand the bad guys' mistakes."

Peter nodded. "Yes. An ordinary way to put it is that you have to understand his intentions before you understand his pettiness. But it's more than that. André Lasker had a romantic fantasy of what he would find, probably somewhere on the far side of the world. The same with the predator. This Rover fellow thinks he's smarter than everyone else. Seldom have I seen anyone more in love with the game. He toys with us, with his sacrificial posing of the victims, his bloodless kills, but it's all about the game with him. With André, I had to understand what happened at the house before I could understand the husband. And Anna herself made the epic, if gruesome, gesture by desecrating their home and jumping from the cliff. She assaulted his romantic image of himself."

"What do you think is left of the husband's romantic plans for his new life?" Sarah asked.

"I wager that he understands that he blew it," Peter said. "I'm counting on him coming home out of remorse. He won't turn himself in. He hasn't given up on his plan totally. Maybe he'll make a grand gesture. Maybe just a visit to Anna's grave. Then he can leave again."

Jerry appeared startled, and Peter knew what he was thinking. Jerry understood that Peter was manipulating the release of Anna Lasker's body for burial by her family. The Regional Lab was holding it, even though most, if not all, the pathology work was complete. Jerry guessed that Anna's mother in Iasi and her cousins in Britain were already complaining that it was unseemly, even irreligious, to refuse to release the body and give them access to the rotting house. Peter would effect the release of both only when he judged that the husband was desperate to come back to Whittlesun, prepared to search out her grave and confront the painful consequences of her self-destruction.

Peter's splinted finger made him clumsy. He took out his hand-kerchief to wipe his brow and André Lasker's gold band came with it. Sarah recognized the ring but said nothing; Jerry faked disinterest. Peter supposed he should have logged it into evidence at the lab earlier, but he had forgotten. He left it on the table for the moment.

"What does 'Kidd's Reach' mean, Jerry?"

"It's a spot along the cliffs."

"In Dorset?"

"Not quite. Still in Devon."

"It sounds like a bantam-weight prize fighter."

"Nope. Named after Captain Kidd, the pirate. There's a story that he hid treasure along the coast. It's unlikely of course. The story probably reflects the fact there used to be a lot of smuggling and violations of the excise laws, shall we say, all along the Channel."

"Now it's refugees and drugs," Peter suggested.

"And perceived terrorists. Tell me about it." He sighed.

"Is there any possibility that Kidd's Reach is precisely six kilometres from the spot where Molly Jonas turned up?"

"Possibly. I'll check."

They gave up the shop talk to order, and Sarah entertained them with stories of her adventures around the coasts of England and Wales. The next hour passed quickly.

The waitress cleared the table and when she had retreated, Jerry looked at the ring. "That your wedding ring?"

"No. It's André Lasker's."

"You are a strange man, Peter."

The restaurant had turned quiet, with only one other table still occupied. A young man, whom Peter remembered as a desk clerk, came over and handed Peter a business card. It was Wendie Merwyn's. Peter read the scribble on the back: "Chief Inspector, I am in the bar?" Peter noted how much she liked question marks.

"You might want to leave the back way, Jerry."

"Ah, the press?"

Peter nodded. Sarah looked distressed for her father. "Jerry, can you see Sarah home?"

"Of course."

"Is this trouble?" she asked. Peter couldn't tell if her sudden fear was based on shrewd instinct, or a more general anxiety for him.

"It's not a problem, dear. Just local media. I'll be at the cottage tomorrow afternoon. Are you planning on a visit soon?"

She sat forward and reached across the table for his hand. "I'll call Mum tonight, let her know you're okay. Maybe I can get there later in the week."

Peter restrained his fatherly impulse to warn her about the many dangers along the cliffs and beaches. But Sarah knew the tides better than he ever would, and he was the one who had fallen from the cliff face into the churning sea.

As for the Rover, he was preoccupied with younger women.

Wendie Merwyn was sitting in a corner of the bar drinking Perrier and thumbing through a notebook when Peter approached her table. She offered him her reporter's smile; she looked fresh and unmarred by studio makeup.

"Chief Inspector Cammon?"

Peter had a funny feeling that he was about to relive the previous conversation with Jerry Plaskow.

"I'm Wendie Merwyn. We've sort of met."

Peter sat down. He was relaxed. "You asked me the right question at the right time."

"I was so startled I forgot to ask the logical follow-ups. Bad journalism."

"That's okay. I wouldn't have responded anyway. How did your broadcast go tonight?"

She frowned. "Okay. Will you respond now? On or off the record?"

"In my experience," Peter said, "there is no such thing as off the record."

She closed her notebook. "I interviewed Detective Hamm, albeit briefly. He called your actions heroic."

"Hardly. When you think about it, that search along the cliffs was probably foolhardy."

"It brought some comfort to the family of Molly Jonas."

"Did it? I hope so."

"But you're not the investigator of record on the Rover case," she said. Peter could tell that she was a smoker, but he didn't suggest they go outside.

"That would be Chief Inspector McElroy, Chairman of the Task Force."

"At the Whittlesun end of things, I meant."

"That would be Inspector Maris."

"It does raise the question of what brings you to Whittlesun, why you were on the cliffs."

"Let me help you out on that," Peter said, tiring of what was threatening to become a tennis match. "I am an official liaison with the Task Force for New Scotland Yard. One of two. Detective Bracher is the other."

"Why were you the one up on the cliffs with a local detective who himself was out of his jurisdiction?"

"I was not outside *my* jurisdiction, since the Yard has a national mandate, although we try not to go where we are not wanted. As for Mr. Hamm, he was under the direction of Inspector Maris, who is a full member of the Task Force. In fact, he's acting chair."

"It sounds to me that he was operating under your supervision."

"No."

"No?"

It struck Peter that the women in this case were the only ones asking penetrating questions. Gwen. Sarah. Joan. Include Mayta in there.

"Can we go off the record?" Peter said.

"No. This is getting good," she said, impishly.

"For thirty seconds?"

"Okay."

"I was assisting him. We both had the same hunch. It seemed like a long shot at the time."

"You went off the record merely for that?"

"I'm hoping that you won't publicize my part in it. The Yard is not asserting lead responsibility in the Rover matter. I have no desire to embarrass, and certainly not pre-empt, either Inspector Maris or Chief Inspector McElroy."

"Not yet," she riposted. "But if the public doesn't see some progress soon, they'll rise up and likely demand that you move in."

"With some urging from the press?"

"Maybe so."

"Until then . . ." he said.

"Are we negotiating here, Inspector?"

Peter sat back out of the light. He signalled the bartender for an ice water, which was brought over immediately. "What do you know about 'Kidd's Reach'?" he said. "You mentioned it in your note."

"I had a brief discussion with Mr. Finter, Chief Inspector McElroy's aide-de-camp. He let slip that the four attacks occurred six kilometres apart." She paused to grin at him. "Add six more kilometres on my handy map, and that gets you to Kidd's Reach. Are you surveilling Kidd's Reach, Inspector?"

"Lord knows," Peter replied, "I can't do everything."

So surprised was the woman that an ancient Yard detective with a tight little grey moustache would tell a joke that she spurted her drink onto the table and burst out laughing. But she quickly became serious again.

"You're a complicated man, Inspector. I came here to talk about André and Anna Lasker, and we haven't done that yet."

"The Lasker investigation is my primary assignment. You see why I don't want to be strongly associated with the Rover business. It might be confusing."

"It might be embarrassing to Inspector Maris if you cracked both cases, you mean."

"Not likely. I was just helping out Mr. Hamm up on the cliffs. He's also on the Lasker case."

"But Anna Lasker committed suicide, you're sure."

"Yes. And I'd better be."

"Is the husband alive?"

"Now we truly have to go off the record."

"It's a deal."

Peter held back, but only for a few seconds. "Yes, I think he's alive. I have no idea where he is, but I am hopeful he'll surface."

"So to speak."

"So to speak."

She stared right at him. "And I can't publish that?"

He held her gaze. "No, but you can call me for updates, from time to time. We'll see what develops."

"Can you give me a number where I can reach you?'

"Why?"

"Because I am guessing you're leaving town tomorrow. *Persona non grata?*"

The waitress from the restaurant came over to the table and handed him André Lasker's ring.

Wendie looked at it. "Is that your wedding ring?"

"No, Miss Merwyn, it's André Lasker's."

She raised one beautifully pencilled eyebrow. "Mr. Cammon, you are a complicated man."

CHAPTER 22

Peter rang Sam at the garage, even though it was 7:25 a.m. In some way, he hoped Mayta would answer, but Sam picked up on the first ring.

"Inspector, we stayed up to watch you on TV last night."

"Lord, Sam, how did you figure I'd be on TV?"

"Psychic. At least, Mayta's psychic. She also watches TV. She's sitting right here. You want to talk to her?"

"No, but give her my best . . ."

"She sends her love. The cameras make you look pale. We're drinking tea. We're in the Little Room. What can I do for you? How's the car?"

"I'm leaving town this afternoon. In disgrace."

"You said the wrong thing to the television?"

"Exactly. But I need to see Martin before I go. Is it too early to call?"

"Inspector, you don't understand. My nephew has called me *four* times. He has never been this happy." Sam exhaled at the end of the line. "Martin always gets to work early. Just show up."

"Thank you. I'll have the Subaru back by noon."

"Whatever . . . Mayta tells me call ahead to Martin, so I will take care of that now."

"Oh, if an Inspector Verden shows up, tell him I'll be there soon."

"What's he like?"

"Almost as charming as Mayta."

"Wow!"

"But not quite."

"I'll tell her that."

The Subaru's SatNav led him smoothly to the Driver and Vehicle Licensing Agency, Whittlesun Branch, on the edge of town. Six people waited at the locked front door for the office to open at 8:30. Peter locked the Subaru and walked around to the side of the brick building and on to the back, where he found an iron door above a loading bay. He rapped on the door, and in less than thirty seconds it was opened by a fresh-faced twenty-year-old lad. His tie was already askew and his black hair flopped over his forehead. He smiled in recognition, in his enthusiasm not bothering to introduce himself.

"Inspector, it's all in my office." He led Peter down a short hallway to a nondescript room with a door labelled *Manager*.

"Is this your office, Martin?"

"No, it's Mr. Kerwin's, but he's not here."

"Where is he?"

"He's never here, mostly. He may actually be on strike. They strike here a lot."

"Your uncle speaks highly of you. And I'm betting you never join the strike."

Martin smiled broadly. "Too many fun things to think about doing. If only someone were interested."

"Show me the material."

The young man had arrayed the files in three precise stacks along the desk. "The government of the U.K. has always claimed that its domestic laws mesh nicely with the EU rules regarding auto exports.

That was, shall we say, complacent of them. In practice, the U.K. never much cared what the EU systems did. Until computerized registration was centralized in Brussels, the tracking of imported vehicles remained problematic. The result was too many people taking advantage of the rules. Kind of a regulatory arbitrage."

"Run me through an example," Peter said.

"Okay. I'm an exporter in Britain. I want to dump my crappy old cars onto the Continental market. I can export them for *parts,* but there's more money if can sell them as *drivable.* But I don't want to pay the expense to bring the vehicles up to standard. Here's what I do. To certify the car as 'disabled,' I take it to an authorized treatment facility in, say, Dorset. As the owner-seller, I don't have to pay for a licence as long as the vehicle doesn't appear on public roads. Then I apply for a Certificate of Permanent Export, an EU-mandated form identifying the car as refurbished and drivable. I count on nobody in Britain or the EU destination country noticing the switch."

"But won't the Customs people in the receiving country notice the discrepancy?" Peter said.

"You'd hope so. But bureaucrats believe the form on the top of the file before they believe their own eyes. As long as the EU form lists verifiable VIN, cylinder capacity, chassis number and a few other things, they tend to be happy. Here's how the scam worked, until recently. The exporting company would simply fill out the EU export application and lie through their teeth about the fitness of the vehicle. They would back it up with a false report from an alleged mechanic stating the car was up to standard."

"You said 'until recently'?"

"The British government finally operationalized its Changes to Current Vehicle Form to standardize all the details at this end to bring it in line with Brussels. But more important, the British and EU form numbers have to match now."

"Did that make André Lasker change his ways?"

"Certainly slowed him down. I can only discover five deals he made in the last year, two of which were legit. These were kosher exports of certifiably rebuilt cars, one to Portugal, the other to southern Italy. The remaining three were the ones you called me about. Actually, the cars involved may have been accurately characterized, but the export companies are hollow shells. Lasker outsmarted himself a bit on those three."

"What about before then?" Peter said.

"Sixteen." He slapped his palm down on the second stack. "All suspicious, using shell companies."

"Then how did you figure they were Lasker's?"

Martin balked for a moment. His look was somewhere between apprehension at revealing his own methods of inquiry, which were perhaps a bit sketchy in themselves, and the urge to launch a fresh lecture on the mysteries of car registration. He smiled. "Two things. Our system supports data mining of EU stats. I ran data sets on companies that sent cars between eight and sixteen years old to secondary markets on the Continent over the past six years. I cross-reffed them against the U.K. Directory of Auto Dealers, Repairers, Wholesalers and Retailers, and if the exporting company listed on the EU form wasn't in the directory, I pulled it. You see, that might indicate a shell company running a scam."

"The second factor?" Peter asked.

"Even with false names all over the form, you have to list a contact telephone number. André Lasker put the legit phone number of his garage on that Portugal export, the kosher one from last year. I simply correlated the phone number against the entire base. Didn't always work, I suspect, but I picked up sixteen cases that likely were Lasker's."

Martin swept a hand over the documents. "These papers won't tell you the ultimate price of the vehicles, or their true value, but they prove that your man was on the shady side of the export business. Look at this one."

He slipped a package of forms from the middle of a stack. The export company was Western Auto, but the signature of the authorizing corporate officer read *Stanhope*. "Fake name but it sure looks like André Lasker's handwriting."

So, thought Peter, Lasker ran an active but secretive sideline in car exporting. He paid cash for old vehicles, minimally fixed them up in his garage and channelled them into the export stream. He often lied about their state of repair, and corporate shells obscured the ownership trail. Lasker potentially faced charges of commercial fraud, tax evasion and conversion under British and European Union criminal statutes. Albrecht Zoren would probably join him in the dock.

But, for the purposes of the active investigation, a crucial question loomed, and Martin was ready for it.

"Can we tell where the cars were shipped to, and if they stayed in the destination country?" Peter said.

Martin smiled. "Sure can. Here's the Country Receiving list."

He passed Peter a single sheet. Of the sixteen questionable exports, three were bound for Portugal, three for Malta, four for Italy (Bari), two for Poland, two for Slovakia, one for Sweden and another for Greece.

Peter looked at Martin, who was still smiling. Peter offered a responsive grin. "Are you thinking what I'm thinking?" he said. "It's a pretty eclectic list."

"Yup. Means two things, for certain. First, he produced cars on order. Second, there was a broker, a middle man involved, with tentacles into all the EU countries. I'll try to find him."

Peter returned the Subaru to Sam's Auto, only to find that Mayta was off doing errands. He had wanted to see her, suspecting that he was saying goodbye to the two of them. In effect, he was in the process of saying goodbye to all of Whittlesun, and, perhaps subconsciously, he yearned for Mayta to snap him out of his self-absorbed gloom. Tommy Verden was already there when Peter arrived and he and Sam were discussing cars, comparing abstruse features of various vehicles they had owned over the decades.

Peter described his meeting with Martin in detail. Sam declared, "He's a bright boy, a bright boy."

Their farewell was outwardly cheerful but there was a definite mood of abandonment as Peter handed over the keys to the rental. Peter got into the front of the Mercedes and waved to Sam. Verden eased out onto the cobbled street.

"Well, boss, are we back to the cottage then?"

"Not quite, and don't call me boss. Just a short call before we leave Whittlesun behind." He opened his phone and pressed the numbers left by Salvez in his message from — what, two days ago, or was it just yesterday? He listened to the phone chime three or four times; the answerphone took over. "This is Father Salvez. I am not available at the moment but messages can be left at St. Elegias Catholic Church administration office." A new telephone number was given. There was no beep; the line cut itself.

He called the church office and got a general message regarding church hours. He asked Tommy to set his SatNav for St. Elegias. This makes no sense, he thought. Why would Salvez employ an answering machine that didn't take messages? He couldn't imagine why Salvez needed to speak with him, but that puzzle was enough to spark his professional instincts. *Had the sick priest remembered something about the Laskers? Or had he seen the Rover?*

He tried the church again. "Hello?" an ancient female voice answered, resentful at this interruption.

"Good afternoon. This is Chief Inspector Cammon of New Scotland Yard. May I speak to Father Salvez?"

"He isn't here."

"I called his house number, but he wasn't there either."

"He doesn't have a house, it's a flat, and he probably was there. Just wasn't answering."

Peter had dealt with hundreds of witnesses over the years, but he still hated confronting the recalcitrant ones over the phone. "How can I reach him?"

"You can knock on his door, the best way. You say you're from the police?"

Peter didn't waver. "I need to see him on official police business."

"I'll give you the address, then." Peter could hear her riffling some papers in the background. She dictated the address, her voice softening a bit. "Can you pick up his messages on your way, and give them to him? There's been a few people calling. He only lives two streets from the church."

"Can't he pick them up himself?"

"Not in the condition he's in."

Twenty minutes on — as Tommy drove — and they were at St. Elegias, which boasted its own graveyard and a small verge of lawn all the way around it. Otherwise, it was a fairly modest Roman Catholic church, its shape not unlike St. George's nearby in Weymouth. There was a seeping frost in the air; Peter got out and looked up at the sky, trying to guess the odds of snow.

A nameplate, which had been riveted to the side door a long time ago, read *Father Robert Clarke* and listed two subordinates in smaller print. Another sign gave the phone number for the administration office; it was the one from Salvez's message. Peter did a full circle of the stone building. Clarke was also identified on the main sign at the entrance. A large encased display on the lawn in front of the church held a statue of the Virgin. Behind it, a sign stencilled in red on parchment paper exhibited the quote of the week: *Have you found your King?*

Peter did not at first realize that the house behind St. Elegias was the rectory. It was a compact, cottage-like home, evidently the residence of Father Clarke. A panel on the railing on the front steps confirmed this and requested that visitors call at the church for assistance. Father Salvez most certainly didn't live here.

Peter hailed Tommy, who understood, and killed the ignition. He got out of the car and waited while Peter descended the steps at the side of the building. He found the right office by following the odour of brewed tea. The old receptionist, whose dried-apple face matched the crotchety voice on the phone, appeared to be counting hymnbooks.

"Sixteen . . . seventeen . . . eighteen," she intoned.

Peter's arrival made her lose count. "Yes?" she snapped.

"Peter Cammon." He entered the office. He wasn't what she expected in a police officer, and that suited him fine. She seemed impressed by his black suit.

She handed over a sealed envelope. "Please give him these, his messages." She paused and said, with unexpected warmth, "Say hello to the Father for us."

"Can I ask you one thing?" Peter said.

"I suppose."

"Why does Father Salvez's name not appear on the list of priests?"

"Because he's not formally associated with us."

Formally associated? Her answer begged the question of why the office continued to function as his mail drop, if little more.

"He's retired," she went on. "He doesn't work here."

"Is he somehow formally affiliated with the Abbey?" For every tidbit of information, the dry, pale woman retrenched behind the battlements.

She scowled. "The Abbey is deconsecrated. Excuse me, officer, but Father Salvez is ill. He's being treated for prostate cancer. He doesn't have formal duties here."

Her compassion was so thin, so grudging, that Peter decided to let it go as hopeless. He stuffed the packet of messages into his jacket and left.

Peter and Tommy decided to leave their car in the church space and walk to Salvez's flat. They found it easily, a beige brick cube of identical units three streets over. The lobby index identified 524 as the priest's flat, although "Father" was not appended to the name. Verden waited for a resident to exit, smiled at her, and held open the door for Peter. The lift was broken and so they took the rear stairs to the fifth floor. Peter knocked on 524. He was just about to knock a second time when the locks began to rattle on the interior side.

The priest was thinner than before, when Peter had seen him in his long cassock, and now he looked deathly. Peter's mother, who was as anti-Catholic as a Huguenot could be, opined that priests often

272

looked like their own undertakers, but Peter felt only a welling up of concern, mixed with alarm, at the stick-man before him. When he saw Peter in the doorway, the priest recoiled in distress, although Peter was certain that Salvez recognized him. He wasn't sure what this meant. They had been on friendly terms; Salvez had saved him at the cliff's edge, and they had left an interesting conversation unfinished, with the implicit promise of meeting again. Had he waited too long to get back to him? The priest stepped back and lost his balance. Verden swooped past Peter and caught the man neatly. He gently lowered him to the carpet.

"This is embarrassing," Salvez wheezed.

"Why, Father? This is a nice soft carpet, isn't it?" Verden said.

The sick man gasped for breath. "It's just . . . nothing."

"'Take up thy bed and walk another day,' the Bible says," Verden pronounced. Salvez tried to laugh, but only choked on his next breath.

Peter's colleague turned out to be a master of practical sympathy. Verden lifted the emaciated man in his arms and brought him to the chesterfield, which faced a small black-and-white television tuned to the news. Peter dipped under Verden's arm and plumped up the three pillows. He took a seat next to the television, so that Salvez could look directly at him. "Father Salvez," he said, "this is Inspector Verden."

"Your first name, Inspector?" The voice was weak.

"Tommy."

"Thank you for the rescue, Tommy."

"No problem. I'll make tea." All business, he left for the kitchen.

The flat was neat, if threadbare. Newspapers and food cartons circled the old man's nesting spot on the couch.

"These are your messages," Peter said. He handed over the sealed envelope, and Salvez tucked it under a cushion.

"Are you all right, Father?"

"Yes. I had radiation treatment yesterday. It's not the first time."

"Has anyone been here with you since?" Peter could hear dishes rattling in the kitchen.

"A neighbour woman came by yesterday afternoon and fixed me something. Oh, and two fellows helped me up the freight lift. The main lift is broken. But mostly I've been sleeping."

Peter hadn't understood the extent of the man's alienation from his own church. He lived in poverty, yet no one from St. Elegias had offered to tend to him. For the fourth or fifth time in two days, Peter thought of his mother: acts of charity are to be done without question. Every man Peter's age knew about prostate cancer; luckily, he had avoided it. The choices were ugly — radiation, hormone therapy, surgery. With radiation, collateral damage to the plumbing around the prostate gland was common, and disabling. Salvez should not have been left alone. But then, he might have lied to the medical staff.

"Why did you call me, Father?" Peter asked.

"Did I call you?" Peter saw that he was troubled, confused.

"Yes, at my hotel two days ago."

"Oh, yes. I enjoyed our talk at the Abbey. I wanted to say goodbye. I figured that you would be leaving soon, and so . . ." The exertion drained him, and he lay back on the pillows.

Peter had problems with this explanation but he didn't challenge it for the moment. Instinct led him to conclude that the call, though it predated the disastrous press conference, was connected to Lasker. Or was Salvez saying his goodbyes to everyone? Did he believe he might not survive yesterday's treatment? Or was he getting ready for his own quiet, self-administered exit? Peter's thoughts slid around crazily. Had Salvez, since he left his message, heard about Anna's suicide? He doubted that the priest had been well enough to watch the television reports the night before.

"Father, can we talk frankly?"

"Confession works in the other direction, Peter."

Peter did not smile. "I don't think so, John."

Salvez suddenly brightened, almost in a spurt of euphoria. He arched his back and flexed his long arms. "You want to know how my health really is?"

"Yes, and what you plan to do about it. This isn't mentally or physically healthy, staying alone like this."

"Okay."

"Wait till Tommy comes back. I want him to join us."

"What?" the startled priest said. "There aren't usually three at a confession."

"This isn't three priests. It's three *men* of a certain age talking honestly. I'm sixty-seven, almost sixty-eight. I won't speak for Tommy, but he's no callow youth either."

Father Salvez continued to look startled, but in his weak state, he let Peter take charge. Peter called Tommy, who brought the tea tray in from the kitchen. Tommy fixed a cup for Salvez and one for himself. Peter leaned forward.

"How bad is the cancer?" he said. Verden didn't bat an eyelash. The priest paused for a few seconds and replied in a strong, direct voice.

"Fatal. The radiation is doing as much harm as good. I expect I'll rebound from this dose, but the poison is spreading. It's ruining my immune system. My doctor warns me about going to the Abbey, but I plan to go a few more times. I love it up there." *Why mention the Abbey?* Peter thought.

There was no point in hectoring the old cleric. The three men talked for two more hours. Verden launched into convoluted, and comic, stories of his travels in pursuit of criminals, stories that had nothing to do with PSA counts. The dying man was soon laughing, spraying spittle across his blankets and letting out deep, rasping coughs, and not caring about either.

While Tommy and Salvez continued to talk, Peter went to the kitchen and found the priest's prescription bottles. They included mild doses of morphine. He took down the phone number of the presiding physician. Salvez eventually fell asleep, and the two detectives caucused in the pantry. Peter despaired. He knew few people in Whittlesun. He didn't dare call Hamm or Willet; the explanations and cautions would take forever. He also wanted Maris to believe that he had already left Whittlesun. The most empathetic people he knew in the town of Whittlesun were Fred Callahan and his son, but he couldn't think of a premise for requesting Fred's help. Sam the Armenian would handle everything, but could hardly be called a calming presence; and he would likely have a heart attack himself climbing the stairs.

He figured it out halfway through his conversation with Joan, whom he called while Salvez dozed. When he explained the situation, she determined to drive down to Whittlesun right away and completely take over the care of the dying priest. He pointed out the impracticality of that approach. She was about to express her serious umbrage at that rejection when Peter thought of Father Vogans. He promised to call her back.

Fortunately, the Romanian cleric was in his office. He agreed to come at once. Peter stated that this was unnecessary, that he and Verden could stay around until seven or eight.

"I'll be there by six," he said. His voice was cheerful. "Let my assistant do the christening."

"You realize that he's not the official, established priest at St. Elegias?" Peter added.

"I like it," Vogans said. "The Roman Catholics need my help. Delicious irony!"

The Romanian knocked on the door at 6:05. He was puffing from the long climb and he carried a basket over one arm. He smiled and introduced himself to Tommy (who later was compelled to comment to Peter that he kept awfully strange company when out on an investigation). Vogans turned grim at the sight of the dying man. The Catholic priest had awakened at the knock of the Eastern Orthodox cleric, and now struggled for awareness. He turned slowly to his guest and stared at the clerical collar.

"Are you coming to collect me?" he said.

"I'm coming to convert you, John. Do you like *ciorba*?"

CHAPTER 23

Inspector Maris loved his wife in a way that wasn't entirely healthy. He had adored her from the first sight of her finely curved legs; that was in senior form trigonometry, two days after his nineteenth birthday. That day, he marked down in his mental inventory her aquiline nose and her cobalt eyes; and he never forgot those details, or anything else about her. Thereafter, he wrote her description down in his notebook over and over, like a shopping list: legs, nose, eyes, hair. And when they eventually married, it was as if he was marrying a memory turned corporeal.

From his standpoint, their engagement was a coup worthy of a band of revolutionaries. He came from the ordinary middle-class masses of Whittlesun, but his courting of her became his way of carving himself out of the pack. Right out of school he joined the police; truth be told, she first loved him for his spiffy uniform. He spent every cent of his salary on their dates. He promised to work his way out of the ranks, and he had. He found that he was good at administration and human resources, and almost as good at criminal investigation, and he moved up the organization chart. All the while, he perceived everything through the lens of his devotion to her and her beauty.

His parents had been pleased, hers less so. On their wedding day, her brother, who had something to do with debt refinancing in the City (and now in the Docklands), took him aside for an inebriated lecture. "She's a sleeper," he had said. He had no idea what the brother-in-law meant on that day but he had never been happier.

On the morning after the press conference, Maris awoke next to his wife, and his first thought was that he wished he had understood his brother-in-law's rant at the time. In the days after the wedding, he had thought it meant that she had hidden depths, that she was a sleeping rose about to bloom. His wife had vague intentions of working in fashion or home decorating. Instead, the brother had meant it literally. She had a sleep problem. No one called it narcolepsy, but she had to get twelve hours' sleep each day, and when she slept it was deathly in its stillness. On this morning, the day after the disastrous press conference, he realized that there was no possibility of her waking up and joining him for coffee in the kitchen. He would have liked to have talked to her about his seething distaste for New Scotland Yard.

But he believed in professionalism more than anything, and he put aside his self-pity as he got out of bed, shaved, showered and dressed. He knotted his tie and felt ready for the day. In truth, his wife was a charming woman, who, when awake, offered him every sympathy for the challenges of his job. She expected greater things from him and was wholly optimistic and supportive. He told her that the Task Force was a real opportunity to show what he could do, and she nodded. It was just that she had gained weight. She was not quite the woman he had married. He was now living with a plump cheerleader who had few ambitions of her own. All things considered, he said to himself, I have a good life. He waffled like this, and it never occurred to him that he was an equivocator, and in this was different from Peter Cammon. He failed to see the ruthlessness in Peter Cammon.

The more he pendulummed between thanking his Protestant God for his blessings and ruminating over the gaps in his life, the more he became irritable. He let things niggle at him. A year or so ago, some

American had come into the station to complain about his stolen passport. Maris had introduced himself as "Inspector Roger Maris," to which the Yank had said, "Oh, like the ball player." Maris knew nothing about baseball. Two days ago, another American had made the same connection, and then said, "Like Maris with an asterisk?" This comment was so confusing that he had felt driven to check the Internet for clarification. It turned out that the American ballplayer had broken Babe Ruth's record (Maris had heard of *him*) of sixty home runs in a season, but there was doubt about his new mark, and thus the asterisk. The inspector was none the clearer, but resolved to be standoffish with all Americans in the future.

As he reached his parking bay by the police station, he tried to think through his strategy for dealing with Cammon. He had left instructions for the chief inspector to be summoned to the police station; then he would call Sir Stephen Bartleben. He arrived in his office to find that Cammon had been unreachable. On the way to work, Maris had been enumerating and rehearsing his grievances against the Yard. Cammon had failed to give him timely reports on his investigation and the family had been hounding him to release the blood-soaked house to them; but Cammon had procrastinated, and now the building was likely unsalvageable. He had brought his wife into the home, for reasons not entirely clear; even Bartleben had agreed that this was unprofessional. Maris was tempted to demand Cammon's dismissal. And Cammon had seduced — not too strong a word — his principal man on the case, Detective Hamm, and almost got him killed on a wild goose chase along the cliffs. The announcement of Anna Lasker's suicide was the final straw.

All the while, Maris felt the threat of pre-emption behind everything these Scotland Yard types, including that Canadian pathologist Bracher, did with the Lasker and Rover fiascos. At one point with Bartleben over the phone, he had suggested that perhaps the Yard should take over the Lasker investigation. Bartleben had buttered him up with compliments about the competence of local and regional police, and Maris had secretly been relieved. Yet none of these efforts represented progress in getting rid of Cammon, and his quiver of strategies was empty.

He hated the glass office. He needed relief sometimes from the pressures of management and liked to play solitaire on his desktop computer. He would have enjoyed a stroll on the Whittlesun Heights, to walk through the heather and feel the salty breeze. But even that was rendered difficult by the constant scanning of the cliffs by the police, most of whom were his own men. But the more he thought about the cliffs, the more he determined to take that walk. He'd done it before.

The red light on his telephone blinked. He waited for his secretary, clearly visible outside the glass, to pick up. She was in his office in seconds.

"Inspector, sorry, but it's Constable Willet."

"Where's he calling from?" She looked hapless. "The field?"

"Inspector." Willet sounded far away. Could he possibly be ringing in from his motorcycle? "Potentially we have another victim."

"Who? Where?"

"Brenda Van Loss. A farm girl, residence less than a kilometre from the sea."

"Has the body been found?"

"No," the Constable replied, seeming confused. "That is, she disappeared last night. She hasn't shown up at home."

"So, Mr. Willet, we can't be sure there's any victim at all. All right, I'll send a squad to help with a search. Where are you?"

"A place called Kidd's Reach."

At the same moment that Inspector Maris was lifting the receiver to talk to Constable Willet in Dorset, Peter was jolted awake by the phone ringing downstairs at the cottage. He had hoped to sleep in late. His plan, after lolling in bed for a while, was to get up, have breakfast and in his organized fashion, work through his list of calls: Bracher, Vogans, Bartleben and maybe J.J. McElroy. He would set up in the shed for the afternoon and write his interim report on Lasker. Although he knew Joan would get the phone, instinct told him that his plan for the day was shattered, and he became fully alert. Now he swung his legs over the side of the bed and gazed out the window, waiting for Joan's footfall on the stairs. The apple trees, and one or two remaining peach trees, held down the eastern side of his property; at an angle, he found the outline of the old fence on the south perimeter, braced by the pile of stones that the landscapers had discarded. On arriving home the night before, he had seen that all the flowers along the drive had died, leaving dry stalks waving in the pre-winter breeze. But he loved this place. He was glad to see that there was no frost yet on the fruit trees. Never had the cottage felt more like a bastion against interference from above, below and sideways.

Joan came in; she had the phone but had turned it off. "Oh, you're up. I took a call from Father Salvez." Tommy had stayed for a brandy last night, and she had heard the full story of their rescue mission.

"How is he?"

"In terrible shape," she said.

"What did he say, specifically?" Peter said.

"That he's feeling infinitely better. It won't do, Peter. He needs constant care, ideally with a heart monitor."

"Does he have a hospital appointment today? I seem to recall . . ."

"Not good enough, Peter. He says he's fine. He's not."

"If a priest adopts a stiff upper lip, do we call it a martyr's lip?" Peter said.

"Don't be flippant. There's something going on with your priest. Not martyrdom, something else."

Peter regretted his callousness. He had slept perhaps too well. More significantly, he trusted Joan's instincts. Indeed, something about Salvez's attitude, his determination to avoid hospital officialdom, bothered him, and he wondered if Joan had the same insight.

She wasn't placated. "I'm going down there myself."

"I'll call Father Vogans."

But the phone in Joan's hand rang at that moment, and it was

Vogans himself. She passed it over. "Hello. Peter, I just thought I'd report."

Peter, with Joan hovering, was careful in his response. "What's his condition this morning?"

"I left an hour ago. He slept through most of the night. The soup helped, he said. I have a woman from my diocese going over later today to feed him and clean up a bit. I'll phone Father Clarke now and see what St. Elegias can organize."

Peter looked at Joan. "Do you think he should be in hospital? He needs monitoring."

"Of course," Vogans said, mildly. "He's declining, you saw that. But he refused my offer to have a full-time caregiver. He insists he'll rebound from the radiation. He wants to go back up to that Abbey."

Peter understood that Joan was ready to start up the car and drive straight to Whittlesun. He would have to go along with her, but he preferred to give it a day.

"I'll check this evening and let you know the latest," Vogans stated. "My Ladies Aid person will stay the day and will report back to me."

"Okay," Peter said, "but he won't answer his phone, so please, you call me."

Vogans agreed to follow up with Salvez's doctors as well. When Peter hung up, Joan had disappeared. For all Peter knew, she was packing a bag. He went downstairs and found her already out in her potting shed. He explained the details of the plan and she nodded but clearly wasn't convinced. He went next door to his study; it was somehow comforting to have Joan working on the other side of the partition. But before he could unpack his material on Lasker, his phone rang again. It was the Canadian himself.

"Just touching base, Peter. You started your report yet?"

"Interim report, at best. No, but I'll file something with Bartleben this week."

"I called to say my report on the Lasker house, and my comments on the automobile forensics, are finished and I've deposited them with Regional. I've sent a copy to Sir Stephen, and I'll courier one to you this afternoon."

"Where are you?"

"Just leaving the lab. Heading up to Nottingham for a consult. I was going to take a last amble up on the cliffs, but did you hear the latest?"

"Which is?"

"The Rover has struck again."

"Oh, Christ. The victim?"

"Local farm girl. Her name is Brenda Van Loss. But he left her alive this time. Actually, she wasn't hurt that badly."

Peter's mind raced. His onrushing thought was that he had left Whittlesun too soon. His instincts told him that something was going to be very off about this one.

"You realize, Stan, that this is the second time he's failed to execute his victim? What do you know about it?"

"Precious little. Something about the creep maybe drugging her, then leaving her on the top of the cliff. But I'm gone, Peter. Have to get to Nottingham." Caution entered his voice. "I thought maybe one of us might want to call McElroy."

Bracher meant that he no longer wanted to serve as liaison to the Rover Task Force, though he surely grasped that Peter was unwelcome in Dorset, and probably Devon too. It puzzled him that Stan was thinking of visiting the cliffs again. Peter was about to ring off, leaving these questions unresolved. He said, "I'll try to call McElroy. Where was the girl attacked?"

"Kidd's Reach, wherever that is."

They hung up and Peter started to unpack his files, but then decided to try Salvez, even though the priest likely wouldn't answer. He got only the recorded voice. His next decision was whether to seek information from McElroy — whom he would have preferred to dodge — or perhaps get the local perspective on the Van Loss assault from Ron Hamm. It was a morning for coincidences. Before Peter could make a decision, Ron Hamm rang his mobile.

"Chief Inspector?" Peter realized that they hadn't talked since that day on the heights, although Peter had seen him on two occasions since.

"I've just heard about it, Ron. What can you tell me?"

"Local girl — from Devon, that is. Brenda Van Loss. Hard to know what he did to her; maybe rape, but she wasn't seriously mutilated. There are bruises to the top of her head, and abrasions on her cheekbones. Odd thing is, she was drugged, and that's different from all the others."

"Yes," Peter replied, "but this is the second one he's deliberately left alive. That's a mistake." He expected the detective to ask him to expound on this theory, but Ron's tone came across as aggressive, more definite and harder.

"I agree. He's toying with us. The location she was found in, on the cliffs, was about six kilometres from the last victim, but he doesn't give shite about the 'Six-K' pattern. And she was drugged. Analysis isn't back yet, but it was something like old-fashioned chloroform, we suspect. I'll ask them to pin it down when I go to the lab."

For all Ron's anger, Peter discerned some hedging. "There's something else, right?" Peter said.

"Yeah. I haven't raised it with Maris or anyone on the Task Force. But the drug, whatever it was, was enough to knock the girl out for twelve to fourteen hours. She didn't wake up until daylight. She could have frozen to death."

"What was the temperature that night?"

"I checked. It was two degrees above freezing. But enough for hypothermia."

"There's something else?"

"Here's my thought. I went up to see where she was found."

"Found?" Peter interrupted. "She didn't wake up on her own?"

"No. Her uncle discovered her. Brenda's father, brother, uncle and a cousin, who lives with the family, went searching when she failed to come home. The uncle woke her up, he told us, though the girl may have been in the process of reviving when he discovered her. That was at sunrise. He said she was laid out, positioned, fully clothed, like a scene from King Arthur, arms by her side, hair brushed, feet positioned together. A scene worthy of the *Morte d'Arthur.* But it was the stone that struck me, so to speak."

"What about the stone?"

"It was a massive slab of grey slate. The surface was smooth, almost polished, and it lay there perfectly flat and horizontal. It was unique to the field it lay in; none of the surrounding rocks were like it. Not that anyone could have carried it there."

"But it bothered you?" Peter said. "It was the natural place to position a body but it still bothered you?"

"It was almost *irresistible* to place the body there, Peter. It reminded us all of Arthurian legends, we all said so. But then, as I was staring at the spot, with the sea in the distance and the wind coming up over the cliff edge, I thought again of Stonehenge. There was no circle of boulders, and there are no standing stones in this area, but it reminded me of one of the pieces of Stonehenge laid on its side. He's a cold son of a bitch."

"And Stonehenge is thought to be a calendar. And, more important, a place for religious ceremonies."

"Exactly. Mocking us or not, the Rover likes his rituals."

Peter exhaled and finally filled the pause. "Ron, I'm likely to be in Whittlesun soon, maybe in four or five days. But I have to avoid your boss."

"That's for sure. Think you can stay on the Task Force?"

"Doubtful. I have to contact McElroy next."

"You haven't heard, then?"

"Heard what?"

"McElroy is out. He freaked, right in his own office. It appears he had been reading the autopsy results on all the girls. Finter told me this. Couldn't take it."

Peter had no response. It occurred to him that Ron, who seemed a little obsessed himself with the autopsies, might never have seen Molly's body; but was it possible that he hadn't viewed the cadaver of

Anna Lasker? He had forgotten to probe Ron about his injuries and now he asked.

"Oh, I'm fine," Hamm said, but his voice was hollow and anxious. "Ultimately just bruises. But the girl in the water . . . Must have been awful for you, grasping her like that. Just awful."

They hung up, although Peter felt that he was setting Ron adrift in Maris's shark pool. He liked the young detective, and he reminded himself to send along a copy of his notes. The shed was cool but still tolerable; he would move a heater in from the house if it got any colder. The pile of Lasker notes upbraided him from the long trestle table. He owed Bartleben an interim report by the weekend.

He arranged his notes in front of him at the trestle table but had trouble concentrating. Hamm had used "awful" twice in the course of one sentence. The discussion had been about the victims, the three that Jack McElroy had obsessed over, and then Molly Jonas, naked, whitened by the sea, and forever linked to Hamm and Peter. And Hamm had mentioned going to the lab. He had no reason to go to the regional facility, unless it was to examine the Lasker vehicle or discuss the long-delayed final autopsy on Anna Lasker. Was he going there to view the corpses of Anna and Molly?

Every one of the girls — including Daniella Garvena and Brenda Van Loss, who were lucky to be alive — was a student and a local girl. Five of the six were very familiar with the cliffs. Forgetting pure opportunism for a moment, Peter considered the reverse angle. *What if the Rover asked the girls where the best caves and lover's lanes were to be found? Could they show him?* Peter tried to work out why so many women would answer without suspicion. *Because he had an innocent premise for asking the question.*

Detective Ron Hamm had more or less invited himself to the Regional Laboratory, and that turned out to be not quite acceptable to the pathology staff.

There were protocols for visitors, including investigating detectives. But he was the coordinating officer on Lasker, as well as an official member of the Task Force on the Rover, and he insisted on speaking with the chief pathologist assigned to each case.

Instead, he got the pathologist on duty for that day, who was not happy. "Both bodies, Jonas and Lasker? Detective Hamm," he said, "this is not a meat market. We prefer not to put bodies out for display without notice."

Ron was ready with his justification. "I was at the cliffs the day Molly Jonas was found. I was one of the detectives who found her in the sea."

They were standing in the Reception room. The pathologist's scepticism showed clearly. If he were to eject the nervous young detective, now would be the time. But it happened that the doctor had in fact attended the autopsy of Molly Jonas and was aware that the two police officers who had retrieved the corpse were being hailed as heroes. The detective's skittishness was bothersome, and he wondered if Hamm had ever viewed a cadaver close up. If not, Molly wasn't a good place to start.

"I can show you the medical report," he tried.

"I've read the preliminary autopsy," Ron retorted. "I'm interested in seeing the bruising pattern on her body, particularly the neck."

His plan had been to appeal to the professional ego of the pathologists by expressing interest in their technical analysis and methods. It worked — at least, the doctor grunted and began to lead him out of Reception and down the big open hallway of the morgue.

He led Ron into a cold room off the corridor and asked him to wait while he checked on the state of Molly's body. After a moment, from the far end of the room, he gestured for Ron to come over to the drawer.

At first, Ron thought that Molly appeared at peace. A sheet was demurely draped over the torso and she lay face up, eyes closed, mouth in a neutral expression. Closer now, he remarked on her paleness. The pathologist pulled back the cover to show the bruises on her throat, still deep blue where they circled the entire neck. The doctor began to describe the injury.

"You are probably wondering. The bruising around the neck remains dark because the scarf that the killer used was pulled very hard, and for a long period until she suffocated. Definitely the cause of death."

Ron Hamm nodded. He managed to lie to the pathologist and to himself. "Thank you. I just wanted to determine how violent this bastard is." Hamm's tone implied that this was some form of closure for him.

The doctor appeared to understand, although Hamm could see there was doubt in his eyes. It was unusual for an investigator to dodge viewing the rest of the victim. The pathologist showed his annoyance. "This bastard is plenty violent, Detective. By the way, the body will be handed over to the family tomorrow for preparation and burial. Unlike Mrs. Lasker, who has been here forever."

This wasn't a lie, since the doctor was unaware that Anna's body had finally been scheduled for release. There had long been confusion about who was authorized — and willing — to receive it.

The pathologist looked at Ron Hamm. "Detective, do you really want to view Anna's body?"

Until then, Ron had managed to conceal his reaction to Molly, but now he felt ready to vomit. *Who has done this? What kind of a man?* There would be no closure until . . . He nodded in response to the doctor. Anna had always been his case. It was overdue that he pay his respects.

Two minutes later, Ron Hamm found himself looking down at Anna Lasker, with her battered face, which would be in repose only if the mortician applied all his skills. Her scarred arms stuck out from each side of the covering sheet. This had been a suicide, he reminded himself, but she had been abused by André Lasker, he still had no doubt. What bothered him was the impossibility of distinguishing between the self-inflicted scars and the impact of the fall onto Upper

Whittlesun Beach. Her left cheekbone had been pressed inward; her hair had been torn from her scalp in two spots. He noted the long slash she had made to her left forearm. His constant thought was that there was nothing left of this woman. He had been in the hollow house and it had been meaningless without her human presence, but now she had flown away, her humanity hopelessly gone. In his state, he let out a curse against Peter Cammon for stalling the release of Anna's body to the mortuary.

Over the rest of the afternoon, Peter made a good start on his interim report on Lasker. It would have an open-ended tone, but the time had come for Peter to write what he knew. He put the Rover out of his mind as he began his iteration of the evidence. About 5:00 p.m., the courier arrived with Stan Bracher's forensics summary, and Peter read it through once before slotting it behind his text as the first appendix. He treated Anna's suicide at length, providing a timeline for her hell-bent journey to the cliff edge. He had no doubt that the evidence eventually would convict André of various counts of fraud, and so he gave those crimes their own chapter; material from Sam's nephew at the DVLA formed the second appendix and was flagged for follow-up action. Given the draft nature of the document, he began to compile a list of next steps. He proposed old Mrs. Lasker and F.R. Symington for fresh interviews, hoping they might identify some chimerical icon — a South Seas island? — that had beguiled the husband away from his stolid British life. In an additional chapter he advised the Yard to send a special alert to the police agencies of the EU countries to which he had exported his sixteen refurbished vehicles over the previous three years.

A quick email to Sir Stephen and another to the director of the Economic and Specialist Crime Branch, SCD6, promised a refined, albeit interim, text within two days, which he would deliver in person. He avoided a direct call to Bartleben; he marvelled that the chief, after the inevitable denunciatory calls from Maris and perhaps

McElroy, hadn't already called. Within five minutes, Sir Stephen sent back his reply: "OK. See U then."

At seven o'clock, he quit for the day and went inside. Joan had dinner ready. She had refrained from interrupting him in the shed, knowing the crucial stage he was at in the Lasker investigation, and what he was up against. Still, the meal was tense. Joan had been left unsure of her role — which she hoped would be a sounding board, now that she had inside knowledge of the case. She wanted to insist that they drive down to Whittlesun and take care of Father Salvez. Peter was entitled to his instincts, but hers told her that Salvez was somehow pivotal to the case. Perhaps it was the geography of St. Walthram's, positioned in the centre of the Jurassic Coast, next to the point where Anna had died and the husband had vanished. St. Walthram's, though she had never seen it, represented for her a gathering place of souls. It wasn't that she had taken on religion; rather, she admired the priest for his preservation of the great Abbey as a repository of spirits; he presided over the Abbey, spending lonely days there shepherding these ambient spirits into the crumbling church in order to preserve them. Peter had told her that Father Salvez planned to go up there at least one more time. She had seen the endgame of prostate cancer, and a trip to the Abbey would tax his every remaining muscle; it would probably kill him in the process.

They discussed other subjects, Sarah's wanderings and the latest non-news from Michael. "Nothing new re the wedding," she stated. She had made the quick trip to Leeds and lunched with his fiancée. After dinner, Peter picked up the local newspaper and read it at the dining-room table. He didn't wish to show disrespect by retreating back to the shed, but when Wendie Merwyn called, he took the phone out to the front veranda.

"Chief Inspector, it's Wendie Merwyn here in Whittlesun. Do you have a minute?" Not a moment but a minute.

"Miss Merwyn," Peter said, formally. He wished she hadn't called; the timing seemed all wrong, and he had no comment to offer on the Van Loss assault. "What are you calling about?"

"Two things, Chief Inspector, but you know I wouldn't call if it wasn't important. First, I rang to give you the coordinates for our streaming video. It's new for TV-20. Have you seen our changed format?"

"I don't get your station up here."

"Hence the streaming video link." She gave him the URL. "We stream our six o'clock news and podcasts of several other specialty news programs."

"What else?"

"They've launched a new team concept, with myself and Parny on the news desk. Our reporters in the field are mandated to come up with an investigative feature every week. Parny and I anchor it, though he still does the weather too. The public likes us. We're being called the Blondie Twins."

Peter had the image of two sets of bright teeth and perfect yellow hair. It seemed to him that her enthusiasm was muted. *Is Parny Moss becoming real competition?* Peter would try out the Internet site, but all this seemed secondary news. He wondered if the real reason for her call was the Rover or Lasker. But then he remembered Wendie's surprising question at the press event. Now, on the phone, he understood that she had called about Lasker.

"You're calling late, Miss Merwyn. You must have wrapped for the evening, so I'm guessing you have something you want to run by me? Off the record, I'll assume."

She surprised him again. "Inspector, do you see any overlap between the Lasker and Rover cases? Because I won't raise it in our feature if you say no. But they both involve criminals operating along the coastal territory around here. Both offenders are unknown, mysterious characters. There's a feeling of evil about both of them. It's like the cliffs are an image that is attracting death."

She was rehearsing her on-air spiel but the tenor she was adopting was excessive, near hysterical, and they both knew it. He shouldn't be judgmental, he reminded himself. After all, he had at one point concluded that he might have to resolve one case in order to wrap up the other — he had never been sure how he would pull this off, but there could be some link there, if he could find it. She was a complex woman, Wendie Merwyn, evidently troubled by the deaths of all these women, but Anna Lasker in particular.

"No," he replied. "There is no link between the two cases. Lasker will be sighted sooner or later. It will probably be luck that catches him. He's certainly not the Rover, if that was what you were implying."

"Not exactly," she said. He wasn't sure that she believed him. "By the way, I interviewed Detective Hamm today, and he's promised a forensics report and a blood analysis on the Lasker home, although I haven't received either yet."

This was spin on her part, merely a teaser to see if Peter would disclose more information. It was likely that Hamm hadn't promised that much. But the young detective had exceeded his authority in promising any autopsy or other forensics. It was bothersome, an amateur's mistake made out of impulse. As for Wendie, it felt odd to him that she was pressing so hard on Lasker, and less on the wraith who had killed four girls and bruised two more. Most reporters would home in the bigger story. He liked Wendie, with her mix of ambition and smarts. And, for a moment, he felt an irrational fear for her safety.

"I'll tell you, Miss Merwyn, I believe that André Lasker is alive. If we arrest him, I promise to talk to you before anyone else."

"Thank you, Chief Inspector."

The cottage was silent. It was too cold for crickets, too quiet to rouse any chained dogs. Peter and Joan talked at the dining room table. He made a deliberate effort to tell her everything in detail. He began with Merwyn's speculative call, recounting the conversation verbatim. He branched out to his theories of Lasker's plan, and by midnight finally connected the thread back to the day Joan had visited the house near the high street — in effect, he told the whole

Lasker tragedy in reverse order. They sat under the antique chandelier, while the rest of the cottage remained dark. He thought of trying Salvez again but decided it was too late. Although it had only been a day, he felt at a huge distance, in time and in psychic space, from the places of death in Dorset and Devon. Neither had been his case, yet he had to take on some of the responsibility for several tragedies. But thus far, had he contributed any more than second-guessing? He'd been called in to do what he could to straighten out the Lasker mystery, an assignment at least consistent with the role of a part-time consulting detective. But it was never in Peter's nature to keep a non-accountable, prophylactic aloofness from the worst, outrageous dimensions of a crime, or to let other policemen dip their hands in real blood while he developed theories in the background. He expected to return to Whittlesun very soon. He owed that much to Anna Lasker and Molly Jonas.

He wondered if André really was alive. The mechanic had embarked on a romantic escape from his old life. He had left his wedding ring behind, in the dead centre of his abandoned clothes. Naked, he walked into the ocean to find his rebirth. If André could sustain his original romantic vision of the sea, he might survive, but it was also the sea that might lure him back.

The telephone rang at midnight. He and Joan looked at it. They let it ring three times, trying to guess who it could be. Peter was startled to hear Bartleben.

"Peter, you owe me a call. I mean, now that you're finished stomping through the tulips in Dorset." No mention of the report. Peter waited. He looked over at Joan; she was smiling benignly, and he was tempted to put her on the other phone line.

"Peter, are you sitting down?" Bartleben said, in a flat tone.

"Yeah."

"Peter, André Lasker has reappeared."

"Where?"

"Malta."

PART THREE

The Cliffs

CHAPTER 24

On November 7, 1974, the seventh Earl of Lucan beat the family nanny to death in his wife's London house, imagining her in the darkness to be his estranged spouse. Then, showing no imagination at all, he beat his wife in similar fashion and fled in several directions, eventually disappearing into the Channel.

The Lucan case had happened at the beginning of Peter's career as a tenured Scotland Yard detective. Now, seated in the air raid shelter at the back of the cottage garden, he flipped through the yellow foolscap pages of the file and realized that the Lucan melodrama might have been the case that had convinced him to look at crime through a literary lens. The archetypes in this instance were not feisty lasses from Hardy or haunted seekers from a Thomas Mann novel. The template here was the domestic children's tale from late-Victorian and Edwardian times, but made topsy-turvy.

The Lucan narrative was replete with nannies and devoted mommies, doting grandmothers, white Belgravia houses with many secret rooms, and party-giving friends who always answered the door when Mummy or Daddy Lucan knocked. The father in such stories is usually a hapless, one-off figure, a bit foolish, seen yielding to the children's requests and laying his benign tolerance on thick. Except that on this occasion the drinking-gambling-philandering father slaughtered the nanny, bludgeoned the wife and left the children upstairs in the bedroom to fend with their dreams.

Although they laid claim to a patrician provenance, there wasn't much to like in the Lucans. When they met and married, he had already dedicated himself to the gambler's vocation. He reportedly worked at a poker school for a while, and perhaps she found this romantic. The files noted that the earl soon abandoned poker for *chemin de fer* and blackjack, which he pursued at private clubs in Mayfair. These games involved low skill and quick gratification, unlike the more complex, paced games of five-card draw and stud. It could be argued that when Lucan lost his poker acumen, he began to lose his wife.

They had three children, George, Frances and Camilla. In keeping with the children's-story motif, Peter would have told the tale from Camilla's viewpoint. George, who stood to gain the title of eighth Earl, was too seriously status-committed to tell it in a balanced fashion, and Frances, as it turned out, became an important witness to her parents' exceedingly bloody brawl and was thus open to endless challenges to her depiction. Only Camilla, haunted by the irony of having slept through the whole fracas, could have been trusted to maintain some objectivity, and possibly return, deeply haunted, to the family tragedy with a memoir later in life.

As it turned out, it was the countess herself who first put an account on the record. Peter cut back and forth between his old files and her subsequent website version. From a legal point of view, and even aside from the inculpatory bloodstains, the evidence of premeditation likely would have doomed the husband in court. He was chronically in debt and hated his wife, to whom he had by then lost custody of the children. He had moved to a flat, while she retained the family mansion in Belgravia. At several dinners he was heard to say that he would be better off with her dead. In the confusion of that fatal night, his pop-up appearances at the Clermont Club and other hangouts smacked of alibi shopping.

Is character destiny? Peter believed that Lucan was undone by the shallowness of his plan. He couldn't even get the victim right. Mistaking the young nanny for his wife in the darkened basement landing — it served him right, since he had unscrewed the bulb (a metaphor for stupidity if ever there was one) — he struck her down with a lead pipe wrapped in tape. The homicide began to resemble the board game Clue. By the time Lady Lucan came down to look for the nanny, he had her stuffed in a canvas sack. He then struck his wife using the same weapon, but she was not easy prey. She grabbed him by the testicles and forced him to back away. There followed a truly bizarre standoff, during which they lurched from the basement to their lavatory and paused, in a pseudo-conciliatory way, in the bedroom to review their options. Somehow, she managed to escape, running out through the white-pillared portal of the house on Belgrave Street.

Much bloodied but still alive, Lady Lucan tottered efficiently down the road to the nearest pub, the working class Plumber's Arms. (In the margin of his original notes, Peter had written: "Who would call their pub that? Shouldn't it have been 'The Plumber's Elbow'?") She burst through the door and articulated: "Help me! I've just escaped being murdered. He's in the house. He's murdered my nanny!"

As his notes reminded him, Peter had doubted the wife's precision at the time. If you are gushing blood in the sudden glare of an indifferent tavern, do you announce yourself in perfect sentences? The Countess had been under siege from the press and conspiracy sceptics for decades since.

As for Lucan, any premeditation collapsed into improvisation. Failing to prevent his wife from escaping, he began an evasive odyssey across southern England. First, he telephoned his mother to ask if she would mind picking up the children. No one knew what he really planned to do next, but his luck now failed him. He attempted to contact old friends, perhaps more for solace than for what they could do for him. Lucan sustained an ingenuous regard for the friendship of his circle, a coterie of hyphenated aristocrats whose main assistance in the long run was to give vague and grudging testimony to the police regarding Lucan's last hours. Some observers hypothesized later that his reluctant friends had helped him out of the country using an expensive speedboat, but there was little sign that any of them knew how to turn an ignition key.

Whichever the case, all these peripatetic roads led to the sea. Lucan parked his borrowed Ford Corsair near the beach at Newhaven and was never seen again.

Over the years, the reports of sightings of Lucan became egregious. He was typically found living in the back of a van or holding down a bar stool in an African village. All identifications proved bogus. The Yard tracked a dozen sightings every year. André Lasker could have read about the case, but there was no way to be sure.

Peter had played a minor part in the investigation in the mid-seventies. Even then, the reports poured in of Lucan surfacing in South Africa, Goa and other classic havens for men desperate to avoid Interpol. Cammon himself, who had just started along his career path when the Yard mobilized to track down Lucan, was sent to Cherbourg to investigate a sighting at a popular resort hotel. An Englishman fitting Lucan's callow profile had stayed there two summers in a row, and was known to take the train to Deauville, famous for its upscale casinos.

Peter interviewed the Cherbourg hotel manager, who was sure that the man wasn't Lucan. Several British tourists had dutifully called the nearest British Consul to swear that they had found the fugitive on the Continent, at the hotel or in the town, but Peter noticed that few identifications were reported by the French residents in the area. Perhaps they liked the tradition of welcoming those who were unacceptable to their home governments. Peter had recently read Somerset Maugham's *The Moon and Sixpence*, in which the Englishman Charles Strickland deserts wife and children to live a bohemian existence in Paris; Peter noted that Maugham regarded the neighbourhoods of Paris as more accommodating hiding places than the provinces.

The hotel guest in Cherbourg was certainly not the murderer.

For one thing, he liked to have his picture taken, and there was even a snapshot of the man on the veranda. He was fifty pounds heavier than Lucan and had a large strawberry mark on his cheek. Lucan was known to eat lamb chops several times a week; the suspect never chose them from the hotel menu. It was the off-season, and Peter remembered that the hotelier tried to persuade him to stay an extra couple of days. Peter, as a junior officer, worried about abusing the Yard's expense schedule, and so refused; but he found out that he couldn't get a train to the French coast until the next morning. The manager treated him to dinner that evening on the closed-in veranda.

Across the table, swirling his wine in the wide bowl of his glass (Peter stayed with a fine Bière de Garde), the manager related the following joke, which he said Parisians liked to tell on themselves.

An Englishman moves to the City of Light with a firm determination to become a great lover, in the French model. ("Beware the man or woman fanatical to live out a cliché," the hotel manager interjected in his own story.) He courts women like a Scaramouche, wines and dines them relentlessly from the moment he arrives. He remains mysterious and nameless, except for the adopted *prénom* Jacques, and is all the more romantic a figure for it. One night, he suggests to one of his amours that they go for a walk along the quay that edges the Seine. He kisses her in the moonlight as the *Bateaux Mouches* sail by. Sweeping her into his arms, he slips on the wet cobbles and she falls into the fast-flowing Seine. He is consumed by remorse. But not quite consumed . . . Within days, his desires overcome his guilt and he seeks out another lover. Again he risks the *bord du fleuve,* and the second girl falls to her watery death. But his ardour — only temporarily dampened, so to speak — wins out, and our Englishman finds yet a third lover and, wouldn't you know it, she drowns as well. There is nothing for it: the man writes a final letter, an ode to Paris and lost loves, and jumps into the river from the Pont Neuf. The body is never found. Thus, he gains an immortal reputation as a romantic, more Parisian than the locals.

The hotel manager leaned across the linen tablecloth towards Peter to deliver the punch line: "Who would have guessed that the man also enjoyed the kill?"

Peter had no doubt that Lord Lucan would have emerged soon after his escape, had he survived. He had planned his crime poorly and mismanaged it from the beginning. The dissolute seventh Earl was descended from the notorious third Earl, who had sent the Light Brigade down that deadly valley in the Crimea, a fact that led Peter's colleagues at the Yard to speak of "generations of screw-ups." Lucan was a hapless mastermind at best: he would have returned to gambling almost immediately. As a titled man, he could never have withstood a life of anonymous penury. As dawn approached, his plan disintegrating, he must have seen the ocean as his only resolution.

Peter knew not to overdo the analogies to André Lasker's disappearance as he read through the musty dossier, but they had one thing in common, and that was the challenge of identity. Lucan didn't know, had likely never known, who he was: in *Brett's* he was listed as the seventh Earl and in the birth records he was Richard John Bingham; to Lady Lucan he was simply John, and to the kids he was Dada; at the Clermont Club his self-chosen moniker was Lucky, although near the end he called himself Blue Lucan. Was he content to depart knowing that his son, George, would inevitably inherit the title of eighth Earl, and an empty bank account?

André Lasker may have been an ordinary man in a provincial town, but he dreamed of a new identity. He had put his affairs in order. He would find his true self in an exotic hideaway on the other side of the world. But the world is a circle, and Anna's self-destruction had put the lie to that dream, and that was why André Lasker would come home.

As Michael had told his father, it was the monkey that she had left him to carry.

300

CHAPTER 25

The Air Malta daily landed at Luga Airport in the blasting light of late afternoon. The flight was stuffed with pasty vacationers, all anticipating that curative sun. Peter struck up a conversation with a Gloucestershire cab driver who made the trip six times a year and now planned to emigrate. Like most other Mediterranean spots, Malta had attracted the gamut of partygoers and elderly couples, many of whom were buying into the condo boom on Malta and Gozo, its secondary island. His seatmate recommended the view from the starboard window as they swooped to three thousand feet and approached the airport from the south. Even through the limited porthole, Peter could see the full dimensions of the main island. Malta was a battleship of limestone, fixed in a sea of unchanging blue. The hill towns at its centre formed a ship's bridge from which an admiral could observe the Mediterranean in all directions, or so Peter imagined. The man beside him identified the highest plateau on the island, which was topped with castle battlements, as the old capital of Mdina.

But Valletta was Peter's destination, and he glimpsed it off to the left as the plane came in to land. The airport was small but crowded with tourists. The Home Office, under whose aegis New Scotland Yard operated, issued all detectives the equivalent of diplomatic passports, and Peter was immediately fast-tracked through customs. He paused to look over at the regular lines, where the other passengers from his flight were queuing up. He was curious about the rigour of Passport Control's vetting of ordinary travellers. He wasn't about to patronize this country; he had no doubt that the Maltese officers were using the latest passport scanner mandated by the European Union, of which Malta was a recent and proud member. But documentation was not the only challenge; that could be faked, and a good customs man learned to read faces and interpret travel patterns. Also, like every other tourist destination, Malta tried to process its cash-loaded guests as rapidly as possible. The line was moving quickly. With a good false passport, Lasker could easily have slipped into the country — and out again.

Outside the main immigration office within the airport stood a short man in a dark blue uniform. Malta Police Headquarters had been forewarned by Bartleben personally; it was a case of deputy commissioner contacting deputy commissioner. The similarity likely stopped there, Peter mused. His host wore the colourful insignia suited to his elevated rank, and his dyed, razor-cut hair and recently trimmed moustache completed the aura of someone parochially important. Peter had expected nothing less from an official named Antonio Albanoni. He reminded himself to choose his words carefully.

The deputy commissioner arched an eyebrow discreetly when he saw Peter approach. Peter had once flown into a tiny airport on the Greek island of Samos to pick up a suspect and found himself greeted in the waiting area by a hand-lettered sign that read, *Welcome Chief Inspector Cammon*; he had prayed that the fugitive wasn't in the airport at that moment. Albanoni extended a hand and offered a pearly smile. Peter was reminded of the Claude Rains character in *Casablanca*.

"Chief Inspector, I am Antonio Albanoni."

"Thank you for agreeing to see me on such short notice," Peter responded.

The Maltese deputy commissioner squared his shoulders and this time raised both dyed eyebrows.

"The prisoner has escaped," he said.

So much for jet-lag recovery, Peter thought. The latest email from Malta Police, transmitted to him via Bartleben's office, had informed him that Lasker was being watched at his tourist hotel in Sliema. How had he escaped the island?

Peter retained sufficient aplomb to fake a benign expression. "Is he still on the island?"

"We don't think so." Albanoni began to explain the situation in a rushed, high voice that took on an Italian rhythm as he speeded up. Peter could barely understand him. "We know that he had a false passport. We now suspect that he had a second false passport."

Peter now had to face the prospect that he and André Lasker had just passed each other at thirty thousand feet.

"Is it too late to meet at your offices?" he asked.

"No, no, not at all! The detectives who were watching Mr. Lasker are on shift until eight o'clock."

Albanoni drove his own official car, an unmarked Saab, into the heart of Valletta. Malta had been one of the countries to which Lasker had exported his used cars, and Peter assumed that this was not one of his vehicles. They passed through an impressive stone arch and into the older part of the capital, where many of the buildings were constructed with soft, yellow stone, giving them an Arabian feel. He caught a glimpse of the fortifications ahead just as Albanoni took away the view by veering down a side street. A minute later they parked next to a modern four-storey office building. Peter observed that it housed both the Police Service and the Security Agency.

The Home Office shared its country briefings with New Scotland Yard; indeed, the Yard provided the crime sit reps for these profiles. Peter knew that since 9/11 Malta had expanded its security capacity, with a new anti-terrorism act to back it up. He wondered if officers from both the police and the Security Agency had been inputting to the Lasker case, since the crossover in manpower and in skills was sometimes useful, although it just as often held the potential for confusion. Many in the police professions believed that the distinctions between policing and counterterrorism were artificial, and Peter agreed, but he was certainly willing to respect jurisdictional lines in a foreign country.

The deputy commissioner led him down a long hallway to his corner office. "You can store your valises here," Albanoni said, "and someone will transfer them to the Marriott."

The usual framed citations hung from the walls, each of these bearing official stamps with the Maltese cross in red. Peter, in his time, had never hung anything in his office at New Scotland Yard. He wasn't impressed by those who did, although the photograph of Albanoni standing beside Pope John Paul II was unnerving.

After washing up in Albanoni's "executive" washroom, Peter repaired with his host to a meeting room on the same floor. Two tough cops, tired and unshaven, wearing their street clothes, slouched on the far side of the table, looking defiant and very unhappy; their dressing-down had already been applied. Albanoni introduced Detectives Bahti and Korman. Peter shook hands, but only Bahti, the younger but evidently the senior of the pair, made eye contact. Scotland Yard was mythical to them, and Peter, in his dark suit and tie, was an alien curiosity. Accordingly, he decided to keep the entire discussion at the factual, procedural level, no matter how the deputy commissioner tried to add a flattering gloss to his descent from London. He was comforted by having two obviously streetwise detectives to work with on this manhunt.

"Gentlemen, first things first. Don't worry about losing Lasker. I've been searching for him for weeks and never came close. Let's start by you taking me through your surveillance."

The two men were mollified by Peter's introduction, though they kept a wary eye on Albanoni. Bahti, the evident leader of the pair, sat up straight. "We have been watching your man for seventy-two hours, maybe a bit less. Rotating shifts, twelve-and-twelve."

"Back it up a bit," Peter interjected. "How did you get the alert in the first place?"

Albanoni answered. "Three days ago, your office cabled a list of names that appeared on British and EU export manifests for three automobiles headed for Malta. We checked for the matching import stamps here on Malta, and we found them; they fit the cars' description. The local signature was in the name Herman Willemsea, and the Customs official recalled that the person showed a Maltese passport in that particular name. We have checked. There is no citizen of Malta with that name."

Bahti jumped in, eager for some credit for his and his partner's initiative. "Your office told us that Lasker could be in Valletta using one of the names connected to the cars. We decided to check hotel registrations for the last week. Hotels here are required to make these available to the authorities. We found him."

"But the hotels don't retain passports?"

"No," Bahti said, "but he was registered at a particular hotel under the name Herman Willemsea, and he showed a passport with that name on it. He never identified himself as André Lasker, and there was no sign of a Lasker passport either at the hotel or at Customs."

The detectives created an expectant pause. "You see what happened, Chief Inspector?" Bahti went on. It was a test. There was a huge contradiction here.

"I do," Peter replied. "Do I have this right? Someone with the false name Willemsea signed the import documents several months ago. But not the same person who used the passport at the hotel."

The one called Korman smiled for the first time. "Right. Mr. Lasker had another, probably British, fake passport that he used to *enter* Malta, and then someone gave him the Willemsea passport when he arrived, to use *while he was here*."

"And therefore," Peter added, "someone had the skill to alter passport photographs, and manufacture fresh passports on short notice. This is a sophisticated operation."

"We began surveillance," Bahti said. "We managed to observe the suspect up close in the lobby. He matched the photograph sent to us by Europol of Mr. Lasker. Not a great picture, but clear enough."

"The same picture was distributed by Interpol and by Scotland Yard," Albanoni added, unhelpfully.

"We were told not to arrest him yet, until you got here," Korman said.

Bahti continued. "We believed that if he abandoned the hotel, there were few places he could hide in Sliema, or even in Valletta. And our people at the airport were on alert for the Willemsea passport."

The flaw in their assumptions was obvious, but Peter restrained himself. Lasker had employed a *third* passport, though possibly the same one he presented upon entry, to flee the country. Either way, the only name they knew was Willemsea.

"When did you lose him?"

"This morning," Bahti said. "The desk clerk was instructed to watch for our man. They have a small breakfast room on the entry floor. He came down at his usual time, had coffee and fruit, and read the *International Herald Tribune*."

"He went out the back," Korman added.

Peter turned to Albanoni. "Does everyone have his picture?"

"Yes, but why are you asking that?"

"Because I think Lasker flew out of Luga today, using a separate passport."

"A third one? Well," Albanoni said defensively, "our Customs Officers were told to watch for the man in the picture."

"What flights leave between, say, 9:00 a.m. and mid-afternoon?"

Korman was the only one who had the answer. "Air Malta to London, British Airways to Heathrow, Ryanair to Barcelona, Alitalia to Rome and Lufthansa to Frankfurt. A few charters returning home to the Continent."

"What about Ryanair to Pisa?" Bahti asked.

"Not today."

It was intriguing to guess at Lasker's preferred destination. Peter believed that the mechanic wouldn't take the direct route back to England — namely, the Heathrow flight — and thereby risk the predictable tight screening at customs. Luton or Gatwick were no less fastidious but, with a disguise, he might have a better chance to get through. Lasker might also have flown to the continental hub that had the most connectors to the U.K.

"Well," Peter sighed, "let's check the most and least likely destinations, and narrow from there. Can we call up the Ryanair site on the web?"

Bahti smiled. "You want to see how he can reach Britain the easiest?"

They trooped down to an open area in the police building where Bahti and Korman had their desks. Each was piled with reports and telephone messages. Bahti tapped the keyboard on the desktop at his station, and the Ryanair homepage came onto the screen. He pressed another key and the destination map unfolded. He clicked on Barcelona and the classic starburst of lines flew out from the Spanish city to a number of European cities, including London.

"Okay," Albanoni said, "let's contact security at Barcelona. Somebody needs to go to the airport to see if anyone of Lasker's description got on the Ryanair to Spain, and check the Rome and Frankfurt flights. I will call Europol in The Hague and Interpol in Lyon."

He was about to dispatch both detectives to the airport, when Peter interceded. "Wait a moment. Do you have the documents covering the three automobiles that Willemsea imported to Malta?"

All three nodded. "We have them in the Lasker dossier," Bahti said.

"Is there a local destination for the cars, and address?"

Bahti understood. "Yes. There must be a Maltese address identified on the forms. Only a Maltese can legally import."

They made another journey down the hall, to Albanoni's file cabinet. The detectives were a bit uncomfortable being in the boss's office. They dug out the dog-eared shipping forms and discovered that the address at the bottom of all three was the same.

"We all know him," Korman said.

"Him?" Peter said

"He is in the import-export trade. All kinds of goods. Sylvio Kamatta. He has an office on the harbour."

"Is he reputable?" Peter said. The detectives smiled and shook their heads.

"Is he known to deal in forged passports?" Peter added. There was no answer but the two street detectives were already reaching for their coats.

Korman and Bahti were assigned to take Peter to track down Kamatta at his office, which was located near the adjacent waterfront of Vittoriosa, while the deputy commissioner went off to find men to handle the airport. This arrangement suited Peter, who preferred to have the two plainclothes officers with him when he interviewed the suspect. Peter understood the reality that there was always at least one tough kingpin at the centre of every elaborate fraud. The interrogation of Kamatta wasn't going to be polite. They needed to pick up the Lasker trail as fast as possible.

The plan went awry almost immediately. They assumed that Kamatta could be traced through his harbourfront office, a short trip from police headquarters, and so, instead of calling ahead, the three detectives, Korman driving, hustled over to the docks. The office was planted on the second floor of a boxy, nondescript block set back a hundred metres from the water. A woman who looked as if nothing, and certainly not three grim policemen, could impress her occupied a desk and chair in the bleak space. The only decoration was a bulletin board that covered one wall and served as Kamatta's invoicing system. Peter scanned the squibs and sticky notes while the woman stared without emotion. Bahti would play bad cop. Korman stood in the doorway, pretty much blocking out the light.

"Where is your boss?" Bahti said in English, for Peter's benefit.

"On vacation." She replied, with a heavy Maltese inflection.

She spoke in a smoker's rasp. Her creased face was heavily tanned. Bahti and the woman then conducted an argument in the Maltese language. It grew louder and more threatening on both sides, although there could be no doubt, in her mind or theirs, that Bahti would get his way. Peter understood that Bahti was warning her of a night in jail if she failed to cooperate.

Bahti turned to Peter and reported: "She refuses to say where he is and when he will return."

By the look Bahti gave him, he knew that the woman understood English quite well. He played along, pretending that she did not. "What was the first thing she said when you asked her where he was?"

"First she told me he was taking a vacation. Then she said that she did not know where he was. Then that he was at the seashore."

This was an island, and so Peter couldn't read all the nuances of that answer. "Does 'at the seashore' have a special meaning in Malta?"

"Yes," Bahti said. "It is what people say when they are going to their home villages. Sometimes it means they are going to a seaside town nearby for a few days, to relax."

"Can we find out where Kamatta is from?"

Bahti asked. The woman spewed out a stream of insults in Maltese.

"She won't say. I threatened again to close up the office and bring her to the lock-up in Valletta."

Peter told Bahti to keep working on the woman, but he winked as he said it. He ushered Korman to the landing outside the office doorway and whispered something in the detective's ear. The woman watched them walk away. They went back inside and Korman took his turn questioning the woman; it was a case of hard cop and harder cop. Although Peter comprehended nothing in the Maltese language, he waited for the key word to come up. It would be the same in both languages.

"Terrorism," Korman said. The woman turned pale. She no longer pretended to be ignorant of English. She looked at Peter — understanding that he was someone foreign, and had special authority — but he shrugged, indicating that he couldn't stop these two aggressive locals. Peter had read the Home Office file. Malta had modelled its terrorism legislation on Britain's, supplemented with model Commonwealth laws developed in the aftermath of the Twin Towers attack. The country had adopted preventive detention as one of its deterrence strategies, significantly with a rather open-ended process for reviewing and revoking that detention. Korman's tone implied that she might languish in jail until her boss resurfaced.

She switched to halting English, perhaps seeking sympathy from the Brit. "Everyone, they know that Kamatta is from Marsalforn. He was born there, but he is not there now. I do not know where he went, but it was not Marsalforn."

"What the Christ does that mean?" Bahti said, in English this time.

"It means," Korman answered loudly, "that this lying old seagull thinks Kamatta will hurt her worse than we will. She knows where he is. I will take her to the town."

The woman began wailing but Korman simply dragged her out the door and down the stairs to the street; Peter heard him instructing her to stay away from the office. All three men knew what was going on, even if the woman did not. They knew Kamatta was likely in his hometown, but they let the lady think she had fooled them.

Bahti and Peter looked in the battered desk and through the papers pinned to the bulletin board. Copies of shipping manifests, business cards and even vacation brochures covered the corkboard; the Maltese coppers would likely confiscate the whole mess. But they found very little to connect the owner to Lasker, though Bahti did find an address that he said was a street in Marsalforn, over on the island of Gozo.

Back in the car, but without the woman, Bahti retraced the route to police headquarters. "We will pick up your luggage and take you to the Marriott."

Peter's excitement rose as he began to see the carrot dangling at the end of the stick, even if the carrot apparently was hiding an island away. Kamatta was likely the key to all of André Lasker's false identities. Peter was tired, from the flight and the heat, but the certainty that Lasker existed and was probably headed back to Britain reinvigorated him. Bahti was so dour that Peter had a hard time reading his face, but he immediately liked him; he had a sense that the man was the ultimate street detective, never happier than when he had explicit orders to do what was necessary to apprehend criminals, and to do it fast.

"What about Kamatta, then?" Peter asked.

"It is probably too late to go to Marsalforn tonight," Bahti replied. "It is on Gozo, the smaller island. But I have a man in Victoria, the capital city of Gozo. He will do what I tell him."

Peter always tried to be alert to the subtleties of the local police wherever he travelled on an investigation. He was willing to push them to faster action, but there was often a way of doing things, a circular way of getting results, that had to be respected, and Peter was adept at picking up on it. Albanoni, on the other hand, appeared not to see the urgency of following every lead in order to find Lasker *before* he reached English territory; his lethargy, born of bureaucratic ossification, was going to be exasperating. Peter had more confidence in Bahti.

"Okay," Peter replied, neutrally. "Do you men know Kamatta?"

There was a pause — and not only because Bahti was busy at that moment swerving around a lorry — while the Maltese detectives thought through their answer. "Yes. Kamatta is Maltese," Bahti said. "We are a small island with many 'invaders' who bring in drugs, illegal refugees, prostitutes, and so on. But when my fellow citizens get involved, I become wonderfully pissed off!"

They turned into Albanoni's parking space (which was a statement in itself on Bahti's part, but which also indicated that the deputy commissioner probably was still occupied at the airport).

"Get your stuff, Inspector," Bahti instructed. "We will go to the hotel, and then, if you are interested, we will go for dinner. Korman, I'm afraid, must run home to his pregnant wife."

Peter immediately agreed to this plan. They reached the Marriott and he went inside to register. By the time he returned, his new partner had made his call to Victoria; Korman had left.

"Here is the arrangement. Marko will drive to Marsalforn right away and check the address we have. He is Gozan. He does not know Kamatta, and he thinks he is not one of the natives of Marsalforn. But Marko knows everyone else who knows anything, and they will tell him if Kamatta is around."

"And Marko is a police officer?"

"Not exactly. He is my cousin. He is reliable."

"I believe you, Officer Bahti. Is that your first name or your last?"

"It is both. It's a long story. Call me Bahti. Obviously."

"Call me Peter. Just for the record, is there a police presence on Gozo?"

"Certainly, and they are very good people. But it is complicated. There are units in Victoria and in Mgarr. Mgarr is the port where the Malta ferry goes. They are used to dealing with tourists and their crises, or with local matters like spousal battery. But it has been a tradition that major cases are supervised from Valletta. In reality, Gozo experiences as much drug and refugee smuggling as Malta. Less prostitution, though. We make sure they save face when we take over a matter — that is the expression?"

"It is."

"Yes, they are getting involved a lot in counterterrorism and refugee exercises. That is because both involve patrolling the coast, along with the navy."

Peter thought he had it straight. Bahti would use his cousin to make discreet inquiries regarding Kamatta's whereabouts. Only then would the detectives decide how to proceed. Peter had no doubt that Korman and Bahti would go it alone if that proved to be the most effective tactic. But just to be crystal clear, he said, "But the expertise on passport forgery is in Valletta?"

Bahti shrugged. "We all learn to read a fake passport. You would be shocked at how many forged papers I see. Malta is a crossroads for illegals moving up into Europe from Africa. Much of the forgery work is excellent, I admit. But we do have a very good forensics lab. You may get to meet them," he added wryly.

He gave Peter the simple directions to the restaurant and they agreed to rendezvous there in an hour. Bahti high-signed several cab drivers parked in front of the Marriott and headed off towards police headquarters.

CHAPTER 26

The Marriott was positioned at the edge of the ancient gates to Valletta. Peter went back to the front desk and retrieved his messages. Of the three, one was from Bartleben and the second from Albanoni, but it was simply a welcoming note that predated his arrival. The third was from Ronald Hamm. Peter got lucky. From his hotel room, the 3G capacity of his mobile kicked in and he heard the phone at Bartleben's end ringing. As usual, he was still at the office.

"Peter! I can hear you fine. Where are you?"

"In my hotel in Valletta."

"How is Malta?"

"When I see it, I'll let you know. Has Malta Police Headquarters reached you in the last hour or so?"

"No. what's the news?

"Lasker was here. He slipped away from surveillance and flew out of Luqa earlier today — ironically, probably about the time I was arriving. Did a Deputy Commissioner by the name of Albanoni contact your office, or anyone else?" Peter could hear him getting up from his desk and walking into the reception area. "Is there something regarding Interpol?" he continued, as Bartleben roamed the office.

"Peter, he called while I was out," Bartleben answered. "The

314

message states he would be contacting Europol, for a start. Wants me to check back."

"That's consistent with our understanding. We're on the track of the man who forged his various passports."

"Right. Here it is; it's on my screen now. Let me see . . . The Europol feed is automatically duplicated on Interpol's standard flow. If it gets a top priority on the one, it will be reflected on the other." Peter listened as Bartleben tapped on his keyboard. Bartleben was adept with the software; he loved to play with his computer, and Cammon thought that that might be why he so often stayed late at the office.

"Yes, here it is," he said. "It says André Lasker departed Luga today . . . Probably for Barcelona . . . might have travelled under a false EU passport in the name of Herman Willemsea."

"Not likely," Peter interjected. "Stephen, I know this is ass-backwards, since I'm the one in Malta, but does it list the possibility of pseudonyms that match the other names on the auto export manifests?" By now Peter knew the names by heart and he listed them for his boss.

"The simple answer is no. The only name on the watch list is Willemsea."

Peter's hotel room phone rang. "Just a minute, Stephen. I have a call on the room line."

It was Albanoni, very excited. Peter juggled the corded receiver in an attempt to let Bartleben overhear the conversation. He had no idea whether or not this manoeuvre would work, and he looked foolish, but there was no one to see.

"Go ahead, Antonio." A little familiarity might smooth the way, he hoped.

"We did not find him," the distraught official stated. "He did not use the surname 'Willemsea,' nor did he employ the other names you gave me."

"I'm not surprised," Peter responded, in a palliating tone. "It is obvious that he has multiple passports."

"But Chief Inspector, what name are we looking for?" The tone was plaintive, and Lord knows how it sounded to Stephen across the Mediterranean.

Bartleben grunted over the mobile phone line. The noise had two effects. It let Peter know that Stephen would take care of Interpol. Lyon would not simply add any name to its list, but if British authorities appended the names to its own immigration watch list, they would immediately be copied to the central Interpol directives in Lyon and distributed to every airline security service in Europe. Of course, Lasker could still be flying around Europe under any of a dozen or more names.

The second impact was to make Albanoni suspicious. "Is there someone there?" he asked.

"No," Peter affirmed. "What do we know about Lasker's clearance to Barcelona?"

Now Albanoni's acumen emerged. It soon became clear that he understood the airline security dimensions of his job. "We have the passenger lists for every departing flight from today. Eighteen of the passengers on the Ryanair flight to Barcelona were booked on the Ryanair plane out of Spain to London. Of course, our suspect could have switched to another airline, and we will look into that, but the earliest arrival time would be achieved by taking the Ryanair connector today."

"When does that flight leave?"

"It has already left. Even worse, it has already arrived in Britain. One hour ago."

The problem, as Peter had expected, was expanding exponentially. If Albanoni had distributed his information earlier, British Immigration might have snagged Lasker under whatever name he was using. But there was no firm reason to conclude that the fugitive was on that particular flight. He could have hopped from Barcelona to some other European capital, and could now be biding his time in anonymity.

Peter brought Albanoni up to date on the tracking of Kamatta and the plan to go to Marsalforn. He left out the bit about Bahti's cousin, but he pledged to report back to the deputy commissioner as soon as they were done. Meanwhile, could Albanoni copy the airline manifests from all other flights that had left in the previous twelve hours, and fax them to New Scotland Yard?

"I will be very happy to accomplish that, Chief Inspector!" Peter understood the importance of keeping the man busy. He hung up the room phone.

"Did you hear that, Stephen?"

"Yes, Peter. I'll take care of Interpol. I'll also work with Immigration on vetting all visitors coming in today or tomorrow. Where do you think he's gone?"

"Everything tells me he wants to get back to Britain as soon as he can. I'm not sure why, but that's my instinct."

"Well, your instinct is good enough for me. What are you going to do next?"

"My best angle is to find Lasker's contact here, which I'm sure is also the fellow he worked with on importing the vehicles. We know where he's likely to be, but I can't get to him before tomorrow morning. We'll see if there's any trace of other false names that our man might be using."

"Let's agree to talk tomorrow afternoon. By the way, is that cell phone you're using secure?"

"Probably not. Last thing, Stephen, but could you call Detective Ronald Hamm at Whittlesun Police? He left me a message here at the hotel and I have no idea what it's about, except that he knows the Lasker case."

"Wasn't he the man you took a dip in the sea with, while pursuing the Rover chap?"

"It's not about the Rover. I hope."

Peter dodged the bright yellow British Leyland buses that circled around the staging terminus outside the Valletta gates. He passed through the ancient stone portal and strolled down the main avenue towards the harbour. Cafés and jewellery shops lined the Triq Republica; lights and strings of ribbons hung above the street, giving it a permanent carnival feel. Arabs, Turks and Crusaders had traversed this area for five centuries and rivers of blood had run between these stones. The town had that self-contained feel that old, walled cities retain; an added effect was the ease with which places could be found inside an unchanging grid of narrow streets, prominent churches and the orderly layout of the stone fortifications.

A small neon sign advertised the restaurant in glowing blue letters: *Giorgio's.* It stood at the spot where the main street began its descent to the Grandmaster's Palace. Peter resolved to find time for a quick tour of what he had been told was a Wonder of the Manmade World, the battlements constructed — and defended to the death — by the Order of the Knights of St. John. He followed the entrance path to a sheltered courtyard, which in turn led to an open terrace. He could not have seen this view from the street, but now he found himself looking out at three fingers of land projecting into a section of the Valletta harbour. The notches between those fingers created vast marinas, all jammed with sailboats and yachts. The view was extraordinary — peaceful, calculated, profoundly blue.

Bahti was waiting at a table by the iron fence at the edge of the patio. He had spruced up a bit but Peter could tell that he was making no real concession to the tourist ambience of the restaurant, and it soon became clear that the manager was happy to have a policeman or two as customers.

"Sit down, Inspector," the smiling host said.

Peter did. Bahti put out his cigarette. "Chief Inspector."

"Call me Peter. There's no need for formality." This was police lingo. Peter was again sending a signal that tomorrow they would be doing whatever needed to be done to find Kamatta. They would be working as a team, and there was no doubt that they would go in heavily armed.

The manager, clearly also the owner, came over and asked if Peter would like some wine. He asked for a local beer. The host, grinning and obsequious, was pleased to recommend a "special" Maltese beer. He left menus, which Bahti ignored, and left to get Peter's drink and a refill of Bahti's Strega.

"Everything is 'special' with him," Bahti said, "but there is only one dish for a visitor to try."

Peter adjusted his chair, but before he could settle in, he was startled to find the manager already back with his beer and a plate of olives. Bahti ordered in Maltese.

Peter had already decided to disclose everything about the Lasker case to Bahti. He spoke non-stop for twenty minutes. A second beer appeared on the table. He reviewed his conversations with Albanoni and Bartleben and the steps that London was taking to distribute the possible aliases that Lasker might use.

"Good," Bahti said, after Peter had finished his long update. "I don't need to phone the deputy commissioner back tonight."

"Did you hear from your cousin?"

Bahti smiled, a combination of family pride and game-is-afoot slyness.

"He is really my nephew and he is seventeen years of age. He is a smart boy, the smartest kid I have ever met. He wants to be a cop. He went to Marsalforn and called me from there. Kamatta has not been seen there today but was in the town either yesterday or the day before, no one was sure. But my nephew did find Kamatta's house. He is watching it."

"He's not exposing himself to danger, I hope."

"He is a smart boy. He will be just another teenager wearing flippers."

"I beg your pardon?" Peter said.

"Marsalforn is a place for sea divers. There are dive shops everywhere, and that's how my nephew knows who to talk to. You see, his friends are in a position to see every new foreigner who arrives in the town."

Peter saw that the detective was building to something.

"And," Bahti continued, "there was somebody new there last week. A Brit."

"Why does your nephew think it might be Lasker?"

"Because the man acted like he was moving there. He looked at flats. He wasn't there to go diving or sail, but he did ask at the quay about boats."

"Your nephew doesn't have a picture of Lasker?"

"No," Bahti admitted. "The man was blond and had a moustache."

As far as Peter knew, André Lasker had never worn a moustache.

The meal arrived and the owner announced: "Tagine with rabbit and couscous!" He seemed pleased when Peter ordered a third beer. They sorted out their meal and began eating.

"So," Bahti said, "do you get seasick?"

"Never."

Bahti smiled. "It will be faster in the morning to take a police launch to Mgarr, then a local man will take us to Marsalforn. We could land at the harbour in Marsalforn, but that will give us away if Kamatta is still in the town. Besides, you will get to see the knights' fort and have a tour of the coast. Very beautiful."

Peter proceeded to recount the saga of his scramble across the Jurassic Cliffs with Ronald Hamm, and their tumble into the Channel. Bahti was soon laughing and tossing back shots of Strega. Peter ordered a fourth beer, and then a fifth.

The four policemen stood on the hilltop looking down on the sleeping town of Marsalforn. They were early, and there was no sign of Bahti's nephew.

A Coast Guard launch had conveyed Peter and Bahti at dawn from the boat slip in Vittoriosa to the ferry terminal in Mgarr, where two Gozo officers met them with a police vehicle. Nowhere was very far on Gozo, and they reached the village in minutes.

It was still early, and the four men shared coffee from a vacuum flask. The pause gave Peter time to appreciate the beauty of Malta and the surrounding Mediterranean, now emerging a special blue under the rising sun. Even in the half-hour voyage from Vittoriosa, he had glimpsed extraordinary sights: the magnificent battlements constructed by the Knights of St. John; the ancient prison where Caravaggio, himself a member of the order, had languished; and the great, crumbling seawall that protected Valletta Harbour. The Maltese were survivors who prevailed by embracing the sea. The Coast Guard boat had cruised past pockmarked and weather-stippled cliffs as forbidding as any on the Channel coast, yet if there was any space at all for a human structure, someone had erected a house, or at least a crofter's shack.

It was a fine spot for a man to hide out. From the top of the S-curve, Peter could see directly through to the scoop-shaped harbour of Marsalforn. A freighter and a cruise ship sat at anchor a kilometre off shore. The senior man, Sergeant Martens, gave Bahti a radio, and they checked the frequency; Bahti concealed it under his shirt. He pointed out the centre of the town and pushed his hand forward, indicating to Peter that Kamatta's flat, and hopefully Bahti's nephew, were lodged several streets in from the water. A short argument followed; it was in Maltese, but Peter grasped that Martens's young partner wanted to join the party in town. The real problem, Peter appreciated, was that Martens and his partner were wearing full police uniforms, a neon warning to any suspect. Peter stood away from the argument, on the verge of the roadway, and gazed down at the quiet village.

The dispute resolved, the four men, Peter in the back with Bahti, got into the car and zipped down the hill into the back streets. Nothing was moving in the town, at least in the main square. Martens let Peter and Bahti off by the bus shelter, which was adjacent to a short canal on one side, with a new hotel flanking the other. The car left, and the Maltese detective at once led Peter down a side street and out of sight.

As they traversed the first intersection offshooting from the canal, Peter glanced to his left and glimpsed the harbour a couple of streets down. As if looking through a gun slit, he saw all the way to the open

Mediterranean, which the Bible called the Great Sea. Bahti remained focused straight ahead along the shadowed street. With basic hand gestures, he stopped Peter at the next corner. He was clearly worried that his nephew, Marko, hadn't appeared. There was still no one about. Peter halted next to his new partner. He was out of breath and for some reason felt bone-weary. He hadn't caught up with his sleep yet, but that wasn't it. Part of it was the constant brightness of the whitewashed rock; the sun was coming up rapidly now, promising to expose everyone and every surface to its spotlight glare. He needed to keep moving, to get this arrest over with, to discover the false name under which Lasker was finally returning home.

Bahti stayed motionless a minute longer. He looked over at Peter; Marko would find them. And so it proved. The boy, making good use of the morning shadows, appeared out of a doorway in the next block. He waved for them to follow. Silence was understood. The boy was lean and tanned. He wore shorts and a dive-shop T-shirt; Peter noticed that his toes, which stuck out of rubber sandals, were calloused and nicked, presumably from surfing, although Peter knew nothing about the sport. He was taller than the average Maltese and had the sleek black hair and olive complexion of a nascent gigolo.

Marko led them to an entrance two more streets along; there was no house number, nor a directory at the doorway. He pointed upwards and whispered in Maltese in Bahti's ear. The detective turned to Peter.

"He does not think that Kamatta is resident in his flat this morning. But someone saw him last night in a hotel bar in the vicinity." Peter noted that Bahti's diction was more heavily accented than before.

The lobby of the two-storey building presented a dark cocoon, and therefore was dangerous. There seemed to be a back door, but it was too shaded to be certain. On the ground floor, several alcoves, of inscrutable purpose, could allow a man to conceal himself, while the narrow stairs meant that there was only one way up. Neither detective was happy about their exposure. Only Bahti was armed, but he carried two guns; he handed Peter a .38. They both removed their jackets and their shoes, but Bahti told the boy to keep his sandals on and wait on the ground level. Without saying so, he was telling him to do his job as a lookout, but nothing more. Peter expected that the boy was carrying a knife under his shirt. Bahti handed his radio to Marko; this seemed to represent a vote of confidence, and the boy smiled.

Peter still didn't like the situation. For one thing, he was unsure about Bahti's plan. Did he even expect the door to be locked? Did he think that Kamatta would be armed? He wasn't entirely certain that Bahti and Marko had worked out their signals. They padded up to the second landing. There were only two flats there, one with a bubblegum pink door and the other canary yellow, both chipped and stained. Both appeared to have solid Yale locks.

Bahti pointed to the yellow one, which showed more pedestrian wear, and knelt down to examine the lock. There was no way of telling if it was engaged, or if the door was booby-trapped, and there was no keyhole. He rapped and quickly stood back. Waiting a timed sixty seconds, he then shook the doorknob. So ended the panto-mime. He and Peter agreed with a look that no further ceremony was justified, and Bahti stood back and kicked in the door.

Conspirators tended to live in strange rooms, in Peter's experience. The criminal life and the need to cover it up breed odd practices and bizarre décor. Look for specialty items, an investigator knew. A mari-juana grow operation must be kept humid as a rainforest, with the windows blacked out. Narcotics operations have to be sterile and well ventilated. A forger may hide his tools, but he needs a large work-bench and a strong lamp. And there it was: a ten-foot table stood along the bigger wall, across from the window, with three gooseneck lamps clamped to it. To be sure, there hadn't been a serious effort at disguise, unless Kamatta had been planning on protesting that he was a watchmaker or a jeweller.

Clearly there was no one in the two rooms, but Bahti knew his professional moves. He pocketed his gun while he searched for any form of booby trap or self-destruction mechanism that could immolate the evidence, and them with it. There was little enough in the flat to search. The whole forgery factory seemed minimalist to Peter. The back room contained a sagging bed, a clothes rack with two shirts hanging from the hooks, and a turquoise bathmat with a grinning sunfish on it. For some reason, the man had moved the bathmat to the bedroom; the atmosphere was anything but cheerful. There was an air-conditioning unit wedged in the bedroom window. Bahti avoided the lavatory for now. In the main room, he slid the table drawers open and came up with various scribing tools, ink pads, jars of glue and textured paper. The only out-of-place indulgence was a dehumidifier under the table.

The two cardboard boxes in the corner offered their best hope. Peter closed the yellow door and placed the two guns on the table. He and the detective each took a carton and opened it. Peter's contained stacks of both blank and finished European Union passports, but every finished one was missing the photograph — that page had been torn out. Bahti's carton contained more official documents, including passports from the United States, South Africa and Switzerland. Peter leaned against the end of the table and scanned the room for clues that plainly weren't there. Bahti sat on the floor against a wall and tapped on the hardwood planks in frustration. The room was stifling.

"Shall I turn on the air conditioner?" he said.

"No."

"We could tear up the floors. Dig in the walls."

"Not very promising," Peter replied. He was thinking — the way he did best. "Kamatta has made a run for it. At least we know he does passports."

"He was Lasker's forger," Bahti said. "He likely gave Lasker the names of real people whose passports he had stolen, tourists probably, and Lasker provided him with photographs of himself."

The room, which had been kept largely free of dust, was now fetid with the exposed glues and inks of Kamatta's illegal craft. Bahti's shirt collar was dark with sweat and he suggested again turning on the air-conditioning unit. But Peter needed another minute, and he held up his hand. There was something wrong with this scene, this ascetic abode of a busy forger. There was something missing.

"Signal Marko that we'll be down in five minutes," he said. The detective wiped away a patch of the grime on the window and peered out to the street. He shook his head; he couldn't see the boy.

There is a chain of logic that will tell me what's wrong, Peter thought. He took his .38 from the table. He opened the splintered door and took in the somewhat fresher air on the landing. This forger is expert at concocting foolproof passports. He uses the stolen documents of real people when he can, though not always. He has to replace the old photos with new ones. *Where does he get those photos?* The client supplies them. Lasker used up at least three phoney passports, one to get into Malta, another to exit the island, and the Willemsea Malta document to use while he was here. He probably had Kamatta make more documents under the other names on the shipping manifests for the exported cars. Peter was willing to bet that he had six or seven done. But Kamatta did good work — he did a steady business, evidently — and that meant he took the portraits himself.

So, where is the camera?

"Bahti," he said, "why did you choose the yellow door instead of the pink one?"

"Because there were more dirt marks — smudges? — around the doorknob and the what-you-call-it?"

"Door jamb."

"Yes. More traffic in here."

They both stepped clear of the sweltering flat and looked down the stairs. Marko was nowhere in sight.

"Did Marko say that Kamatta lets this flat only, or both these flats?"

"He did not say. I assumed just this one place."

Bahti went downstairs in his stocking feet and padded out the door. In a moment, he returned with Marko. Bahti put on his trainers, since there was less need for a silent approach now, and they brought up Peter's shoes too.

"You want me to break down the pink door? It will be a bit easier with shoes on."

"Marko, you have a knife in your belt?" Peter said.

Marko brought out a narrow filleting blade with a black plastic handle, and handed it to Peter, who slid it into the groove between the strike plate and the frame, prying the metal loose. He had noticed that the Yale lock on the other door was lighter than it looked; he probably could have opened it with a credit card. With the next twist of the knife, Peter felt the *thunk* of the brass shaft withdrawing, and they were in. Bahti pushed the door open on its oiled hinges, and since he had retrieved his gun, he entered first. But Peter could already see, straight ahead of them in the revealed room, the mantis figure of a photo enlarger and the clotheslines from which two dozen film strips hung. They reminded him morbidly of the stockings wafting from Anna Lasker's shower rod.

The light on the landing darkened a tone as a form at the bottom of the stairs filled the doorway. Bahti was inside and didn't notice, but Peter and Marko turned to the shadow at the same second. Peter received a faceful of plaster as the first shot bored into the ceiling. He estimated that the gunman had centred himself in the opening. Peter launched himself across the landing at a downward angle. The shooter was making the mistake of firing his full cylinder as fast as he could, thereby reducing his accuracy. The second shot sheared the plaster on the wall by the yellow door.

Peter drew the .38 and pumped shots wildly down the stairs. He dragged the boy to the floor but not before the attacker's third bullet seared a bloody groove along Peter's left forearm. Peter had been shot at before, and he knew the sound of an automatic revolver with a double action hammer. The amplified noise in the funnel of the stairway was deafening, but he was able to pick out the rough sound of each explosion, something you wouldn't get in a pistol. Unless the gun was relatively new, it would contain no more than six shots.

Three to go.

The fourth hit Marko in his left foot, which had projected beyond the top step when Peter pushed him down. The boy screamed and blood arced over his and Peter's body like a fan of sea spray. But by now Bahti, who had also hit the floor inside the pink room, had slid out into the landing, his left arm projecting between Marko's ankles. He snapped off five shots downwards, hoping for a ricochet if he hit the sloping ceiling of the staircase, and praying that the spewing blood from his nephew's foot did not cause his pistol to slip out of his hand.

But that was the last shot. Bahti's scattered but rapid fire had deterred the assailant, who simply ran from the entrance, leaving the three men bunched like players in a rugby scrum on the confined landing. Bahti rolled over on the slippery platform and turned to examine the wounds of the others. Peter, who was already pulling out his belt to use as a cinch on Marko's lower leg, shouted: "We're okay. Go!"

Peter watched as Bahti reached the stone base in one long leap and propelled himself into the street. The explosions must have wakened the entire town, Peter thought. His own arm throbbed and leaked bright blood across everything near it, but he was more worried about the boy. The foot has twenty-six bones and many blood vessels and tendons to tie them all together. By sweeping away the heaviest blood, he saw that the bullet had hit one or more tarsal bones and perhaps even the tibia of the left foot. Triage principles demanded that he control the bleeding first, and this he did with his belt. The second task was to get him to a podiatric surgeon, and that had to mean Valletta.

As Peter was considering whether to drag Marko into one of the rooms, Bahti rushed into the house and vaulted back up the stairway. He assisted Peter in tying off the belt tourniquet and instructed Marko in Maltese to stay quiet. He checked the boy's eyes and found them clear, no fogging of the lenses. Marko had been carrying the telephone and it had tumbled to the base of the stairs. Bahti wiped the blood from it and tapped in a stream of numbers. He began an awkward conversation half in English and half in Maltese with Martens up on the access road. They were to call an ambulance — Peter was immediately able to hear a thin voice in the background start to shout into a different mobile line — and only then to intercept Kamatta. Bahti looked over at Peter, who understood that Kamatta had no choice but to take the hill route. The fugitive would reach the top of the road in minutes.

Peter lay back. He was sinking into medical shock and there wasn't a thing he could do about it. He tried to stay calm. Bahti took off his own jacket and wrapped Peter's peskily bleeding arm. It was funny, Peter thought there on the landing, where the three men lay entangled like shipwrecked refugees on *The Raft of the Medusa*, what affects you in a crisis. The last thing he remembered before passing out was the shift of Martens's voice through the line to a cold, diamond-hard sound as he said, in clear English: "We have to go."

CHAPTER 27

On any other day, Sir Stephen would have loved Malta. He could always use the sun.

Guilt, frustration, worry, a slipping thread. And Joan Cammon, a woman who, Bartleben now realized, knew him better that his own wife did. His four-hour flight from London, sitting next to her, had proven this. It was very disconcerting. He felt like a fraud. All these years, he had been glad to pose himself next to Cammon as a *team*. He sent Peter into the field while he backed him up from the London office. No other operational detective had Stephen's home number. Peter often expressed surprise that Bartleben usually picked up the phone himself (office or house). He would always answer, it was accepted; his staff were instructed to find him, wherever he might be, short of the Palace or Number 10. If only Cammon knew the bureaucratic steeplechases Bartleben ran to keep up his end of the bargain. He'd had to sweet-talk that déclassé local fellow Maris at Whittlesun Police, and had browbeaten Stan Bracher, his brilliant but oddly footloose Canadian, to stop his wanderings long enough to relocate to the region for a week and put himself on call for Peter. A day ago, at Peter's request, he'd made the call — he a deputy commissioner — to that front-line detective, Hamm, in Whittlesun. Actually, that had been fine, given the information the fellow had supplied.

It was daunting, mobilizing everything to give Peter Cammon what he demanded, and troubleshooting all the time, but, standing in the corridor of Valletta Hospital, Sir Stephen accepted the more compelling reality. He had sent his man into danger too often, too blithely, and now he was wounded, scarred. Peter had danced with death twice in the last week (and on the most ordinary of assignments, Bartleben thought). The imbalance, in terms of risk, had been too conveniently in HQ's favour this time. He must make amends, even if it meant being held captive by Joan Cammon.

Sir Stephen had to come to terms with the fact that Peter was a man he didn't really know. Joan and Peter were the real team, and, as he and Joan stood waiting in a corridor painted pale green and pink pastel, just like London hospitals, the Malta sun kept out by screens over the windows, and with little left to say between them after that long, uncomfortable flight, he saw that only one of them understood how Peter had been living in his own mind over the last three weeks. Joan had known the toll the Whittlesun crimes were taking. But for now, standing there, she and Bartleben were talked out.

For the second time in those weeks, Peter Cammon found himself lying half-dressed on top of the covers on a hospital bed, and again he was on the brink of walking out in defiance of his doctors.

Though the bullet had burnt a channel down his forearm — the brand would be picturesque — and generated a lot of blood, ultimately the wound would be classified as superficial by the Yard's consulting physicians. The Maltese paramedics, who had run him to the helicopter pad just up the hillside from Marsalforn, couldn't be blamed for thinking it worse, given how much Peter's blood, combined with Marko's, saturated everything in the ambulance. They had injected a morphine sulphate dose into his leg. This wasn't the right treatment for a man facing hemorrhagic shock — Joan later raised an eyebrow — but it certainly calmed him down. He remembered asking repeatedly about Marko, who lay on the gurney next to him in the back of the ambulance. As Peter sank into morphine delirium, the madcap, jostling ride up the hill turned to grim farce. Bahti, uninjured himself but perhaps the bloodiest of the three, had tried to reassure Peter that Marko would make it, while the boy kept up a stream of Maltese curses each time they hit a bump. The presiding paramedic tried to sponge off Peter's face, but with little effect.

As they reached the hilltop turn, Bahti shouted at the driver to pull onto the verge. He raised up Peter by the shoulders and cried, "Look!" Peter recalled looking where the detective was pointing and seeing the stern expression on the face of Lieutenant Martens, but nothing else before he fell back on the gurney. He did remember smelling smoke.

Peter turned as the door opened. For a flash, he expected Sarah to come in with his shoes. It was Joan. This should have been a surprise, but the residue of morphine had shifted him into a surreal hospital ward in some Neverland, and he simply said matter-of-factly, "I'm ready to go."

Joan came close and stroked his head. It was neither patronizing nor done out of anxiety, but it wasn't a gesture she would have offered, say, five years ago. She wasn't sure what was different about this time. Perhaps, if the touch meant anything, it was concern that their partnership was aging, that the potential for severance was greater now. She said nothing in reply to his statement, but quickly, since Bartleben was waiting in the hall behind her, raised his bandaged arm. She was tempted to unwrap it, and would at some point soon, but the work seemed competent enough. Even better than Sir Stephen, she understood that their main job was to get Peter home. She sensed the endgame. Her husband couldn't remain in Malta while André Lasker was wandering around England with his intentions unknown.

But he had a haunted, druggy look that caused her to reassess. "Can you walk?" she said.

He perked up, fell for her sucker line. "Yes. I'm ready to go."

"How do you know you can walk? I bet you haven't tried."

"Let's get going, Joan."

"Here's your deal, Peter, take it or leave it. We go to the hotel, fly home tomorrow." He groaned. "Sir Stephen is in the antechamber, wants to talk to you. Tell him you're cooperating."

"With whom?"

"All of us. Say what you need to. You'll be in my care, even if that's only vaguely true."

"Meaning," Peter said, "you want me to get *him* to go home immediately."

Joan leaned over the bed and whispered, "I'd rather not have to sit next to him on another flight to Heathrow. He hates not controlling everything. I hate sitting next to a fidgeting, under-occupied bureaucrat for five hours at a go."

"Lasker's back in England."

"I have no doubt," Joan said. "Ten minutes with Stephen, then we check out. Unless you want more bed time."

"No," he said.

Sir Stephen gave her a worried look as she exited. They passed like exchanged prisoners at Checkpoint Charlie. The worry was for himself; she remained self-possessed. He approached Peter's recumbent figure but he couldn't find a comfortable place to sit to conduct the conversation. The chair placed him too low to the bed. He finally chose to sit on the end of the mattress. He hated hospitals. The smell of disinfectant had penetrated his suit, and he was glad once more that he hadn't gone the Harley Street route.

"How's the boy?" Peter said.

"Several bones broken in the left foot. Two transfusions. I'm told there was blood all over the place. The paramedics had trouble figuring out who was shot and who wasn't. They operated on the lad last night, and he should be fine."

"Does that mean he'll walk?"

Bartleben smiled ruefully. "Your partner, Detective Bahti? I spoke to him this morning. He'll come to see you. Tough customer. He told me to tell you the boy will be surfing again in a month."

All this time, Peter had been stretched out on the bed, dressed but for his stocking feet. His body aching, the bandage on his left arm a little too tight, he swung to a sitting position on the edge of the mattress. Bartleben hesitated to help him; he hated feeling like a boxer's manager wondering whether to aid his bruised fighter after the match. He knew there was little time remaining alone with Peter before Joan re-entered, and he had business to cover. Peter winced with the effort of sitting up. He was struggling, Bartleben could tell, but there were some matters they never made explicit. Peter was never prone to depression or self-pity; his frustration was more likely to surface as anger at various bureaucracies — hospital rules, police management, or whatever was at hand.

"Damned morphine knocked me out," Peter said. He didn't say that he still felt a bit disoriented, not in command. "What happened on the hill road? I wasn't awake for that."

"Okay, here it is," Sir Stephen continued. "Kamatta's dead. I understand he ran from the building after blasting away at the three of you, got in his car and took off from the town on the only road out. There was a police car waiting at the top of the hill."

"Martens and his partner."

"Did Detective Bahti warn them? I presume so, but he didn't actually tell me. In any event, they were waiting, guns drawn. From what Deputy Commissioner Albanoni informs me" — Peter grunted at the name — "they opened fire on the car immediately and the man veered off the hill. The car burst into a ball of fire."

Peter vaguely remembered the smoke. "And the flat? Kamatta's second room?"

"We hit the jackpot. He had a box full of altered passports, although none with Lasker's picture in them. Very professionally done. But even better, we found a list glued to the bottom of a drawer that included all the false names our man used on the export applications over the years, and a number of others that might have provided aliases for Lasker. Albanoni told me about an hour ago that he matched one of the latter with the name of a departing passenger on yesterday's flight to Barcelona."

"What about Barcelona to London?"

"Still waiting for Interpol to pin down the flight schedules out of Barcelona yesterday and today. I made sure the Spanish authorities had the names from the list kept by the late Mr. Kamatta. Of course, Lasker could still be in Spain. But do you think he's headed back to England?"

Peter understood that his boss had accomplished most of this from the plane. *Within earshot of Joan?* He looked straight at Bartleben. *Why did Joan comprehend what Bartleben failed to?* "He's already there."

Sir Stephen decided to change direction. "I have what may be even better news. You asked me to call Detective Ronald Hamm?"

"Ah, yes, the phone message."

"Do you know an F.R. Symington?"

Peter called up the image of the stage of the Whittlesun Community Theatre, the red seats. "Yes, I interviewed him. Lasker volunteered at the local theatre."

"Well, it seems that a man reported to Whittlesun Police that his wallet and passport were stolen from him six months ago. When asked why he was carrying around the passport, he said that he regularly takes the Newhaven-to-Dieppe Ferry, which was a reasonable enough explanation. But the reason he waited six months to report it was that he finally began to suspect that it was stolen while he was at that very theatre. You see, he performs in their plays."

"So, why did Hamm become suspicious of Symington?"

"He didn't, initially. But he checked all the recent reports of lost passports, both in the local files and with Immigration, and found another filing of a stolen passport three months before the first theft. He called the fellow and asked if he had any connection to Whittlesun Theatre. The man seemed quite proud of his turn as Captain Queeg."

"Was that passport stolen while he was at the theatre?"

"Not that one. It was taken from his house, he believes. He always kept it in the same desk drawer." Bartleben recomposed himself on the end of the bed. "But here's the loop. Both names showed up on Mr. Kamatta's list. We didn't find the passports themselves, and so perhaps he finished them, and handed them over to Lasker for future use."

"We need to check entry points across Britain to see if either character crossed through customs."

"I've started the process, but I need to get back to London."

"When are you leaving?"

"I have an Air Malta connection in two hours."

Bartleben saw the idea flit across Peter's face: he waited for Peter to ask him to arrange tickets for himself and Joan on the same flight. But Peter didn't say it; in fact, he didn't come close to saying it. He winced again as he flexed his bandaged arm.

"And what else do we know about Symington's involvement?"

Sir Stephen moved to the window. The disinfectant smell increased. For some reason, there was no view to be found of the great Valletta Harbour. "How well do you know Detective Hamm?"

"We had our adventure together. I seduced him into danger, I'm afraid. A good man."

Bartleben turned back to the bed. "Here's the story, the way I understand it. Hamm went to see Symington. Maybe he was still in the flush of his good detective work regarding the passports, though I expect he was just being fastidious. After some evidently aggressive questioning, Symington admitted he knew of Lasker's plan to disappear. And now we know that Lasker was planning to abscond with a considerable amount of skimmed profits from the garage, and the proceeds from the shady export scheme. But Symington denied knowing that Lasker was organizing a fraud; he claimed he knew nothing about the cars."

Peter finished the line of logic. "But he wasn't in a position to deny knowledge of the theft of the passports from his crew and cast."

"Symington is in serious trouble. Aside from the aiding and

abetting charges that Hamm says will be preferred, he's likely to be fired from his teaching job and dismissed from the theatre."

Peter had liked the philosopher in Symington, but had no explanation for his role in the escape. He suspected that he had bought in selectively to the romantic elements of André's plan and had failed to consider the potential for havoc. Naiveté is also a romantic's impulse, the belief that all will work out well if motives are pure and trust is established. Taking someone into your confidence is a con man's first principle. The passport dodge should have alerted Symington to Lasker's nasty side.

Bartleben returned to his bedside; he began to fidget, and tapped on the iron frame of the hospital bed.

"What are you not telling me?" Peter asked.

"Hamm struck the man. The theatre director's filed a complaint of police brutality. This all comes from Hamm himself over the phone."

"Very unlike the Ronald Hamm I know."

"He told me it was just after he viewed the corpse of Anna Lasker."

Bartleben moved off a pace, towards the wide door. The conversation wasn't so much ending as fading out. It had been short, almost abrupt. Stephen had come a long way to offer comfort, and Peter felt a need to offer something back. Unfortunately, Peter's wrap-up comment came out as a seer's prediction. "He'll head back to the cliffs."

Peter regretted having to confront his doctors, who were merely doing their professional best. After all, their Hippocratic tradition stretched back to the knights themselves, the Hospitallers, who had established the most humane clinics in Europe for their time. The young resident in charge of his case wanted him to remain for observation — echoes of Whittlesun General — but Peter resolved to go. The doctor was intimidated by Joan's nursing qualifications, and by his patient's promise to see his own physician as soon as he reached England. The head of surgery — the whole staff knew that a Scotland Yard detective was under their care — argued that Peter needed skin grafts on his forearm, but, at age sixty-seven, Peter wasn't concerned about cosmetic repairs, and Joan, having forced the staff to unwrap his bandage, expressed optimism that the wound would heal without their monitoring.

But it was Detective Bahti who finally pulled off their exodus. He showed up an hour after Bartleben left for Luga Airport; he had actually shaved for the visit. He appeared nervous to Peter but claimed to be at the hospital merely to check on his nephew. He lightened up as he recounted the events in Marsalforn after Peter passed out, the rush to the helicopter and the flight to the Valletta hospital. To Peter's amusement, he and Joan hit it off. Since she had been reading Conan Doyle, Joan had acquired a taste for skulduggery and international intrigue. Bahti reminded Peter of Tommy, in his easy way of embellishing stories of criminal mayhem. Crowded around the hospital bed, the three of them spoke in hushed tones, although there was no reason for it. Bahti eventually suggested that he take on the role of chaperone to the two Brits for their remaining day in the capital. Peter perceived that the detective might be angling for a job in the U.K. — he mentioned the Metropolitan Police three times — but as the impossibility of this became self-evident, Bahti had the discretion to drop it. He went to see Peter's young doctor (to whom he claimed blood links) and recommended that he guide the couple to the cathedral, as a test of Peter's stamina. The detective guaranteed that Peter would return for a final examination at the clinic. Only then would the decision be made to let him fly home.

As it turned out, their visit to the church of the knights wasn't quite the lark their little cabal planned.

At first, the doctors resisted Bahti's test: the cathedral would be extremely crowded in the early afternoon; it would be better to rest for a day more. But, as the trio escaped into the Mediterranean sun, Joan and Bahti watching Peter for signs of enervation, the fresh air and the opportunity to leave behind the banality of the clinic to engage in a "tourist experience" revived Peter, and they maintained their happy, conspiratorial mood.

Bahti led them through the side streets of old Valletta, up from the seaside hospital, until they emerged onto Republic Street and found themselves facing the pillared entrance to the Co-Cathedral of St. John. It was referred to as the "Co-Cathedral" since it shared primacy on the island with the church in Mdina, the old capital. The mass of tourists, as had supplicants for centuries before them, waited in an obedient line that trailed down the dusty front steps. Peter again noted the Arab influence in Malta; much as the Knights of St. John might have resisted the Ottoman assault in the Great Siege, the East had everywhere shaped the look of the island. The detective ignored the line of visitors and led them past the crowd into the cool antechamber, the air and shadows anticipatory of the sacred rooms beyond. Bahti approached the nearest custodian. His whisperings led the docent to shake his head in sympathetic sadness, and he looked over at Peter with concern. Bahti led them around the ticket booth, picking up audio guides on the way. He paused before they could gain the interior of the church and reached for Peter's hand.

"I promise to pick up two British Airways tickets out of Luqa for the morning. I will call you on your mobile to set a rendezvous time. If Albanoni will let me, we will meet again at the airport."

Peter shook his hand and Joan kissed him on the cheek. Left alone, they stopped to get their bearings, always a wise approach in a cathedral cavern as vast as this one. He had experienced Chartres and Toledo and other great churches, and he had felt a competitive tone to most of them, an impulse towards excess in decoration and dimension, designed to outdo other monuments to God. He at once felt the difference here. Yes, every corner was filled with carving and embellishment, each side chapel lavishly honouring a suborder of knights, but this house of God, entirely baroque in its formal style, displayed another sensibility: defiance. This, it was immediately evident, was a warrior's church, not so much built to glorify the deity as to exalt His soldier servants and commend, unapologetically, their armoured souls to heaven.

Although he had visited hundreds of churches, Peter never knew where to begin in exploring the many-mansioned maze of a Catholic cathedral. In this church, erected by the knights to memorialize themselves, the altar down the long nave to the left seemed to both him and Joan a good place to start. Alone in a church, Peter often experienced a kind of gestalt, a claustrophobic reaction to the hermetic chapels and tombs: *how did I get here, at the exotic end of the world?* But this time, with Joan accompanying him, the sensation was different. They were on an adventure together, and this new, absolute and self-contained universe suited their mood. He felt good, the drugs suppressing the pain in his arm but leaving him fully awake. As they wandered up to the altar beneath the great vaulted ceiling, cherubs by the hundreds vying with full-feathered seraphim on every gilded pilaster, Joan whispered, "I never remember the difference between rococo and baroque."

"I don't know either," Peter whispered back. "Why don't we just count the angels?"

There were no depictions of the Annunciation on the walls over the altar, but he did discover a fine painting of Mary's visit to her sister Elizabeth, at which she announces her miraculous conception. Peter pointed to it, but Joan had already stepped well back from the altar and was examining the amazing inlaid floor that ran the length of the nave. The knights had commemorated all their comrades who had perished in the Great Siege of 1565, and then made room in the cathedral floor for the gravestone panels of successive Grand Masters. The stones set into the floor, one after another, were elaborately decorated with pieces of white, black and orange marble; most pictured skeletons holding scythes or weapons, resulting in a Grand Guignol, Halloween impression. But the displays, replete with escutcheons and banners, helmets and pikes, honoured noble dying as the precondition to eternal living. Each tomb was annotated with prayers of intercession and encomiums to the heroic deeds of these Soldiers of God. The defiant Knights of St. John knew all the angles on Death.

Back a few more metres into the nave, Joan's eye was caught by a panel that depicted a smiling skeleton jauntily poking a bony finger at the shield of one of the Grand Masters, a Knight of Provence, who had died in 1601 and was now interred in a direct line from the main altar. She read the inscription: *In mortis starabo ante Filium hominis.*

"In death I will stand before the Son of man," she translated. Peter had by now wandered off to a side chapel in search of Annunciation scenes, but the acoustics allowed him to hear her clearly. He went back to the nave, avoiding stepping on the inlaid tombstones, and stood beside her. She repeated the inscription.

"I bet he'll stand before Him as an equal," Peter said.

They passed two hours in the cathedral, entered all the chapels and read every inscription. They were eventually drawn to a separate chamber that held the Caravaggios, huge paintings depicting the *Beheading of John the Baptist* and *Saint Jerome Writing,* the latter showing the saint contemplating a skull. The former scene depicted the seconds before John's bloody execution. On a floor panel placed equidistant between the masterpieces, a rictus-grinning skeleton was shown climbing out of a long coffin. The cathedral provided a full education in the notions of death and eternity, of great deeds and salvation. They left chastened and quiet, and not quite prepared for the afternoon sun.

They went only as far as the terrace outside the cathedral, where they ordered lemonades. Peter checked his messages and found that Bahti had succeeded in getting them a midday flight the next day.

Freed for the balance of the day, he and Joan wandered to a café on nearby Theatre Street and ate a leisurely meal. Peter ordered a Cisk beer, and a second. His arm had begun to throb from about the moment they entered the chapel with the Caravaggios, but he didn't tell her. They toasted one another. It was time to get back to England, to begin the final act of the tragedy of Anna and André Lasker.

CHAPTER 28

The coppers had come up short. Had doomed themselves with their hackneyed Big Story. Had begun to believe it themselves. The Rover despised them. They told everyone they were scribing the arc of a chronicle across the cliffs, and all they had to do was wait. They would soon preside over his dying fall into a screaming sea; it was inevitable, they said. But his fate — neither biblical, nor mythical, nor tabloid lurid — wasn't in their hands.

Not until they saw through their own disgraceful, slack assumptions. They took solace in their bureaucracy. How dare they consign their faith into mere *watching* to get the job done? You have to *deserve* to win. They kept a vigil and patrolled and scanned the serrated shoreline, the saw blade that slashed back at the sea, that was now giving in by measures to the massed tides.

In this killing zone, where was there room for the rational, the settled? They imagined the shore to be linear, like their thinking, but how could that be correct when the rocks fell in sections each day and reshaped themselves each night into images no more fixed than figures in the clouds? Viewed from space, the land shifted no less than the hurricane whirls around its eye, day after day fragmenting the hunters' best maps into useless fractals.

No wonder they couldn't find him. He'd baited them with spurious clues. "Six kilometres" was a false, nonbinding mark on a sextant; he could kill from any distance, and planned to do so very soon. He had looked up "6." It was the day of Man's creation, a lucky number on the die and the mark of Pythagorean luck. And there were six senses. There were seven senses if you counted prescience. Maybe tomorrow he would switch to "7." Or seven could signify sex, the strongest sense.

He would never be caught by the policeman's linear arithmetic but only, maybe, by the mystic's algorithm. He preferred to kill in sanctified places within sight of the ocean waves, but he wasn't wedded to them; he could kill under an oak tree for all it mattered to him. He liked the ritual, but there are many rituals. That's what makes a horse race, or a religion. God, he felt good. He might perform his rituals in another county, another country, or on another shore. Scotland might be nice.

As the saying goes, he wasn't looking for trouble, but he was looking out for trouble. There were hunters with tiny pieces of the puzzle. That detective in black, who asked some of the right questions but failed to read between the lines of the answers. The others had shunned him. There was the girl in the cloak — why did she dress in a cloak? That bothered him — who showed up like a wraith in unexpected places along the coast. There was the reporter and her competitive drive to confirm every one of the trite morality tales peddled by the Task Force. She might venture out on the rocks once too often. First, he would reward her: one more girl should blow the story national and give her the scoop she craved. The story would be irresistible; it sure was overdue. They couldn't suppress it any longer. For the endgame, he would change his "pattern" and go after the damsel in the cloak.

Let the games begin!

Finally, there were an irritating number of policemen doing just about everything but look for him. What the devil did they think they were doing out there on the cliffs? It was getting so crowded. It was probably a good time to move on.

Oh, and there was one other, a new one. Looked like a hermit, dressed in that cloak. Was it possible that he was a kindred spirit?

They wouldn't find him, because not one of them could integrate the pieces. There was no tried-and-true, no plodding towards the truth. Only a mutation could catch him. Only a mutation could catch a mutation.

But first he would snare the cloaked girl, the one with the red hair.

The ache in Peter's arm refused to fade away. It was all the more irksome, since he needed to be in fighting trim for his descent to Whittlesun. He had taken the train up to London to St. George's, the hospital that served the Yard, but his doctor would prescribe only time and low-level painkillers for his wound. It had been three days; the gash had stayed clean, thanks to Joan. The doctor, a man older than Peter by several years, promised that it would heal with an "ugly but not angry" scar. He thought that Peter, almost Frankensteinian already with scars, might like the imagery. As a novice policeman, Peter had been horrified by his first cicatrix, a slash wound from a Liverpool brawler, but now, like much else in his profession, superficial wounds were exactly that, nothing more. He was indifferent to the surgeon's joking. "Your corpse will be easy to identify," the doctor added, making Peter think of Bartleben; it was his kind of bureaucrat's joke.

At the cottage, Peter assembled hiking gear, heavy boots and gloves, along with a squall jacket; he also dredged up a set of Royal Marine–grade binoculars. He called Tommy Verden and they compared lists of equipment. Tommy would pick him up two days forward. In normal circumstances, he would have notified Maris and Jack McElroy, but the hassle was too much. If they met Task Force operatives on the heights, he would explain their presence as best he could. Peter wouldn't be alone. As well as Tommy, he would mobilize Bartleben to reinforce his expedition from London. Jerry Plaskow, with his tabulations and his knowledge of the coast, would be invaluable in their search for Lasker. Finally, he would enlist Ron Hamm in the cause.

Above all, he would find Gwen Ransell and be guided by her.

At noon on the second day back in Britain, he retreated to the shed with a plan to sort through the entire Lasker dossier again. Yard Headquarters had failed to identify the airport through which the mechanic, in disguise, had entered Britain; none of the Kamatta aliases showed up in any of the scans of the gate checks or the airline manifests. But Sir Stephen had assigned the tracing probe to an assistant deputy, name of Masters, whom Peter knew quite well, who was known to have the habit of blaming his shortcomings on poor-quality input from his colleagues. Peter called him in London and immediately got back a whining response: "We don't have a decent photo as a reference point. Lasker's driver's permit photo is so blurry there are virtually no useful points or comparison. His old passport picture is so old it makes him look prepubescent. In any case, the scanners don't work that well. One little moustache will throw them off."

Would Peter come up to London, Masters asked. Instead, Peter asked to be passed on to the officer doing the actual work on the file (an old trick with Masters), who turned out to be an enthusiastic career officer named John Fitzgerald Carpenter.

The young man knew Peter only by reputation, but that sufficed. His voice indicated Cambridge. He suggested that Peter call him Fitz. "I know you must be busy, Chief Inspector. How can I help?"

The flattery was subtle. Carpenter had to know that Peter was semi-retired, and perhaps not so busy. Peter smiled to himself. "Call me Peter."

"Sir, we've checked every Passport Services record involving a landing in the U.K. on the day in question, and crossed them with known, or possible, aliases of Lasker."

"With what result?"

"No result, sir. No matches. Even on date of birth."

"Why did you work entirely through Border Control, instead of contacting each airline?"

There was an embarrassed silence. There were thousands of passengers, hundreds of flights. "Because it was easier," Carpenter admitted. "There's no central registry of airline manifests."

"Tell me what you did find."

"I believe, based on discussions with Malta Intelligence and Mr. Albanoni at Malta Police Services, that Lasker took off on a ticket using the name Watson. But he never landed, if you know what I mean."

"How is that possible?" His abrupt questions implied impatience, but that wasn't Peter's intention.

"A Mr. Thomas Q. Watson, one of the stolen identities found in Malta, made a booking from Barcelona to Dublin and then on to Manchester. Two different Ryanair flights. But he appears not to have landed in Manchester."

"Okay. Why?"

"Well, it took me a while to figure it out. I worked at customs for two years before joining the Yard and, in fact, it's why they hired me for this job. I saw this once before. A passenger uses one passport when he leaves the launch country, then switches to the second forged passport when he passes through the gate in Britain. Not that hard if all your passports are EU-issued. By the time Manchester might have noticed a mismatch with the passenger list, he was home and dry."

"Do you have the name, the one that didn't line up?"

Carpenter sighed. "Not yet. You see, Manchester never bothered to compare the lists. And there's been a delay getting the manifest from Ryanair. May take another day."

"Okay," Peter said. "You know what would be extremely helpful?"

"You would like the video from the Border Agency? So would I. I ordered them up, should have them by end of day."

Peter sympathized with Carpenter, who faced a long, bureaucratic slog through miles of grainy footage. "Mr. Carpenter, anything *visual* would help. Then we can . . ."

"Sorry to interrupt, Chief Inspector, but I've just been handed the passenger list for the Manchester leg. If you'll just hold on a quick sec."

"You'll check it against the passport entry list?"

"Yes," Carpenter replied, distantly. There was a pause as paper was shuffled. Peter got up and took the phone to the window of the shed. He watched Joan topping the expired flowers in the garden bed by the corner of the driveway. Carpenter came back on the line.

"That was quick," Peter said, to offer encouragement.

"Got lucky. Triangulated the Ryanair manifests and the arriving passengers in Manchester. The man we want is Quentin Calvert. He's the odd man out."

"So, he had yet another forged passport we didn't know about."

"He was well prepared," Carpenter offered.

"Exactly."

Carpenter promised to scan the Manchester tapes when they arrived. Peter gave him Bahti's cell number in Valletta so that he could check directly with one of the few people to have ever seen Lasker in disguise. He hung up. The call made him think idly about Sarah, something to do with the fact that 'Fitz' and his daughter were aligned in age. He didn't think beyond that spark, though he resolved to give Sarah a ring.

Instead, he called Ron Hamm. He waited through four rings. The shifting temperatures in the shed as the day aged alternately warmed and chilled him. He flexed his bandaged arm, and longed to unwrap it.

"Peter!" Hamm said.

"I'll start by apologizing, Ron," Peter said. "I owe you a call."

"No apology needed. But it would be good to have you here."

"Congratulations on the passport angle. Excellent job of digging. We just found out that Lasker used one of the names from the theatre people to re-enter at Manchester."

"Bastard. I funnelled all the records to the Yard's London office. By the by, what was the name on the passport?"

346

"Quentin Calvert."

"Ah, yes. Bloke about Lasker's age. Different hair, I recall. His statement's part of the file."

"Listen, Ron, are you in the office right now?"

"No. I'm following up a lead at Lasker's Garage. Haven't finished talking with the staff, Albrecht Zoren in particular."

"You know the receptionist there, Sally, died last week?"

"Yes." But Hamm seemed surprised. "You were there in the last few days?"

"Went to look at the ledgers of auto exports before I flew off to Malta." He switched to the issue at hand, the confrontation with Symington.

"He quoted Shakespeare to me," Hamm said. "'Thy tender-hefted nature shall not give thee o'er to harshness.' Jesus, Peter."

Peter recognized *Lear*. All men over sixty-five avoid *Lear*. *Talking about which daughter? Regan? In context, was Symington referring to Anna Lasker? To Brenda? To Hamm himself?* And then Peter knew: the teacher was referring to himself. But he let Hamm go on.

"Condescending bastard. I had him red-handed about the passports. He gave me grief. I pressed him if he had seen Anna's fractured body. He said he hadn't, had no opportunity to. Had no reason to want to. He made it clear he didn't care."

Why, Peter thought — because he saw the world as a Shakespearean plotline?

"Ron, how much did he give over about Lasker's plans? I understand he provided makeup, supplies."

"Yeah, he told me that. But then he clammed up. Told me nothing else. That's when I said what I said. That's when I . . ." His voice quavered with revived anger.

Peter let the silence go on for a minute, but he was ready to hang up once Hamm got the self-pity out of his system. The only thing for both of them to do, he knew, was to reach the Whittlesun Heights, to explore them together once again. "Can you perhaps join us when we get down there?"

"Sure." But his response was half-hearted. "He's out there, isn't he?"

In his mood, Peter didn't care which wanted man Hamm was referring to.

Peter went back to his files on the Rover case, laying out the manila folders in which he had slotted police reports, news clippings, sporadic forensics analyses and a few photos. The puzzle was irresistible. He shuffled the categories until he had about twenty folders. He had to set aside the Lasker material and push back several shadow boxes-in-progress to make room on the trestle table. Nothing was timelined; the material formed no linear plot or Cartesian framework. The order was in his own mind, sensible to no one else. From the reports and statements of fifty witnesses, he mined for small truths and the false notes that seemed tiny but wouldn't be made to fit, no matter how he reordered or rationalized them. He pondered, for example, the problem of transportation: the predator appeared without warning, the witnesses stated, yet how did he traverse the rocky heights without being seen? At the same time, neither Daniella Garvena nor Brenda Van Loss could remember the man's face before he struck them down. Peter realized as he fought through the murky evidence gathered by the Task Force that he was having trouble concentrating; the Rover remained his secondary focus. It had never been his case, and he could tell himself that he was brought in for Lasker only, and so his focus was in the right place. Peter imagined what Stan Bracher would say to this. "Bullshit," he would say. Peter understood, with all his instincts applied, that this Rover was asking to be caught. It would take a professional to catch him and Peter was, above all, a professional.

To prime his analytical juices, while fully realizing that he was mixing the two investigations, Peter undertook an artificial exercise. Looking at a case from an oblique angle sometimes helped. This little diversion almost amounted to one of Father's word games. He was aware that the women in Whittlesun could hold the key to both investigations. For one thing, they were all — and he struggled for the word — "honest"; in their various ways, each possessed the innocence of the martyr and the clarity of the seer. Whether it was Anna with her desperate understanding of André's desertion, or Molly's naked body rising to confront her murderer, the women challenged their attackers with raw truths. He took a sheet of paper and listed the women:

Anna Lasker

Selma Mitter, JayJay Evans, Anna Marie Dokes, Molly Jonas
(the dead girls)

Daniella Garvena and Brenda Van Loss

Mrs. Lasker

Guinevere Ransell

Mayta

Wendie Merwyn

He looked over the list; obviously it was too broad, but that wasn't the point. *Do they have anything in common?* For one thing, he supposed, they wanted nothing *from* the Rover or Lasker (Anna excepted), whatever they were justified in seeking to do *to* their abusers. He read and reread the list. The benefit of lateral thinking, Peter knew, was that it could lead to answers you weren't even pondering. He read and reread the list. There was an odd woman out: Wendie Merwyn. She was the only one who could profit materially from the investigations. He tried to pinpoint his instinctive concern about her. During their last telephone conversation, she had stayed with Lasker and had refused to engage at any length on the Rover Task Force. But if Wendie were looking for a career-maker, the Rover case had to be it. Her decision to focus on Lasker was a professional judgment call, but he wondered about her choice.

But then he read the list again. He understood that Wendie had been told to downplay the Rover scare. For the first time, he comprehended the force that Regional officials had brought to bear. They hoped to solve the Rover problem before the story broke open.

Lasker would be a welcome diversionary success if Peter could nab him. He pondered the question of how much Bartleben was complicit with the politicians.

Peter had resisted the meds; he told himself that he needed to be clear-headed for Whittlesun. But it was late afternoon, and after three hours of close work on the files, the ache of his wound had tipped him into dysfunction. He walked back to the house for a painkiller. Joan examined his arm, pronounced him okay and got the pill for him. She understood that he needed a long nap; they would share a late dinner. She ushered him up to the bedroom and made sure that he took off his shoes and jacket and prepared to sleep for a while — he was just as likely to burst out of the cottage in five minutes to examine some piece of evidence out in the shed. Lying on the master bed, he began to drift off even before she left the room. Downstairs, Joan moved through the house silently, letting her husband sleep. But she didn't go outside, beyond hearing range. She felt alienated when he got like this — relentless, irritable — and she hated this phase of a case, yet part of her annoyance was born of fear for his safety. She knew perfectly well that he had no fear of confronting violent criminals, that he was capable of killing, and had killed people. And, of course, she loved and trusted him.

No one who knew Peter would have been surprised that he precisely understood his own sleep patterns. As he sank quickly, he knew, as he crashed, that he would experience wild dreams. But he maintained, even into his subconscious, an atheistic disbelief in the symbol-heavy dreams of Freud and Jung. Hopes, and especially fears, don't vary much (he argued with himself) and anxiety can express itself in any object. Peter Cammon felt superior to psychology, in the way that many people do who have never studied it. When all the debunking challenges to Freud had emerged a few years back, Peter had read them with satisfaction. In his line of work, he cared nothing for the packaging of the id, ego and superego by, for example, zealous prosecutors, defence psychiatrists and behavioural sciences types. They showed up constantly as blithe labels in sentencing reports, but they rarely helped him glean the motivations of evil men; they were slots for cliché neuroses. For instance — and he didn't complete this thought as he sank into sleep — he had worked on the Yorkshire Ripper and Lord Lucan muddles, and inklings of their childhood fears and sexual traumas hadn't helped anyone at all in the investigations.

Some decades ago, he had seen a psychologist who regularly dealt with the problems of police officers, the Yard's people her specialty. He had been working a case in Manchester involving several arsons and accompanying murders. Peter always recalled the count: twelve victims in six separate immolations. Yet the killer's pattern seemed to be no pattern at all. Back then, the Yard liked to pair older, veteran detectives with junior officers in the field. Peter worked the first four crime scenes in Stockport with an old hand named Evans, who chronologically was only a few years older, but had many more years in. The case stalled, even as the incidents mounted, with some of the bodies left unidentified for weeks. The local command centre ordered all the victims to be held in the morgue until all were attached to names. Peter remembered viewing the charred bodies in a gruesome row. Two were children. But then, out of desperation, Evans sent him back to London to run data sets, a tedious and fruitless job.

"Peter, we lack a motive. No connections among the victims, no lunar cycle, no profit. If the arsonist-murderer lacked overt motive, other than some vicious misanthropy, what patterns can there be? How do you hunt down perversity? Just do your best."

This was the era of Son of Sam, when an alert beat cop in New York had thought to check parking tickets in the vicinity of a lover's lane, and thereby traced the killer. By the time of the Stockport arsons, forensics labs everywhere were stacked high with all manner of spreadsheets covering parking infractions and low-grade citations and cautions, and Peter spent his days with keypunch operators and mathematicians borrowed from King's College. Modern profiling wasn't in use much in those days. Peter was stuck in London when the case broke in Manchester. An intemperate word by a laid-off machinist led to a knock on the door; the arsonist was found dead with a stomachful of lye. A day later, Peter's senior had a major heart attack and was forced to retire. During that period in London, far from the fires of Manchester — Peter never got to see the last few bodies — he experienced a recurring dream. Its central antagonist was a snake, a viper the size of an anaconda, who confronted him everywhere in the dream. As he wandered through strange houses, the snake would rear up in doorways, or wait, coiled up, in the corners of empty rooms. As in a video game, various odd weapons, hammers and scythes, were presented to him. Whenever he attacked the snake, the weapons disintegrated into dust. Always, in the repeated dream, he was trying to reach Joan. Peter, who dutifully reported his distressing dream saga up the line, was ordered to see a shrink, who in fact was Viennese, and she made him sit in a big, soft chair facing away from her. She had read his career file and the first thing she said when he described his serpent dream was:

— You're normal, perhaps the most normal police officer I have met.
— Is that supposed to be a compliment?
— Yes. [Her *s* was sibilant. Was she the snake, his dream anticipatory?] Your orderly mind stands you in good stead. Keeps you sane.
— I'm cured, then?
— Didn't say that, Mr. Cammon.
— That isn't what I expected from a psychiatrist.
— What did you expect?
— Reticence? My impression of psychology is that the restoration of order defines psychiatric success.
— Nothing wrong with that.
— But what if my dream is the new order, within my own mind? Like some kind of looping videotape? The viper coils and uncoils in front of me. He greets me everywhere I go, like Dodgson's Caterpillar.
— That seems to me a literary conceit. The snake is not real, and, no, it is not just a cheap symbol.

— He's in every dream. I try every time, in every room, to get past him.

— Your life is not a cinema story that follows one repeating plot. You cannot rely on your dream of a snake to last. Maybe that's why they call movies the "flickers." They are evanescent.

— I see only disorder. I'm worried, Doctor. I find only unaccountable crimes and the potential for violence in my dream.

— Yes, and it is such disorder, the violence, that plagues every detective. It is to be expected that the images of close-at-hand death haunt them. But the solving of crimes ultimately braces them and they go on.

— Are you saying that the dream will get better by wearing itself out? [*With a Prozac prescription or two,* he thought.]

— Probably. Here's what I mean, Inspector. It is a difficult life in your profession. You have to decide it is for you. But I sense that it is indeed your vocation.

— Do you say that to every detective?

— Certainly not.

— So I should just go out there and solve cases?

— It is more complicated than that, but that is your definition of job satisfaction, isn't it? But I see that something else is bothering you.

— My problem may be the reverse. I tend to deal with crime as an abstract puzzle. I'm too isolated from the victims.

— My dear Inspector Cammon, let me suggest that the prescription is the same. No, not tranquilizers, which would only distance you further from the emotional connections you seem to crave, but the opposite.

— Namely?

— Like others in your trade, I am sure that for you solving crimes is its own reward. I know that you are good at this process, yet you plead disengagement. Well, the best natural drug is endorphins. To get to the fundamentals, Inspector, you should go where the action is. Accompany arresting officers a few times, or go along with patrols in the inner cities. And as you engage real people along the way, make your decision about what is typical and what is unique, what is normal and what is abnormal about human beings.

Not once did she mention Freud or Jung, nor did she ever address the archetypal snake. But she was right. What interested him in every case was getting inside the mind of the criminal — and that started with grappling onto what was abnormal and perverted. Unless he understood the reasoning process of the thief, the murderer, the rapist, he claimed no success. This became a workable method for him, although he began to worry that the victims too often shared many characteristics with the offenders. Criminality wasn't an abstract puzzle, he conceded, although he held back on telling anyone, including fellow detectives, that he had sometimes approached violent crime this way. It was about evil and the human emotions behind it. Tommy Verden once said (with admiration) that Peter never hesitated to walk through a door. But Peter "solved" his crimes when he understood the criminal, and not until then. You had to walk through the door of the mind.

In the bedroom, with Joan moving silently one floor below, Peter went under. This time he had a new dream, and there wasn't a snake in sight.

In his dream, he stood in a rocky desert in Africa. The sky blazed orange and a molten sun reddened the landscape. It was neither day nor night, the sun a science fiction orb in a garish heaven. His task in the dream world was to get to the horizon, yet he knew that he couldn't make it without perishing of thirst. He dutifully trudged across the endless sand. His vantage point within the dreamscape shifted, like an edited film scene, and now he was flying, hovering over the desert, looking down in search of human forms. He knew within the dream that he couldn't expect to see faces; that was a dream rule. And then he was standing on the desert floor again, a few yards from where he had started. Clouds, puffballs revolving in the sky, showed black undersides and rotated again, turning alabaster. They roiled overhead as in a black-and-white movie, very Bergman.

They shattered into feathers and disappeared, leaving a sickly green sky. Once more, he floated in the stratosphere; he watched savannah grass emerge from the sand, turn green then brown, and shrivel and die.

On the ground, no closer to the horizon, he watched a black cross glide to earth. It transmogrified into a man cloaked in black. It was the Archangel Gabriel from a typical Renaissance depiction of Mary's Annunciation. Yet there was no Mary in the dream. Gabriel, moreover, displayed no wings or facial features, but apparently he could fly. The wingless, falling angel landed neatly in the obeisant kneeling position from the Annunciation. The obsidian cavity where his face ought to be angled up towards the orange horizon, while his thin body continued to tilt in supplication.

A flock of grey sheep — the only colour he could think of was the grey of Confederate soldier uniforms in the American Civil War — appeared, unherded and thirst-panicked, on the desert plain in front of Peter. All of them, the angel as well, began to move in a mass to a vanishing point below the distant, hovering sun. The levitating angel held out a leafy sprig in his right hand; in his left, he hoisted a thin rod, much like a conductor with a baton. Gabriel spoke only one word, but repeated it six times in a flat, deadened voice: "Chervil!"

Dreams can be foolish, was Peter's thought as he rose to consciousness. He tried to hold onto the aftertaste of the reverie. It was semi-dark in the bedroom. He managed to summon up the main points of it. He flexed his bandaged arm; it no longer throbbed. There was no doubt that the dream had been instructional. He really ought to review all the evidence again, he thought. He would see Guinevere as soon as he reached Whittlesun and ask her about it.

But then he appreciated that what had brought him out of the dream was the phone downstairs. The upstairs phone wasn't in its cradle in the bedroom; his mobile remained in the shed. He heard footsteps on the stairs, and Joan tapped at the door.

"Peter?" she said.

"Who? What is it?"

"It's Father Vogans in Weymouth."

She entered and turned on the overhead. In other circumstances she would have been more heedful, giving his eyes time to adjust. He saw the dread in her face.

"Hello. Peter Cammon."

"Inspector, this is Nicolai Vogans. I'm here in Whittlesun."

There could be only one reason for the priest to be in Whittlesun rather than Weymouth.

"I'm here with Father Clarke. It's Father Salvez. He's dead. He took his own life."

The sadness came in as a slow wave. Ruefully, and incongruously, Peter let it close over him with the identical rhythm of the descending black angel in his dream.

And Peter knew, right then, how the priest had done himself in.

Vogans continued. "This is certainly a tragic circumstance for you and for me, Inspector, but he leaped from the cliffs onto Upper Whittlesun Beach."

"Near the Abbey," Peter said.

"Yes, just below. They found his body at sunrise. A woman walking her dog along the shore."

Lying motionless in bed, Peter re-tasted the anxiety underlying his desert nightmare. Later, he was never able to account for his next question.

"What was Father Salvez wearing?"

Vogans hesitated on the line. "Why, since you ask, an old leather coat, work trousers, gardening boots. Peter, I went to the mortuary an hour ago. He was skin and bones. Skeletal."

Peter barely remembered what they exchanged next. He pinned down the funeral home location. The ceremony was scheduled the day after next at 10:00 a.m., at St. Elegias, with Clarke doing the eulogy. He promised to be there.

It was a small coincidence that the moment Peter hung up, Tommy Verden reached him from the car in London. After Peter delivered the news, Tommy asked for Vogans's mobile number. "Salvez was a rich character," was all he would say, other than to arrange to pick up Peter and Joan at the cottage early the day of the funeral.

That evening, Peter and Joan sat at the dining room table with the lights off and drank brandy. He recounted the story of the palliative efforts of the three aging men to comfort Father Salvez. She had heard much of the story before from him, and the embellished version from Tommy, but she nonetheless listened intently.

"I wonder what will become of the Abbey restoration?" Joan said.

CHAPTER 29

Peter endured a dreary day getting ready for both the funeral and his trek across the Whittlesun Cliffs. He would wear his best black suit to the funeral; no matter that it was identical to all his other suits. In the afternoon, with little better to do, he set up the streaming video feed that Wendie Merwyn had promoted. It proved surprisingly simple, requiring only the downloading of a flash player and the straightforward bookmarking of the site. He hoped to trace archived material in addition to the live feed, but it turned out that old material was selectively available, and not of much use. There was some break-up of the sound feed, but Peter expected that the channel would fix itself eventually. He planned to make regular use of the site.

He searched for any and all reports and public announcements of the death of Salvez. As well, he was generally curious about the level of sophistication of TV-20's operation, watchful for any indicators that it was increasing its market share and therefore its overall impact in the Whittlesun community. He wasn't sure why he did this; perhaps he worried that TV-20 would somehow undermine the search for the Rover by moving to more sensational coverage. He also looked for the storm forecast for the Jurassic Coast for the rest of the week; again, for reasons uncertain to him, he used the TV-20 reports rather than one of the weather channels. Yesterday's news and weather modules were still up on the TV-20 site. There they were on the noon news, the Blond Bookends, Wendie Merwyn and Parnell "Parny" Moss, like Teutonic twins, positioned against a robin's egg blue backdrop. Moss played the huckster role, at one point sliding from the news-desk stool to prance in front of a digital weather map. The shifting meteorology of the English Channel zone was spun out like a Victorian melodrama. High winds were predicted for the length of the coast.

Impatient to get to Whittlesun but unwilling to drive down the night before the funeral, Peter killed the balance of the day by ensconcing himself in the shed with the maps and charts that Jerry had supplied. After three hours of close examination, some of it with a Holmesian magnifying glass, Peter had developed a few notions of where to look for André Lasker. At sundown, Joan knocked and came into his side of the shed. Normally she would have called from outside, but as one of the funeral party, and given her contribution to the investigation of the Lasker killing ground, it was assumed, by both of them, that she was entitled to pose questions about the expedition.

"But wouldn't it be pretty cold holing up in any of the caves?" she said, scanning the topographical and marine charts of the coast, and noting the neat red circles. "Wouldn't he hide out anonymously in some bed and breakfast, and just pay cash?"

"He has his reasons," Peter replied, unintentionally sounding like a judge delivering a ruling.

After supper, Peter tuned in again to the TV-20 feed to watch the current newscast. There they were, Wendie and Parny at the desk, except that this time Moss was presenting the top news item while she played sidekick.

"Our top item tonight," he began. "Sources in the Task Force that is investigating several assaults, disappearances and killings in Devon have told TV-20 that the serial attacker, who has been roaming the cliffs along the Jurassic Coast unimpeded, has planned his assaults at regular intervals. This is known within the Task Force as the 'Six-Kilometre' theory and, as the label implies, the attacker has been moving in six-kilometre intervals along the coastal terrain."

The camera cut away to aerial shots of the cliffs. The obvious fact that this was promotional tourism footage showed how cheap the TV-20 operation was. What did impress Peter was the stage presence of Moss, who had lowered his voice to an authoritative baritone and seemed more mature. When the camera returned to the desk, Peter could tell that Wendie, despite her posed persona, was not happy. Did she resent Parny's toothy aura as a threat to her senior position at the station? Peter appreciated her shrewdness nonetheless, and perhaps she was attempting to separate herself from the Six-K theory.

"If the Task Force calculation is correct," Parny intoned, "the Six-K Killer will soon cross into Dorset. We will obtain a statement from Dorset Police on the impending threat to our community."

In spite of the alliterative new label, Peter doubted that it would lodge in the public mind. "The Rover" was just too easy to say.

The next morning, Tommy arrived early enough for them to take a few minutes for coffee on the veranda. He'd had the Mercedes washed before leaving London, and it sat gleaming beside the driveway fence. The bright autumn sun belied the sad circumstances. The three of them had been friends forever, Peter reflected. They had endured nearly five decades of crime and public crises: the Yorkshire Ripper, the IRA, the Brixton riots, Vietnam and the protests, the Underground bombings by terrorist fanatics. Peter flexed his bandaged arm — it had become a habit — and for the first time wondered how the scar would look. He and Tommy, stripped naked, would have presented a kaleidoscope of scars, a muddled tablet of a half century of crime. For Peter, his latest wound told him that he was still in the game.

"It's a sad day," Tommy stated.

Joan, who had watched Peter from the sidelines, and waited for him, for so many years, nodded. Her assistance that day in the bloodied passageways of the Lasker home had somehow changed things. She felt that she was an insider now, at least where the alien town of Whittlesun was concerned. The idea made her more protective of Peter and Tommy than ever.

"Tommy, you took to Father Salvez, I gather."

He was old-school gracious. He looked at her, but Peter too. "In the interests of professional disclosure," he began, "I called Father Vogans to express my condolences. A half hour on, I got a ring from Father Clarke. Asked me if I wanted to say a few words. Thought I might."

Tommy parked a street over from St. Elegias, since the parking strip was pretty much full, and the three walked to the crowded front entrance of the church. It had been overcast when Peter and Tommy first visited; now the midmorning sun was out, though it failed to redeem the ponderous building with its chiselled, bulbous stones. The coastal damp and Victorian chimneys of the town had stained the grout to a purply colour. No wonder Salvez preferred the Abbey ruins. At least the ironwork was formed in an authentic Gothic style. The encroaching ranks of flats made the contrasting church seem lonely. Peter wondered how large the congregation was these days.

Friends of the deceased clustered at the edge of the steps, as if reluctant to enter. They were a mixed group. Peter assessed two knots of mourners: priests from other churches and a fresher-faced contingent of men and women in their twenties. Peter assumed — hoped — that they were preservationists associated with Salvez's Abbey campaign. He noticed several nurses, likely from the neighbourhood hospital, but there was no sign of the crotchety woman from the admin office of St. Elegias. He scanned the crowd closely from the church steps, on the lookout for Vogans, whom he spied in a ring of clerics; the priest acknowledged Peter with a we-need-to-talk-later glance. Peter was surprised to see Mrs. Ransell in the crowd, standing alone, though apparently quite content, over by the corner of the church. He pointed her out to Joan.

Reverend Clarke, a burly man with a goiterous neck, presided over the two-hour High Mass. The ceremony stayed in a minor key while he held the pulpit. Clarke delivered a tepid homily laced with platitudes about service and devotion to Christ. His baritone was steady, but Peter knew that Salvez would have preferred that the singing of the choir be in Latin, however middling the choir itself. There was something perfunctory about the effort. Only when the time came for giving witness was Father Salvez truly allowed into the church, made flesh and blood by a half century of friends. The throng was brought to tears by a young woman who had worked with the priest up at the Abbey cataloguing the remaining stones and writing an updated history of the grounds, which, "out of necessity" as she put it, she would dedicate to him. Her encomium became the Eucharistic prayer Clarke should have given, as she spoke of Salvez's mystical blending with the sea and the cliffs.

The tributes flowed, anecdotes of Salvez's time at the seminary, his good works in the community and his love of games and puns. Tommy Verden stepped to the rostrum and recounted their visit to the sick man's flat. Tommy possessed hitherto buried talent as a comedian.

"I'm a policeman. Coppers and priests may seem to have little in common. Okay, we both appreciate a tidy confession. But a priest ministers to many troubled souls and I know that Father John Salvez comforted thousands in his lifetime. I only wish I could make that claim. But here's the thing. I appreciate toughness in a man, what the Americans call a 'stand-up guy,' and although I met Father Salvez exactly one time, I understood immediately that he was one of the tough guys. A tough guy who had a soft side, who loved puzzles and an old church on a hill. What more can you ask of a man?"

Local ladies served coffee and tea in the downstairs common room but the day remained mild and most of the crowd regathered on the lawns. They couldn't hope to fit on the entrance stairs and naturally spilled over to the pocket-sized park across the way, where several benches had been placed beside the display case holding the church's schedule. Peter wandered, or pretended to, not quite aware that Vogans was his objective. He wondered if Ron Hamm had attended.

Joan walked next to him as he moved down the church steps but then she went off to give Tommy Verden a big kiss on the cheek.

A middle-aged woman, about fifty, came up to Peter and introduced herself as Salvez's niece. Her sad look may have been entrenched, or merely a response to her uncle's suicide.

"I'm his only niece. He mentioned you twice in the days before his death."

Peter could only guess who had pointed him out to the woman; probably Vogans, surmising that his continuing investigation of Anna Lasker might lead him again to the Abbey ruins, and that he would be interested in what she had to report about John Salvez's last days, however anecdotal. Peter felt tears welling up. Any visit to the Abbey would feel hollow and transgressive now. "What did he say, Mrs. . . . ?"

"Murray. He mentioned your help in the last days, you and Mr. Verden. Father Vogans called me that following morning. Thank goodness. I thought Outpatient Services had lined up the home nursing. We were able to straighten it all out, no thanks to the church. Anyway, thank you, Detective."

"I assume you're tasked with clearing out the flat?"

"Yes. There's a mountain of paper about the restoration. The Preservation Trust is taking all that."

She was close to tears herself. Peter tried to hold her attention. "Did he keep any papers, files up at the Abbey itself?"

Her brows furrowed in puzzlement. "I never go up there. What would he keep up there? The Preservation people will take care of it, no doubt. I suppose."

Father Vogans, breaking off a conversation with Father Clarke, threaded his way over to Peter. They all shook hands, and Mrs. Murray immediately left for the parking area.

"A sad day, Peter," he said, finding what seemed to be the refrain for the day.

"Tell me, Father, when did you see him last?"

"Ah, always the Sam Spade," Vogans said, missing the mark by a few degrees. He wheezed loudly. "I feel guilty enough, I do. That time, I stayed into the next afternoon. He as much as kicked me out. Said he was feeling better, but so did Lazarus at one point. I left and never saw him again."

"Did he call you?"

"No, no." Vogans shook his head.

"Me neither. You shouldn't feel guilty. It was exceptional, what you did. And I understand that you helped his niece with the home care after that." It occurred to Peter that someone must have helped Salvez get up to the Abbey that last time. It might have been Vogans.

Peter and the Romanian were tough men of an ancient generation, and neither was inclined to euphemism. Vogans exuded authority, and Peter supposed that he did too, in a way; he felt the crowd stand back from the two of them, nearly slip away. Vogans sensed it too but let the moment pass. "I feel guilty because you always feel bad when a good priest dies."

"Is suicide still a mortal sin in the Church?" Peter said. At once he understood his mistake, lumping all denominations together.

"Technically, for the Roman Catholics. But I see hundreds of young people, several generations younger than us, Peter, who wouldn't stand for an edict like that. Young people see it among their peers too often." There had been no mention of suicide during the ceremony. Vogans's eyes swept the sky. "No, Peter, I didn't imagine he would take his own life. If I'd believed that, I'd never have abandoned him for even an hour."

Peter said he would be in town for two or three days. The priest invited him to visit at St. George's in Weymouth. Peter nodded but made no offer to update Vogans on Lasker. They were both far too aware that Salvez had jumped from the rocks not very far from Anna's fall. Peter prepared to leave, having failed to spy Ron Hamm anywhere among the mourners. He looked around for Joan and was surprised to see her chatting with Mrs. Ransell in front of the big display case. He hastened over. Joan looked up and smiled her polite smile. "Mrs. Ransell tells me she has lived here all her life."

The old lady might have downed a shot or two already, Peter estimated. "Mrs. Ransell, could I drop by your house later this afternoon?"

"I guessed you'd be along," she said.

"Why is that?"

"Because Guinevere said you would be around."

"But how . . . ?"

Peter couldn't justify badgering the Ransells on this point. He had postponed so many meetings with Gwen that she had no reason to count on his promised appointments. Joan must have noticed that he was undone by the Ransells, he was sure. She looked bemused. He wanted to ask about Gwen's epilepsy, had she had more episodes, and was she taking chances out on the cliffs. But his solicitousness was inappropriate to this scene. The old woman also seemed to understand that he shouldn't be asking such questions in advance; better to visit without prejudice, receptive to whatever Gwen decided to tell him about Lasker. Peter also comprehended that Mrs. Ransell was a member of this church, and had every right to be among the grieving crowd.

"You're most welcome to visit," she said, piercing the fog that had enveloped him. His arm was aching again; it had become a cue to his mood, paining him whenever he was anxious. Mrs. Ransell was looking at him; evidently her invitation did not extend to Joan. Above the spire of the church, the sky darkened and the predicted winds, the vanguard of new ocean storms, moved in.

Each claimed to have a gun. Neither did. But one possessed a Highlander skinning knife, slotted down his sock, out of view. The other carried a right-angled chunk of iron in his pocket. It was crude, but he told himself that it suited his spontaneous style of attack and defence; he had picked it up on a farmer's lane.

The Rover and his Assistant. The New Order. The New Model Army. The New Broom, now getting a bit old. The New Best Friend.

He did that, the Rover, spun phrases until he found the one that worked. Name something and you begin to control it. He enumerated the options in his head. The Dynamic Duo. Burke and Hare. Green Hornet and Kato. He couldn't find the fit. He, the List Man. Oh well, lists were made to be broken.

But the Cloaked Man knew something that the Rover did not think he knew. Lasker had figured out the Rover's non-pattern. Oh, he had struggled with the "Six-K" thing; TV-20 had made a big announcement of its "Six-K" calculation, even labelled the pervert the "Six-K Killer," but it hadn't stuck; it was still the "Rover." But the Cloaked Man had sorted it through and more or less ignored Six-K, and moved to the next square on the Parcheesi board. Except that in the absence of a pattern, that meant the Rover might kill just about anywhere. But then, he thought, Six-K was a ruse and a diversion and that fact might hold the clue to his next set of moves.

Lasker shivered in the October air. Why had the Rover come this way — towards Whittlesun — and not, say, farther towards Land's End? His prey, evidently, lived everywhere, in abundance. So why this direction, not that one? Two possibilities came to mind. First of all, opportunism was only so much fun. Stalking was a better kick, the Cloaked Man deduced. And now it was pretty evident that the serial killer was stalking *him*. Otherwise, he probably would have switched to the other direction, but somehow the Rover had discovered *him*. Lord knows, he had made his presence obvious. If the Cloaked Man kept up with the news, likely the pervert did too.

Or, second, the Rover had a *specific* woman in mind this time.

Anna's death had been a reprimand. She had confronted his desertion in the — what? — *slyest* way. She knew that her death would draw him back. He had no religious faith, but he understood the need for penance perfectly well. She had won, with her sense of duty, her family, even her religion.

The Cloaked Man and the Rover sat in mutual silence — that is to say, it was a tactic for both of them. Each thought he could outwait the other. The Rover wanted something, to seduce the scruffy fellow, and he was content to wait. He had already said his piece the first time, and the offer was on the table — the tablet — the funeral bier — the sacrificial altar. For his part, Lasker used the waiting to figure out the rest of it, what he was already envisioning as the end-game. Let the killer believe they were striking an unholy alliance. He must know that it was going to be very short-term. Winter was coming. If the Rover's pattern was a non-pattern, then it could all end abruptly. The worst thing for André was for the Rover to walk away. Mutual seduction, that was the ticket. He only had to get close enough one time. He would kill the Rover, do justice to Anna. Of course, meanwhile he might have to offer up something to bring the pervert on side.

CHAPTER 30

The mission to the Ransell cottage got off to an awkward start. After the funeral, the three old friends drove to the Sunset Arms. Tommy had exhausted his supply of Salvez anecdotes at the podium — there seemed to be nothing left to say — and Peter's rendezvous with Guinevere Ransell overshadowed their lunch. He had described Gwen to Joan only in vague terms, but she had picked up on his captivation with her; she saw his neediness when her name came up.

They talked over the logistics of Peter getting across the fields to the Ransells'. It was Joan who solved the dilemma. Tommy would drop Peter off and return for Joan, and then convey her home. She, meanwhile, would take "a very long tour of downtown Whittlesun." Peter agreed to call both of them later, when he knew where he would be spending the night. So it was agreed. Peter paid the bill in the restaurant and kissed Joan goodbye. He wondered idly if her rambles would take her past the Lasker house.

Tommy and Peter got lost on the back trails to the cliffs and had to ask directions of a grizzled crofter at the roadside. Peter was tempted to ask him if he had glimpsed anyone who might be the Rover, but he refrained. They arrived by late afternoon; the light had already turned sallow and wintry, and the wind off the Channel was building. Peter had changed at the hotel and now carried his heavy boots in a beat-up rucksack. Tommy let him off at the end of the rutted track. To test telephone reception, they separated to about a hundred yards and Peter called Tommy's mobile number. After some initial static, the connection became better than either expected. Peter waved and walked over the final hillock towards the front door of the cottage.

There was no delay when he knocked; Ellen Ransell was expecting him and she opened the door wide. He placed his bag just inside the entrance. In his polished black brogues and his dark turtleneck and canvas pants, he was a mysterious visitor from an Edward Gorey tale. A fire crackled away steadily, and he smelled sandalwood. Mrs. Ransell was very drunk.

Guinevere glided out of her bedroom. She wore her usual layers, and her hair hung in gorgeous disarray. She was barefoot. Peter interpreted her manner as welcoming, but then, she had that way about her anyway, an ability to put others at ease. She gave her mother a warm glance, yet as she made eye contact with Peter, she at once promised full engagement with him. Thus it was with a seductress, he thought.

"Are you well?" he said.

"Very well."

"Your mother told you I'd be coming by?"

"Yes. But no. I'd been expecting you anyway."

Before now, was the implication. Peter was starting to worry that he had left it too long. She moved to the chesterfield and took up the same spot as before, at the end of the cushions. She did this quickly, and Peter read the movement as mildly confrontational. Perhaps he was overreacting. Mrs. Ransell had busied herself in the kitchen, and Peter couldn't tell if she was monitoring their conversation, but he sensed hostility from her, too.

Before Peter could speak, Gwen said, "You've been getting close." It was a factual statement. Her verb tense confused him a little.

"How close?"

Evidently the question bothered her. She let a minute pass. As he had been doing since entering the cottage, he looked for a path to connect to her, but he respected the lull and kept quiet.

"I'd make a terrible police officer," she said.

"Why?"

"Because I don't have the police officer's all-consuming desire for endings."

"You mean, putting closure to a police investigation? I'm hopeful we'll find André Lasker soon."

"Actually," Gwen said, "I was talking about the one they call the Rover."

Peter sighed, and said only, "It's easy to confuse the two."

"I'm not confused. I see no reason we can't talk about both, and keep them straight. Take the Rover, for example. Are you close to finding him? Do you know who he is, *what* he is?"

She was in a philosophical mood. He was not. Peter felt something he had never anticipated: exasperation. *Is she playing games?*

She continued. "You don't know where he was born, where he was christened, what colours he liked, his favourite shows on the telly, and so on."

"I wish I did know. We'd have our killer."

"Then what would you do with him? I know, you'd put him in prison for life. Or in an asylum."

"That would certainly be closure."

"Not for him."

"My role, without being callous, would be over."

"But then you would never know what he really thought about evil. You've stopped him from killing again, but does it bother you that he squats in a cell and continues to ponder his crimes, that he makes no distinction in his mind between past and future deaths? What does he really think about the girls out there that he hasn't killed?"

"Jesus Christ, Inspector!" Peter turned to meet the dark red face of Mrs. Ransell. She stood six feet away in an unsteady crouch, a tumbler of vodka in her hand. She raged forward; he smelled her

370

fumes. "You can't see him clearly now? Listen to the girl. We both know your next seven questions, Inspector, but you can't understand the answers. Your next question, am I right, is whether Gwen has been out there on the cliffs? We are both out there on the cliffs. You're not close, no matter what she says." She waved her free arm in disappointment, returned to the kitchen counter for her Koskenkorva bottle, and clumped into her bedroom.

Gwen remained calm and let another full minute go by. In that short time, something changed in Peter. He had been beguiled by Gwen, but he was also a policeman, a professional. He needed her special insight, but not at any cost. He decided that there would have to be limits on how much of the investigation — the two investigations — he would disclose.

"Should you comfort her?" Peter said.

She looked at him. "Peter, what do you think is going on out there?"

He didn't have an answer, but her mother's outburst and all the talk about closure made it obvious that Mrs. Ransell and Gwen had been talking as one: both knew all the possible endings. Out there.

"I'm sorry," he said, "but have you been along the cliffs much?"

"I live here, Peter. Sure. Do you believe in the Six-K theory?"

"No. I don't trust the theory," he answered, understanding that she was changing the subject in order to control the conversation.

"By my calculation," Gwen said, "another six kilometres beyond the last attack wouldn't place him very close to here. On the other hand, there's the husband. Maybe he's . . . closer."

Peter tried to lighten the mood. "I'm sorry. It seems every time we discuss one case, we end up talking about the other one."

She frowned. "But isn't that true generally, when you talk to other policemen? I'd think it would be irresistible."

And just like that, Peter broke through one of his longstanding quandaries. She was right; there was no need to compartmentalize his thinking about the Lasker and Rover dossiers. André might be close, or he could be in Barcelona or Manchester. The Rover could be six kilometres closer or somewhere far to the west. He could keep them straight.

As usual, Gwen was ahead of him, making a different point. "Okay, Peter, let's start with Anna and André Lasker. Do you want to fill me in?"

He hesitated and finally said, "We have to be clear about this. Much of what I'm telling you is internal police information. I may call a halt at some point."

She nodded, apparently not at all concerned. His consultation at the feet of the oracle had become a negotiation, and give-and-take would be the rule.

He recounted his trip to Malta to arrest André Lasker, the shooting in Marsalforn and the death of Kamatta. He left out the bloodiest parts. He laid out for her the details of the auto export scam and the factory operation that spewed out false passports. He summed up the itineraries the husband could have essayed to get back into England and, warming to his own saga, he offered his views on why Lasker would return to England.

She asked him to list every known alias Lasker had adopted or might have obtained from Kamatta's stash in the flat with the yellow door, and Peter enumerated them from memory. He also recited the names used on the Malta import manifests. Impressed, she nodded and sank back into the cushions to consider the list. For his part, having summarized just about everything, he thought the overall case file of the Lasker investigation amounted to a feeble showing.

Eventually, she looked up at him. "One detail, then. Our Mr. Lasker's a bit of a joker. He's been toying with the police. He used the name Willemsea on one of the documents?"

"Or Kamatta did."

"No, I think it was the husband. Herman Willemse swam the English Channel in 1959. He was the first Dutchman to accomplish it. Convert the last syllable to 'sea' and you have Mr. Lasker's idea of a bon mot."

"How the devil did you know that?" he said.

"I live here," she said, for the second time. "What is it that bothers you most about André Lasker, Peter?"

He paused to regroup. "I'm afraid that, out of guilt for his wife's killing herself, he'll commit suicide too. Then I'll never understand why he concocted his elaborate scheme. What drives a man to that, to leave his wedding ring exactly in the centre of his clothes and walk into the ocean?"

"I don't know," Gwen said, "but it illustrates the point, doesn't it? Death isn't always closure. Death can stay around to haunt the living."

They sat in the quiet. Finally, he looked at her and said, "What about a *dream* of Death?"

"Ah! So, that's it. What have you been holding back?" She smiled for the first time. It seemed that she could read his every thought.

"Because the dream is probably about the Rover, not Lasker," he said. It sounded pitiful even as he spoke. He was willing to tell her the entire dream but he secretly hoped that it would turn out like his session with the police psychiatrist years ago, who had dismissed the worrisome elements of his nightmares and told him to go back to work.

He narrated his dream to her, and managed to recall most of it. He tried to convey the vividness of the desert, which he speculated was the Sahara. He described the flying black figure and the flock of sheep, and emphasized the underlying anxiety through it all. He elaborated on his hobby of tracking down scenes of Mary's Annunciation and how that motif was reflected in his dream. Finally, he repeated the chant at the end of the nightmare: "Chervil!"

Gwen smiled at this ludicrous word. Peter had asked Joan about it, for he knew that it was some form of bush, and she had told him that it was a harmless, scrubby plant like parsley, and could be found everywhere; it was one of the herbs used in French cookery. Peter waited. He expected Gwen to highlight the religious icons that were threaded through his dream story, but she leaned forward and gently touched the back of his hand.

"Peter, the dream isn't about the Rover, it mostly concerns the other one. Lasker. The Cloaked Man."

"Why do you call him the Cloaked Man?"

"Because he wears a cloak. It doesn't matter, Peter." She didn't want to be confronted on this point.

He moved on. "Are you sure? The dream, I mean."

"My mother's better than I am at this, but let's try. Tell me about the sheep. Close your eyes and picture them . . . What colour were their faces?"

With his eyes shut, he conjured up the scenes that built to the stampede of the flock of sheep. "They started out as clouds, puffy like sheep's wool. They were grey on top. Then they turned over and showed white on their bellies. At some point they transmogrified into sheep."

"Their faces?"

He opened his eyes. "They were white."

"The chanting of the word 'Chervil.' Who said it?"

"No one. It just came out of . . . the environment. I heard a voice repeat it five or six times."

"Well," Gwen said, and got up from the chesterfield. She began to pace around the Persian rug in her bare feet. "It's obvious."

"Don't toy with me."

She laughed, and faced him. "Chervil is a plant, a bit of a weed, not so good in salads. It has medicinal properties, but that doesn't concern us here. You can find it everywhere. Chervil is just your mind's trick for homing in on the cliffs. It represents the cliffs, if you want. You probably saw lots of it. Maybe it represents a wasteland, depending how you feel about the cliffs these days."

"I was in a desert," Peter said.

"Yes, that. The desert is in Australia. It's not the Sahara."

"How do you know that?"

"One point of clarification. Did the chant stop, then start again, later in the dream?"

He ran the dream plot in his mind. "Yes, I think so."

"And was the word the same, 'Chervil'? Could it have been 'Cheviot'?"

"I don't remember."

"Because the sheep you describe are Cheviot sheep. They have distinctive white faces."

"Found in the north of England mostly," Peter added. "Where's the connection to Lasker in the *north*?"

"Oh, there are at least three farms around here that raise them. The word could also reference Chesil Beach, which is just up the road, well within the Jurassic Coast."

"That's it, then. Chervil-Chesil-Cheviot. All in the neighbourhood."

"No."

"Well, why not?" Peter said.

"I don't think so. The connection is in Australia," she said. "Do you remember Harold Holt?"

Of course he did. "Australian prime minister who drowned in the sea. It was an accident. He went swimming in a riptide. There were conspiracy theories at the time. One had it that secret agents had picked him up offshore in a submarine. But no doubt that it was an accidental drowning."

"The body was never found, was it? That's probably why you dreamed it. Another case not closed. And, I might add, another example where Death still haunts us."

"Australian sheep?" he said.

"No. Cheviot sheep. Harold Holt disappeared on a beach. What was it called?"

Now he remembered. "Cheviot Beach."

He sat there in astonishment. Even if she had searched the Internet, how had she thought to seek out the death notice of Harold Holt, an almost forgotten Australian prime minister?

Gwen was tracking his thoughts. "Peter, the Great Dream Master, whether his name is Freud or Jung, loves puns. So, chervil becomes cheviot. Lasker turns Willemse to Willemsea."

"I'm almost afraid to ask, but what about the black figure in my dream?"

"Was he good or evil, benign or hostile?"

"I assumed he was evil, maybe an avenging angel. I thought he was the Rover, and then he might be André Lasker, your Cloaked Man."

Gwen took her place again on the chesterfield. "He's neither Lasker nor the Rover. He is obviously Father Salvez. Maybe the Annunciation image meant that he was 'announcing' something to you. He was all in black, like Salvez. His face too?"

"It was black where the face should be. Because he was dead?"

"I'm not so sure. In dream symbology, the white face is the Mother, but a blacked-out face isn't necessarily the Father. It can be Death, but I'm not so sure. My mother's better at this. Black is the void. A human figure all in black is inviting you to fill in the void."

"Please don't tell me that Salvez was summoning me to find my faith, find my way back to the Church?"

She laughed. "No, this was the dream of a Scotland Yard detective. Probably secular, then. At least your dream is some kind of progress."

She leapt up from the cushions. "Time to go, if we're going at all. The light fades early these days."

Peter went to the entrance to the cottage and unpacked his hiking boots. While he was putting them on, Gwen went to her bedroom and retrieved a pair of bright purple Nike trainers. He stared at her outfit.

"What?" she said. "You need to dress for the cliffs. These shoes are perfect. You think we're attending the Celtic Fair?"

Her dream interpretation was still buzzing around his mind. He felt as if he had just left a fortune teller's tent. "Where are we going?"

"Three caves I want you to see. Conceivably, a person could hide out in them for a long time. Bring your gloves if you have any. It'll get cold."

"Why these three?"

"Don't fairy tales have three of everything? Three hibernating bears, for example."

"Three witches?"

"No, that's Shakespeare. We're leaving him at home today, along with all those sheep. Banquo's ghost won't help us this time."

They were outside on the stoop of the cottage, just about to close the door, when Peter's mobile rang. They moved back inside while he answered it.

It was Joan; the reception was good. "Peter, are you there?"

He hadn't expected a call from his wife and was thrown off balance. Mrs. Ransell, her hair a Gordian knot and her face ruddy from sleep, burst out of the bedroom. Even though it was impossible, Peter understood from her look that she had known right off that Joan was on the line. They had met only once, at the funeral, although he had no idea what they had discussed. The old woman came close and made to grab the cell.

"Just a minute, Joan." He fiddled with the buttons on the side of the device. "Hello? Hello?" He was satisfied that he had succeeded in putting the call on speaker. The three of them, Gwen and Peter baking in their heavy clothes, huddled around the mobile to listen to Joan, her voice tinny coming out of the miniscule speaker.

"Yes, what's wrong?" he said.

"Two things. Well, nothing's wrong at all. But Stan Bracher has been trying to call you."

"Well, I'm here."

"He's nearer you than me. I don't know why he can't get through. He's on the south coast."

"What's he doing here?"

"He wouldn't say. He was very coy. But there's something else. The church."

Peter had encountered so many churches over the last two weeks that he wasn't sure which one she meant. As usual, she read his thinking process.

"The church today, Peter. Did you notice that big, enclosed display case at the end of the front path?"

"The one with the Bible passage in it?" He was thoroughly confused. He caught Ellen Ransell nodding, as though she understood where Joan was going with this. *What did these women talk about?*

"Did you read it?"

"I don't remember it."

"It was from Luke 21. It said: 'That ye may be accounted worthy to stand before the Son of man.' Underneath was printed *Luke 21:36.*"

"It was a different quotation when I was there before. Something about kings."

"Not now. I think it was put there recently, maybe especially for Father Salvez's funeral. You know how a picture in a sealed glass case can wrinkle after a while if it isn't framed properly? Well, this sign was fresh, no water spots."

"What bothers you about the Bible verse?"

"When I read it — I was talking to Mrs. Ransell at the end of the path . . . "

He interrupted. "She's right here."

"Hello, Ellen . . . Well, something stuck in my head, but I didn't figure it out until a moment ago. When we were touring the cathedral in Malta, I read out to you the inscription on the Grand Master's tomb. It said, *'In mortis starabo ante Filium hominis.* In death I will stand before the Son of man.' How can an obscure biblical reference on a knight's grave suddenly show up at a Catholic church in Whittlesun, Dorset?"

Peter certainly didn't have the answer, but after his dream interpretation session with Gwen, it wasn't a day to reject coincidences out of hand. "That is weird." He didn't know what to say; he was anxious to get out to the cliffs. Mrs. Ransell tried again to grab the phone. "Joan, Ellen wants to talk to you."

The old lady roughly took the device. She addressed her words to Joan, although the others could hear.

"Joan, the Bible is best read in Greek, whether or not Matthew, Mark or St. Paul originally composed it in Greek. It's what scholars use when they study the meanings of the fine text. There might be Hebrew and Aramaic scholars who disagree."

Joan's voice sounded metallic out of the speaker. "But the reference in the display case was in English, not Greek or Latin."

Mrs. Ransell was not to be rushed. "Greek is the preferred language because it is precise. For example, if you want to be sure whether two people in the Bible are 'cousins' or 'brothers,' or 'uncles' rather than 'stepfathers,' the Greek is your best source. But Latin is next-best, and that's what your Maltese knights were familiar with."

"Are you suggesting that I read the passage in Greek?"

Mrs. Ransell heaved a frustrated sigh, though more with Peter than with Joan. "No. I am suggesting that you compare, read the quotations carefully. Pay attention to the similarities but also to the differences. It may in fact be a mere coincidence."

Mrs. Ransell was drunk, and Peter saw no point in her lecture. He remained confused, and he also sensed Joan's distress. If Mrs. Ransell was delivering a clue, Peter couldn't find the trail. It was time to get back to business, and that meant embarking on their search of the cliffs.

"Peter," Gwen said, "didn't Father Salvez like word games?"

"Yes. But why the same quote?"

"First of all, it isn't exactly the same — that's what Mum is saying — and it isn't much of a coincidence to find that two religious men, even centuries apart, would anticipate their pending encounter with Jesus, the Son of man. To really know, it would help to verify if Salvez was behind the homily at the church."

Peter understood that Joan felt isolated as they bickered in the cottage so far away. But the distance gave her perspective on the discussion, and perhaps that was why she identified the next logical question. "You may be right, Gwen. Peter, did you tell Father Salvez about our visit to the Cathedral in Valletta?"

"No. I never talked to him at all after Malta."

"Well," Joan said, "if it turns out that the Latin on the Grand Master's tomb matches the Latin Bible verse from Luke, what does that tell us?"

It told them, Peter knew, that, coincidence or not, John Salvez was trying to send him a message.

"Oh, you two!" Mrs. Ransell shouted. "Let me talk to Joan. Go do your walkabout. Come back later, by sunset, Gwen." She kept the mobile and bustled into the bedroom, slamming the thick oak door behind her.

CHAPTER 31

They had been walking on a shallow downward angle for ten minutes, and Peter was already lost. Guinevere was relentless, steadily leading him towards the setting sun along sharp defiles in the grass-crowned dunes behind her cottage. Over that time, he couldn't make out the sea at all, and she kept them below the horizon, in black shadows, as they moved west. She finally stopped; there was nowhere to go but up.

She turned to him. "Shelter your eyes when we come over the knoll. We'll come out facing west and the sun will be directly at us."

The vertical path was deceptive, becoming rough limestone as it climbed. The depression they had been following was merely a silt fosse for soil swept by the wind from the top plates of stone. Gwen reached back to help him over the lip of rock. He gained the upper rock plate, stood up and arched his back, and looked out to the east. The vista along the Channel recalled the wake of the Great Armada, fleeing out to the open sea. Looking westward, he made out the shape of Whittlesun and its harbour, and even with the face-on sunset, he thought he glimpsed Whittlesun Abbey. He looked at Gwen and she nodded.

They alternately descended and remounted the heights as they progressed to the first cave, although Peter thought at times that they were no longer moving west by the compass. She moved with full confidence, and he had no choice but to trail behind. She never hesitated when the path diverged. Whenever they succeeded in reaching an open perspective on the Channel, his sightline was inevitably blocked by the salients of rock. She kept them away from the edge; he well knew the risk of suddenly falling into one of the hollowed-out bays along this erratic shore.

Finally, after they had been walking for several minutes on a relatively flat plateau with a clear view of the water, she halted on a massive stone and called out against the crosswind.

"The cave is thirty feet below. First, I'll take us up there" — she pointed to a rock mound ahead — "so that you can orient to the shoreline, get some idea of distance from the town. It'll be stormy."

They found handholds along the sides of a defile ahead, and in two minutes they emerged on the pinnacle. He poked his head over the fissured rim, found the wind tolerable and hoisted himself onto the topmost rocks. Talking was impossible; they used hand signals and gestures to communicate. The relatively straight line of the shore to the west surprised him, as if erosion had been largely resisted in that sector. Gwen pointed to his pocket and he took out his military binoculars. He followed her pointing finger to several spots along the shore, in both directions. She wanted him to identify promising indentations that might have provided hiding spaces for Lasker.

They descended and began working their way towards the rim of the cliff. They had to crab-walk and crawl against the rising wind off the Channel. The final goat track down to the cave inscribed another narrow maze, but Gwen moved with assurance. She paused twice to check for signs that someone else might have visited recently. They came out onto a sloping hill that ended in the sea some two hundred yards away. Their position gave them an open view of the coast below. From there, with Gwen's guidance, he spied two dark indentations in the rock face opposite.

"Caves," she said. "We can get to them in twenty minutes."

The trek took thirty minutes. The path narrowed to a mere trace at times; Gwen knelt down and fingered the gravel, like an Apache tracker. Gorse and sedge grew in clumps and encroached on the track, threatening to obliterate it. Where it widened, she pointed to plants that had taken hold in the rich silt. "Buckthorn, whortleberry, horsetail."

The first cave was disappointing. Sea winds had etched out a dry grotto in the cliff wall fifty yards above the Channel. Peter nervously held back from the rim of the cave. The hollow extended into darkness and the beam from Peter's torch disappeared into the gloom. It was a good enough hiding place but no one had been here. Not even crisps wrappers or condoms, he noted.

The sky over the Channel had now ashened with the nascent storm and the fading of daylight, lending some urgency to their return to the cottage. After only one discovery, the heart had gone out of their plan. There were too many possibilities, and they had failed to narrow down the search criteria. He had been naive, he saw. Even if André Lasker had holed up in one of the caves the night of his escape, he might not use the same refuge now. He could be anywhere, including a location much farther west, on the other side of Whittlesun.

The claustrophobic effects of the labyrinth of paths wore on them. "Let's go to higher ground," he pleaded. "I'm disoriented."

As they climbed to a safer level, and inland a few hundred yards, Peter found a perch on a boulder that gave them a silhouetted angle on the row of cliffs in the distance. He paused for a last look at the grey clouds, with the dun water below. He began to see the meaning of his dream, or at least the part with the flying black figure. (To be fair, Gwen had never presumed to explain all of the dream.) A sea bird — Peter identified it as a skua — migrating along the Channel shortcut swooped past them, fighting a contrary wind as it struggled for a purchase in the rocks. The black figure was Salvez, but *why* had he flown into the dream? She was right, that most of the dream was about André, fed by the urgency in Peter's subconscious to track him down, but there was something else. The figure was equal parts priest, angel and hovering bird. It floated above the scene for a good reason: there was something it had wanted to point out to Peter.

They stood on a broad, lonely plateau strewn with boulders. Even with the wind howling and battering the zone around them, Gwen noticed the change in him. "What is it?"

"The black angel. It's a premonition."

And then they were no longer alone.

Gwen knew the route back to the cottage and they were soon in sight of the farm roads that demarcated the fields from the cliffs. Their return would be faster once they reached a country lane. Behind them, the weather closed in. Peter turned to catch a last look at the sunset and thought he saw something sticking up above the horizontal plane. Gwen threw him a questioning look. He took the compact binoculars from his pocket, and aimed them towards the sea, adjusting the focus as he scanned the horizon. The dark figure jiggled into view and he steadied the binoculars with both hands. The figure stood sideways, but was gazing out to the Channel. Peter recalled the iconic scene in *Wings of Desire* where the angel stood poised on a rooftop overlooking the city. The man turned, full on. It was Ron Hamm. The face remained in half shadow, but Peter was sure.

After a few seconds, Hamm stretched out his arms from his sides, and turned in place. He raised his face to the heavens, like a Druid, or a Native shaman completing a sacred ceremony. He lowered his arms and resumed his solitary vigil.

Peter handed the binoculars to Gwen, who watched for several minutes. "He's not moving."

"Can we catch up to him?"

"It's at least a half mile. The fastest way is the road over there, then find a path to the rocks."

"Where do you think he parked his car?" He remembered the Vauxhall; there were many places the clunker could never reach.

"Possibly the Abbey. But that's six miles or so beyond where he's standing now. Besides, we don't have a car ourselves . . . Wait, he's moving. Look."

He realigned the binoculars and found Hamm again, but he was edging up the shoreline, out of sight. The grey mist would soon roll in and gobble him up. In an instant he was gone.

"Damn! What's going on here?"

"We could phone him," Gwen said.

"Your mother has my cell."

They trudged back along the farm road to the Ransell cottage, light rain in large drops spattering the dust around them. Peter filled Gwen in on Hamm's confrontation with F.R. Symington and its genesis in the young man's reaction to the corpse of Anna Lasker.

"So is he hunting for Lasker?" she said.

"Perhaps, but I wonder. There's no reason he couldn't be looking for the Rover as well." He was saying that Ron Hamm had freaked out.

"Except that the Rover has never operated this close," she said.

What he really feared was the possibility that Ron Hamm was looking for both of them. He had grown to like the young man. He wanted Gwen to say something. She hadn't referred to the Rover as the Electric Man yet during this visit, and he would have welcomed her saying it now. They were almost at the cottage. Peter said, "Gwen, do you know who the Rover is?"

"No," Gwen said, "but it's possible my mother knows."

Mrs. Ransell was asleep in the bedroom when they entered. Peter's mobile phone sat on the counter beside the Koskenkorva bottle. The fire had subsided to glowing coals. There were a dozen things to be done urgently, yet the spectre of Ron Hamm had undone Peter, and all he could think of was to reach out to the young detective. The number, as he expected, was not being answered, and so he called Constable Willet.

"Surprised to hear from you, Chief Inspector." He had reached Willet at the Whittlesun station. The reception was clear, although Peter's battery was down to a half.

"Why is that, Constable?"

"I dunno, sir. Maybe because you've been considered out of the loop on the Lasker thing of late. Not me saying, you understand, sir."

Not you, but Maris. Willet's tone, however, was friendly enough, indicating that he was making an effort to stand apart from the friction between Maris and the Yard. But Peter resolved not to tell the Constable of his presence in Whittlesun.

"Can you bring me up to date?"

"The Lasker home has been released to her family. A bunch of uncles and cousins, I can't tell them apart. As you well know, sir, the house needs a replastering, and more. I've been fielding complaints about that. And there are superstitions among the Romanians."

"Is there any thought of declaring André Lasker dead?" He knew there wasn't, but he wanted to move the conversation along without offending Willet.

"Dead? No, and there won't be until we find him, in one condition or another. You think he's back in England, sir?"

"Yes. We're optimistic about tracking him down with the passport angle. What do you think, Mr. Willet?" He felt some relief in talking to the constable. He had had enough of the Ransells' strangeness for one night.

"I'd have to agree, from what I'm told, which is little enough."

"And what does Detective Hamm think?"

Willet paused; he clearly understood where Peter was heading with this. "That was clever police work, his figuring to look at complaints of stolen passports."

"Have you talked to him today?"

"Not today. Not for five days."

"What's his status?"

"They're calling it administrative suspension. Pending an investigation of Symington's complaint, that is."

"What happened?"

Willet cleared his throat. "Kind of lost control with Symington. Told me he had delayed viewing the corpse for a long time, but it was his duty as the main investigator on the case. It affected him."

"I want to put this carefully, Mr. Willet," Peter said, "but has he been just as obsessed with the Rover?"

There was a longer pause this time. "Mr. Cammon, I have a theory. It may sound a little grand . . ."

"I want to hear it, Constable."

"Well, Mr. Hamm changed when you and he found the girl's body that time. Maybe it was coming that close to his own death. But I think it was finding the girl. He's been off the beam since."

In Peter's recollection, Hamm hadn't seen the bleached and scarred body of Molly Jonas rise, naked, from the sea; he had been unconscious at the time. He was sure now that Hamm had asked to see her at the morgue, probably just after viewing Anna's remains.

"Mr. Cammon," Willet continued, "you know what my father said to me? He said, our true natures will always come out. Don't tell Ron I said this, but the most important thing in his view of himself is to be considered a professional, a copper's cop. He's always worried he isn't tough enough for the job."

"He's a good man. A compassionate man."

"Yes, sir, and this true nature may be what's tripping him up. Hopefully just temporary."

"I'd like to talk to him."

"I'm not authorized to release his new mobile number to you, Chief Inspector. He's not using his police number any longer." There was no point in challenging Willet's interpretation of the rules. There were ways around the problem.

"I understand. Can you reach him and ask him to call me?"

"Yes," Willet said, knowing there was more to come.

"I have another favour to ask. Do you think Hamm has disappeared?"

"Disappeared? How?"

"Gone off the rails. Done something, or gone somewhere, that puts him at risk."

"I hope not, Inspector."

"Could you do me a last favour? Look at his work station? Just the loose stuff on his desk. See if he's jotted down any appointments, anything like that. Or any piece of paper with a question mark on it."

"Anything unusual."

"Exactly. And call me tonight on this line. Tonight for sure, you understand?"

"Sure. Inspector?"

"Yes, Constable?"

"Mr. Hamm does have twin girls."

As Peter hung up, Gwen emerged from her mother's room and shook her head. Mrs. Ransell was down for the count. She crossed to the kitchen and brought him some tea. He sipped it appreciatively; she had guessed, somehow, that he took milk, sugar. He caught her glancing at his arm; blood had seeped through his bandage.

"You could rest the night here, Peter," she said.

He had already decided not to stay. He carried painkillers but, with or without the pills, he feared that he might dream again. He wasn't a child; awakening in a strange house from a nightmare wouldn't panic him. But he might have a portentous dream, a premonitory hallucination, and, at least for the next twenty-four hours, he needed to come back to his policeman's plodding ways. Gwen would know right away if he dreamed. She would want to interpret his dreams and, while that was one of the key reasons he had come to see her in the first place, a mortal consulted Guinevere in moderation. He also had calls to make, to Joan, Sarah, Bartleben, and, most important, a call-back from Willet. His first dilemma was getting back to town. Tommy would come but it would take two hours, and that was an unreasonable imposition, even for his willing partner. It was entirely black outside now, the wind howling around the cottage. No taxi would hazard the trip on back roads. The Ransells were safe here. A room at the Sunset Arms would his best choice, he reasoned.

He promised Gwen that he would return tomorrow, and he meant it. The answers were here, he felt. But he had to try to find Hamm, to see what hell-bent course he was launched on. Also, he had to fit in a visit to the Abbey.

He didn't expect Sam to be at the garage in Whittlesun at this hour, but there was a slim possibility that he was closing up or that Mayta was working late on the books. There might be an "in emergencies" number on his machine, although Peter could only guess at Sam's definition of an emergency. Long ago, Peter's mother had described his favourite aunt as "excitable and unflappable at the same time." That was Sam.

As it turned out, Sam was there, but Mayta answered the phone. To "Sam's Auto," Peter offered a tentative "Hello?" He did not identify himself.

"Inspector! How are you? How is that arm? Every time we hear from you, you've done damage to yourself. Is it a curse we've put on you?"

Peter had to laugh, a release of a long day's tension. "What do you know about my wounds, Mayta?"

"I hear a drug dealer shot you."

"That's truly amazing, Mayta. That information wasn't in the press."

"Skype. Friends in Malta, everywhere. And you're one of our favourite hits on the Net."

"I know it's late to be calling . . ."

"I'll put Sam on. He's in love with you. I'm pretty hot towards you myself."

"Mayta, what are you talking about?"

But she had gone, and Sam took the receiver. "Peter, how's your arm? Do you need a car?"

"Fine, Sam, and yes. Mayta is amazing."

"True. She has many Skype friends, chat groups. They gossip about me a lot. And try inputting *Scotland Yard shootout*. Mayta should be a police detective."

"Your whole family should be in the business," Peter said.

Sam's tone shifted. "Give me your SatNav coordinates. I'll pick you up."

"It's a long way."

"It's okay."

"I actually don't know them," Peter confessed.

Gwen wrested the mobile from Peter and introduced herself. She smiled as she listened, nodded often, and said: "Yes . . . Right . . . Okay." A Gwen–Sam conversation had to be bizarre, Peter thought. She giggled. She held the mobile so that she could read the screen, pressed a series of buttons and recited the longitude and latitude coordinates for the cottage.

Peter took the phone back from her. "Sam?"

"He's already left," Mayta said. "What are you doing putting beautiful girls in range of my Sam, Peter?"

They walked out to the road using Gwen's pencil torch. The winds had fallen off, leaving the whiff of summer's end, as if winter were holding off for a more propitious time. Peter was glad that Mrs. Ransell remained asleep, even if she knew the Rover's identity. Of course, it was Gwen who surmised that her mother knew; Ellen Ransell had made no such claims.

"It's not safe for you out here," he said, worried for her.

"As safe as it ever was," she said, in an even voice.

She shone the light at the path, leaving their faces in darkness. His mind was occupied by images from his dream, especially the black figure and the Day-Glo orange of the landscape. But it was the Rover who, however illogical Peter's thought patterns, sprang to his lips. "He'll never stop."

"The Rover? No, he will never stop. But Peter, don't worry. He's close."

He took that to mean she encouraged him. She had used similar words before. It was this message that he misinterpreted, and only later did he understand that Gwen never spoke with the intent of flattery or discouragement. She spoke objectively: he was close. But as a veteran policeman he knew he couldn't wait for the Rover or André Lasker to come to him. He had to take charge.

Sam's headlamps joggled through the swales and turns on the tiny road leading to where they stood. He parked the vehicle, an old but rugged Land Rover, catching Gwen fully in the lights.

CHAPTER 32

The one who rejected the label of the Rover watched Peter and Guinevere Ransell from a secure distance. He was sure of himself, his safety guaranteed by the simple fact that he had no intention of attacking them. He could have shot them through the eyes from there. No, no attacks tonight. He was still learning the ins and outs of this new domain, much farther to the east than he had ever ventured. Better to wait.

There's an interesting point, he reflected, as he monitored the pair waiting in the pinprick glow two hundred yards off. Why not execute the men too, do them in pairs? Pairs of lovers. It made sense. His pursuers were pairing up, more and more. Abbott and Costello, Sonny and Cher. The pocket-sized detective and the exquisite girl. There was that navy man, now with some girl in hiking clothes; they put ashore from time to time, to no purpose that he could tell, and walked the sand. And the paired-up coppers fumbling all over the cliffs. No, he wouldn't kill by twosomes, though he loved new numbers. He had integrity in his methods. Besides, he wanted to meet their expectations, for now.

He wandered to changes that disturbed him more, though he was prepared to meet them head-on. The girls were no longer so innocent. There had seemed to be an endless supply at one time. The police had distorted the landscape. Where once the plump teenagers had to sneak away to meet a fellow, now they were not allowed out alone. There were a lot of horny boys getting a lot less thanks to that Task Force.

But he wanted the police to explore the cliffs in false hope. He appreciated the earnestness of these young constables. They craved experience, not a picnic, and that was admirable. If they told themselves they were only larking about, then that was no good, no good at all. A message to the young constables and to the remaining girls and their escorts: this is a killing zone, ladies and gentlemen, not a playground.

He made a mental list of his pursuers. This was fun to do, and kept the knife-edge honed. It struck him that so many of the bobbies, especially the newest ones, wandered in shells, in their carapaced uniforms. There were coppers in blue, in trenchcoats and in slickers. They reminded him of little figures in a Fisher-Price set. Then there was the young detective wrapped in his layer of fat, and the old woman moving in her cloud of booze. He himself had his rain gear, which was a very good disguise. Let them send twinned coppers out to stand on the edge and look out to sea like stunned bullocks or dull sheep. He was more protected every day. He was the Electric Man.

And this line of thought brought him, as many times before, to decisions about what to do next. He was always the one who changed without them seeing that he had changed. Fighting the previous war. He was the plastic trickster. They saw him and didn't fear him, for he was looking inland from the sea. All islands live in apprehension of the flood, yet tell themselves that the water circling them is a moat. He played the defender in order to remain the invader. You can live with anything on an island after a while: erosion, flood, corrosive wind or someone calling your young women to be taken away out to sea.

He watched the Land Rover arrive and take away the detective. It was time to get back to what he had become.

Back to the salt air's electric cackle.

Back to the Druid shores.

I am concealed because I have melted with the rocks. Just as they have grown to pinnacles of silt through layers of time, shaped by geological pressure, I have added levels to my tower. And here's the thing they don't get, yet.

I don't plan to finish the tower.

Peter was amused to see Sam, when he got out of the suv, go over to Gwen, bow and kiss her hand. It did seem appropriate, her standing there wrapped in her cloak like a Greek statue. He had only ever seen her interact with her mother, and briefly with Hamm, but now she smiled with matching grace.

"Thank you, Sam," she said.

"You are welcome, Miss."

But there was little need for more chatter, and Sam and Peter got into the car. Peter rolled down the window. "Go back in now. I'll call you tomorrow."

"Yes, you should," she answered.

"Stay safe."

She may have nodded, he wasn't sure. She faded back into the dark.

At the wheel Sam was all aggression, forcing the beat-up Land Rover back up the double track and disregarding the eroded shoulders.

"Thank you, Sam," Peter said.

"No, no, it is for me to thank you."

"Okay, what the devil is going on? Mayta was coy as anything on the phone."

"My nephew is very, very excited, and he demands to thank you himself if you have the time in Whittlesun this visit. Even next week."

"What exactly did I do?"

"You told the Scotland Yard bosses to show him around. He was up to London yesterday."

"I told my senior, Mr. Bartleben, that Martin had been very helpful and maybe he'd like a tour of our Criminal Information System in London."

"No, it was a man, Blaikie, showed him around the Statistics Section and the computers, Martin told us. Two hours! He has never been happier."

In fact, Peter had made a call to Bartleben, who delegated the job to Keiran Blaikie, an old Yard man, an amiable mentor and right for this task, with a modern sensibility for number crunching and applied stats.

"You know what else?" Sam continued. "You know what else, Peter?"

"Frankly, I don't," Peter said.

"He got a big tour of the Regional Lab out on the edge of town." Blaikie had gone all out.

"Did London arrange that visit, do you know?"

"I assume so," Sam said. "A Mr. Bracher?"

"Stan Bracher?" What was the Canadian doing in Whittlesun? He thought he had fled to somewhere in the North; it was a sign of Peter's fatigue that he couldn't remember Stan's itinerary. Perhaps he had merely set up Martin's tour from London, or some other distant port of call.

At the hotel, Sam tossed the keys to Peter, gave a quick wave and disappeared into the bare nighttime streets.

The chief inspector propped himself up against the pillows and wrote out his list of calls. The lounge had been shuttered when he collected his room key but he had cadged a pint by slipping a pound to the night porter. Willet stood at the top of his list, but he had to wait for the constable to reach him. He owed Joan an update on the day's events and some reassurance of his safe return from Whittlesun Heights. What really puzzled him was Stan Bracher's intervention, probably well intentioned, to help Martin, and he drew an arrow from the Canadian's name to near the apex of the list, just below Keiran Blaikie. As usual, he was left with a pile of impossible priorities.

This fussing with his little catalogue clearly showed his level of exhaustion and, in the end, he called Joan, and let all the others slip away until morning. She started by apologizing for interrupting his expedition to the Ransells'. "I really felt bad calling you there. It's just that it was such a coincidence, with the Knights and Father Salvez quoting the same scripture. What do you think it might mean, Peter?"

"What do you think it might mean?" Peter said, sounding like one of the psychiatrists he liked to dismiss.

"Probably nothing, is my thinking," she said. "They're not exactly the same words. I looked up a Latin Bible on the Internet, and the phrase from Luke is close to the Grand Master's inscription, maybe off by a word or two."

"There's no way I can think of that Salvez would know anything about Malta, and neither of us told anyone about the tombstone. Did Mrs. Ransell have any other theories?" he asked, betting she did.

"Oh, we had a good chat," Joan said. "She's a strange bird, but very bright. Very intuitive between the drinking." Peter hadn't noticed many interstices between her drinking bouts. Joan had become part of the investigation again, and Salvez's little game had brought them together. Peter was patient with her. He was now doubtful that the priest had anything at all to do with choosing the quotation for the display case.

But then he knew.

"Peter, are you still there?" she said.

"Do you have a Bible nearby?" he said.

"You have one in the bedside right next to you," Joan said. "Look up Luke 21:36."

Each heard the other riffling pages. He read: "'Watch ye, therefore, and pray always, that ye may be accounted worthy to escape all these things that shall come to pass, and to stand before the Son of man.'"

"So what?" she said.

"It could be a warning," he said. "That first part of the quote."

"Of what?" she said. Peter worked it through. Joan grew impatient. "Do you think he's warning you about the Rover?"

Peter was inherently cautious; decades of policing had made him that way. "I'm not sure."

"Maybe he suspected the identity of the Rover," she said. "The reference to 'escape' could mean the manhunt for the killer. Yes, I think he knew who the Rover is."

"No, Joan, he was sending me a message, but it was about André Lasker. That's what Ellen Ransell was telling us to do. To figure out what Salvez was saying — whether in Greek, Latin or English. Salvez loved to play games, but he wouldn't mislead me."

"So, dear, what *is* the message?"

"I'm willing to wager that he encountered André somewhere near the Abbey," he said.

"Yes, but for crying out loud, what does the message *mean?*"

"That's the game John Salvez was playing, *is* playing, from beyond the grave. The message — 'pray always that you may be accounted worthy to escape' — was meant for all three of us, André, me and Salvez himself. Something about Lasker escaping."

"Listen, Peter, how about I ring up Father Clarke and ask him whether John wanted the whole verse on display?"

"Wait until tomorrow afternoon. I'm going up to the Abbey in the morning. If I find what I'm looking for, I'll call right away. I'll call anyway. We need some closure on Father Salvez, on a number of things."

"Is Tommy going with you to the Abbey?"

"No," he responded. "It won't be dangerous. But I'm asking him to come down the day after tomorrow." This, of course, came out all wrong (the extra irony being that the job he wanted Tommy Verden for would very likely prove dangerous).

She was about to ring off when she remembered: "Oh, news on the home front. Sarah called. I have the feeling she is more or less dating Jerry Plaskow."

Peter had learned from decades of marriage that one of the worst mistakes a husband can make is to hold back information about a child's significant other. His daughter had surprised him several times in the past week, but her choice of Jerry wasn't one of them.

"Oh?"

"They've been going out on his boat, or one of his boats. Apparently he's been taking her to sites for her marine research."

Peter shifted to the obvious issue. "I want her staying away from the shoreline for at least the next three or four days."

"She may not."

"It's a reasonable request. Only four days."

"There's your likely mistake — telling her what to do."

"I'll call Plaskow."

Joan understood the depths of Peter's exhaustion. She also knew that the pressure was rising, and that it would play itself out on those very cliffs. He wasn't off base. "No, it's okay. I'll make the call — to Sarah."

They agreed to talk about it tomorrow. Finally, as the call ended, Joan said, "Father Salvez might have warned you more explicitly."

"I think I know his reasons," Peter said.

"I'm a detective, like you," Sarah had said to him in the hospital, or maybe it was on the way to the Callahans', but it wasn't true. She was a wanderer, yes — restless, a seeker — but not like him. She had realized this during the dinner at the hotel with Jerry. She kept wondering why the two of them talked so obliquely about death — the naked girl, Dad's fall from the cave and Detective Hamm, whose concussion was only a few heartbeats from death. They dodged the subject, not out of fear and certainly not bravado, nor cynicism. If anything, her father had a right to his weary resignation after forty years of confronting the violence perpetrated by angry men, and Jerry was starting to get those squinty furrows around the eyes that showed him heading the same way. The distance they kept from mortality, from the mortal remains on the slab, was finely measured, learned from experience. It was also necessary. They did a disservice to the dead women if they lost it in public; giving in to rage in private would be even worse, she supposed. She liked her dad even more for his calm that night at dinner in the hotel. She mostly kept quiet and listened. She had faith that her father would gather the evidence with relentless purpose: he would serve the needs of the battered wife and the slain teenagers.

She looked up at the cliffs now, not all that many miles from the Abbey. Sarah believed in serendipity, even Jung's synchronicity; it was why she liked fossil hunting, leaving all of the evolution debate to one side. She finally understood her dad's vocation: a detective prepared his case, then prepared some more, so that when the unusual, the mutation and the unique perversity of evil popped up above the horizon, the detective would be ready. He often said that luck would catch André Lasker, but it wouldn't be luck at all. Grinding work would produce serendipity. Sarah imagined her dad right now on the clifftop, fussing in the ruins of the ancient Abbey for who knew what. Just as she was doing down below.

With the tide out and the waves in abeyance, she picked her way through the creatures they had left on the wide strand, which was like a field of soaked potter's clay. She liked Jerry because he was dashing and a man committed to life on the sea, who understood the roll of the Channel and the ebb and flow of the tides. He was a good detective too; Dad had confirmed it. But he wasn't her dad, not the man whose passion for justice underpinned every breath. Might be easier to live with, though, she thought. She pondered her relationship with Jerry a while longer as she moved up the beach, keeping an eye on the tide. She had met Jerry's Mr. Smith once, on the big motor launch, and had watched them work together in oiled unison, communicating mostly by eye contact. She had known right off that he was SAS; she saw them from time to time training along one coast or another. It occurred to her now that maybe Mr. Smith was the other twenty-five percent of Jerry, the ruthless and relentless part that her dad embodied in one black-suited, bowler-hatted soul.

It was time to retreat from the tide. She had almost reached the end of the accessible beach anyway. Looking up the strip of sand into the sun, she saw a silhouetted figure approaching. In the quivering mirage of rising heat she made out a cloaked person, who seemed to glide across the shore towards her. The figure raised an arm and slowly moved it back and forth in greeting.

CHAPTER 33

Peter got up by six and skipped breakfast in order to reach Whittlesun Abbey as quickly as he could. He departed the hotel without making any of the numerous calls on his list. Just as he unlocked Sam's old Land Rover, his mobile chimed. He checked the screen. The one person he really needed to reach was Willet.

"Good morning. Did you contact Mr. Hamm, Constable?"

"Left a message again, and your number, sir. But I did take a gander at Mr. Hamm's desk, like you asked."

"And?"

"Tried not to disturb his papers, mind. Did find a volume of Shakespeare. Thought it odd for a detective's desk. He's put verses down on various bits of paper."

"Handwritten?"

"No. Typed."

"Printouts?"

"Yes, I suppose. Some of them. The thing is, they were all about murder."

"All from Shakespeare?"

"I suppose so. But they all contain the word 'murder.' Here's the longest one."

He read:

Thou shalt do no murder, and wilt thou then,
Spurn at his edict and fulfil man's?
Take heed, for he holds vengeance in his hands,
To hurl upon the heads that break the law.

"Did you keep the others?"

"No, sir. There were only four short ones. Recognized one from *Macbeth*."

Peter rubbed his palm against his eyes. *Richard III*, he recalled. What was Hamm doing Googling *Richard III*? He wasn't. He was simply pairing words in a search, and they were "murder" and "vengeance." Hamm was passing the time, obsessing, gearing up. *What for?*

Necessity is the mother of the parking space, and Peter had no option but to leave the Land Rover on the cement pad where Anna Lasker had met her end. There wasn't a human being in any compass direction; still, he was uncomfortable about advertising his arrival like this. He locked the vehicle, pushing his service revolver, the old-tech Smith & Wesson, under the tyre in the wheel well in the boot; Tommy Verden, he knew, carried a newer Glock 17, favoured by bodyguards. He might have nursed the SUV along the path closer to the Abbey, but he also might have broken an axle, and he was content to hike down the slope. It took only ten minutes. The trail fed into the notch between the two hills inland from the Abbey and emerged by the crumbling steps where he had first met Father Salvez.

He started by trying the massive oak doors that gave onto the cliffs at the front of the church. Local police had added a fresh cordon of yellow tape without removing the tatters of the old tape, which flapped in the morning inshore breeze like streamers at a fair. They framed the section where the old priest must have jumped to his death; they served no security purpose. As he had expected, the doors were locked. Any safe access point would do. He soon found a useable path back along the spine of the Abbey, on the eastern flank. He knelt down to examine shoeprints in the fetid muck, and concluded only that they were recent and they were made by an old pair of boots. The path led to a hinged door cut from fibreboard and jammed shut with a block of granite. He was quickly inside and found himself in a covered section of the nave about halfway down the concourse.

For all his preparations at the hotel, he had forgotten his torch, and now he stood in the Gothic gloom adjusting his vision to the shattered interior of St. Walthram's. Towards the front, a column of eerie light arrowed down from the fractured roof, but only served to shield the transept with its contrasting shadows. He had a clear notion of where to search for the crypt. The tourist brochures hadn't mentioned the existence of a crypt, but he was sure there was one, even if stove in and obstructed over time. Salvez was the kind of man who loved hiding places, secret rooms and their mysteries. He also needed a place to sleep on the nights he lingered at the Abbey. Peter hadn't found any of his possessions lying about; they had to be stored somewhere.

He picked his way through the ruins around the transept. Small, shadowed chapels fell away into the dimness on either side of the nave. The front section did have a roof, though it was punctured and offered limited protection against the weather. The haphazard roofing had the dual effect of preserving two of the chapel bays almost intact, while accentuating the Catholic melancholy of the altars within. He examined the chapel on his left and found no succeeding chambers or niches that might hide a door to a crypt. The room to his right, however, presented an array of masked alcoves, arches and hollows emptied of their icons. Normally, a crypt would include a readily seen staircase, wide enough for embalmed bodies and their caskets. The stairs might have been sealed off for safety reasons.

He found it in the darkest recesses of the right-hand chapel, behind an archway that, at first, seemed to lead nowhere. An oak door, ordinary and plainly painted, opened smoothly when he pulled it back by the edge. He sincerely regretted leaving his torch behind. Without much hope, he felt for a light switch along the inner wall of the entrance to the crypt, and encountered his first miracle. A string of small bulbs, strung the length of the staircase, lit up with a sepulchral glow. To be safe, Peter stepped back and noticed for the first time that there was a dusty light switch on the outside wall that would have served just as well. Perhaps, after all, the old priest had used a little of the Preservation Trust's funding for his own comfort.

If so, he hadn't overspent. The lights traced a route downwards to a small room off the base of the narrow steps. It was the kind of space where an ascetic cleric or a custodian of the Abbey might mark time. He pulled the string on another light bulb, and the small room was half-illuminated; it was unheated but fairly dry, a rough sanctum, almost an oubliette, though perhaps not conducive to meditation. The chamber was furnished with a cot covered by a blanket; two more blankets lay folded and stacked at the foot of the bed. A crucifix hung above the pillow. A small desk and chair filled out the tiny cube, and the computer on top of the desk felt oversized in the confined space. He noted that two cables ran from the computer into the granite wall behind it. A tunnel appeared to flow farther back into the church, but there was no way to tell how far without a strong torch.

The ledge behind the desk, partly occluded by the computer, served as a bookshelf; it held a dozen religious texts. The front panel of the desk unfolded forward to create a writing tablet, and the drawer behind it revealed a series of slots containing pencils, a rosary and several small notebooks, which turned out to hold accounts of expenditures on the Abbey. The only colour in the space, aside from the ruby glow from the rosary beads, was a sign printed in orange ink on ragged-edged parchment, which Salvez had taped to the side of the monitor: *ars bene moriendi.* Peter turned on the CPU and was amazed when it fired up; the monitor soon lit up with its blue face, and immediately displayed the homepage of the Abbey. Worried that the power might brown out, or be cut off entirely by the weather, Peter found the icon for the priest's email and clicked it. Automatically updating itself, the system listed a half dozen new messages, but all were routine missives from other church groups, so to speak, post mortem.

Out of curiosity, and no particular purpose, Peter checked the history of Google and Yahoo searches. Nothing showed for the last four days, but the listing for the previous week, which the computer helpfully archived, charted what could only be termed a massive search for references to the Rover. Peter counted two hundred news sites that addressed the four murders and two assaults, as well as the Task Force's official page (accessed ten times) and various speculative sites, the kind that always spring up with major crimes; Peter's own adventure on the cliffs was also catalogued. Salvez's interest, nearly a fetish, regarding the Rover disturbed Peter, because he saw no point in it; it correlated neither to the priest's character nor to his professed interests.

More distressing was the complete omission of any sites covering the Lasker tragedy, which at minimum was relevant to the Abbey by the proximity of Anna's death. Also, Peter was now certain that the message from the Book of Luke dealt with Lasker.

Peter shut down the computer and turned his attention to the three words on the casing of the monitor. He had naively hoped that Father Salvez had left behind a personal message for him, but *"ars bene moriendi"* didn't resonate with him. He thumbed through each of the books on the slim shelf. Salvez owned a King James, a New Standard and an elegant New Testament by William Tyndale, which Peter had studied in his English Literature years. Tyndale, if he recalled accurately, had died at the stake during the same campaign of persecution that had sent Henry's railers to pillage sanctuaries like this one. He took down the King James and turned to Luke 21:36, reading aloud to the Abbey stones: "Watch ye, therefore, and pray always, that ye may be accounted worthy to escape all these things that shall come to pass, and to stand before the Son of man."

Salvez had underlined the passage.

A telephone rang in the depths of the crypt.

At first, Peter thought it was the computer announcing its automatic rebooting, but then he knew that it was just his mobile echoing oddly in the hollow chamber. Ron Hamm's name appeared on the screen. Through a blur of interference, he struggled to make out Hamm's voice; if there was panic there, Peter couldn't distinguish it from the static.

"Inspector, this is Ron Hamm." Further words were swept away. Peter moved towards the feeble light of the stone stairway, and the reception improved.

"Where are you, Ron?" he shouted.

"I can't hear you too well, Peter. I'm in town."

"Did Willet reach you?" He was shouting now.

"Not to worry. I'm close. Where are you?"

Close? *What does that mean?* "Close in what sense?"

"I have reason to believe that Albrecht Zoren helped Lasker with his plan." Possible, Peter conceded. "I also know that Zoren killed the bookkeeper, Sally, to keep her from finding out about the cars and the shell companies." Peter thought this impossible: he had seen Zoren's face the day of the funeral. "I'm going over to Lasker's."

"Where are you?" Peter called into the line. The signal faded. The wind in from the Channel was audible down in the crypt. It seemed to be building. The door at the top of the stairs slammed shut.

Peter called out: "Ron?" The phone still worked, but he was losing Hamm. The lights went out in the crypt, leaving merely the lonely screen of his mobile.

"Don't hang up, whatever you do!" he shouted. He scrambled to the top of the steps in the dark. He banged his left arm on the rough wall, hitting his recent wound. Finding the door by touch, he pressed against it. It didn't budge; it didn't appear to be locked, only jammed shut, but the steep pitch of the staircase made leverage against the inner side of the door difficult, his position on the top step precarious.

"Are you there, Peter?" Hamm said.

"Ron, I'm at the Abbey. Stuck in the crypt. The entrance is off the chapel east of the transept. I don't know if I have much air. Can you come over and open up?" There was no answer at first, but then Peter thought he heard a muffled "Yes."

Peter called into the fading line: "Stay away from Zoren." But he was met by dead air.

It turned out that he had plenty of oxygen. What he lacked was light and a firm prospect of rescue. He tried to shoulder his way through the door, but it held fast. He found the inner light switch, but it appeared to be dead. Slipping and stumbling down the steps, he paused in the little room to reflect on his options. The glow from his phone was pitiful, but at least the bars showed that his battery had a half charge remaining. He called Hamm back, only to be greeted by the "no reception" lady. Grappling towards the chair next to the desk, he oriented himself to the tiny room and called up his speed-dial list. He even considered trying to reach Verden or Bartleben. Sam's Auto was promising, he thought. But there was a better choice: he called Constable Willet.

There was no reception.

He called Sam, Tommy, Joan, Sarah and the Regional Lab in Whittlesun. He called Vogans. He tried Hamm again. Nothing.

His telephone light would last no more than two hours. He could try the upper door again, but he wasn't hopeful. Feeling round the desk, over and under the computer and along the bookshelf, from which he dislodged half the volumes, he touched the on/off switch on the CPU. He flipped it On. The blue screen arrived like a friend. Peter had never participated in what Michael and Sarah called "social media," other than using email, but now he was faced with choosing his most reliable Best Friend. He considered a quick SOS — filled with exclamation points — to Willet, but that could alert Maris and everyone else on the police network to where he was sending from, and he wasn't eager to explain. Sam or Vogans risked a heart attack climbing these hills and, besides, at least one of them might have legitimate reservations about breaking into a Roman Catholic church. In the end, he emailed Tommy with directions to the crypt. Tommy was the one most likely to check his inbox at least once an hour, and, most important, he would browbeat the Whittlesun force to send someone out to the Abbey.

He prayed that the feed to the computer would stay alive. He turned off the mobile and marked the passage of the minutes on the monitor clock. In the spooky blue glow, Peter decided to pass the time by completing his search of Salvez's possessions. He flipped through the remaining tomes in his library, feeling in the dark beside the desk for the upended volumes. He found a few prayer cards, used as bookmarks. But when he took down a well-thumbed volume of Aquinas, a folded sheet fell out. He opened it and read:

Dover Beach
The sea is calm tonight.
The tide is full. . . .
. . . .
. . . . the cliffs of England stand
. . . . out in the tranquil bay.
. . . . the night air
. . . . the long line of spray
. . . .
. . . . pebbles . . . fling
. . . . up the high strand
. . . .
The eternal note of sadness

All of the next stanza was missing, except for the final phrase.

. . . . the distant northern sea
. . . .
. . . . the breath
Of the night wind. . . .
And we are here as on a darkling plain.

Peter had hoped that Father Salvez had left behind a message for him, but this wasn't the sign he craved. Salvez had simply been playing a word game with himself; it wasn't a puzzle meant for any other reader. He had copied it for solace, or for amusement. He had chopped down Arnold's poem to the physical details, which happened to match the topography just beyond these Abbey walls. He had borrowed them in order to affirm his reality, his presence here on this hilltop during his final stay. No doubt the fragments of the poem had comforted him. His only concession to mortality was the partial line, "the eternal note of sadness."

Yet the truncated poem was written in a fine hand, not unlike an illuminated manuscript, by a practised amateur calligrapher, presumably Salvez himself. It was a beautiful thing in itself. Peter pulled the tiny square of parchment from the side of the monitor and held it in the glow of the screen. He read the words in yellow-orange, *ars bene moriendi*, and turned it over. On the back, in the same lettering, he found: *Th a-K.*

The typeface. The font. He had seen them before. It was a sign-painter's font. The letters carried modest serifs, with a distinct clerical tone but with a commercial impact too. The font was not derived from the elaborate alphabet of an illuminated manuscript. The colour cinched the debate: the draughtsman of the pious homilies on display in the case at St. Elegias was the craftsman of *ars bene moriendi*. The parchment had been a token from the painter. Salvez had practised his own journeyman calligraphy on "Dover Beach," but this gem was the work of a professional.

He scanned the short bookshelf for Salvez's copy of *Imitation of Christ*. He thought that he had the English translation clear but he paged through the chapters until he found the precise reference. Thomas à Kempis had been full of catchy sayings, including "Man proposes, God disposes." *Ars bene moriendi* translated effectively as "the art of dying well." No, Peter concluded, Father Salvez would have spun it another way, as an exhortation to himself: "You must die a good death."

In his last days, the old priest had resolved to find that good death.

Father Salvez had persuaded Father Clarke to place the verse from Luke in the casement for his parishioners, and all the town, to see. He had played on Clarke's sympathy for a dying man, making a final nuisance of himself. And perhaps it was for André Lasker to see, if he decided to attend the funeral.

And so Clarke had cut it back. The reference to man's "escape" from fate had been omitted. Salvez had loved games, even when they were shaped by apprehension of his imminent death. Salvez knew what the Knights understood. They too had deleted any reference to "escape" — "fugere" — on the final gravestone. The Knights of St. John were convinced that their leader, if he lived a good life and made a good death, would leapfrog the Reaper and land in heaven to stand before the judgment of the Son of man.

Salvez had sent Peter a message, and a puzzle to ponder. *Who was worthy of escape?* He was asking Peter to decide the right answer.

As he rested in the basement gloom, he half dozed and recalled snippets of his dream. Father Salvez was the black figure, flying out over the desert-sea. Had Peter been able to count the blank-faced sheep, he bet the number would have been thirty-three. Thirty-three buttons on the cassock.

He took the sheet with "Dover Beach" on it, bent it in half and slid the parchment between the folds. A small fossil sat on the shelf, a pyritized ammonite that the priest must have collected down at the shore. He picked up the three items and put them in an envelope from the drawer. Last, he picked up the red rosary and slipped it into his pocket.

Hamm checked his pistol and inserted it, safety on, in the door slot beside the driver's seat of the Vauxhall. The man on the phone had been clear about the murderer, and Ron was grateful for clarity. Oh, the caller had sworn him to tight secrecy, and he wasn't a chap whom Ron would normally be inclined to trust, with his glib manner, but everything he said made sense. It was about goddam time someone nailed it down.

The caller confirmed what Symington had guessed at, that Albrecht Zoren had been pivotal to Lasker's escape plans, helping to conceal cash and complete the paperwork for the off-ledger export scam. It was Hamm's own deduction that Zoren had eliminated Sally the bookkeeper to prevent her from pointing the way to the gaps in the accounts.

Ron had been less certain about nailing Zoren as the Rover. The caller had been persuasive, pointing to what Ron already knew, that the mechanic had two previous charges for assault, though no convictions; he had to admire the caller's research skills. With access to an unlimited supply of cars, Zoren could move fluidly across the road network on the cliffs.

But perhaps it was the pure momentum that got to Hamm. He had known for a week or more that he was close to the Rover. The attacks on Garvena and Van Loss, as Peter had emphasized, were mistakes that demonstrated a breakdown of discipline. But Ron had been influenced most by the sight of Brenda Van Loss, pale and bruised and luckily rescued no more than a couple of hours away from death by freezing. There was an extra callousness in that one.

Ron tried to be honest with himself about the rendezvous. He wasn't out for glory, but he wanted his measure of vengeance. Momentum again — and it had been launched with the Symington confrontation. He had not intended to strike him, but the teacher's arrogance had been too much. At first he denied his guilt, then threw lines from Shakespeare in Ron's face. He tried to push all the responsibility onto Zoren.

Ron approached the side streets and stopped out of sight of Lasker's Garage. He contemplated the scene ahead. It was possible that he wanted to prove his professionalism to Cammon and Maris, he thought, but really it was the momentum. If he could stop the Rover now, he would forget the torn bodies of Molly and Anna.

411

And the caller had been persuasive.

He had visited the garage once before, when he first interviewed Zoren, and recalled the messy work bays, which extended on to several back rooms. The caller had advised that Zoren slept on a cot in one of these rooms, but had no idea which one. Ron crept to the front entrance, which was recessed from the road, and stopped to listen. No lights were on inside. He needed to be inside before he announced himself, and so he tried the doorknob to the front office. To his surprise, the door swung open and a faint glow from the street established that the room was empty. He entered with his pistol in his right hand, a small torch in his left. He noted the gouge in the reception desk but moved on to the opening that led into the work area. Within, he remarked on the open bonnet of a sedan by a work pit; the garage wasn't all that busy, he observed, and the whole place gave off a spooky, semi-abandoned feel.

"Mr. Zoren? This is Detective Hamm, Whittlesun Police."

He waited in shadow for a full minute. The noise came from the entry behind him, unexpected. The man walked into the beam of Ron's torch and smiled. He was utterly self-possessed. Ron's first one-off reaction was that the man could have been wearing one of the disguises F.R. Symington had conjured up for André, with makeup and hair gel.

"Thank you for coming, Detective. Have you found Zoren?"

"Not yet. Do you have reason to think he's here?"

"I think so, but I'm glad to have the police find out. Have you checked the back rooms?"

"Stay here. I'll do it."

Weapon drawn, Ron edged past the cars in the work bays and around the open pits. The room was a dangerous obstacle course. It became necessary to turn on the switch by the doorway leading off the large space into the back, and as the neon tubes flickered on, at once he felt overexposed. It seemed safer to move into the next small room.

A cot had been set up in the corner, but Albrecht Zoren was not on it. He had propped himself against the opposite wall and now lay slumped to one side. Death had arrived at least twenty-four hours ago, for the body had stiffened and the sallow skin on the man's face had begun to tighten as the features moved towards full rictus. Ron knelt beside the dead man and immediately discerned the effects of a cocaine overdose. Not only was there white powder on his nostrils and chin, but he had wrapped himself in a panel of canvas for warmth. Cocaine reactions often included the shakes. As Ron examined Zoren, the furnace beneath the garage fired up and hot air began to blow out of the vent right next to the body.

The man, composed and smiling, was waiting in the big room for Ron Hamm to return.

"Zoren is dead," Ron announced.

The man held back until Ron Hamm was parallel to the work pit and then reached out and cut the detective across the jugular. Coincidentally, the tool that Albrecht Zoren had threatened Peter with lay on the floor between them; but the Rover had brought his own familiar, sharp knife. He stepped back to avoid the spray.

As Ronald Hamm toppled to his right into the pit, he heard his mobile chiming its familiar ring.

CHAPTER 34

It was a sign of Peter's fatigue that he was dozing off in the stiff-backed chair, deep in the blue aura of the computer, when Willet began pounding on the door. He was floating in a reverie, making his detective's lists. Whom did he trust? Well, that answer was constant: he trusted Gwen. She had identified the Electric Man, and he believed in her.

Peter recalled his list of women. He supposed that the one who still niggled at him was Wendie. She was strong, though not in the way that Gwen was self-assured. It bothered him that she seemed more interested in the Lasker case than the Rover, when surely the biggest, showiest news story was the serial predator. He wondered if she had an undisclosed connection to Lasker. Then again, apropos of the Rover, Wendie had been the one to twig to Kidd's Reach.

Still groggy when the second rap came, Peter imagined the gong being rung at the opening of a J. Arthur Rank film, the reverberations sweeping through the crypt from no single direction. He forgot his half-dream as he revived.

He met the constable at the landing; the door had opened about six inches. The man wore his motorcycle goggles and ancient leathers, and still resembled a flying ace.

"Thank you, Mr. Willet. How did you know to find me here?"

"I received two calls, one from Mr. Hamm and a second from Mr. Verden, to the same effect. Stand back for a moment, if you will." Peter retreated as Willet kicked the door wide.

"Just a minute, Constable." Peter trotted down to the room and shut down the computer. He tested the light switch at the top of the steps and it worked fine now; evidently, the lights closed down when the door was closed.

They made their way back along the nave and out around the Abbey to the set of steps. Willet's motorbike was parked below, with an extra helmet on the seat. Peter held back in order to take a couple of deep breaths.

"What did Hamm say?" Peter asked.

"He was a bit coy, I must say. Said he's made a breakthrough. He'd report back later about it. I had started my late shift when he called."

Willet ferried him back to the car park by bike, after which they formulated their plan. Willet would lead the way to Lasker's Garage. He would likely get there faster than Peter in the Land Rover, but he was to park a street or two away and wait for him. Peter had recorded Hamm's number from the young detective's incoming call. He now dialled it as he drove down the hill. This time he connected to his voicemail service and left a message: "Ron, stay away from Zoren. It's a trap."

In the Land Rover, he careered down the hill, with the SUV fishtailing on the muddy verge. He was seeing the power of a coastal storm for the first time. Until now, he had only the tourist's experience of bad weather, encountering the dull fixity of grey mists and drizzle, but now the sleet, fog and cold had rolled in together. Even at this speed, he began to lose Willet's tail lamp in the distance. He turned the wipers to high, and wondered if it might rain forever.

He was safe as long as he followed the only passable road to the town limits; from there he would know the way to Lasker's. He felt, rather than saw, the cloudbank overhead. The storm was moving in from the sea like an invader; it would hover over the land until it completed its assault, leaving wind damage and flooded cellars. Between curtains of rain he glimpsed farmhouse lights. A van with a decal of a satellite dish logo on the side huddled near a farm entrance; the power feed to the area had held so far, but, Peter thought, television service must have become problematic for the entire heights.

He reached Lasker's much faster than he expected. He desperately hoped that he was in time. Willet had pulled his machine into a lay-by on the cobbled street that led to the garage; he had removed his helmet. Peter pulled in behind. He dug in the boot for his Smith & Wesson, which was fully loaded, and ignored the sleet that was angling into his face from up the road. They padded side by side to the lot, where only three cars occupied the apron out front. The pull-down garage door next to the parking area was shut and padlocked. They had a clear view of the entire exterior, but that didn't count for much when any entry to the interior would require blunt force, with the accompanying racket.

Ron Hamm had blundered into the ultimate misinterpretation of the evidence. For a fortnight — had it been longer? — Peter had struggled to keep Lasker separate from the Task Force, if only for day-to-day efficiency, and to avoid crossing wires with the searchers along the Whittlesun Heights and with the Task Force analysts back in Devon. Peter, during the time he was assigned to the Lasker case, had served as a token member of the group. Hamm never had that luxury: he was formally appointed to both and had taken on substantial, perhaps clashing, duties. He was ripe for seduction. Ron Hamm had decided that Albrecht Zoren was the Rover, and he had been persuaded of this by the Rover himself. The convergence could be fatal.

Hamm was new to the world of pathology. It had been a mistake for Peter to conceal Anna's suicide from him. Ron couldn't be blamed for concluding that Zoren had contributed somehow to her humiliation. While at the Regional Morgue that day, he examined Molly Jonas as well, her bloated, white body showing every bruise and desecration of her innocence. But Peter also suspected that Brenda Van Loss was important too. Ron had been early on the scene. He had described the tableau to Peter on the phone, noting the near-freezing conditions that night. The Rover had beaten Brenda about the face, in contrast to Daniella, and left angry abrasions on her arms and forehead. The resemblance to Anna was compelling. Later, the Rover had reinforced the link to Zoren. After all, Hamm had reasoned, Lasker himself had left England before the attacks on Daniella and Brenda. So Zoren was the Rover.

All it had taken to get Ron to Lasker's Garage was a call from the Rover himself.

Followed doggedly by Willet, Peter approached the office, to find the door locked and the shade pulled all the way down. Taking off his coat, he wrapped it around his fist and punched in the window. No sound came from the office, or from the depths of the work bay area beyond. Reaching around the frame, Peter released the door-knob. Followed by the constable, he paused in the office to check the shelves on which Sally had ranged the binders of company invoices. The books were in their places; the intruder hadn't been interested. Peter had a sense that the business had slowed considerably, and the condition of the work bays confirmed the fact. Only two sedans, neither less than a decade old, were waiting for attention, and the open bonnet of one indicated that only desultory repairs were being done.

He needed to move swiftly, but with a high degree of caution. The interior of the garage afforded many hiding places; chasing down a suspect would entail dodging every kind of obstacle, and there were multiple egress points allowing a fugitive to get away. Basic police training for entering a building was the same everywhere. Willet drew his service pistol and fell into rhythm behind Peter as they shifted strategic positions from the doorway to the first parked vehicle, and then to the second. Peter made sure not to block the Constable's line of fire, since the reaction of the first man would likely be to drop-and-shoot while the back-up would shoot to kill. Peter reasoned that an ambusher would place himself at the back of the work zone, although Peter had never been this far into the facility. Also, there was bound to be another door through which he could flee.

417

But there was silence. It was the kind of silence that rings hollow and seems to expand, that birds feel before the advent of a storm; the sensation that someone has left a room a minute earlier.

The two policemen moved efficiently to the rear exit of the garage and around the full interior perimeter, checking off each place of concealment. Willet finally lowered his weapon and looked towards Peter. He understood when the constable took out his mobile phone and punched in numbers. Peter wheeled a hundred and eighty degrees as a ring tone sounded behind and *below*. The two men followed the sound to the rim of the rectangular hole in the garage floor, and gazed into the oily pit. Ron Hamm lay on his back, his left arm contorted under his body.

Peter scrambled down the short ladder into the pit, unmindful of the grease. Hamm had struggled; his coat was thoroughly soaked with oil and grime. Peter found no pulse and tried CPR, to no avail. On closer examination, he understood that Hamm had been unconscious, probably mortally injured, before he fell; the slash across his throat wouldn't have been instantly fatal, but was enough to throw him off balance and make him give up resistance as he turned to his gushing wound. Arterial blood had flooded over the man's shirt, down to the beltline, and sprayed ahead as he fell, coating the side of the work pit. He had bounced and twisted on the slippery cement, rotating onto his back, where he bled out entirely.

Willet dialled 999 and requested both ambulance and police. The responding dispatcher, a woman, was initially confused, but he patiently led her through the basic information she needed to do her job. He explained that a local police officer had been killed, that he too was a Whittlesun officer and was wearing black pants and a leather jacket, and the arriving officers should refrain from shooting him. He gave the address of Lasker's Garage and stated that the door to the small shack, set back from the street, was unlocked.

"We're in one of the work pits with the body of the victim. Once you send Ambulance Services, please call Inspector Maris at Whittlesun Police HQ, top priority."

"Are you sure the officer is dead?" she said, her voice now as cold as his. There was a special code for Officer Down.

"Definitely. CPR has been applied."

"Is anyone there with you?"

"I am with another policeman."

"Whittlesun Force?"

Willet rolled his eyes in exasperation. "No, New Scotland Yard."

"Do you know the identity of the deceased person?"

"Yes. He was a good policeman."

The ambulance arrived in seven minutes flat. Police vehicles began to pour in two minutes later, and Willet met them at the door to the office. The paramedics and police investigators trailed into the work bays and relieved Peter, who was down in the bloody pit cradling Hamm in his arms. His arms cramping, woozy from the damp and the blood smell in the hole, Peter was grateful to climb up top. He followed the instructions of the first detective to arrive, a tall man in his fifties named Perlmutter, and waited outside on the asphalt apron in front of the office shack. Witnesses, even if both were police officers, were to be separated, and Peter respected the rule. He was alone for a moment as the pedestrian traffic spun around him. He knew that Maris would be only seconds behind. Peter's mobile battery was almost exhausted but he tried, with success, to get a clear line to Tommy Verden at home in London. He provided a brief status report on Hamm's killing and asked Tommy to rendezvous at the Sunset Arms as soon as he could drive down to the coast. Peter went over next steps, the agenda for the night, and instructed him to prepare for an intensive search along the cliffs, and to bring along a fresh coat and gloves for Peter himself.

"It's a bastard of a storm moving in, Tommy," he said.

"And weapons?"

Peter answered with only one word, but Verden understood. "Kershaw," he said, invoking the bloody shootout with the sixth man Peter had killed.

419

Peter ended the call just as Maris, bundled in a trenchcoat and leather gloves, was disgorged from a panda car. He asserted immediate ownership of the scene. He came right up to Peter, who was leaning against the door jamb, trying to avoid the broken glass on one side of the doorway while dodging the medical and police personnel trundling in and out.

"Cammon," he said, "how did my man die?"

Peter was in for a long night, and he didn't have the time. He had never expected that he could "start from the beginning." Resignedly, he decided to respond in a direct and literal manner to all of Maris's questions. Maybe he could get out of here in two hours or so. The tough part would be keeping his own evasions straight.

"Do you have anyone to take notes?" Peter said, not unkindly. He was signalling that he wouldn't try to upstage or finesse Maris in any way. He knew perfectly well that Maris was on the firing line when it came to explaining this cock-up to the press. He had been the one to suspend Ron for — what would Stan Bracher call it? — straying off the reservation.

"Start with the basics, Cammon. Full statement at the station."

A young female constable stepped forward. She sensed the need to get Peter's statement, and his professional characterization of events, down on paper quickly the first time. "I can do it, Inspector."

For all Maris's chronic annoyance, the loss of young Ronald Hamm had affected him, and he tempered his reaction to the woman officer. "All right. Constable, you sit at the desk in there. Chief Inspector, over here."

They moved inside. The officer, Maris, Perlmutter and Cammon. Peter made it clear that he would stand. It was an awkward venue in which to take a formal statement. The chatter of a dozen men and women intruded from the garage, while rotating cherry lights flashed across the sightlines of the four in the office. Perlmutter realized the problem. "I'm not needed for this at the moment. Let me finish up with our man." He left for the crime scene inside.

"Cammon, do you know who did this?" Maris said.

"I think so."

"Well, then, who?"

Peter paused and gathered his thoughts. He took a recharging breath, which Maris interpreted as the prelude to more dissembling. "Can we take it back an hour or two?" Peter said.

"Cammon, if you know the killer, you must agree that time's of the essence. The garage has been closed for two days. The interim manager is a strange fellow named Albrecht Zoren. Willet confirms that Detective Hamm interviewed him early in the course of the Lasker investigation. Was that before or after the incident with Symington?"

"Before."

Maris was growing exasperated with his grudging responses, Peter could tell. He was trying to be forthcoming (he really was, he told himself); it was just that so much had to be concealed from Maris.

"When was it, then?"

"What?" Peter had been distracted while Maris was talking. He heard a change of tone from the interior, a raising of voices. He tried to work through the Rover's risky move in killing Hamm.

"When did Hamm interview Zoren?"

Peter didn't respond.

The medics removed Hamm's body bag through the garage to the ambulance waiting on the street. Perlmutter came into the office a moment later. He looked worn through.

"News. We've found another body."

Peter had a good idea who it was, but he didn't dare say it in Maris's presence. The Inspector turned pale. "My God, who?"

"A mechanic. Big man. Willet says it's Albrecht Zoren. Works here."

Maris looked over at Peter, as if the coincidence were amazing. Peter knew that no coincidence had occurred at all. He wasn't surprised at the news. Perlmutter was watching Peter and couldn't help himself.

"You met him, Mr. Cammon?" Perlmutter said.

"Once."

Maris leaned forward. "Did Zoren kill Hamm?"

"No sir," Perlmutter interjected. "The mechanic's been dead twenty-four hours, though it's hard to pin down."

But Peter was surprised at how calm Maris had become, despite his impatience. He watched the Whittlesun chief preside over the chaos — paramedics, detectives and uniformed officers streaming in and out of the garage, several stopping to seek instructions — with an even, authoritative demeanour. Nonetheless, Peter did not benefit from this new-found forbearance.

"So, Cammon, did Hamm kill the mechanic?"

"No." Peter thought it unfortunate that the inspector at that moment came across like Lestrade in a Sherlock mystery. Of course, perhaps Peter himself seemed to Maris to be posturing as an English Poirot.

"No," Maris agreed. "Why would Hamm return to the scene of his crime the next day? Perlmutter, are you sure about time of death?"

Perlmutter leaned against the back wall of the small office. "I did my time with the Drug Squad, Inspector. It looks like cocaine overdose to me. Now, cocaine intoxication, as they call it, is difficult to assess, but there is inflammation around the mechanic's nostrils and evidence of a heart attack. It's still hard to be sure, but cocaine in large doses often causes the shivers and shakes, and sends the addict into spasms, which elevates the pulse rate to extremes. The drug high starts to fight against the hallucinogenic high and heart attack may occur. We found Zoren half wrapped in a canvas tarp sitting next to the heat vent for the garage."

Maris's gaze swivelled towards Peter. The young policewoman stopped writing on her pad.

"When did you meet Zoren?"

"Just after the bookkeeper, Sally, died. He was depressed, blamed himself."

"Hamm came here to see Zoren after that?"

"Yes."

"Let's be clear. Why?"

This was the crux of it. If Peter was going to head down the road of the full truth, there was one right answer. If he was going to lie, he might as well lie big.

"Because someone advised him to."

Maris leaned in closer. "Would that be André Lasker?"

"No," Peter responded truthfully. "It was the Rover."

Peter endured three more hours at the Whittlesun station before Maris saw fit to release him. As Peter explicated his theory that Hamm had been shocked into vengeful action by the sight of the dead women, Anna Lasker included, it occurred to him that he might be wrong, that Hamm had been after André Lasker himself, and that the threads connected to Lasker through Symington and Zoren were logical, and presented a completely self-contained scenario. Yet if Peter had presented this storyline to Maris, he would have been in the interview room in the old insurance company edifice forever, looking foolish, running either/or theories all night.

Ultimately, Peter discounted his own alternate story and stuck to the Rover angle. In fact, relieved of the need for equivocation, he became a forceful advocate for a massive hunt for the Rover along the coastline. He needed Maris, in both his capacities — as Whittlesun chief and interim chair of the Task Force — to mobilize the dragnet. The idea that the Rover was moving east wasn't new, and Maris was susceptible to it in any event. Hamm's murder had happened within the County of Dorset. The threat had changed. The whys and the where-nexts could be reasoned out later; there was a chance of catching the killer tonight.

There was another reason for urgent mobilization, Peter felt: the Rover had something special planned for the first winter storm of the year.

CHAPTER 35

Tommy's Glock 17 and Peter's sturdy Smith & Wesson, its bullets unchambered, lay on the mattress. Two separate boxes of ammunition accompanied the guns. Tommy hadn't bothered with shotguns. He had brought three knives, of different types; one was for Peter, a feather-light SOG folding blade, painted flat black. Two walkie-talkies, smaller than the pair Peter had used that fateful day on the cliffs, would provide the best means of communicating during their expedition. Waterproof torches were likely to prove the most useful items in the entire arsenal; it was all too easy to stumble into a crevasse or sprain an ankle on the rudimentary trails.

"Skipped the high-voltage Taser," Verden said, looking sanguinely at the equipment. "Would have liked to, but it's soaking out there. Start sparking like Guy Fawkes Day."

Peter had no affection for the Taser. For one thing, its maximum range was a hundred feet; if they managed to get that close to the Rover, guns would already figure in the mix, they could be sure.

He unfolded a map and placed it on top of the weapons on the bed. Blotchy red circles marked regular distances on the wide zone between Abbotsbury and Exmouth.

"Here's what I persuaded Maris to do. He wasn't reluctant to call out the constabulary for Devon and for Dorset and, to his credit, he isn't deterred by the storm. He promised to enlist other forces tomorrow, if this thing goes on that long."

"I'm having a devil of a time reading this coastal weather," Tommy declared.

"Join the club. The rain, maybe some snow, will play hell with lines of sight. You and I will have to stay close. The teams will be confined to the main access routes, significant roads, landmarks. Searches will proceed in twos. Manpower for tonight, despite Maris's promises, will be limited. It leaves about six kilometres per team."

"With all respect to our colleagues," Tommy said, "the temptation to move from one warm hearth to the next may be irresistible. And Peter, you know I have to ask this: what are we looking for, exactly?"

"A man."

"Okay."

"A man who shouldn't be there. He doesn't belong on the cliffs. But I think he has a specific target in mind."

Unsubstantiated or not, his fear was that Guinevere Ransell was to be the Rover's next victim. Worse, the Ransells had toyed with him, were playing too many cute games.

Tommy proceeded with the greatest efficiency. He folded up the map, and began to assemble a cache of gear by the bed, along with a rain jacket. A knock on the hotel room door caused Verden to toss the comforter over the arsenal on the bed. Peter cast an expectant look at him.

"Should be all right," Verden whispered, while keeping one hand under the comforter. "I called Jerry Plaskow."

"What?"

"He has the equipment I wanted."

Peter opened the door and simply gaped at what he saw. Mr. Smith stood there, carrying an ordinary shopping sack in one beefy hand. It was the most natural thing in the world, it appeared. Of all the questions that might have crossed Peter's mind, his thought was: *How come Mr. Smith is bone dry? It's raining out there.*

"Plaskow asked me to make a delivery," the SAS man said.

Peter stood back to let him in. He would have been happy to shake his rescuer's hand, but somehow it didn't seem the right thing to do. Mr. Smith entered and nodded to Tommy.

"Tommy Verden, Scotland Yard."

"Falklands too?" Mr. Smith said, finally smiling (or his mouth smiled; his eyes didn't).

"Something like that," Tommy said.

"Brought you what you wanted." Smith moved to the bed, and Verden swept away the cover, revealing the weapons. Smith scanned the equipment and nodded. "Good," he said. "Leave the Taser and the stun guns at home, that's wise. But these should help your odds."

He spilled the contents of the bag onto the bed. The goggles tumbled out like two small squid made of rubber.

"Got night-vision goggles here. ATN Thermal Imaging System, intensifier multiple up in the forty thousand range." Like Tommy, Smith often dropped the subjects out of his sentences. "Spot movement at a hundred yards, read a map in total darkness."

"I like it," Tommy said, trying on a pair. "Glad they're bino. Don't like the single lens version much."

"I agree. Only workable if you're in a fixed position. These're better for walking around. You can strap them to your head, if so inclined. I don't recommend it. Tendency to bump right into terrorists. Mr. Cammon."

"Yes?"

"They cost three thousand pounds a unit, so try not to drop them in the drink."

They invited Mr. Smith to stay. Peter laid out the plan for searching the coast. The SAS man appreciated the need to move fast, but he advised that rapid movement across the cliffs in the dark was asking for accidents. A question hung in the air, and Smith answered it. "I'd love to join you lads, but we aren't authorized for a civilian mission like this. Good luck."

They agreed to take Sam's old Land Rover after Peter suggested that the starting point for their explorations should be the rugged terrain around the Ransell cottage. Peter understood very well that it was long overdue that he lay out his thinking for his partner, and he did so now, but, as was often the case with the veteran chief inspector, he took a roundabout path to the core of his plan.

"Tommy, it was my underestimating of the Rover that got Ron Hamm killed. I zigged and he zagged. If I had seen where he was heading . . ."

"Meaning?"

"Hamm became fixated with Anna Lasker, once he finally got around to viewing her remains."

"Yeah, I remember your being surprised he hadn't seen the body before."

"He'd been involved from the first day. He and Willet handled the call. So, I thought, why wouldn't he have seen the body? Well, these things happen. Maybe he was waiting for the final autopsy, which, you recall, was slow. But I should have seen the problem."

Tommy peered into the pelting rain. He told Peter to slow down as they reached the higher elevation beyond the Abbey. Peter continued. "One way or another, her body was kept on ice longer than usual. One day he drove out to the lab and viewed the corpse. The organs would have been out, the flesh turning blue."

"Now, there's a question," Tommy said. "Can you just drop by the Regional Lab and expect to be welcomed into the mortuary to examine a body?"

"Well, he was the investigator of record on Lasker, at least until the Symington fiasco." But Peter wasn't so sure. He debated, based on no evidence whatsoever, whether Stan Bracher might have been Ron Hamm's interlocutor with the staff at the lab.

He continued. "At first, Hamm wasn't thinking about the Rover at all. Our mishap on the cliff upset him, but he hadn't seen Molly Jonas, like I had. The abuse of Anna set him on a beeline to find the husband. His success with the stolen passports and his exposure of

Symington's key role in the whole scheme encouraged him to believe that he was close to André, very much alive. And then he found a reason to believe that Albrecht Zoren was the Rover."

"Which was?"

"The Rover suggested it. He called Ron Hamm."

Peter had to slow down as they entered the grassy hills around the Ransell cottage.

"If he wasn't yet onto the Rover, why would the killer bother to make the call?" Tommy said.

"The obvious answer is that the Rover wants us to believe that Zoren was him. Hamm called me up at the Abbey to say he was going after Zoren because the mechanic *knew who the Rover was*. This was false. For whatever reason, Hamm misled me. Until the killer made the call, Hamm wasn't sure at that point. Zoren, of course, had no idea of the Rover's identity. The killer telephoned Hamm, anonymously of course, to plant the idea. By that time Zoren was dead."

"I still don't see why Hamm wouldn't have told you his theory that Zoren was our man."

"Because, even with the call, he wasn't sure. He was prepared to beat the truth out of Zoren."

"Peter," Tommy began, "isn't it possible that André Lasker did all this? That the Rover wasn't involved? Lasker called Hamm to lure him to his old garage. Zoren knew where Lasker was hiding, and Hamm was getting close. He created the opportunity to kill both of them."

"Zoren committed suicide, or maybe just OD'd. He didn't know where Lasker was. That's a tragic irony. Lasker hadn't been in touch since fleeing Malta — in fact, since leaving England. When I saw Zoren last week, he was bitter that his old boss had abandoned him and the business. He'd been promised a piece of the company. Oh, Zoren may have helped with some of the phoney paperwork on the cars, but I don't think it was too much more than that. Hamm was in a state of agitation when he called me that went beyond mere vengeance. He thought he had a chance to nab the Rover, but in the back of his mind was finding Lasker as well. I confess, he's not the only one to have trouble keeping them separate."

"There's one additional question."

"Yes, there is," Peter said.

"Why did the Rover bother setting this up if Zoren knew nada about his identity?"

Peter kept silent and waited for Tommy to turn off the motor. They were on the back road just short of the Ransell house. He had worked it out while sitting alone outside Lasker's Garage, waiting for Maris, and now he had to tell someone. If he couldn't tell Tommy, who could he trust?

"Because he wanted to send a message to André Lasker that he was smarter. By killing Hamm he proved he was the master. It's a game between the two of them. You see, Tommy, André Lasker is on the hunt for the Rover."

From the Ransells, Peter encountered something he hadn't expected: open hostility. Leaving the Land Rover as close as possible to the front lane, he and Tommy struggled the last fifty yards through daunting rain squalls. He was alarmed to be greeted at the door by a carrot-topped, freckled policeman, no older than twenty.

From behind Peter, barely sheltered by the overhang, Tommy said, "Who the hell is this?"

The youth wore a sidearm but the flap on his holster was buttoned. Still, he looked ready to resist intruders, and didn't immediately give way to his saturated visitors.

"Constable Grahl. Who might you be?"

Peter fished out his identification and offered the boy only a cursory look at it, but it was enough to make him take a step backward. Tommy flashed his ID for good measure. The detectives came inside; the constable continued to eye Tommy's rucksack, which gave off heavy metallic sounds as he hefted it onto the mat. Grahl retreated another step, but maintained his protective stance. Verden found it tiresome and strode to the centre of the room.

Peter, too, was eager to settle in, and stepped around the constable. The cottage would serve as their headquarters, a staging ground for their search of the zone; it was, foremost in Peter's mind, also a defensive perimeter around Gwen.

From the start, it was evident that Ellen Ransell viewed the crisis differently. She stood in the kitchen with her back to the three policemen, and shot a sidelong sneer their way as she fiddled with something in the sink. A fresh bottle of vodka stood on the counter. A half dozen paraffin lamps lit the space; a fierce fire kept the room warm.

The boyish constable whispered to Peter, although the old woman could hear him. "They say they're just fine. The electricity is out, and so is the land line. My mobile is functioning, so you might want to test."

"Mrs. Ransell," Peter said, across the constable. She turned, but remained leaning against the sink by the refrigerator. "Is Guinevere here?"

"This isn't Paddington Station, Chief Inspector, despite appearances. I want young Mr. Grahl to leave. We won't be needing your protection either."

"I understand," Peter replied. The door to Gwen's room stood open a few inches. The awkwardness continued as Mrs. Ransell, refusing to respond, remained motionless by the fridge. Neither man had been invited to take off his wet coat. Verden looked impatiently for a spot to unfold the map. He succeeded by laying it flat on the Persian carpet. He took off his coat and waved Grahl to his side, and they knelt down to examine the welter of red spots on the chart.

Peter went over to Ellen Ransell and said quietly: "You need to be careful outside."

"You're presuming to warn me against the evil out there? I've lived here thirty years. I can handle it."

"We have a supply of weapons."

"Not all the weapons are in that bag." Somehow she didn't seem

430

drunk. "Tell me, Inspector, why conduct your search tonight? Why did Maris go along with it? You'll never find him in this weather." She stared at him. "You want to drive him this way, like beaters flushing a tiger?"

"Something like that."

"Tell me, Inspector, what are you out there — the Tiger, the Beater, the Hunter, what?"

"I don't play those roles."

"How nice for you."

In his own defence, Peter struggled to declare himself. "The constable will leave. I'll send him back to town. Verden and I will stay."

"Say what you mean to say."

"All right. It will come down to the four of us against the Rover. That's what I have prepared for, and you as well, I think. He can't be redeemed or cured, or deterred from killing again. There's a chance of stopping him tonight."

"You know the irony in that statement, don't you?" They were embarked on a tense debate.

"Yes. The Rover plans to stop killing. His habits in the last fortnight show what he's about. He followed a geographical pattern for the first four girls. He quite deliberately held back on Garvena and Van Loss, not because he stopped craving the kill, but simply to throw the police off. He likes the game. The Six-K theory was another tease, and no more than that. Can I ask you something?"

"Go ahead," she said.

"Do you see it the same way?"

"Yes, for the most part. I agree that's the danger now: he plans to stop killing. He'll disappear like fog off the Channel and reinvent himself somewhere else."

"Except that he has one more task to complete before he goes. If someone knows his identity, he has to take care of it. Does Gwen know who the Rover is, Ellen?"

She shook her head, but it was simply frustration; Peter didn't believe she was answering one way or the other.

"If there are four of us to do this job, then each of us must play our role," Mrs. Ransell said. She took out a metal flask — it was the flask she had been filling earlier — and had a drink. "The predator is the Electric Man. Which man are you, Inspector? And Mr. Verden, who should he be? Are you familiar with the expression 'judge, jury and executioner'?"

"Of course."

"Then Mr. Verden would make a pretty good executioner, don't you think? And Father Salvez, hovering like a bird above the flock of sheep, he could be the judge, don't you agree? I'll be the jury, if you like. That leaves you with . . . oops, no role to play."

Peter had arrived at the Ransell house without much expectation of any grand revelations from the Ransell women. It was down to hard-slogging police work. If the Ransells could tell him the name of the Rover, well, they hadn't before and wouldn't now. They had their reasons. But he and Tommy were veteran policemen. It would come down to force *after* the police work of tedious tracking and the culmination of grinding, day-after-day effort that, at the time, might seem to be dumb luck, but wasn't at all. Oh, Peter believed in luck — it was what made him a romantic — but luck was always two-edged. You were unlucky when lightning struck you but lucky you survived to play another round on that golf course. As a copper, you got shot at, but with luck the bullets merely whiffed on by your head. The tenacious detective was an underrated breed when it got to the endgame of arresting criminals.

"Is Guinevere okay?"

"She had a seizure this afternoon."

"Can I see her?"

Mrs. Ransell paused. "Yes. She'll wake up if you go in. I'm going for a smoke."

She said this in the tone of a cryptic sibyl's prediction. She gathered her layers of shawls around her and went outside to the front landing. Peter entered Gwen's room with a silent, measured step, but

432

the second he reached her bedside, her eyes opened and she fixed him with a stare.

"Hello, Peter. Where have you been?"

"Just in the outer parlour. In the last few days, I've been at my home. Ron Hamm is dead."

"I know. I'll go to his funeral." She sat up in the bed, pushing forward several blankets; there was no heating in the room, and little warmth came through the doorway. "Tell me again where you've been, where you explored this last week."

Her voice was kind, if a bit dreamy. He understood that she meant St. Walthram's. "The Abbey. I went there and found the crypt," he said. "Salvez used it as a kind of monk's chamber."

She nodded. She closed her eyes, as if a headache had unexpectedly struck her. It passed and she looked at him again. Peter wasn't familiar with the aftershocks of epileptic seizures, and he proceeded carefully.

"Are you okay?"

"My mother is angry with you."

"I see that."

Peter heard a phone ring in the outer room. He judged from the tune that it was Grahl's.

"You keep leaving and coming back, you know that, Peter? You haven't spent a lot of time in Dorset, when you add it all up. She thinks you haven't spent enough time here."

"Time for what?" he said, annoyed.

"Do you know who's in the Abbey crypt? Bodies, I mean."

"Uh, no."

"Nazis."

"Nazis? I didn't see any." It sounded glib.

"That's my point, Peter. There's a rumour around here that two German soldiers are buried in the crypt of St. Walthram's Abbey. They were S.S. officers who were smuggled onto the coast in 1942 as part of Operation Sea Lion. The local people saw them land and captured them right off. They killed them on the spot and hid the bodies."

"Interesting."

"Yes, interesting. One more bit of local colour. But maybe, my mother thinks, details like that might have helped you to understand the heights before now. Your dream was telling you that, too. The black figure floating over the desert was all-seeing. At the same time, his face was a blank — he wasn't physically able to see anything. The black figure was you, Peter."

Her face was sallow, her lips bluish; yet her eyes focused on his with clarity and conviction.

"It has arrived at this, Peter. You waited too long. Mr. Hamm is dead, and it remains to be finished by the people who live here, who know the cliffs, who *are* the Coast itself. The policemen out there will soon retreat, leaving it to those who understand this Rover, who has outraged them with his horrible game."

She had exhausted herself and Peter helped her lie back against the pillows. He had come here because of the threat to Guinevere Ransell, but also because he craved her inspiration. He had innate faith in her perspective on both Lasker and the serial predator. But now he knew she was wrong. The Rover wouldn't be netted by the villagers collectively surrounding him. There was no Tiger and no Beaters driving the monster to the cliff's edge. There were only Hunters, and he and Tommy were the efficient — and well-armed — pursuers.

She quieted, and seemed on the verge of sleep. He backed up towards the big oak door but her eyes opened, and she stared at him again.

"Peter?"

"What is it?"

"Sarah is safe."

He came back to the bed. "What about Sarah? What do you know about Sarah? You've never met her, have you?"

"I met her on the beach at Solomon Cove two days ago. She was digging trilobites out of the rock face near the shore. I told her it was no longer safe that far east. She accepted my advice. She left, Peter."

"My Sarah?"

"Yes." Peter couldn't imagine his daughter giving in to the admonitions of a stranger on a beach on a sunny day in the south of England. But, then, this was Gwen.

He turned back to her, but she had fallen asleep.

He returned to the big room, leaving the door to her bedroom slightly ajar. He was profoundly disturbed by the thought of Sarah on the coast. He prepared to regroup with Tommy and Constable Grahl, having decided to leave Grahl behind to guard the Ransells — in spite of his promise to Ellen — while he and his partner went hunting. He understood the story of the S.S. soldiers as a cautionary tale about the lost innocence of the citizens of Whittlesun. But another kind of innocence had slipped away. The Rover was the Modern, the ruthless predator descending from the Outside World and deracinated from the parochial life of Dorset. He exploited them with some ruse they hadn't yet figured out, and he moved among them with impunity. He was different, electrifying, the Electric Man.

Peter expected to find Tommy and the young constable still strategizing over the map, but Grahl was standing by the door with a chagrined look on his ruddy face. Ellen Ransell had yet to return. Tommy had folded up the chart and it lay, apparently discarded, on the rug.

"What's going on?" Peter said.

"I'm sorry," Grahl began. "That was my chief, Mr. Maris, on the line. We've been called back. All of us."

"What does 'called back' mean?"

"The weather has gotten too bad. He says we're going to lose men if we send them out on the rocks in these conditions. We've been instructed to get some sleep, assemble at the station at 0600."

"All of you?"

"Yes."

Peter wanted Grahl out of earshot before he reviewed his options with Verden. He had hoped, indeed, that the manhunt would serve exactly like a tiger hunt, to the extent of driving the killer off the main roads and out of the obvious locations where he could conceal a vehicle. What the Rover possessed was guts and stamina, and Peter wanted to turn these strengths towards recklessness and headlong misjudgment by confining his killing zone.

There was the added problem of Grahl's own safety. He appeared to have walked some distance to reach the cottage.

"Where is your vehicle parked, Mr. Grahl?" Peter said.

"Up the Fen Road a ways. Maybe a mile gone from here."

"Do you want Mr. Verden to accompany you?"

"Not necessary. I know the way very well. Thank you, Chief Inspector." In fact, there was no worry in his voice. He probably wanted to get away from these odd Scotland Yard codgers, Peter thought — these Outsiders.

Both Peter and Tommy walked out to the front path with Grahl. The rain had let up, but the gale was a banshee. Peter had the anomalous thought that the wind was forceful enough to blow a bullet off its trajectory. Ellen Ransell had disappeared.

Although it was difficult for Peter to be heard, he called: "Mr. Grahl! Why didn't Maris send a second man with you?"

Grahl leaned forward and cupped his hand over Peter's ear. "We were pretty stretched out by the time we assigned officers this far east. I grew up only two miles from here. I'd met the Ransells before, so I volunteered."

Tommy smacked his hip to show Grahl that he should keep his pistol at the ready. He handed over one of his military grade torches and nodded. Grahl turned away and was swallowed up in a blink by the darkness.

CHAPTER 36

Mrs. Ransell had gone, but Peter, who suspected that she had come outside to drink, more than to smoke cigarettes, had no intention of looking for her. If she failed to return in the next half hour, they would do a circuit of the cottage. But Tommy took him by surprise. The moment they re-entered the building, he halted. "I'm going to take a look around, maybe track down the old woman. But if I'm gone more than eight minutes, come calling."

Alone in the central room, Peter felt the hollowness of the isolated cottage. Verden had placed the bag in the centre of the Persian carpet. He was right: time to unpack the guns and set out. Gwen was in the other room and Peter had the overwhelming urge to talk it all through with her. There was much he didn't understand about the Rover. She had been his guide all along; even when he had missed their meetings, she had been in his consciousness, telling him where to go next. He understood the need to stay close to her, and he wondered how he and Tommy were going to build that challenge into their search of the grid around the cottage.

The ringtone of his personal phone resonated in the room.

"Hello?" Peter answered, on the edge of shouting. He was habituated to expect weak connections anywhere near the Channel.

"It's Stan." Bracher's flat Canadian voice came through distinctly. Peter was stunned into momentary silence. "Peter, it's Stan. Where are you?"

Cammon wasn't about to be specific until he ascertained Stan's location. And why was he calling at all? "I'm in the Whittlesun area. Where are you?"

"Peter, I tried to reach you earlier but you didn't answer. Plenty of static due to this cursed British weather. Jack McElroy says it's the first winter storm of the season."

"Jack? Where are you?" he repeated. *Why is Stan with Jack McElroy?*

"I'm with Jack."

"At the lab?" was all Peter could think to say.

"No, no. At Jack's place, his home. In Devon."

Peter began to understand. Stan's peripatetic ways reflected a deeper nature. He liked people and made friends easily, because he had no grievances with anyone, criminals excepted. The Brits sometimes ascribed his loose friendliness to a shallow character. He was unpredictable, restless, but his wanderings obscured a strong impulse to help people. Canadians were supposed to be undemonstrative, but Stan Bracher loved the grand gesture — and the minor gesture too. Peter guessed that he had discovered something and he had gone to see McElroy with it.

"How is Jack?"

"He's right here. He's had a mild incident, but he's on the way back. We've been at it for two hours straight."

Peter wanted to address Jack McElroy's breakdown, to say he was sorry for not calling, but he understood that the best support he could offer would be to take their news seriously, whatever it was. "What have you fellows got?"

"We have DNA," Stan said. "We know who the Rover is."

Ever the detective, intrigued by methods as much as outcomes, Peter couldn't help asking, "Which girl?"

"It was the third one, Anna Marie Dokes. Semen evidence. I've been back and forth from Regional three times in the past week, working on the tests. I'll never get used to driving on the left."

Peter heard Jack McElroy grunt in the background, trying to steer Stan back on track. "We tapped into all the databases on it, hit the jackpot on the central Youth Offenders Repository. It took us two days, but Jack here, I tell you, missed his calling as a computer wizard, a potential hacker."

"Aren't Y.O. records sealed?" Peter said.

"You tell me. But yeah, they're protected, unless we can justify an enhanced disclosure of the full criminal record. The suspect had a sexual assault charge at the age of twenty. This adult charge served to open up his previous charge record, from when he was seventeen. A sexual assault count then, too. He was convicted as a youth on that one. Came from some small village in Northern Ireland. Even Jack's never heard of it."

"Got a name?"

Stan seemed to be reading from a file. "Paul 'Sandy' Lebeau. He'd be twenty-six at this point. Raised in a group home for boys. Orphan, no family."

"French?"

"No reason to think so, despite the name. We're twisting arms to get a photo."

"When do you expect to get one?"

"Jack's calling in every marker he has. Trouble is, the Belfast files aren't digitized from back then, and the other charge was up in Manchester and it appears to be buried deeper than the *Titanic*. By the way, Jack thanks you for finding Molly Jonas. It puts his mind at rest."

There was muttering in the background, and Peter heard Stan guffaw. "Jack says they found the *Titanic*, too."

Peter checked his watch, and exactly at the eight-minute mark, Tommy came back in. He shrugged off the rain and the chill. Peter debriefed him on Stan Bracher's shattering news. Several things bothered Peter about the tombstone data on Paul Lebeau, the first being the lengthy gap of three years between his last youth offence and his arrest in Manchester for sexual assault. Even if he had succeeded in restraining his urges, something must have triggered his homicidal outbursts over recent months. The rapes and killings along the Jurassic Coast displayed inventiveness and attention to detailed planning. No doubt the Rover had reinvented himself when he settled in Dorset or Devon, but perhaps he hadn't come very far. He had probably killed women before.

"I'm getting worried about Mrs. Ransell," Tommy said. "She's been out there a long time, and it's bloody cold."

On instinct, Peter glanced towards the kitchen counter. As he had expected, she'd taken her flask outside with her, but the full bottle of Koskenkorva was also missing.

They went to the rucksack and unloaded the *matériel* for their expedition. The guns, knives and goggles were arrayed on the carpet much as they had been on the hotel room bed. Tommy racked the slide of the Glock and loaded half the box of ammunition into the chamber. Peter did the same with his pistol. Each watched which pocket the other carried his gun in; it was an old partners' habit. Soon, each man was equipped with a pistol, knife and a set of goggles; Tommy would carry the remaining torch, and Peter the map.

Peter went over to Gwen's bedroom and eased the door wide. The covers were heaped in the centre of the bed. He walked farther in, in order to see if she had simply snuggled under the blankets.

Gwen had disappeared.

"She's not in the room," he said to Tommy, through the doorway.

Verden was zipping up his jacket over by the front door. "She got out?"

"I was here. She couldn't have slipped past me. Impossible."

Tommy, always a beat faster on the uptake, opened the front door and stepped outside; he didn't care how she had evaded them, but he checked to the right and left corners of the cottage. Peter ran out behind him. He was almost as quick as his partner, for now he understood what Gwen already knew, and was on her way to take care of.

The Rover was hunting Ellen Ransell, just as she was hunting him.

The two detectives walked out into the teeth of the night wind.

It would have to end, the Rover concluded.

Six sluts, so sad. It shouldn't have taken *six* for them to pay attention. The Footballer had wanted to publicize early on (he had stolen the draft announcement off Finter's desk in that interview), but the politicos had shut him down. He had attacked two more, left them alive, but they even shut down Garvena. The Media caved (there was a good pun in there somewhere) to the politicos once again. He had believed in the Media (a way for an ambitious young man to get known), but no longer. They analyzed — Freuds of the Tabloids — but concealed even the bare facts. Where was the integrity in it all?

A Date with the State. Look what they'd done to him, beamish Borstal Boy. And now to suppress the panic. Manic Panic. Outrage Outage. The Garvena girl had been the ultimate. Not even allowing TV-20 and the wire services to disclose it. Conspire the Wire. (Just because her repressed Italian parents asked — nice to have *any* parents.)

No more Six-K. Refrain from the Refrain. They were too close. There was nothing left to do but kill the Girl in the Cloak and get out. Take care of the Man in the Cloak, too, and get out.

Start up the Game somewhere else.

As Peter and Tommy crouched down on the shoulder of the farmer's road, Peter thought of the Knights of St. John, who never seemed to have doubts; they were convinced that they would stand before the Son of man, but only if they walked in a forward direction, without a backward glance. How nice for them, he thought. But Ellen Ransell had been right: there were times as a police officer when you had to decide whether or not to take on the role of judge, jury or executioner. Yes, Peter thought, but then you let events sort out which role you were always destined to play.

They were cued in to any man-made light that might appear anywhere in the kilometre zone around the Ransell cottage; the goggles would make the light seem like a starburst. But first they had to accustom themselves to the opaque night. Tommy hiked himself up onto a fence railing and scanned three hundred and sixty degrees with a pair of regular binoculars. It was an awkward manoeuvre, since it was pitch black and he expected to see absolutely nothing, aside from a faint glow from the cottage itself. They would move quickly towards any other source of light. Satisfied with these preliminaries, the two detectives put on their night goggles and adjusted the focus. Peter opened up the square of topographical map that Tommy had torn out of the larger chart, and with hand signals, pointed out the way to his partner. They moved down the farm road towards the east. The rain had ceased, but heavy crosswinds continued to buffet the path, and Peter was tempted to take his chances in the fields, where they would be less exposed. Within two hundred yards, they found a wisp of a trail, no more than a flattening of the grass, that led off towards the cliffs, and they took it. The goggles made it easy to follow the track, but they were soon on rocky terrain, where the trail faded out. The choices at first seemed infinite, since the moraine, a field of both small and gigantic stones, offered no natural pathways towards the sea; the ground became more treacherous, too, and they proceeded single file. Peter estimated that they must have crossed the route he and Gwen had taken in their stymied search for caves, but he failed to recognize any landmarks. Tommy felt the same disorientation and, as their methods dictated, they began to pause every fifty yards to reconnoitre.

The infrared settings within the goggle lenses meant that any luminosity, other than stars or ambient radiance from the sky, would flash in the viewfinder. The eyes of an animal or a human would show as brilliant beads. The devices projected their own light forward, although only the wearer could see it, and the detectives performed slow two-hundred-seventy-degree scans ahead. Peter was looking at a sharp angle to his left when Tommy, on his right, saw the figure rush past. He later swore that the body was dressed in flat black clothing but there was an odd, bright flash about the head.

There was to be a gathering on the heights. André sensed it.

He had come to love the ocean. He had escaped into it, swum back from it, explored the borders of it, and now he would seek redemption at its very edge. He was the most rational of men, but the cliffs were luring, seducing everyone to a strange meeting place overlooking the sea. He now understood what Odysseus endured when the sirens sang. He had idled away hours in hiding reading a dog-eared paperback of Homer, and now he got it. The song of the sirens made you fall in love. The sea had seduced him back and made him fall in love with Anna again, and his debt to her would be repaid when he netted the killer of women.

He was perfectly ready. He knew the shore better than the Rover. Hell, he knew all the killer's weaknesses. He'd said just enough to panic him, convince him that he had to kill the strange girl. It wouldn't happen. André congratulated himself. The Rover was eager, and André had seduced him with pictures of the Sacrifice. "Your best ritual yet," he had called across the plateau of stones, speaking in the voice of a local boy — the Rover had such a smooth, contrasting timbre. Apparently the predator hadn't quite believed he would do his part. The enticement of Detective Hamm — Hamm had been close to nabbing both of them — had been nasty and unexpected, a provocation.

But André would certainly attend the ritual, reshaping it the way he wanted. He wondered who else would show up at the altar for the ceremony. Whatever. He was ready to preside over the ritual.

Waiting in the cold room, he flipped the pages by the light of the torch. The tragedy for Odysseus had been that he couldn't stay. He had lashed himself to the mast. André pondered how he himself would feel when the time came to sail away.

Taking encouragement from Tommy's glimpse of the Rover — if that's who it was — they pressed ahead with some confidence, making swift but efficient judgments about which way to go. The track was filament-thin, but the goggles highlighted the bent-back grass and saved their legs from missteps into the clumps of brome and thorn. Still, there was nothing inevitable about their route, and they paused every few yards to scan the horizon. They certainly weren't going to track anything by sound, since the wind bayed like an attacking animal. *Where are the Ransells?* worried Peter. There was always the possibility that they were being led into a trap, but Peter couldn't help thinking that the players in this chase were all converging towards one significant spot on the cliffs.

The grassy depression through which they had been rushing gave way to barren rock, with weirdly wind-carved stones looming up to block their progress. Peter ordered Tommy to stop. The next section, between their location and the rim of the cliffs, was too treacherous for any attempt at speed. Tommy looked at him; they were two green-lit monsters, out of breath and hot beneath their masks, despite the wintry air. Peter mouthed, "Dead slow," and they took shelter in the lee of a granite spire.

The rock formations here were different from any seen on Peter's earlier forays onto the Whittlesun Heights. The others might find the plateau equally difficult to cross, but Peter and Tommy were the only hunters with night vision capacity, and they could use it to advantage. With arm movements, Peter instructed his partner to scan the area ahead, to their left, for large, flat boulders, while he did the same for the quadrant on the right.

Peter thought he saw something ahead, lit green and spooky in the lens. He drew his pistol; Tommy did the same.

Peter led the way towards the irregular ring of boulders fifty yards off; strewn with pebbles, branches and other detritus, it was a poor man's chapel of stone, but the giant rock in the rough centre of the circle was perfect as a sacrificial altar. There was every reason to wait for the Rover here. He had no concern of imminent ambush, since the area was unlit and the semi-circle of rocks blocked at least half of the lines of sight. With the night goggles, they would see him coming. Peter moved forward another ten yards.

A movement to one side, around a vertical boulder, caused both men to swing their weapons that way. Guinevere Ransell slipped into the path; she looked remarkably composed given the fierce wind and the danger about. She signalled for them to remove their goggles, which they did. They struggled with night blindness for a full minute, and she waited for their eyes to adjust.

"He was here," she hissed in Peter's ear.

"Where is your mother?" Peter called back.

"I don't know. I'm looking for her. You have to come with me."

The landscape was rendered even darker by the displacement of the night-vision apparatus. Gwen turned on a torch and pointed it in the direction of the sea, then back at the detectives. The beam bore into Peter's retinas and he turned to one side. What startled him even more was the risk she had chosen to take by lighting up their location, however faintly. But she pointed the light away from the chapel of stone and swept ahead on an invisible trail; he and Verden had no choice but to follow.

In daylight, the plateau would offer a panoramic view, but now the rim of the cliff was invisible. He guessed that they were on an old smuggler's path that eventually would take them down to the shore. They edged downwards through crumbling rocks left by cataclysmic upheavals thousands of years ago. Peter could hear the surf now, but the rush was muffled. There was a smear of light from the sky off in the direction of the French coast, and he could see that a collapsing rock face to their left had become a heather-coated hill pointing to the Channel. He doubted that this was a useful direction in which to head, but he deferred to Gwen's local knowledge. They stumbled on for ten minutes until they were on another bare escarpment exposed on three sides; there was nothing but the sea ahead, and only one route back. He had no inkling of what she expected to find here.

Peter's instincts told him that the girl had led them astray. He turned his gaze back towards the rock chapel and thought he saw a light wavering along at an upward angle. When he turned around to confront Gwen, she was gone.

The light moving up the hill seemed far away, but Peter knew this was a trick of the darkness and that she could not be far ahead of him. Tommy hadn't noticed; he appeared to be struggling with his goggles. Peter put on his own goggles again and a burst of light up on the hill flared in the lens, as if an explosion had been set off. He recoiled but quickly recovered and began to move. He started to run along the flattened path through the soaking grass. His gun was out again.

He tripped twice on the trail but kept going. Tommy was somewhere behind him. Peter could not face the bonfire's glow directly through the lens of his goggles, and so he focused on the path. But it was the night-vision apparatus that saved him, for by the time he reached the heights, his eyes had adjusted to the fire, and yet he could still see into the blackness surrounding it. He knew that the Rover's cunning would keep him in darkness until the last minute. The Rover was a night creature.

Peter circled to the upward slope, all the time on alert for Gwen. He must be close behind her, he calculated. From a vantage point slightly uphill from the stone chapel, he scanned the area beyond the big stones. Mrs. Ransell, vodka bottle in hand, stood in the centre of the killing ground and waved the fire upward, though in fact it was dying down now, threatening to extinguish itself. Peter waited a minute longer. Mrs. Ransell continued to wave her arms in an incantation.

After less than a minute, Peter spied the Rover at the far edge of the fire's glow. His left arm held Gwen Ransell around the neck and he held a weapon in his right hand; Peter guessed that it was a box cutter or knife of some kind, but he had little doubt that the killer had come armed with a gun as well. Ellen Ransell failed to see him.

Peter circled to his right until he was less than thirty feet from the killer, who had moved a few more steps towards the fire. His blond hair gleamed in the firelight. Mrs. Ransell turned and realized her mistake in one horrified look; her trap had failed. Waiting, Peter hoped that the darkness concealed him, but a flare-up from the bonfire must have revealed his location, for Parny Moss turned his way. Peter saw that a .38 had materialized in his right hand. *Where did that come from?* Still, the light from the goggles gave Peter the advantage, allowing him to see the entwined figures clearly. Moss took a step to his right, away from Gwen but still clenching her collar in his left hand. The bright fire flashed into Peter's lens and he was tempted to remove the goggles. He aimed the Smith & Wesson, its grip and its weight so familiar.

Moss fired first, a single shot that went wide. Peter waited, alert to the reasoning of the gunman. Peter wanted to take his time, but any movement by Moss towards Gwen, any turning of the pistol, would force him to shoot. As it turned out, the men fired at the same moment. Perhaps Moss was a little faster, for he got off three shots before Peter fired his one. Peter's bullet slammed into Moss's left shoulder. Despite the surreal green landscape inside the viewing lens, Peter's shot landed precisely on target, slamming the killer backwards and releasing his grip on the girl.

Peter was accurate, but Moss was lucky. One of the bullets from the .38 raked the left shoulder pad of the detective's coat and spun him back, so that he fell, losing the goggles in the grass. His head cracked against a boulder.

Tommy later told him that he was out for only five minutes. Tommy had encountered his own problems on the trail, spraining his leg and arriving at the sacrificial site too late to do anything but limp over to Peter and administer first aid. By this time, Ellen Ransell had jumped onto Moss, clubbing his gun away with the vodka bottle.

Peter awoke to see the bonfire flaring again.

He couldn't immediately discern what was burning in the centre of the pyre, but it appeared that the flat rock itself was ablaze. Peter and Tommy limped together to the edge of the flames. The heat drove them back. Peter began to see the outline of a human body, lying supine and motionless. He moved forward, ignoring the heat, in hopes of making out the facial features: he was a cop, he had to be sure. All he could smell was burning hair, and maybe alcohol. The orange and red flames illuminated the charring outlines of a face.

The inferno hypnotized him and undermined his judgment. He moved even closer. From behind, Gwen grasped him by the upper arm, and then let go. He turned, tears on his blackened face. But it wasn't Gwen. Ellen Ransell stood behind him, calmly sipping straight from the forty-ounce bottle of Finnish vodka.

"Where's Gwen?" he shouted.

"Back about a hundred yards, watching from the dark. Safer there. My daughter does what her mother tells her."

"Can we save him?"

"He's dead, but let's make sure, shall we?"

Ellen Ransell screwed the cap back on the bottle; there were only a few ounces left. She hefted it like a Molotov cocktail, which it surely was, and lofted it onto the blaze. It exploded in a cloud of fire.

"When did you know? When did you know it was Moss?" he cried.

"Don't kid me, Inspector. You knew who it was, too. I saw it in your eyes in the parlour."

"Who the hell is Moss?" Tommy said.

Mrs. Ransell watched happily. "Why, he's the Electric Man."

CHAPTER 37

"Press conference at 2:00 p.m.," J.J. McElroy said. "Who wants to be there?"

Stan Bracher and Tommy Verden, lounging against one wall of the suite in the Sunset Arms, shook their heads and groaned. Peter Cammon reacted with a frustrated murmur. Despite the solemn reason for their meeting, they were giddy.

"Wasn't I booted off the Task Force?" Peter said.

Stan laughed. "It's happened so many times, I can't remember if he's on or he's off."

"Come on, gentlemen," McElroy continued. "I've already made one media statement this morning. Least you can do is offer me some back-up at the two o'clock. You were there."

Peter stood up and flexed his shoulders. His whole body ached, including the persistent wound on his forearm; a first-degree burn, looking worse than it was, covered the left half of his face.

The three Scotland Yard detectives had no intention of participating in the press event. At the best of times, on principle, none of the veteran police officers was forthcoming to the media, Stan excepted, and he had not been on the cliffs. McElroy's man Finter was scrambling to come up with a plausible narrative to explain the

Rover's personal history and how he ended up raging through Dorset and Devon Counties. It was going to be a hard sell. Nothing could adequately account for a young man, with no roots in the south coast community, descending like a hawk on six innocent local girls and doing it with impunity for so long.

"Not to gild the lily, Jack," Tommy said, "but maybe you could fill *us* in on Moss."

McElroy picked up a thin dossier from the coffee table, but he didn't open it. He paused, gathering his thoughts, rehearsing for the media session.

"Partnell 'Parny' Moss had at hand the best bag of tricks a serial rapist could ask for. He had access professionally to every kind of map of the whole Jurassic Coast. Weather forecasting has changed. It's all done through computer models and digitally constructed mapping. In the guise of being extra keen at his job at TV-20, he downloaded every aerial, topographic and thermographic map of the coastline. He was able to pick out every nook and cranny along the entire rim of the Channel."

McElroy opened the folder and took out several professional head-shots of an over-groomed young man with gleaming yellow hair. Peter was surprised that the file appeared to contain no candid photos. He knew that Task Force investigators had been at the television station most of the night. He expected at least a mug shot or two.

"He had no criminal record as an adult, no fingerprints on file. He grew up in an orphanage in Belfast, then a series of group homes and foster placements. The records are best characterized as minimal. Maybe the best we can say is that the only places he could call home were the town radio stations who hired him over the years. There were three of these, all six- or seven-month stints at most, and he was still using his birth name. Then he disappeared, right after the assault charges in Birmingham were dropped. The next thing we know, he has the job with TV-20, starting a year ago."

"He reinvented himself," Stan added, "starting with dyeing his hair."

"Any incidents of sexual harassment in the radio jobs?" Peter queried.

"No. We interviewed Wendie Merwyn at length at TV-20 last night. There's an embarrassed woman — forever linked to the other Blond Twin. She didn't like him, thought he might be gay, though that was just competitive snarkiness. He wasn't known to date anyone at the station, or in Whittlesun. If anything, the station manager was chagrined that he hadn't noticed anything out of the ordinary with our boy."

"Didn't he notice that he checked out the station's weather van a little bit often?" Tommy said.

Collectively, the four detectives had little sympathy for the management of TV-20. They had shown a lack of due diligence in checking out Moss's credentials. The station had groomed Merwyn and Moss as a brace of fine young role models, and "a vital part of your community," whatever that meant.

"The Parny Moss we saw on exhibition was a package invented by the station manager," McElroy continued. "You're right, he always volunteered to go out on location; you know, those remote broadcasts at shopping-mall openings and used car lots."

It seemed a good point to take a break, and they gathered round the tray of coffee Jack had ordered up. McElroy turned to Peter, although he didn't mind if the others heard.

"Ellen Ransell's role in all this is strange. She says she saw Moss on television, and she knew. It would have helped if she had actually told someone. She calls him the Electric Man, because of all the computer graphics he used in his weather forecasts. Those little, jagged lightning icons they use for storms. She's a drinker. But she said she was pretty sure right away, whatever that means."

Peter sipped his coffee. "I think the daughter knew, too. Gwen Ransell saw Moss driving around the country lanes in the TV-20 Weather Cruiser. That's what the manager calls it, anyway."

"They should have notified the Task Force. The easiest thing. Of course, if you're planning on killing the killer, all bets are off.

Reminds me of those Buddhist priests who set themselves on fire in the middle of intersections in Saigon."

"Are you charging her?"

"With what? We may. What the hell. The evidence is in ashes. She hit him over the head with her vodka bottle. Then she dragged him out to that stone, laid him out like a dead Viking, or a Knight Templar, poured vodka over him and fired up a ritual sacrifice. Wait till that comes out."

The TV-20 vehicle was discovered in a public lot four miles away. McElroy hadn't mentioned that although Parny Moss had delivered over thirty remote forecasts over the past year, no one from the Task Force had thought to question him.

McElroy's voice hit a lower register. "You know, Peter, we would have had a hard time convicting him. He was meticulous. No prints, no victim connections, just that one mistake with the DNA, and that was open to challenge in court, Stan tells me. He reinvented himself, and the Ransells were the only ones to see through it."

And to see what had to be done, Peter might have added. Never trust a man who adopts too many identities, he thought. Lord Lucan. Greydon Kershaw. Parny Moss. André Lasker and his multiple passports. You soon forget who you are.

Peter drove the Land Rover up to the Abbey a few minutes after 1:00 p.m. He went alone. If challenged, he would say that he had unfinished business, and that would have been the truth. But he told no one where he was going, and his excursion coincided with missing the press conference at the Whittlesun station.

It seemed appropriate to travel light. For one thing, he had thrown his bowler hat in the bin for good; he felt silly wearing it. He had also left his pistol with Tommy.

He parked at the now familiar concrete pad on the hilltop and walked at a slow pace down the swale, swampy from the rain, and mounted the thousand-year-old steps to the grassy border of the

Abbey. He wondered again how the Preservation Society would maintain the church. The Jurassic Coast having been declared a World Heritage Site, St. Walthram's Abbey could not be demolished, and so it might have to be rebuilt, he reasoned. Perhaps the bottomless pockets of the Olympics Committee would fund the reconstruction.

He circumnavigated the ruin, and for once the breeze off the Channel was light. On the western flank, he noticed for the first time that an archaeological dig had been underway a hundred yards from the main structure, and he took this as a hopeful sign. He completed his formal circle at the big oak door and took a seat on the steps overlooking the sea. He set his mobile phone to the off position.

Peter knew little about Catholic church architecture. Off in the scrubby weeds to the west stood a stone hut that resembled an outdoor privy, but he supposed that this couldn't be its function; whatever it was, the door was obviously sealed. Ahead and to the east of the front steps, the monks of the Abbey had erected a small, rectangular outbuilding, a crude cloister perhaps, that had been refurbished in recent years. It was windowless and slightly recessed into the ground. Again, he was puzzled by its purpose. Sunken into the rock, which the builders must have excavated with great effort, the hut could have served as a root cellar or gloomy quarters for servants.

Peter waited patiently for ten minutes, as he knew he must. The door to the hut opened and André Lasker stepped out and mounted the two slate steps to the lawn.

He was thinner than Peter had expected, but Peter could have easily picked him out of a crowd, or from an identity parade at the Whittlesun station. His chin showed three days' growth of blond beard, and his hair was ratty. He squinted at Peter, trying to sort out who he might be. Peter's face had appeared on TV-20 only once, and never in relation to the Task Force. There was no recognition in his eyes. Yet perhaps he understood who Peter could be.

"Am I under arrest?" His voice was tired, and it croaked a bit from lack of use, but he was neither fearful nor belligerent.

Even if Lasker didn't yet understand, this was already an

arrest-in-progress, and Peter was unperturbed. He knew how it should go. He wasn't about to let the initiative shift, and so he stated: "I'm Chief Inspector Cammon of Scotland Yard."

Lasker considered this information for a full minute. "You're the one who found me in Malta. Very clever."

That was it. Peter recalled Mayta telling him that his name had appeared on an Internet site based in Valletta. "Your accomplice, Kamatta, is dead. He went over a cliff outside Marsalforn."

Lasker offered a wan smile. "I heard that. Sad. Did he do that?"

He gestured to the bandage that peeked out from the policeman's coat. Peter had reopened the wound during the search last night and had replaced the dressing, with Tommy's help. "A hazard of the job."

They stood there for another minute; the wind picked up from the sea.

"Do you want to talk?" Peter said.

He had no intention of entering the church. He recalled the dangers of the crypt. But he grasped that Lasker, like most fugitives who have spent too much time alone, needed to talk. The only question in Peter's mind was whether he would seek expiation or justification; Peter didn't anticipate anger or violence.

Lasker looked back at the hut, and gave the reply Peter hoped for. "We can talk out here."

Lasker re-entered the hut and brought out two rough-hewn benches, which he set on the lee side of the building, but still in the afternoon sun. Peter did his best to appear relaxed.

"Mr. Lasker, you know that you'll be charged with the offence of fraud in relation to exporting automobiles."

"I'm willing to face up to my responsibility." *I suppose you would, if that's the total of it,* Peter thought.

"Do you want to tell me about your original plan?" Peter said. "I'm curious."

"My wife and I lived in a marriage that was based on mutual contempt. I'd reached my limit. She had reached hers. She wanted children, I didn't. Those damn trips to Romania. Her mother."

Lasker shook his head, mostly in sadness, but there was a residual resentment in his voice. He hadn't explained anything. Again, Peter recognized the tone of a man who had too much time to replay his sins. Lasker had started out believing that his journey was an epic one, and in unintended ways it had been; walking out to sea, with no turning back, must have been terrifying. He had fled, shedding his accumulated identities in layers until he reached a fishing village on tiny Gozo. Had he awakened one morning to the canary yellow sun and the blue Mediterranean and checked his passport in order to see who he was that day?

"How did you get out of the country?" Peter asked.

"I had a boat offshore. It wasn't all that hard. Swimming naked into the cold sea is challenging, but it was more weird than anything else."

"You rowed to France?"

"Like I say, it wasn't that difficult. With Kamatta's passports — he did seven of them for me — and a bundle of Euros, and a set of clothes, I became a new man."

"But Anna guessed that you were leaving."

Lasker grasped his implication: the new man had carried the old life with him. Her suicide had made sure of that. The monkey on his back. "I made it to the French coast by early morning. The sea was calm all the way." Peter felt the echo of "Dover Beach," but said nothing. "From there, the train to Paris, and a quick flight to Malta."

"What was Symington's part in all this?"

Lasker stood and paced behind the bench. He kept his hands in his pockets. "Inspector, I tried to do this alone. I didn't aspire to be unique or rich or something that I'm not. It was just me. I tried to do this solo. Symington and I became friends. He thought my plan was romantic, swashbuckling, I don't know. It wasn't romantic at all, as it turned out. He helped me out with makeup and disguises."

"And he helped you find cast and crew with passports," Peter said. Lasker had easily identified the addresses of male volunteers in the theatre and had broken into their homes. He chose men of the same age and general features. It was easy, and Symington had made it easier. "How did you hear about your wife?"

"Jesus! I went on the Internet one day, in Malta, to check on the news about myself. The local television station here in Whittlesun had recently expanded its website to include streaming video of its newscasts. I'd been in Malta for a few days by then. First, they reported that I was wanted for murder. Then, sometime after, they said that she had killed herself. I couldn't believe it. I told her that all I wanted to do was disappear. I said it wasn't her fault. I didn't imagine that she would do that."

"You came back. Why not turn yourself in at that point? Your crimes were limited and we knew she'd committed suicide."

"I spent a lot of time walking that beach in Gozo, I can tell you. Part of it was that you still might charge me with murder. I wasn't sure that I had much of a defence. You know the other reason I returned, and why I couldn't surrender."

"Because you decided to trap the Rover. As your penance?"

"If you like. Even before I heard that she had killed herself, I had decided to come home. I needed . . ." Lasker stumbled over the words, but it still sounded rehearsed. "Everyone knew I wouldn't murder my wife. I just needed to visit her grave. Even then, some son-of-a-bitch . . ."

"That son-of-a-bitch was me. I told the lab not to release her remains. Your penance was to trap the Rover?" Peter repeated.

"Yes. How did you know?"

"I looked at the computer in the crypt. I couldn't imagine Salvez showing that much interest in the predator. I guessed it was your two hundred search hits."

"It was. I sneaked into the Abbey and used it. But I figured it out before then, in Malta."

"How did you identify him when no one else did?"

"I was watching the broadcasts from TV-20 on the web in Sliema. I knew it right away. The eyes. Too smooth. Too focused on the weather on the coast; he sounded obsessed. It was perfect cover, wasn't it?"

"How did you find him?"

"Simply followed him. I watched the studio where he worked. He had a flexible schedule. He wandered everywhere, believe me. If anyone challenged him out there, he would say that he was 'broadcasting from the field.'" Lasker moved forward into the sunbeam that reflected down from the roof tiles of the outbuilding. "I met him. He tried to enlist me."

"You're saying that you found him and tracked him alone?"

"Yes."

Peter knew that he was lying. Lasker had launched himself on a second convoluted adventure, but he had help.

"Mr. Lasker, we don't do anything alone in this world."

Lasker took a deep, preparatory breath and began. "Father Salvez, that's what you're talking about, isn't it? When I arrived back in England — passport number six — I came to the cliff, the car park where Anna abandoned the family sedan. It was the middle of the night. I saw a light down here. Of course, it was Salvez. When I came over — I made no effort to conceal myself — I found him out at the edge of the rocks. I thought he was going to jump right then."

"But he didn't."

"No. But he was very sick. He'd been living here, finishing out his last days. Anyway, I talked with him. We went over everything. I guess you'd say he heard my confession. I told him about Anna. I'm not Catholic, Inspector, but he granted me absolution for my sins. He had a room in the crypt and made space for me. Three nights ago, I woke up and he'd disappeared. Of course, I couldn't find him, but I soon realized that he had jumped over the edge. Just like Anna."

"But you decided to keep after Moss?"

"Anna haunted me. My penance, you're right, was to find the murderer of those girls and eliminate him."

"You were on the hill last night, weren't you?"

Peter felt Lasker turning inward. There was a solipsistic aura to him. His voice turned querulous.

"It was complicated. Trapping Moss required patience. We were supposed to rendezvous near where he planned to take his next girl, the stone chapel on the hillside. Can you believe that he wanted to collaborate? We hadn't actually met, just talked from a distance, from behind boulders. I planned to get him when he reached the big rock."

"Wasn't he armed?"

"He had a knife, but that didn't worry me. I'm not a helpless farm girl."

"How did you plan to subdue him?"

"A big, whacking dose of morphine."

"Father Salvez's morphine?"

"Yes."

When it comes to witnesses, Peter knew, small falsehoods presage major ones. Lasker was twisting the details. For one thing, he inflated his role in the taking of Parny Moss. Ellen Ransell had discovered Lasker wandering the cliffs. She listened to his penitential plan and agreed to work in collaboration with him to lure Moss to the stone chapel. She had consented to his proposal to use Gwen as bait, his final ritual. But she had every intention of killing the Rover herself. He hadn't mentioned Ellen at all. Lasker had been in the area — it was his form, with the dyed blond hair that was part of his disguise, that Tommy had caught in the beam of his torch, not Moss's — but she never trusted him; he never got any closer to the sacrificial site. In the final moment of judgment, it would be mother and daughter.

Peter looked for repentance in André Lasker's eyes, but it was the dream that instructed the detective once again. The hovering figure that emerged from the black cross had been both Salvez and Peter himself. The dream had contained its own clever code. The face of the angel had been blacked out, a void: that was Salvez, rendered incomplete, faceless, by the manner of his death. The figure had also been Peter, a man in a black suit, equally incomplete in his ignorance. In the dream and through the clues Salvez had left behind, he had been asking the detective from beyond the shadow to resolve this state of limbo, for the salvation of both of them.

Lasker told a sentimental story of the priest's last days. He implied that Salvez had climbed the hill those last few times to selflessly hide Lasker himself. Indeed, the dying man had made a final trek to the Abbey with a firm plan to end his own suffering. But Lasker's small lie again pointed to larger deceptions. Peter understood that Salvez took pride in walking up to the Abbey as often as his strength would allow; it had been a recuperative exercise. That first day, Peter recalled wondering why the priest in his black costume wasn't blown off the heights. He had concluded that Salvez was so emaciated and the robe so tight-fitting that the risk was small. But that wasn't it. A man wearing a constricting garment like the priest's cassock could not have walked that hill up to the Abbey. He wore street clothes to get there, but always changed into his black robe at the church. It was the kind of ritual that a dying man would maintain. It was a ritual that preserved his dignity by presenting him to the wide open world as God's priest, defying King Henry and Canute's tide alike. Had Salvez chosen to jump, he would have been wearing the black outfit — he was Gwen's Black Man — and for a moment would have been visible floating above the seventh wave, the thirty-three sheep and the graves of Anna Lasker and Molly Jonas. Instead, he had been found wearing his leather jacket.

Peter didn't display any urgency, although Lasker clearly comprehended that he was being arrested. "What else do you need to know, Inspector?"

"What else do you need to tell me?"

"You mean, am I ready to turn myself in?" he paused. "Yes, I am. I trapped the Rover because someone had to stop him. Maybe it's some recompense for what I did to Anna."

"Did Salvez leave you a note, Mr. Lasker?"

"No."

"He left me one. Do you know Latin?"

"Never studied it. Not so useful in the trades."

"*Ars bene moriendi.* To die a good death."

"Where have I heard that before?"

"It was taped to the side of the computer in his office. It goes with another of his favourite phrases: *to be worthy to stand before the Son of man.* Salvez would never have committed suicide."

"Why not? He was days from death in any event."

"Because suicide is still a sin in the Catholic Church. And in the Romanian Orthodox Church. Your wife knew that, and by committing that unforgivable sin, she implicated you, in every sense. But André, you killed Salvez, threw him over the cliff. He wasn't going to let you kill Moss, because that was a sin as well. I'm guessing that he also told you to surrender to the police."

"He would have stopped me from eliminating a killer of young girls." Lasker moved away from the bench. "You can't prove it."

As a detective, and a connoisseur of these things, Peter was disappointed in André Lasker. He could have been home free. Why hadn't he ignored the priest and tracked down the Rover while Salvez lay in his morphine dreams? The mechanic hadn't killed anyone at that stage.

And Peter knew that he could prove everything.

"A colleague of mine, a Canadian, telephoned me an hour ago. He's a pathologist. Salvez's body was pretty beaten up, but the lab found a skull fracture that was not caused by the fall. André, you had a stronger reason to kill Salvez. He was going to turn you in. And your plan all along was to disappear again, once you visited your justice on Parny Moss. Were you going to swim the English Channel like your ancestor, Herman Willemse?"

Lasker stood with his back to the cliff's edge. The afternoon light caused Peter to back up and hold his hand up against the sun. In the glare, he perceived that André was heading towards the low building — but now he halted. Peter moved out onto the barren lawn and stepped out of the sun's direct angle in order to see what the mechanic was doing. The wind dropped and the flapping police ribbon quieted.

Peter spied her then. Lasker kept his gaze on him and failed to see her at first. Wendie Merwyn, her golden hair pulled back in a knot, a fashionable wool scarf wrapped around the collar of her suede jacket, was pointing a digital camera at André Lasker's face. He couldn't evade her. The reporter said nothing, but clicked picture after picture as Lasker moved backwards to the cabin. She pressed herself upon him liked a fanatic paparazzo until he started to wave at her, as if batting a cloud of wasps. He turned to face the sea and walked past the entrance to the hut.

"André!" Peter called. Lasker turned, one raised arm blocking Wendie's camera angle. "When you were in Malta, did you ever visit the cathedral?" It was the one thing Peter couldn't make sense of in all this. There was no rational link between the inscription on the Grand Master's tomb and the homily displayed at St. Elegias.

"No!" he shouted back from the rim. "I never made it to the church."

André Lasker kept walking beyond the stone cottage. Wendie Merwyn stopped and finally lowered the camera. She failed to catch the money shot as the man stepped out into the sky above the English Channel.

EPILOGUE

He stood in supplication before the old lady; she had been waiting for him to call.

The chill seeped up through his thick black shoes to his knees, and he shifted from foot to foot to repel the November frost. The Thames hadn't frozen over in two centuries, but it seemed possible this winter.

In one's youth, he reflected, there are signal acts of determination, or mere impulse, which may set your course for life. He had never believed in the irresistible sculpting of wind and tide; he put his faith in the conscious choices of men. At the age of nineteen, Peter had taken the midmorning bus to the headquarters of New Scotland Yard, which was still in its digs at the Victoria Embankment. It was a decade before the move to the new HQ building, but the plans had already been revealed. The staff were divided into two camps: those who were frustrated with the old lady's decrepitude, and those who loved her traditions. But Peter had loved the mother house on sight.

The kindly officer from Admin, Mr. Cape, came down to the lobby to greet him. They talked for an hour.

"Of course," he said, "your idol Holmes would never have joined the Metro Police Service, such a bureaucratic fate."

Nevertheless, a brochure and a lapel pin had been enough to recruit him to the Police Service life. They required a university degree, and so he read English Literature. A month after graduation, he started at the Yard.

He was her supplicant, but he didn't wait for her to answer. Echoes were enough. He scanned the sooted pillars and the lateritious stone, and her spark began to fade for him. He would retire. He would go to his other home and embrace his smart wife and his clever children. He would endure, far from ocean waves. Or so he told himself. Anything was possible. The ice parties on the Thames were being revived, he had been told.

The grey mass of the River lay only a few feet away. Peter walked over to the thick iron railing, took Father Salvez's red-beaded rosary from his pocket and tossed it into the flow.

He would return home to the fields, the lane, the shed, his books. He would wait for the phone to ring.

ACKNOWLEDGEMENTS

I wish to thank the staff at ECW Press and in particular Jack David, Crissy Boylan, Rachel Ironstone and Simon Ware. May I also highlight the invaluable editorial advice of Emily Schultz and Peter Norman. Additional comments by Ann Ratcliffe, Anne McAllister, Diana Whellams, Laurent Lecavalier and Chris Parsley are greatly appreciated.

At ECW Press, we want you to enjoy this book in whatever format you like, whenever you like. Leave your print book at home and take the eBook to go! Purchase the print edition and receive the eBook free. Just send an email to ebook@ecwpress.com and include:

- the book title
- the name of the store where you purchased it
- your receipt number
- your preference of file type: PDF or ePub?

A real person will respond to your email with your eBook attached. And thanks for supporting an independently owned Canadian publisher with your purchase!

Get the eBook free!*

*proof of purchase required